THE FAMILY WE MAKE

Dan Wingreen

A NineStar Press Publication

Published by NineStar Press
P.O. Box 91792,
Albuquerque, New Mexico, 87199 USA.
www.ninestarpress.com

The Family We Make

Printed in the USA
First Edition
March, 2020

Print ISBN: 978-1-951880-69-9

Also available in eBook, ISBN: 978-1-951880-68-2

Warning: This book contains sexually explicit content, which may only be suitable for mature readers, references to attempted sexual coercion by a male professor toward a male college student, references to a female high school teacher having sexual relations with unnamed underage male students, references to past sexual harassment.

Spencer Kent gave up on love a long time ago. As a twenty-eight-year-old single father with a fourteen-year-old son, Connor, he knows his appeal to the average gay man is limited, and when you factor in his low self-esteem and tendencies towards rudeness and sarcasm, it might as well be nonexistent. But that's okay. A man is the last thing Spencer needs or wants.

Tim Ellis's life is falling apart around him. After four years of hard work at college, he finds himself blacklisted from the career of his dreams by the professor he refused to sleep with and abandoned by the boyfriend he thought he was going to marry. Even though he was lucky enough to land a job at a bakery, he still feels like a failure.

Tim and Spencer's first meeting is filled with turbulent misunderstanding, but Tim makes a connection with Connor through a Big Brother/Big Sister program, and both men put aside their mutual dislike for his sake. By letting go, they may help each other find their way into a life they never could have imagined.

To Mom, Dad, and Nate.

Thank you for always being so supportive.

Chapter One

"Yo, Mr. Kent!"

No, no, not now!

"What do you want, Jamal?" Spencer Kent asked, not glancing up from his phone as he furiously tapped the screen. *Commanders of Warfare 3*, a *Four Square* clone where people built up a character and "conquered" real-world locations, was his latest obsession, and he was *so close* to reclaiming his rightful spot as the Great General of Laurence Tureaud High School from the little *prick* who kept taking it away from him. Whoever CaptainSpock77 was, Spencer knew he had to be a student, because he never knocked Spencer off during class. It was always right before school or during sixth period—which he assumed was the bastard's lunch period—and Spencer was determined that this would be the day he'd vanquish his foe forever.

Still, even with most of his attention focused on glorious conquest, he couldn't help noting that being able to recognize one of his new students by the sound of their voice six days into the new school year was never a good thing. Spencer once had a dog who'd, according to his parents, gone through three different names before he finally remembered to keep calling him Avery. Personally, he doubted the accuracy of that story, but he'd be the first to admit he was pretty shit at remembering names unless the person in question was a Bringer of Stress.

And, sure enough...

"If I didn't do the essay, but I still read the story, do I still get credit?"

Spencer stifled his first exasperated sigh of the day. "No, Jamal." He winced as his commander lost half its health bar. "The whole point of the essay was to *show* you read the book."

"But I did read it."

"And how am I supposed to know that if you didn't do the essay?"

"You could trust me?"

Spencer didn't have to look up to know there was a cheeky grin on the kid's face. He could *sense it.*

"I could also throw myself in front of a train. Doesn't mean it's a good idea."

A decent number of kids chuckled. "That's cold, Mr. Kent." *Not as cold as the icy ball of despair that will form in the chest of CaptainSpock77 when I win this battle.* "My pops says all this literature stuff is bullshit anyway, and I ain't never gonna use it in the real world."

"Language," Spencer droned. "And your dad's right. You *aren't ever* going to use anything I teach you outside of this class unless you decide to study literature in college. But. You're still *inside* my classroom for the rest of the year, and until then, you need to do the work you're assigned, or you'll be right back here next year doing the same—*son of a bitch!*" he finished with a hiss as his commander fainted, and two adorable, blushing anthropomorphic ambulances carried it off on a stretcher.

How the fuck did I lose? I had it!

"Language, Mr. Kent."

The bell rang, signaling the beginning of first period, and the end of Spencer's noble crusade to free the school from tyrannical bondage. It took more effort than he'd care to admit to keep from throwing his phone at the wall. Fucking mobile gaming was going to kill him.

What kind of shitty algorithm picks a school as a command center anyway?

Spencer glared up at Jamal. The kid standing in front of his desk was ridiculously tall for a fourteen-year-old, and Spencer was a short man who liked to keep his chair as low to the ground as possible, so some of the intimidation factor was probably lost. Sure enough, there was the cheeky smirk.

"Class," Spencer called out, not even trying to keep the growl out of his voice. He was pleased to see a few flinches from the more perceptive and easily rattled students. "Be sure to take the time to thank Jamal for the surprise quiz you're going to be taking today."

There came a chorus of groans and some scattered "fuck you, Jamal's" he decided to ignore. Jamal scowled, but Spencer merely raised an eyebrow and pointed at his assigned seat toward the back of the room. "Unless you want a desk closer to me, I suggest you take your seat and get out some paper. I'm thinking this test will take the form of an essay question." He raised his voice. "Hopefully, the rest of you got some practice writing essays over the weekend."

His words were met with another louder round of groans. Spencer smiled to himself.

Spreading the misery rarely failed to improve his mood.

*

Much later in the day, the bell rang at the end of Spencer's relatively problem-free fourth-period class. After more than a week of the usual post summer "what the fuck am I doing with my life?" funk, it was nice to once again feel like he was starting to get a handle on things. Especially since, through a clerical screwup of miraculous proportions, Connor was in his class.

And speaking of the kid...

"Connor!" he called. "Can you stay behind for a minute, please?"

Connor paused, adjusting the large backpack weighing down his narrow shoulders before nodding and walking over to Spencer. The classroom emptied rapidly, and when they were alone, he reached over to help Connor take the pack off before it tipped him over.

"Dad, stop," Connor said, ducking away and somehow keeping from upending himself despite a precarious wobble. Spencer glanced around the classroom, but they were alone, so he didn't bother reminding the kid to call him Mr. Kent at school. "I'm just gonna have to put it back on in two minutes anyway."

"It's gotten bigger." Spencer had no idea how that was even possible, but his kid's bag was at least twice the size it had been at the beginning of the year. Logically, he knew Connor had been carrying around a bag nearly as packed full of books and crap all through middle school, but being able to see how much weight his son had to lug around in the middle of the day was a brand-new experience this year. "How can you even lift this?"

Connor rolled his eyes in pure-teenage disdain. This particular expression had popped up over the summer, and part of Spencer still wanted to scream into a pillow at the thought of The Teen Years finally kicking into gear. "I've been carrying it around all day with no problem. It's not gonna suddenly throw me down the stairs just because you noticed how full it is."

"You don't know that."

"Did you really hold me back to talk about how heavy my backpack is? I'm gonna be late now."

"Ah, but that's just one of the perks of your dad being a teacher." He leaned over his desk and pulled a small slip out of a drawer before brandishing it with a flourish. "Nepotism. In the form of unlimited late passes. Now you can even make it to your locker to get your lunch before your next class without being late like you're always complaining about."

This has to be worth at least five dad points.

Connor stared flatly. "What lunch?"

"The one I made you before I left for school." Spencer frowned. "You didn't see it?"

"You didn't make me anything, Dad."

"Of course I did. I left it right on the kitchen table in a bag like I always do."

"No, you didn't. There was nothing on the table but the coffee pot. And a new burn mark."

Spencer shook his head, but before he could say anything, he remembered his phone buzzing earlier that morning as he filled his thermos. There had been a notification from his game telling him about a special deal on Command Points, and he bought five hundred of those fuckers and used them to train the shit out of his commander and...

Then I got in the car and drove to school. Shit.

"Oh." Spencer rubbed the back of his head. "Did you pack one yourself, then?"

It wouldn't be the first time his son had to take care of himself after Spencer left for school at ass o'clock in the morning, but no matter how often it happened, it never stopped making him feel like a shitty father. That it had been happening more and more as Connor grew up was just the icing on the Spencer-Sucks-at-Parenting cake.

"You never went shopping this weekend. There's no food in the house."

Right. Shopping. That thing I kept putting off.

He needed to delete every game on his phone the second his next class ended.

"Shit. I'm so sorry, kid," he said, pulling out his wallet. "Do you need..."

Of course, I don't have any cash. Fuck me.

"I don't suppose the lunchroom takes Visa?"

Connor snorted. "They don't even take twenty-dollar bills."

"Sorry..."

Connor shrugged as well as he could with the straps of doom digging into his collarbones. "It's okay. I took some money from the lock box under your bed I'm not supposed to know about."

"Ah." Spencer winced. "Can we...maybe pretend you're too young to know what any of the other stuff in that box is? And then completely forget about it?"

"Too late. It's already filed away for my inevitable therapy sessions when I get older." Connor flashed him a rare in-school grin, and Spencer couldn't help being struck by how much the kid looked like him. Everyone had said so pretty much since Connor's birth—although fourteen-year-old Spencer had very much disagreed that he looked anything like the mushy lump of skin that was newborn Connor—and their similarities had only become more obvious as he grew up. Aside from the slight Asian slope of his hazel eyes and his naturally tanned skin, he was the spitting image of Spencer as a teenager. Same mop of soft black curls, same sharp nose, same chin, same short stature—although Becky had been tiny for her age too, Spencer remembered; poor kid never had a chance in the height department. Sometimes looking at his son was like peering into a mirror fourteen years in the past. Kid even had the same facial expressions. Thankfully, those similarities made him ridiculously easy to read.

This particular grin was a perfect match for Spencer's *I'm-fine-now-but-I'm-also-trying-to-cover-up-how-not-fine-I-was-a-few-hours-ago* expression.

Time for damage control. The last thing I need is this coming up in front of my parents when I've just started living down the "Grandpa, do you shave your pee pee like Daddy does?" incident. Fuck, the kid really is gonna need therapy one day...

"I'll just...give you the rest of the money in that box when I get home. And then, you know, hide it better."

And then drown myself.

"Dad," he said, eyes wide, "there was like six hundred dollars in there."

"Really?" Connor nodded. "Okay, revising my statement because I can totally use that kind of money—I'll give you a hundred and hide the box. And we can go shopping together right after school, just so you can make sure I actually make it further than a block."

Because Spencer was self-aware enough to know the odds of him actually going through with deleting his latest time sink was pretty fucking low.

"Can I get a frozen pizza?" Connor asked hopefully.

"I'm giving you a hundred dollars! You're gonna make my house smell like pizza too?"

Pizza was the bane of Spencer's existence—well, one of many, really—and ever since he'd graduated college he tried as hard as he could to keep it from tainting his living space.

"Pleeeeeease?"

And there go the big, pleading eyes. Fuck. I'm such a sucker.

"Fine. But no more pizza until you're at college."

"*Dad.*"

"Or next month, whichever comes first."

Connor rolled his eyes again, but Spencer could see him trying not to laugh.

"All right," he said, tossing his kid the late pass. "Get to...what do you have next?"

"Math."

Spencer winced again. "Ew."

"*AP* math."

Spencer shuddered. "The *worst*. You should skip."

"You're a pretty bad influence."

I know, but you like pizza and math despite my best parenting efforts, so hey, failure all around.

"Yeah." Spencer sighed. "Okay, how about I pretend I just gave you a speech about how important your schooling is, and you'll pretend I'm not horrified my kid actually likes math, of all things."

"Math is *so* easy though!"

Spencer shook his head. "My son is a freak."

"What did math ever do to you?"

"It's more the fact that it exists, if you know what I mean."

"Oh my God, are you really quoting *Harry Potter* right now?"

Spencer's lips twitched. "Always."

Connor groaned. "And you think *math* is bad."

"It is!"

"And *Harry Potter* isn't?"

"*Harry Potter* is *genius*."

"*Tolkien* is genius."

"You were raised wrong." Spencer paused. "Or really, really right. I can't decide."

"I'm leaving," Connor said, sighing.

"Don't forget to take a nap next period," Spencer called after him. "That's what math is for!"

Connor didn't respond as he ducked around the few kids who bothered showing up before the warning bell and disappeared into the hallway. The kids followed him with their eyes and then turned their attention to Spencer, seeming surprised, amused, and, in the case of one mousey girl Spencer had always secretly thought of as the biggest nerd whoever nerded, horrified.

Worst teacher ever.

"If you tell anyone what I just said, you're all writing me a four-page essay on Steinbeck's use of adverbs," he said, fixing them with his best teacher glower. "By *hand*."

They very quickly found other things to be interested in.

*

"Don't forget to finish the book by the end of the weekend!" Spencer said as the final bell of the day rang. "And don't give me those looks; it's a short book. And you all have at least a rudimentary understanding of the English language; it won't be that hard. There's going to be a test *and* a report when you're done, and both will cover things that aren't in the Cliff Notes *or* on Wikipedia, so no shortcuts."

He took note of which students seemed particularly dismayed by his last statement and tried to commit at least their faces to memory. Troublemakers he'd happily throw off Navy Pier and never give them a second thought, but the ones who refused to learn he took as a personal challenge. They would have one fact about at least one of the books he made them read rattling around in their heads on their deathbeds if he had to cut them open and shove the books in their skulls himself.

Once they left—and he could be sure none of them were going to come running in with a last-minute question—he let out an exhausted sigh and collapsed in his chair. Summers off or not, if someone had told him being a teacher was going to be more tiring than college, he would have...honestly, he probably wouldn't have done anything. He'd already abandoned a journalism degree for a teaching degree, and he seriously doubted even his overly indulgent parents would have paid for another pointless semester. Not when they'd also been paying for Connor's...everything, really, at the same time.

He shook himself out of his thoughts and made a halfhearted attempt at going through some of the homework he had piled up on his desk as he waited to see if anyone would show up for their scheduled detentions. Most likely, they would; few freshmen were up to skipping so early in the year, and the ones who thought they could get away with it didn't make the same mistake twice after Spencer tracked them down. Spencer smirked to himself, then settled in to do some grading.

The best part about teaching literature the way he did was he could substitute work with reading and discussion more than most teachers, but the downside was most of the work he did assign were essays and other assorted written crap. No succulent, mouthwatering, easy-to-grade multiple-choice tests for him. Or, not very many, at least. And definitely not in the summer homework, which he *still* hadn't finished grading.

Spencer couldn't be sure how long he'd been slogging through, but by the time he got to the third different "the

Old Man should have just went to Jewel-Osco and got some Chicken of the Sea" joke, he figured he deserved a break.

The halls still had kids roaming through them as he made his way to the cafeteria vending machines, but by the time he remembered he didn't have any money and changed his destination to the teacher's lounge, they'd mostly emptied out. As he walked through an area of the school he hadn't been in for years—while desperately pretending this detour wasn't the biggest adventure he'd been on in almost as long—he came across two older students—boys probably, but he couldn't tell for sure from this angle—crowding a freshman-sized student against a row of lockers.

"Hey!" he barked, enjoying the way his voice echoed down the deserted hallway almost as much as he enjoyed watching the little shitbags flinch. "What's going on here?"

Voice deepened for intimidation? Check. Threateningly neutral question? Check. It's been too long since I've been able to do this. Please let this little freshman have a split lip or a bloody nose or something visible, so I can hand out some sweet, sweet suspensions.

"Shit," he heard one of them say. "Come on, bro."

Spencer gave a halfhearted shout for them to stop as they ran off, but he knew it was pointless. Only freshmen ever listened to the "get back here and wait to get in trouble" stuff. He resigned himself to letting them go right up until he came closer to the kid they'd been harassing and found himself staring into his son's wide hazel eyes.

"Connor?"

"D—uh, Mr. Kent..."

Spencer saw red. He hated bullying at the best of times, but seeing it happen to his kid right in front of him, hearing the slight tremor of fear in his voice... All of a sudden, he was back in his own high school years; a small terrified boy who couldn't take care of himself, let alone the tiny life growing inside a girl he'd exchanged maybe eight sober sentences with. The hall was so quiet he could almost hear the echoes of long-ago taunts and jeers.

"So, is your baby a little faggot too? Or is it just retarded?"

"I can't believe that chink's actually letting you raise her kid. I would have got rid of it the second I found out it was yours."

"So, what are you gonna feed it anyway? Dogs and rice balls? Or just a steady diet of dick?"

He didn't even realize he'd started to take off after the kids until he felt a hand grab his wrist, trying to hold him back.

"No, Mr. Kent, stop! Mr. Kent! *Dad!*"

Habit stopped him, more than anything else. Neither one of them wanted it to become common knowledge that Connor was Mr. Kent's son. Spencer because he loved having Connor in his class, and Connor because he already had a hard-enough time without being known as the son of the most hated literature teacher in the school. Hearing Connor call him Dad in the middle of the halls had him glancing around to make sure no one had overheard, which had the side effect of freezing him in his tracks.

Fuck it. It's not like I can catch them now anyway.

Spencer took a deep breath and turned to his son.

"What the hell was that?" he asked as he pried Connor's hand off his wrist. "And I swear to god if you say 'nothing,' I'm gonna shove you inside a locker myself."

"You can't actually put a person inside these lockers. They're too narrow. I think they were designed like that on purpose so no one—"

"Don't change the subject," Spencer said, crossing his arms. He'd never been tall, but he'd had years of dad experience in using every centimeter of height he did have to *loom threateningly.*

"It's noth—"

Spencer raised an eyebrow.

"Okay, it's not nothing," Connor admitted, worrying at his lip and refusing to meet Spencer's eyes. "But it's not a big deal. They're just a bunch of idiots who like picking on younger kids."

Spencer clenched his jaw until he was sure he could speak without yelling. "I could quote suicide statistics that prove how much of a 'big deal' shit like this can be." Connor opened his mouth, but Spencer steamrolled right over whatever he might have said. "And even if this is just an isolated incident of two bored losers pushing someone around because he's too small to fight back, you're *my* kid, so that makes it a big deal to me."

"It *isn't* though." Connor's voice was barely above a whisper.

Spencer refused to dignify that with a response. "I want names. Now."

"What? No!"

"Connor."

"No way, Dad," Connor said, sounding panicked. "If they get in trouble, they'll know I turned them in, and then it'll get so much worse."

"They'll know it was you? So, they're not actually bullying other kids?"

"They never got caught by a *teacher* with anyone else!"

"I could just say I recognized their faces."

Connor started shaking his head before Spencer had even finished. "No, Dad, I'm not risking it. I'm *not* gonna be their punching bag for the rest of the year. No way. Please just let this go. *Please.* I promise it's nothing I can't handle. Just please don't make this worse for me."

He'd never been good at resisting his kid when he begged for something, but this time his anger outweighed the usual guilt that came along with being a middling-at-best single father.

"I could ground you for the rest of the year."

"I'm home alone more often than not." Connor said it straightforward, like it was just a fact of life and not anything particularly bad, but Spencer still mentally flinched. "You get back right before dinner, so that's like four hours of grounding time before bed every day total. I could deal with that."

Spencer could have reminded him about weekends, or the fact that he was only so late on days when he had to supervise the ninth-grade detentions—a task that had fallen to him as the newest freshman teacher—but he recognized when his son was going to be stubborn about something no matter what logic he used.

"Fine," he ground out. "But I'm going to find out who those kids are on my own, and when I do, they'll be spending so much time in detention they won't have a spare second to think about who might have turned them in."

"Dad, no. Please just forget about it."

"I can't do that."

Connor's eyes hardened. "*Fine*. I hope you enjoy it when I start coming home with *broken bones* every day."

In an impressive feat of strength, he grabbed his bulging bag in one fluid motion and ran down the hall.

"Connor!"

Connor flipped him off over his shoulder right before rounding the corner.

Spencer sighed. "That went well," he informed the nearest locker.

The locker wisely stayed silent.

He sighed again and rubbed at his too-dry eyes. If there was one thing he absolutely hated, it was fighting with his kid. Even when he was in high school and college and his parents were raising Connor more than he was, he'd always felt like it was the two of them against the world. It had taken a few years and more than a few lectures from his mom before he could bring himself to discipline Connor instead of finding ways to excuse his misbehavior, but even now when he had a better handle on all the parenting crap, he couldn't help feeling horribly alone at times like this.

And he's only barely fourteen. How the hell am I gonna deal with the next five years?

Although, Spencer had pretty much been asking himself the same question since *he* was a teenager, and his answer had always been the same. As long as Connor didn't get anyone pregnant, Spencer could deal with anything. He believed that. He had to because the alternative—that he couldn't do this by himself—wasn't even an option. Becky was gone, his parents were almost four hundred miles away, he couldn't afford a nanny, and guys weren't exactly lining up to have their shot with the neighborhood's twenty-eight-year-old single dad. No, Spencer was on his own, and being on his own was something he'd made peace with a long time ago. He could only do what he'd always done: muddle through, hope for the best, and occasionally take his frustrations out on any student stupid enough to give him an excuse. Lucky for him, he had the perfect two already lined up.

All he needed to do was find them.

Chapter Two

"Are you coming home for Christmas, Timothy?"

Tim Ellis barely kept from sighing audibly enough for his phone to pick up the noise. He hadn't even been talking to his mother for five minutes, and he could already feel a headache coming on.

"Mom, it's the middle of summer. I have no idea what I'm doing for Christmas yet."

"But it's Christmas! How can you not know? It's not like I'm asking when you're getting married. Although you should keep in mind your father's knee gets worse in the cold weather, so a summer wedding would—"

"I might be working," he said quickly. The lecture he might get for cutting her off would be a million times better than the five *thousandth* rendition of "I Just Want To See My Son Married In New York Before I Die." "On Christmas," he clarified, just in case his mom thought he was referring to his mythical wedding date.

"On *Christmas?*" she repeated, sounding predictably aghast. "Who works on *Christmas?*"

People who desperately want to avoid you, I would assume.

He grimaced as a guilty weight settled on his chest. His mother wasn't really *that* bad. Just...trying, at times, especially when she got on one of her tangents. Like Tim getting married, or Tim moving back to New York, or Tim not being around to pick his father up from one of his many—and, Tim secretly suspected, at least 75 percent fabricated to make him feel guilty—doctor's appointments, or Tim being four states away for the holidays. She would have been the quintessential Jewish mother if not for the fact that she was a mostly devout Catholic. Only mostly, though, because while she didn't believe in divorce and had very specific views on sex before marriage, she was surprisingly liberal in her views on sexuality. She was even a card-carrying member of PFLAG. Literally. Her official business cards read "Mary Ellis, Owner, Slice of Heaven Bakery and PFLAG Mother."

"I just got hired. I'm not exactly the first person in line for time off on Christmas," he said, only half lying. He *was* new, but the owner was his junior-year college-roommate's older sister, and she thought Tim was the greatest thing since instant coffee. Even if they were open on Christmas, if he asked for time off, she'd probably give it. The problem was, Tim had been making the twelve-hour trip from Chicago to New York every year since he'd moved out to go to school. Now, after finally graduating and getting his own place, he was determined to spend at least one year not crammed into a Greyhound going across one of the busiest highways in the country at the busiest time of the year.

There was a beat of silence from the phone.

"Is this about not getting into your graduate program?" his too-perceptive mother asked. "Are you falling into a depression? Our family is prone to that, you know."

With effort, Tim pushed down the by-now-familiar feeling of failure and betrayal. "It has nothing to do with that." *Oh God, the lies. You were right, Mom; it's hard to stop lying once you start.* "And I'm not depressed. I just don't know if I'm going to be able to get the time off."

His mom made her skeptical humming noise, the one that used to make Tim feel like she was reading into his soul when he was a kid and that he would never admit to using on some of the younger center kids when they acted up.

"If you say so," she said, and Tim could tell from her tone this was going to come up in every single conversation they had until he either admitted his supposed depression or he woke up in a hospital bed after a suicide attempt to find her standing over him telling the doctor, "I knew all along he was depressed, but he wouldn't listen to me and *now* look what's happened."

"Will you at least try to come home, sweetheart? Your father and I miss you very much, and we aren't as young as we used to be. God forbid this might be the last holiday we ever have as a family before one of us dies. And with all his health issues, you know your father is going to go first. I'll probably walk in one day to find him dead right there on the kitchen floor. You'll feel so horrible because you never got a chance to tell him you loved him one last time, and I'll be all alone in an empty apartment, crying my heart out, with my son halfway across the world and probably dying too at that very moment, leaving me even *more* heartbroken and alone."

The. *Guilt.*

Tim steeled himself. He was an adult now, freshly graduated from college and everything. If there was ever going to be a time to resist his mother's emotional manipulation, this was it. All he had to do was firmly tell her she and Dad would be fine alone for one year and to stop being dramatic. A simple, firm refusal and he could maybe feel like some part of his life was finally back in his control.

"I…" *Dammit. I can't do it…* "I'll…try, Mom."

Which pretty much meant he'd be having overcooked chicken in New York again this year.

"That's all I ask." There was another pause, most likely for his mother to close her eyes and savor the sweet taste of victory, before she deftly changed the subject. "So, how is that new job anyway? Do they overwork you? Do you still have time to volunteer? You know, at the center?"

"The job is fine. It's…you know. It's fine."

"Timothy…"

"No, really. There's nothing wrong with the job, I promise." *Aside from the fact that I'm back in a bakery because I have four years of psychology credits and Professor Asshole Douchebag wouldn't let me into his graduate program unless I sucked his dick metaphorically* and *literally.* "I'm just a little upset. I had to move halfway across the city, and now the center's too far away for me to get to easily."

"Oh, sweetheart! Don't tell me you stopped going. You *loved* volunteering there!"

"I know, but my job's more important." *Not nearly as important as what I wanted to be doing with my life, but keeping myself from sleeping on the streets is important to me, if no one else.* "And it's not like that's the only center in the city. I found another one closer to my apartment I'm going to check out this weekend. Hopefully, they have a similar program or something."

"I'm so sorry, honey, but I'm glad you're keeping a positive outlook. Depression runs in our family, you know. Your grandfather jumped right in front of one of those police horses after he lost his job. Of course, the only thing he accomplished was bruising his tush when the thing knocked him over and worrying my mother to death, but he still made the attempt. I never want to go through anything like that again, especially with you." She made another one of her patented noises, this one halfway between a scoff and a coo. "But enough about sad things. I'm sure these new kids will love you just as much as the old ones did. They'll be good for you, and I know you'll be good for them."

For the first time since seeing his mom's name on the caller ID, Tim smiled. "Yeah. Yeah, I think so too."

"See? Positivity! There's my Timothy."

He could practically see her beaming smile; the one that added ten years of lines and wrinkles to her face and yet somehow made her beautiful at the same time. If nothing else, he missed seeing her smile in person. Especially when he was feeling down.

"It's important to keep a positive mindset," he said, mostly for a lack of anything else to reply with.

"And he's so smart too. How these schools aren't begging you to be in their graduate programs, I'll never know. You sound like a shrink already. Don't you worry about a thing, sweetheart. Next time they'll snatch you up, and in a few years, we'll be laughing about all this over our yearly traditional Christmas dinner, you'll see."

A surprised laugh forced its way out of Tim's throat. "Jesus Christ. You never quit, do you?"

"Don't take the Lord's name in vain!"

Tim rolled his eyes. "Sorry, Mom. Sorry, Jesus."

His mom made another noise, this one sounding suspiciously like choked-off chortle.

"Well. Don't forget the Commandments just because you're living on your own. God sees all. Even in Chicago. Which means no wild sex parties either."

"Mom, stop."

"I'm just saying. Now that you're single again, I don't want you going crazy with the sex. I know how young people are these days, and you're a handsome young man. It wouldn't be hard for you to drown yourself in loose boys who are probably filled to the gills with disease."

Tim groaned. Personally, he thought his mom was vastly overstating his appeal to the gay youth of Chicago. Sure, he'd had a few boyfriends over the years, and more than a few that wouldn't qualify for the title under even the loosest definition, but they mostly tended to get bored with him once they realized he wasn't into clubbing or the drug-fueled orgies his mother was probably imagining. Tim took dating seriously these days, and there weren't very many college guys looking to settle down. There were even less older guys looking to settle down with a twenty-two-year-old assistant baker.

"What's that noise about?" his mother asked suspiciously. "You're still single, right?"

"Y—"

"Please don't tell me you've gotten back with Rudy."

"Oh, God. No, Mom. No way."

"Are you sure? I don't want you lying to me."

"I'm not lying. I promise. I'm *not* back with Rudy. Rudy is...an asshole. And a bigot. And—"

"And he was incredibly rude to your father and me."

Tim closed his eyes. *Of course, this is about how he treated you.* "Yes, he was very rude to you guys that one time you met him for five minutes."

"He was!"

"He barely said two words to you."

"Exactly! He ignored us—your parents! On our first meeting, even. Why are you still defending him?"

Because it's barely been two months since we broke up. Because our relationship was nine months of unhealthy codependency and emotional manipulation, and I spent half of those nine months ignoring or making excuses for the truly awful parts of his personality and the other half stupidly thinking I could fix him. Because I so desperately wanted just one relationship to last. Because if we had stayed together a few more months I probably would have asked him to marry me like the idiot I am. Take your pick.

Tim sighed very audibly. "I have no idea. I'm sorry. You're right. He was rude."

"And bad for you."

"And bad for me."

"Because of the rudeness."

"Because of a lot of reasons."

"Hm." She paused, probably trying to decide if she was going to accept that or push to get Tim to admit Rudy was a shitty boyfriend solely because he was rude the one and only time they'd met. "Good. I'm glad you finally see that. Very well named, that one."

Tim stared at the floor and muttered an agreement. Then he muttered several more to the various other disparaging comments she decided to make about Rudy. The conversation drifted, as conversations with his mother tended to do after she got past the things she called to talk about, and by the time they hung up, Tim could barely keep his eyes open even though it was barely five in the afternoon on his day off. He loved his mother, he really did, but there were very definite reasons he hadn't even tried to look for colleges within two hundred miles of his childhood home.

Tim tossed his phone on the small Ikea coffee table and then collapsed back onto his threadbare couch, trying to ignore the all-too-familiar way the lonely silence of his tiny apartment started creeping back in. It didn't help that their conversation had brought up several things he'd been trying very hard not to think about for the last few weeks. Opening a bakery six mornings a week was not how he'd been expecting to spend his postgrad years. The work wasn't hard—he'd been baking with his mother since he was seven—but moving halfway across the country just to end up alone and doing the exact same thing he'd been doing since he was old enough to work felt like the worst kind of failure.

He kind of wished he was as religious as his mom. She'd always said God never gives a person more than they can handle, and he ached for a reason to be optimistic. To not feel like he was hanging onto the edge of an icy cliff seconds away from plummeting into a bottomless pit.

Tim groaned and covered his face with his arm. God, he wished he could just fall asleep; waking up being optional, of course. He briefly played around with the idea of downing some NyQuil and passing out for twelve hours, but he'd been dosing himself a lot lately, and the last thing he needed was an addiction to cough medicine to go along with his probable depression and the unhealthy way he kept repressing his problems. Of course, he could be wrong; psychologists weren't supposed to diagnose themselves, after all. Not that he was one, and he probably never would be either. Not if Professor Carmichael followed through on his threat to smear him to every professor he knew running a graduate program, which was a pretty screwed-up way to react to being turned down. If college taught Tim anything, it was that fully grown adults could be as petty and childish as actual children.

I need to stop thinking about this. Today hasn't been great, but tomorrow can be better. Things aren't as bad as they seem. You still have things in your life that make you happy.

Tim took a few deep, calming breaths, closed his eyes, and kept repeating those words like a mantra over and over in his head, trying to force himself to believe them. Tomorrow he'd make time to go visit that new youth center and see what he needed to do to sign up as a volunteer. Tim always felt better when he was helping people, and he really should have gone down there weeks ago.

As for today? Well. Maybe another twelve hours of nothingness wouldn't be such a bad thing after all.

Chapter Three

Three weeks later, Spencer wasn't any closer to finding out who was harassing his son, though not for any lack of trying. Nearly every free moment he had was spent patrolling the halls during his one free period and between classes, hoping to spot some of the bullying Connor claimed was happening to other people. He wasn't sure if the kid was lying or if bullies had gotten smarter about avoiding teachers since his day, but the most detention-worthy thing he saw was a senior getting what looked like the world's sloppiest blowjob from his girlfriend in the boys locker room. He spent the entire walk to the principal's office listing every kind of fungus that grows on locker-room floors and making pointed comments about how the skin on the girl's bare knees seemed like it might be starting to fall off. Fun, sure, especially when he started throwing around phrases like "health hazard" and "epidemic" and "need to inform your parents" but ultimately disappointing.

At least things with Connor had finally started getting better. The fight they had after school the day Spencer found out about the bullying was easily one of their top five worst. By the end of it, his usually even-tempered kid was red-faced from screaming at him, and Spencer was little better. The few days after were incredibly tense, and even when things calmed down, there was this uncomfortable undercurrent of tension any time they were alone in a room together. Nothing had been resolved, and they both knew it. Connor was still determined to suffer in silence, and Spencer was still determined to find out the names of those kids and rain unholy hellfire down upon those who dared lay hands on his boy. It didn't help that, in his effort to catch the bullies in the act, he'd started watching the kid closer than he ever had before and made more than a few discoveries about Connor's life that really bothered him.

"He doesn't have *any* friends!"

It was Thursday afternoon in the teacher's lounge, and Spencer was gesturing wildly as he paced back and forth, his lunch of cafeteria chicken nuggets and a bottle of Snapple forgotten on the small round table next to him. Across from his abandoned food sat Cassandra Baker, the middle-aged home-economics teacher and one of the only staff members Spencer actually liked. Mostly because she was the only other unmarried ninth-grade teacher with a family—her own son, Jason, was off at his second year of college—and when Spencer first joined the faculty, they'd quickly bonded over their shared experiences as single parents.

"I mean, that can't be normal, right?" He abruptly stopped pacing. Cass was leisurely chewing her sandwich, seeming content just to watch and observe. "Even *I* had friends in high school. Well, friend. Well, sort of a friend. We hung out a bit, and he was the only person who didn't drop me like fashion dropped the fanny pack when it came out that I'd knocked up Becky. Probably because it stopped most of the rumors about me and him having sex in the janitor's closet every day but still. I had *someone* to hang out with, and even just one person was a lifeline. Connor doesn't have *anyone*. Except me."

Spencer forced himself to shut up and leave an obvious opening for comment in the conversation. Cass languidly finished her chewing, but instead of taking another bite, she placed her sandwich on a napkin and sat back in her uncomfortable plastic chair.

"Your histrionics are showing," she said calmly.

Spencer glowered. "I'm aware. Do you have anything *else* to say? Maybe something actually pertaining to the thing I've been *histrionicing* about for the past twenty minutes?"

Cass didn't react to his scathing tone at all aside from a short pause to make sure he was done talking. She tended to deal with life with an equanimity Spencer both envied and was grateful for since it meant his occasional slip into being a piece of shit didn't drive her away. The week before, as a joke, Cass had sent him a link to this new-age website that supposedly described a person's personality based on their favorite color. The whole thing was mostly a bunch of neo-hippy garbage that didn't have a shred of basis in anything even remotely resembling reality, but he'd been struck by how eerily accurate it was in Cass's case. She was a brown through and through: steady and dependable with stamina and patience aplenty. Come to think of it, it kind of worked with Spencer too since purples tended to be temperamental, fastidious, sensitive—or *over*sensitive in his case—and sarcastic. Of course, they were also supposed to be artistic, witty, and dignified, so what the hell did some stupid website actually know?

"Look," she said eventually. "It doesn't really sound like that big of a deal. He has you, right? So, he's not alone. As long as he doesn't go around telling other kids his dad is his best friend, I don't really see a problem here."

"But what about when he doesn't *have* me?" Spencer asked, lowering his voice. They were alone in the lounge, but he hated admitting his failures as a father out loud. "My parents are either back in Ohio or traveling around the country in their RV, so when we're fighting, he's all alone."

"He's been away from his grandparents for a while now though, right?" Spencer nodded. "So, why is this a problem now? And if you tell me you and your son never fought before, I'm going to laugh in your face."

Spencer shook his head and collapsed into his own plastic chair. "Of course, we've fought before but not like this. And I know I sound like every single 'oh my God, my kid's growing up not my little baby' parent ever, but he's not ten anymore. He's a teenager with hormones and mood swings and ideas about how things should be that don't line up with mine. We're not...making up like we used to."

"And are you sure you're worried about this being a Connor problem? Because it sounds more like a Spencer problem to me."

"Of *course* I have a problem with it! In every important way, he's all I've got too, but even I have you to talk about this stuff with. He doesn't have anyone. I've never seen him open his mouth to anyone at school unless it was to ask them to borrow a pencil or something. When I'm being 'unfair' or 'not getting him' or whatever, he doesn't get to complain to anyone; he just sits in his room and stews. And I *know* how much that shit *doesn't* help." He glanced at his soggy nuggets for a moment, but his stomach was still too twisted up for him to seriously consider eating. "Didn't anything like this ever happen with Jason?"

Cass smiled sympathetically. "Jason was a pretty popular kid. My problem was getting him to spend any time with me at all. Whenever we had really bad fights, he had dozens of couches to go sleep on."

Spencer felt vaguely ill at the thought of Connor running away after a fight and said so. Cass only laughed.

"He wasn't *running away*. He just needed some time away from home. Whoever he stayed with, their parents always called to let me know where he was, so it wasn't like I was up all night wondering if he was dead in an alley somewhere. And honestly? I needed the time away from him too. It helped both of us calm down."

"And Connor doesn't have any of that," Spencer said. "He just has his room that shares a wall with mine."

"And that might be okay for him." Spencer started to protest, but she cut him off. "It *might be*. My point is you don't know. You two don't have long, drawn out teenage hate fests, not yet anyway. Even this fight you're having is pretty pathetic by teen standards."

"How can you *say that*? I've never felt further away from him!"

Cass rolled her eyes. "Has he said he hates you?"

"What? No."

"Did he say he wished you were dead?"

"Of course not!"

"Did you throw his Nintendo out into the street?"

"We don't have a Nin—" Spencer paused. "Wait, did *you* throw *Jason's* Nintendo out the window?"

Cass nodded. "Oh yeah. And we lived on the eighth floor. Smashed it into a million pieces. I was lucky it didn't land on anybody."

Spencer worked his jaw as he tried to form words. "*You* did that? You? I...I don't think I've ever seen you raise your voice."

"No one can push your buttons like your own child," she said with a shrug. "Now do you see why it was for the best we had some time to cool down away from each other?"

"Shit yeah," he said. He couldn't imagine getting so angry at Connor and then having to coexist in the same house together.

"And you two haven't even gotten to the name calling yet."

"He said I was being unreasonable," Spencer pointed out.

"Oh. No," Cass said, deadpan. "I hope you got out the belt for that. If you don't reassert your authority, he might knife you in your sleep."

Despite himself, Spencer laughed. "Okay, fine. Maybe our fight was lame in hindsight. But it still feels wrong, you know? And I still feel bad he doesn't have anyone else in his life he can talk to."

Cass hummed thoughtfully, then hesitated. "Can I say something without you getting pissed off?"

Spencer thought about it. "Probably not," he admitted.

Cass's lips twitched. "Well, I'm gonna say it anyway. Do you think, maybe, what you're feeling isn't so much about Connor as it is about you?"

"You already asked that. And I already said I was upset about fighting with him."

"I don't mean the fight. I mean..." Another uncharacteristic hesitation. "I know what it's like to be a single parent. It's hard, and it takes up your whole life, but even though your son is your only focus, it can still get lonely."

"I'm fine," he reassured her. "Like I said, I have you to talk to."

"I'm not talking about friendship," she said. "I'm talking about—"

"If you say 'getting laid,' I'm leaving."

"*Falling in love.*"

Spencer shifted uncomfortably. "I'm perfectly fine on my own."

Cass raised an eyebrow.

"What?" he asked.

"I'm trying to figure out if the only reason I can't actually smell the bullshit is because the stench is so overwhelming, it's shorted out my sense of smell altogether."

"I'm not bullshit! I mean, it's not—I'm not lying."

Smooth as always, you fucking loser.

"Oh, you're bullshit all right," she said. "And I know exactly how much too. Being alone *sucks*. There were times when I would have *killed* to have someone to share my life with after Dick left, but at least I had a marriage as short as it was. You're half my age, in the prime of your life. Don't even try to tell me that if you didn't have Connor, you wouldn't either be in a relationship or actively looking for one."

Spencer couldn't meet her suddenly too-intense gaze. "But I do have Connor," he said to the table. "It doesn't matter what my life would be like if I didn't—and that's not something I even want to imagine." *Not when it could have so easily happened.* "And it's not like I haven't tried, you know? I've done the dating thing, and this may come as a surprise, but being a dad isn't really very attractive to potential gay boyfriends." He paused. "Well, not unless 'Daddy' has a very different meaning."

Cass rolled her eyes. "And when's the last time you had a date?"

Spencer pretended to think. "I'm not sure, but it got cut short because his unit was being deployed to fight World War II so…"

She snorted. "And you don't think that maybe you should give it another shot? You're not that young anymore—"

"Thank you for that. Because being an *old* single dad is so much more appealing to the average American gay than being a teenage single dad."

"You're not *that* young anymore," she repeated. "Which means your potential partners aren't that young anymore either."

"Oh, totally. You know, I can just see going up to my ex and saying, 'Hey, remember how we dated for two months in college, and you dumped me when you found out I had a five-year-old at home? Well, now I have prematurely graying hair, I haven't exercised since Bush was in office, and that five-year-old is in the middle of puberty. Wanna get hitched?' No way that could fail."

Cass's sigh was almost artistic in how many different levels of exasperation it managed to convey.

"Stop exaggerating. You don't have a single gray hair, and if you even try to say you're fat when I'm sitting here with this gut"—she poked her belly—"then I'm going to hurt you."

"I do so have gray hair."

She made a point of studying his head. Spencer squirmed. He hated being examined. "I don't see a single one."

"Great. That means they fell out, which means I'm probably going bald too." He tilted his head toward the nearby window. "Shh. If you listen real close, I think we can actually hear a line of guys starting to form outside my door."

"You're being ridiculous."

"Oh! They just started beating it down."

"You're not even gonna try to listen to me, are you?"

"That's the plan." He smirked, but the expression quickly faded when he saw the disappointed frown on Cass's face. He *hated* that look. The one that said someone had expectations of him, and he'd fallen completely short. He let *himself* down enough. He didn't need to see visible proof other people knew how much of a failure he was. "Look, I know you're just trying to help, but I promise you it's pointless. Even if—*if*—I was lonely, the amount of effort I'd have to put into finding a guy who was not only attracted to me but could put up with my shitty moods, my terrible personality, *and* my teenage son would take up hours upon hours of my life I don't have to spare. Perfect guys don't just fall out of trees."

"Or you could find the right guy the first time out of the gate."

"Did you miss the bit where I briefly outlined a few of my many flaws? And that was me lowballing it. I'd be here all day if I listed all the reasons no one would ever want to date me."

And even if by some miracle someone does want me, no one ever wants us.

"And I could be here all day shooting every one of those reasons down. Trust me. As someone who's sampled more than her fair share of assholes, you're not really all that bad."

"It's amazing I ever got hired without having you to quote as a reference," he said, sounding snippier than he intended. Cass—beautiful, wonderful Cass—didn't even blink at his attitude.

"You never know what you might be missing if you don't try," she said. Then, in a roguish display of utter disregard for every piece of body language Spencer was sure he was currently displaying, Cass reached across the table and squeezed his hand. "You don't need to find the perfect guy, Spencer. Just the perfect guy for *you*."

Spencer opened his mouth fully intending to give *that* kind of Hallmark schmaltz the scathing ridicule it deserved, but what ended up coming out was more bitter and honest than he was prepared for.

"I'm not even sure those exist."

He pulled his hand back and glanced away. The last thing he wanted was to see the pity he was sure was written across her face.

"Can we please just drop this?" he asked quietly.

Cass sighed again. "All right," she said. Spencer risked a glance a minute later, but she was eating her sandwich and not even paying attention to him anymore. He felt incongruously annoyed.

"I'm gonna get back to my classroom," he muttered.

"Okay," she said. Spencer waited, though he wasn't sure what he was waiting for, but when she didn't say anything else, he stood up and started to leave. "Spencer, hold on."

Spencer cautiously stilled.

"If you're really worried about Connor not having anyone to talk to, Dick helps run a youth center a few blocks away from where you live. It's got one of those Big Brother Big Sister mentoring programs you could probably get him into."

Spencer was slightly thrown by the sudden shift back to his original concern, but talking about helping Connor was much more preferable than getting advice on his pathetic love life. "Isn't that kinda like buying him a friend? I don't want him to feel like a loser."

"The center's nonprofit, so you don't need to pay anything. The most they'll ask is for a donation." She took another bite. "Probably several if Dick is there."

"I can't believe you're recommending me a place your ex-husband works."

"He's not completely useless. I kept his name after the divorce for a reason, after all," she said with a shrug. *Oh, please. The only reason you kept his name is because you didn't want to have to get new credit cards again.* "Besides, it's a good center. Jason still volunteers there sometimes when he's home from college."

"In this Big Brother thing?"

"Mmhmm," she hummed around another mouthful, swallowing before going back to her words. "He says it helps shy kids especially."

Spencer scrunched up his nose. "I dunno. Sounds kinda...institutional. I want Connor to have a friend, not a therapist."

"It's not like that. Not really." She finished the last of her lunch and glanced up, clearly noticing the skeptical expression on his face. "I'll text you a link to their website later, and you can look it over. If nothing else, it'll get Connor out of the house and used to talking to someone who isn't you. Maybe that will give him confidence to talk to more kids his own age."

"Maybe," Spencer allowed. He might have said more, but the bell rang, signaling the end of his lunch break.

"And now *I* have to get back to my class." Cass grimaced. "First cooking class of the year."

Spencer snickered. He'd heard enough stories about freshman home ec cooking to be very happy with his chosen career path. "Try not to empty out too many fire extinguishers."

Cass let out a noncommittal hum. "I'll send you that link later."

Spencer nodded, then waved over his shoulder as he left the teacher's lounge.

*

Spencer sat at his kitchen table with his phone in his hand, which was probably the first time in weeks him having his phone out had nothing to do with gaming or texting his son. The site Cass had sent him was a lot more professional than he'd been expecting when he heard the words "nonprofit youth center," and even though it gave off kind of a retirement-home-recruitment vibe with all the pictures of laughing kids and fresh-faced adults with unrealistically wide smiles, he was still able to get answers to most of his questions.

Cass had apparently been telling the truth about the Big Brother program. There was no therapy to be had, though the words "life coaching" had, distressingly, shown up more than once. If anything, the program seemed like free babysitting, which in a city probably *filled* with single parents, he had no idea why there was still a big banner reading Spaces Open! Sign Up Today! At first, he thought the page might be out of date, but there was a helpful bit of scrawl at the very bottom informing him the last update had been three days ago. The slight air of This Might Not Always Be Available implied by Spaces Open was almost enough to have him dragging Connor down to the center right then. It was the same weakness to marketing that had Spencer spending hundreds of dollars on collector's editions of video games he didn't even really want to play, but this time he managed to resist. He'd suffered through too many years of kiddie sports leagues when he was a child to sign Connor up for anything without talking to him first, and he wasn't about to start now.

"Connor!" he called. "Dinner's ready!"

A minute later, the kid thumped down the stairs, then navigated the smooth wooden floors in socked feet with unconscious grace, which Spencer had never quite gotten the hang of. He smothered a jealous scowl, but he couldn't help longing for Connor's first real teenage growth spurt and the inevitable gangly awkwardness that would follow. Connor, unsurprisingly, had already changed into his pajama pants and an oversized sleep shirt even though it was only six thirty. The kid hated wearing proper clothes at home—one of the many ways he'd taken after Spencer in more than just looks.

Hopefully he doesn't react the way I would to what I'm about to suggest…

"Is that stew?" Connor asked, raising his eyebrows in surprise at the slightly steaming pot on the stove.

"According to the package, yes, but I make no promises about the taste."

Connor glanced at him suspiciously. "You hate stew."

Which was true, more or less. Spencer hated any food with a strong smell. Connor's constant complaints about their "bland" meals were as close as they used to come to reoccurring fights, and Spencer hoped that making the stew would put him in a better mood for their talk.

"If you don't want it, I could toss it and bake some chicken breasts—"

"No, I want it!" Connor's eyes widened in panic, and it was all Spencer could do to keep from bursting out laughing.

"Get a bowl and sit down then."

Connor had the cabinet open and a bowl in his hand before he seemed to notice Spencer sitting at an empty table.

"Are...you gonna have any?" he asked, hesitantly reaching up for another bowl.

"Nah, I got something to eat on the way home."

Totally the wrong thing to say, judging by the reappearance of the suspicious look.

"O...kay." Connor closed the cabinet slowly. "Um, can I go eat in my room?"

Spencer smiled. "Nope." He kicked the empty chair across from him out from under their small kitchen table. "Fill up and take a seat."

Connor did so slowly, looking like he'd rather be doing anything else.

"You're not in trouble or anything," Spencer said as the kid started eating. "I just wanna talk."

Connor didn't relax one inch. If anything, he only tensed up more.

"I'm not telling you their names," he said quietly, staring down at his bowl. Spencer had to bite his lip to keep from demanding Connor do just that. *Don't start a fight. This isn't about fighting.*

"That's not what I wanna talk about."

Slowly, Connor glanced up through his long eyelashes. He was ridiculously adorable, like a furless berated puppy, and Spencer had to fight the sudden urge to pet his soft curls. "It's not?"

Spencer shook his head. Connor still seemed like he didn't believe him. Which...hurt in a way Spencer wasn't really prepared for. He'd always made a point to be honest with his son, ever since the very first day he'd laid eyes on him. Connor was even the first person he'd come out to, tearful and shaking, terrified the week-old baby lying on his chest would open his eyes and look at him with the same hate and disgust he saw every day at school. It ended up being the most liberating experience of his life up until that point, and for the first time, Spencer had felt like he *could* be honest. Not just with Connor, but with himself too. For the first year or so of Connor's life, Spencer tended to treat him like a living diary, pouring out his fears, hopes, and dreams to his baby's soft little face. He'd stopped after Connor started talking because Spencer had seen too many TV shows where the parrot repeated incriminating lines of dialogue at the worst possible time not to be paranoid about his secrets being spread through toddler talk. But even after he stopped pouring his heart out, he'd never once lied to him. He thought Connor understood that.

"What do you want then?" Connor asked.

All Spencer's carefully prepared openers disappeared from his head like early morning fog in the midmorning sun. That was stupid because telling his kid about a program at a youth center didn't nearly warrant this kind of stress, but then Spencer had always been amazing at making mountains out of molehills as his mom liked to say.

Instead of trying to say anything, Spencer slid his phone across the table. Connor stared at its darkened screen for a moment, then glanced up, apprehension written across his face. "You're not showing me something weird, are you?"

"No!" Spencer glared. "Just...read the page I was on, okay?"

Connor glanced nervously down at the phone, but miracle of miracles, he actually did what Spencer asked without any more lip. His expression turned to confusion when he unlocked the phone and then to dawning understanding after a few minutes of reading. By the time he finished, his face was impressively blank.

"So?" Spencer asked, wincing when his voice was a bit too loud for the still silence in the kitchen. "What do you think?"

Connor stared at the phone for a long while. When he spoke, his voice came out so soft Spencer could barely hear him. "Is this because I won't tell you who's picking on me?"

"Not directly, no."

His son glanced up with tears shining in his eyes. "Then why are you sending me away?"

Spencer felt like he'd taken a baseball bat to the chest. He reached across the table, almost upending Connor's forgotten stew bowl in the process, and snatched the phone back. He had visions of some technical fuckup opening a page for military school or something equally horrible by accident, but no, it was the same page he'd spent the last forty minutes diligently scouring—which didn't at all explain his kid's reaction.

"I'm not sending you away—"

"Yes, you are!" Connor's shout seemed to snap whatever control he'd had over his emotions because the moment the last word came out of his mouth the tears started streaming down his cheeks, and his breath came in quick ragged gasps. "You—you don't—you don't want me—anymore..."

Dammit.

"No-no-no-no-no." Spencer got up and, after rushing around the table, scooped his son up out of his chair and sat down before pulling him into an aggressive cuddle. Connor struggled but not nearly as much as he usually did ever since getting "too old for hugs." That alone would have showed how upset he was. "I *do* want you, okay? I'm not sending you away. I promise. You're not going anywhere you don't wanna go. I want you here. I'll *always* want you here."

He kept it up, holding Connor tight and murmuring reassurances.

Fuck, I hate this.

It didn't happen often, but every once and a while someone—usually Spencer—managed to do or say something to hit on some deep insecurity or fear Connor had buried inside him. When that happened, it usually came out the form of a sudden crying fit or a panic attack. Thankfully, they never lasted very long, and the one therapist Spencer had spoken to years back had told him they were nothing to worry about, that they were just the way Connor's mind dealt with a manifestation of his dread or something. Of course, no amount of assurances made Spencer feel any less like a piece of garbage for almost always being the thing causing them. Especially since he was pretty sure going away to college had been what messed Connor up in the first place. Even though Spencer's parents had done most of the parental stuff, Connor hadn't dealt with Spencer being away for most of the year well at all. They even had to temporarily move the whole family five miles down from Spencer's university for his last two years, just so Connor wouldn't freak out. The kid had kind of clung to him ever since.

And that probably means it's my fault he doesn't have any friends. Awesome.

"Come on, breathe for me, okay? That's it. In...and out. In...and out. Nice and slow. You're doing great, raisin."

The old childhood endearment was familiar on his lips even though it had been years since Connor had very emphatically made it clear he'd outgrown it. No matter how much he claimed to hate it, though, hearing the old name when he was upset rarely failed to help calm him down. It worked this time too, and a few minutes later, Connor stopped hyperventilating and went limp in his arms.

"Sorry," he mumbled, his voice thick with embarrassment. Spencer didn't need to see his face to know his cheeks were probably bright red.

"Nothing to be sorry about," Spencer said, giving him one last hug before letting go. Connor hopped off his lap immediately, taking a few steps away and rubbing furiously at his eyes. Spencer politely turned away, knowing how much Connor *hated* when he lost control like that, especially when tears were involved.

"Why don't you get some more stew?" Spencer suggested.

"'Kay."

They both ignored the still steaming bowl sitting on the table as Connor busied himself with pouring a new one. The same way they ignored how it took him nearly ten minutes to scoop three ladlefuls of stew into a bowl and take a seat in the chair Spencer had started out the evening in.

"You okay?" Spencer asked as casually as he could.

"'M fine."

"Do you wanna talk about it?"

Connor shoved a large spoonful of meat into his mouth and started chewing. Slowly.

Okay then.

After a few minutes of silent eating, Spencer pulled the other bowl over and took a small sip of the beef broth. *Oh, God. This is disgusting.* He made a face at the taste, and somehow managed not to collapse in relief when Connor's lips twitch in amusement.

"So," Connor said around a mouthful of meat chunks, "what's that thing about, anyway?"

Spencer hesitated, but if Connor wanted to act like nothing had happened, then he'd take his cues from the kid and do the same. If nothing else, the tension following them around these last few weeks seemed to be gone now.

So, Spencer quickly explained about the center and the Big Brother program, trying to emphasize the parts where it seemed cool for a fourteen-year-old boy to be friends with a college-aged guy and glossing over the mentoring and life coaching bits. Connor barely glanced up from his dinner the entire time he spoke, but that was pretty much normal, even without the kid feeling embarrassed. He seemed to be listening, and maybe even interested, although it was impossible to tell with teenagers sometimes.

"So, what do you think?" Spencer asked.

Connor poked at the dregs of his stew as he contemplated. "It kind of sounds like you're buying me a friend."

God, I love you.

"Nonprofit youth center. Everything's free. Well, free for us anyway. Nothing's really *free* since everything costs money, and that money needs to come from somewhere.

Remember that when you get older. If someone is offering you free stuff, they're full of shit. Especially if they're running for office." Spencer nodded once for good measure.

"Still sounds like you're forcing someone to spend time with me."

"They're volunteers, Con. They wouldn't be there if they didn't want to be."

"Yeah but..." Connor crossed his arms and let out a sound of frustrated teenage disgust. "Whatever. You don't understand."

"Then explain it to me."

"You sound like Grandpa now."

"Grandpa's pretty smart, so I'm gonna take that as a compliment. I'm also not gonna ignore the totally unsubtle way you just tried to change the topic there either." Spencer pushed his own cooling bowl of stew away. He didn't need that horrible stench right under his nose when he was trying to have a serious conversation. "Tell me what's wrong, or I'm going to start guessing, and who knows what kind of crazy shit I might come up with."

Connor glared. "Have fun."

Stubborn little shit.

"Okay," Spencer said, meeting his glare evenly. "Could it possibly be you think that, while these volunteers might want to be there for kids in the general sense, there's no way any of them would ever want to spend time with *you* specifically?"

Connor looked like he'd been slapped.

"I know we don't talk about it a lot," Spencer said, answering the question written all over his kid's face, "but I'm not that much older than you. My days of teenage insecurity aren't so far behind me, and, I'm gonna be honest, adult insecurity isn't really all that different. Sometimes I look at you and you're like this mysterious puzzle that exists in dimensions I can't even see. Other times, I swear to God I'm looking in a mirror, and I can almost *hear* what you're thinking because I've already been there, thinking the exact same thing. And you know what? In this case, I was *just* as wrong back then as you are now, raisin."

"Don't call me that. And I'm *not* wrong," Connor said, his voice quiet and sullen. "No one wants anything to do with me."

"That isn't true at all."

"Must be why I have so many friends."

The glare had returned, but this time Connor spread his arms wide and made a point of searching around their tiny kitchen as if to emphasize all the friends he didn't have. Spencer felt an involuntary pang of sympathy for anyone who'd ever had to deal with similar melodrama from him.

"And that's why I really think you should give this Big Brother thing a shot."

"So I can be ignored by someone outside my age range for once?"

Spencer had to fight not to roll his eyes. "So you can talk to someone who doesn't have any preconceived ideas about who you are. Wouldn't you like that? Just hanging out with someone who doesn't know *anything* about you? Who hasn't spent an entire school career slotting you into a box in their stupid cliquey hierarchy?"

Spencer would have killed for something similar when he was Connor's age. Even now he couldn't stand when people he barely knew tried to put him in boxes.

An emotion Spencer couldn't identify flickered across Connor's face, and Spencer hoped he was striking some kind of chord with him.

"*You* don't do that," Connor said.

Spencer smiled sadly. "You need more in your life than just me, Con."

It was one of the most difficult things he'd ever had to say, mostly because he couldn't help picturing a phantom Cass standing over Connor's shoulder giving him a knowing smirk.

"You're the only one who likes me."

"I'm the only one who *knows* you. Tell me this, does anyone at school make fun of you? *Besides* Those-Who-Must-Not-Be-Named, I mean."

Connor frowned. "No?"

"There you go. Kids are mostly awful little shits. If they didn't like you, you'd know."

"That makes no sense."

"Then prove me wrong." Spencer sat back and crossed his arms. "Go do this Big Brother thing for a week. If the guy hates you, then you never have to go back. I promise."

"Is that supposed to be a *bribe*?"

Spencer hesitated. *I'm probably about to set a* really *bad precedent here, but...* "You know what? Sure, why the hell not. It's a bribe."

Connor stared at him incredulously. "Seriously?"

"Yeah. But don't get too excited, this is a one-time thing because I really think this will be good for you, and I don't want to force you."

"I..." Connor chewed his lip. "That's...not a very good bribe, then?"

Spencer smiled. "So, make me an offer."

Connor glanced away again but not before Spencer saw the calculating glint in his eye.

I have you now.

"Okay. If I go...you have to get me my own PlayStation 4," he said, shooting Spencer a challenging stare and obviously expecting him to back down.

Oh, kid, you sell yourself so low. You could have held out for a dog.

Not that he'd be giving in so easily. He might be setting a shitty precedent, but he wasn't going to set it without at least *trying* to teach the kid something useful.

"How about I let you take the PS4 we already have out of the living room and keep it in your room?"

Connor blinked. "You're *really* gonna pay me to do this?"

"I don't lie to you. I said I would, so that's what I'm gonna do. Besides, we've already started negotiations, it's too late to back out now. You made your offer, and I made my counteroffer; now it's your turn. You either accept the counteroffer or try to see if you can get more out of me. But—" Spencer held up one finger. "—don't ask for anything worth more than your original offer. It'll make you look like you have no idea what you're doing, and if I don't respect you as an equal negotiating partner, I'll do my best to screw you over."

"What are you talking about?"

"Basic bartering. If we're doing this, we're making it as educational as possible."

"But...people don't barter anymore."

"You'd be surprised," Spencer said, thinking of the few times he'd tried to sell things on Craigslist. "Now, do you accept my counteroffer, or do you have one of your own?"

The poor kid seemed utterly confused. Any other time Spencer would have been merciless—no one ever learned anything from an easy lesson—but today was a panic attack day. Not even Spencer was heartless enough to push hard on one of those.

"So, a hint? I would have been willing to go a lot higher than a new PS4, which means I'm already coming out ahead on this deal. I'd be willing to accept literally anything legal that's equal to or under the price of a brand-new console."

Connor frowned again. "How much would you have given me?"

"That would be telling." *And I'm really hoping you've forgotten about wanting a dog.* "Counteroffer?"

Connor opened his mouth, then slowly closed it. Spencer was very pleased to note the kid actually seemed to be thinking about his response.

"Um. Could I take the PS4 into my room *and* get a new TV?"

Not exactly a confident offer, but they could work on confidence some other time.

"How big?"

"Forty inches?"

Spencer thought about it. He could probably find a cheap forty-inch TV online for about three hundred dollars, but he knew the electronics trade-in store three blocks away had a better selection of bigger ones that were put together much better than anything he could find for such a low price at a different retailer.

"Tell you what," he said. "I'll get you a bigger one that might even have a chance at being name brand *if* you let me take your old one to trade in down at Electronics World."

"And I still get the PS4?"

"And you still get the PS4."

It wasn't like Spencer didn't have five other game systems hooked up in the living room to play. Honestly, he should have let the kid game in the privacy of his own room years ago.

"Deal!" Connor shouted, practically tripping over himself to get the word out. Spencer bit the inside of his lip to keep from laughing.

"Deal," he said solemnly.

They shook hands across the table.

Chapter Four

The Michael Crichton Memorial Youth Center was very different from the centers Tim was used to. The building itself was laid out more like a rec hall than the more familiar, slightly run-down, one-floor school design. The reception area was spacious and inviting, the receptionist was professional and didn't smell like menthols, and there was even an indoor gymnasium complete with basketball and tennis courts. The facility was very impressive, but there was a vitality to the place that made Tim uncomfortable. He'd gotten accustomed to the air of neglect and the painfully obvious need for more money that clung to taxpayer-funded youth centers. Those centers *needed* volunteers, people who would stand as a crumbling seawall against the tsunami of gang culture and poverty that ruined the lives of so many good kids who desperately needed positive adult role models.

He didn't like to think of himself as the kind of person who would rank children based on how well-off they were, but it was hard for him to imagine the kids who would go to this kind of center truly *needing* him. The few he saw wandering around appeared clean and well-fed with properly fitting clothes; nothing like his last group of kids. A sharp disdainful voice inside him questioned whether these children—though most of them seemed to be teenagers, another difference Tim hadn't been expecting—even deserved a center like this. Surely their parents could afford babysitters if they didn't want to actually take care of their own spawn.

If his inner voice had sounded even a little less like Rudy, he might have actually listened to it. Instead, he marched up to the receptionist, asked about volunteering, and was immediately whisked off to a small office for the strangest intake interview of his life.

Richard Baker—"Call me Dick, please"—the co-director of the center was a walking contradiction. He was tall and wiry, with flinty-gray eyes, a stern, heavily lined face, and thinning black hair combed severely back off his forehead. He sat straight-backed and stiff, exuding an air of confident authority Tim had rarely seen in civil servants. Tim's first impression of Dick was that he looked like Clint Eastwood and Burt Reynolds had a kid who grew up to be a drill sergeant.

He was also the most genial and open person Tim had ever met, greeting him with a wide smile and a manly shoulder clap like they were old war buddies before inviting him to have a seat in one of the two chairs in front of his desk. Dick sat next to him, abandoning the comfortable-looking desk chair he'd been using when Tim came in, and proceeded to tell him what seemed to be his entire life story. By the time he stopped talking, Tim knew the names of his parents and extended family, what they all did for a living, what they thought of Dick's job as co-director of a youth center, that Dick had been divorced for five years and he had a son slightly younger than Tim who was away at college in California. He'd also been hit up for donations to the center five different times. Tim felt like he'd been through a hurricane; not even his *mom* talked as much as Dick.

"Well," Dick said after nearly an hour of one-sided conversation, "now that the pleasantries are out of the way, what can I do you for?"

Pleasantries? Dear Lord. And "what can I do you for?" People actually say that?

Tim shook himself. "Um. I'd like to volunteer?"

"You sure about that?" Dick asked. He raised an eyebrow before laughing loudly and slapping his own leg. Tim had absolutely no idea how to react. "All right then. I guess I should start with asking about your qualifications."

Now Tim felt even more off balance. He'd volunteered at a bunch of youth centers over the years, and this was the first time anyone had asked him about qualifications. Usually they just ran his name through a database to make sure he wasn't on a sex offender's list. *They were all pretty desperate for volunteers though.* Maybe privately funded places could be pickier?

Tim really hoped he wasn't about to be turned away. He *needed* this.

"Oh, okay. Uh. I've volunteered at a bunch of youth centers before. Public ones. Most recently Heart of Youth across the city. And I have a BA in Psychology from CSU and..." Tim started to sweat under his collar. He hadn't prepared at all for this. After everything that happened with Rudy and Professor Inappropriate, he needed something that *relaxed* him. He needed to be helping people, not defending his ability to help. *I don't think I can do this. What if he asks who my teachers were? What if he calls for references? What are the odds that he won't call Professor Carmichael? What if that bastard ruins this for me too?*

Tim cleared his throat, desperately hoping his voice wasn't about to crack. "I guess that's it, really. Um. I babysat for some of the parents in my building when I was a teenager, too, if that counts…"

Tim closed his eyes. There was no *way* he wasn't about to be thrown out.

"Wow. A Psychology BA from CSU, huh? That means you must have studied under Professor Carmichael, right?"

Of course *he knows Professor Asshole by name. Why wouldn't he?*

"Yeah," Tim said quietly.

"Hm." Dick didn't say anything for a long moment. Tim refused to look at his face. He had enough experience with expressive *hms* to know Dick wasn't exactly pleased with his answer. "Are you going into his grad program?"

Tim flinched. "No."

"Good."

Tim finally opened his eyes, more than a little surprised by Dick's blunt statement. Dick's smile held a trace of sympathy.

"Never met one of his grad students that I liked," Dick said, answering the question Tim hadn't quite dared to ask. The almost knowing glint in his eyes, though, had Tim suspecting there was more to his seemingly benign statement.

Maybe he knows how *he picks his grad students.*

"So," Dick said, easily changing the subject. "What are you planning on doing with your degree? Going into another grad program? Or do you already have a job?"

"I…" He probably should have expected someone besides his mom to ask these questions, but for some reason, he hadn't. Well. Okay. Not *for some reason.* He didn't think anyone would actually care. The people in his life rarely did. Even Sarah, his boss at the bakery, never really asked about his career plans, and she was practically his only friend in the city. "I'm not...I have a job. Not in psychology though. I...work in a bakery."

He wondered if he'd ever be able to say that out loud without feeling like a total failure.

"A bakery, huh?" Dick asked. *And here it comes. The air of confusion, the judgment, and the assumption I couldn't handle pursuing a real career.* "Do you get an employee discount?"

Tim blinked. Out of everything he expected Dick to say, that wasn't even on the list.

"Yes," he answered hesitantly.

"Does it extend to family and friends?"

"It can..."

Dick grinned. "When do you want to start?"

Tim blinked again. "What?"

"Well, that might be a bit premature, I guess. Gotta run your name, make sure you're not here to feel up the kiddies." He fixed Tim with a hard glare. After the last hour or so, it actually seemed out of place on his craggy, unforgiving face. "You're not, are you?"

"No!"

The grin returned. "Then we shouldn't have any problems aside from what you wanna do around here and when you wanna do it. So, what were you thinking?"

Tim had no idea what to say. Was this really it? The whole interview?

"It's okay if you don't know exactly what you want to do right now," Dick said. "Lots of volunteers don't. Though, I will warn you, there are probably going to be a *lot* of bakery field trips in your future no matter what you end up doing. With me if nothing else."

"Field trips?"

If anyone had even suggested taking kids out of the last center he volunteered at, they would have had the cops called on them. The idea of field trips was completely foreign to Tim.

"One of the reasons why we vet our volunteers. Private organization means we get to make our own rules, to a degree, and I've never thought keeping kids cooped up in a center is the best way to help them."

"And their parents are okay with that?"

"Of course. That's what permission slips are for."

"But..." Tim had no idea why he kept asking questions. It sounded like he wouldn't be thrown out after all, but this whole setup was so new and confusing to him he couldn't help himself. "You didn't vet me though."

"I'm a good judge of character." Tim stared at him in disbelief. Dick met his gaze evenly. "You sat there and listened to me go on about things you couldn't possibly care about for almost an hour, never interrupted, never let on you were bored. You're polite, you're sensitive, and to be honest, you're easily the most qualified volunteer I've ever interviewed."

"I...only have a BA..."

"We have a woman here with half a high-school education who abandoned her own family because she couldn't handle being a mother. The only reason she volunteers is to try and ease her guilt. She's also one of the best volunteers we've ever had. School certificates aren't everything."

Once again, Tim was at a loss for words.

"The only thing I care about is what's best for the kids," Dick continued. "We're going to do a background check before you get within shouting distance of any of them, but we wouldn't even bother with that if I didn't think you'd be good for them."

Tim *hated* the way his eyes started to water at Dick's words. He used to be so confident in himself, in his dreams, and his ability to accomplish them. The Tim of a year ago never would have felt this pathetically grateful because a man he'd just met thought he would be a good influence on children. That Tim hadn't been ground down to almost nothing by his relationship with Rudy or months of emotional manipulation from a man who had been his mentor. That Tim had been a rubber band, able to snap back into shape no matter how much life had stretched or contorted him.

The Tim of today felt like a thousand-year-old piece of parchment. A rough tap would be all it took to send him crumbling to dust.

"So," Dick said. "Any ideas on where you'd like to spend your time? Or do you wanna table the talk and hit the cafeteria for some late lunch? We don't have a bakery, but we should be able to scrounge up some pretty mean mac and cheese."

Tim choked out a laugh. "I'm not really hungry." More lies. Tim's stomach had groaned at least a dozen times while Dick had been speaking. He'd been so nervous about coming here that he hadn't been able to eat anything all day. "I do have ideas though. Um. I used to spend a lot of time with the younger kids. Around six or seven. I'd really like to stay with them. I think I'm probably best with that age group."

"Everyone always wants the young ones," Dick said, his expression radiating sympathy. "Truth is, we don't get many of the young ones here. Most of our kids are between twelve and seventeen, and we already have too many volunteers focusing on our younger kids..."

Tim's heart fell. "Oh."

"Is that gonna be a deal breaker?" Dick asked. "I know teenagers are tough, especially ones that find their way to centers like this. If you don't think you can handle it, I wouldn't blame you."

Even if Tim hadn't spent the last four years of his life studying psychology, Dick's attempt at manipulation would have been obvious. Considering everything that went on with Professor Carmichael and Rudy, it should have pissed him off, but for some reason Tim wasn't bothered. Maybe it was because the professor and Rudy had always manipulated Tim for their own gain while Dick seemed to be pushing him, *daring* him to step outside his comfort zone. It had been so long since Tim had been given a challenge that wasn't about making him reliant on his professor or turning him into a clone of his boyfriend. It was...refreshing, in a way Tim never would have expected. Even the *implication* of someone believing in him was enough for a tiny spark of drive and ambition to flare to life in his chest.

"I...can handle it."

"Great!" Dick grinned once again. "Then you're gonna fit in perfectly here."

To his surprise, Tim found himself smiling in return. "You know what? I think so too."

*

As it turned out, fitting in at the center was a lot harder than either Tim or Dick expected.

After Tim had agreed to volunteer with the older kids, Dick had almost immediately started telling him about the center's Big Brother program. Tim had heard of similar programs, of course, and really this one wasn't too different aside from a few less restrictions on what "Big Brothers" were allowed to do with their "Little Brothers," but he was reluctant to get involved. Helping one kid was great, but Tim had always gravitated toward group activities. They were what he knew and what he was used to. Jumping into one-on-one mentoring was definitely stepping outside his comfort zone, but Dick was so *passionate* about the program and seemed to have so much confidence in Tim it didn't take too much convincing for him to sign up.

The first disaster wasn't anyone's fault, really. Tim and the kid—a blond fifteen-year-old boy named Austin—actually hit it off pretty well. Austin played football, and Tim had been on his high school's basketball team—for one season where he played maybe half a game, but still—so they bonded pretty quickly over sports and trading funny stories about their respective teams over lunch in the center's cafeteria. Where it all fell apart was when, after an uncomfortably detailed twenty-minute retelling of Austin's latest cheerleader encounter, he asked Tim about his own history with girls. In hindsight, even if he'd *had* a history with girls, he probably should have deflected the question, but Tim didn't really have much experience with teenagers, so the question caught him just enough off guard that he answered honestly.

"I don't have any girl stories."

"Come on, man, you can tell me. I'm not gonna say nothin' to anyone."

"I'm being serious."

"You're telling me you went through *four years* of high school without ever popping any bitches?"

Tim didn't know whether to be amused or horrified. "That's what I'm saying. And is that how you pick up girls, by the way? By calling them 'bitches' and saying you wanna 'pop' them?"

Austin rolled his eyes. "You sound like my mom, dude. Wait, are you one of those male feminists or whatever? Is *that* why you never got laid? Holy shit, dude. Are you a *virgin*?"

Tim had to laugh. "No," he said wryly. "None of that. I'm just gay."

"What the *fuck*?"

Even though he spent his life living in pretty liberal cities like New York and Chicago, Tim wasn't exactly a stranger to homophobic freak-outs. Still, Austin's was more...enthusiastic than he was used to. Dodging what was left of their lunch, a thrown chair, and falling on his ass as he scrambled away from a teenage boy he outweighed by at least fifty pounds was not one of the high points of Tim's life. After a few staff members managed to drag Austin away—still screaming obscenities—to calm down in some other part of the building, Dick came rushing up to him to apologize.

"I am so sorry. I should have told you about Austin's violent reactions to homosexuals."

Tim, who at the time hadn't been feeling anywhere near as forgiving or understanding as he would be a few hours later, glared at him. "You *think*?"

Dick winced. "In all fairness," he said, holding up his hands in a placating gesture, "I had no way of knowing you were gay. Or that you were going to tell him the first time you met."

"You could have *asked*."

"Actually, I couldn't. Even though you're a volunteer, I'm still technically your employer. I'm not allowed to ask about your race, ethnicity, religion, or sexual orientation."

"But you can ask me if I'm here to molest the kids? Because that's a thousand times more offensive than asking if I'm gay."

Dick shrugged. "Welcome to Chicago."

It took another twenty minutes for Tim to feel like talking civilly, and in that time, Dick explained a bit about Austin. Apparently, his parents were both textbook neglectful alcoholics, and he'd been raised mostly by his older sister. About a year ago, she'd gotten married to another girl, and they ran away together, leaving Austin behind. He didn't take it well and transferred his feelings of abandonment and betrayal from his sister to gays and lesbians in general. There had been a few incidents with other kids at the center before, but this was the first time he'd ever gone off on a volunteer.

"Then why didn't he have a Big Brother already if he got along with the staff?" Tim asked.

"He was abandoned by his actual sister. It took me a while to convince him the program would be good for him. A lot of wasted time as it turns out," Dick added with a sigh.

Tim felt a pang of guilt. "I could talk to him again, maybe? It would probably be good for him to see that an older, sibling-like figure wants to stick around whether they're gay or not."

"I agree," Dick said with a small smile. "But Austin's already made it pretty clear that he's not coming back here any time soon."

"Oh."

"Don't take it personally." Dick squeezed his shoulder. "Nothing about what happened was your fault."

Intellectually, Tim knew Dick was right. It didn't really make him feel any better.

"We can try again next time, okay?"

My life is an endless series of next times.

"Yeah, okay." Tim took a deep breath. "By the way, I'm Catholic, white, my mom's family is Polish, and my dad's is from Ireland. Just in case there are any kids who have a problem with any of that."

Dick's lips twitched. "I'm sure we can find you someone who doesn't hate white Irish-Catholic Poles."

Disaster number two came in the form of Julius; a lanky mixed-race boy who lived with his father—who held three jobs and was almost never home—and his senile grandmother. They didn't bond as quickly as he had with Austin, but after a few afternoons spent together, Julius slowly started to open up, telling Tim about how hard it was to be at home alone with an old woman who kept confusing him with her son or her dead husband. He told Tim about his girlfriend and how he used to spend most of his time at her house before her father caught them doing what Julius called making out, but Tim suspected was probably a lot more, and forbade them from seeing each other. After that, he'd started coming to the center on his own just to get away from his house. Tim opened up in return, telling Julius about his own need to escape his home to put some distance between himself and his mother; he even talked a bit about his own romantic troubles. He'd thought things were going well between them right up until the day when something Tim said convinced Julius to steal his father's car and run away with his girlfriend—something Julius very helpfully explained in the note he'd left behind for his father.

The conversation he had with Dick after the police left ended up being a lot less comforting and apologetic than the one they'd had after Austin.

"Out of all the people who volunteered here, I didn't think I needed to tell *you* to watch what you say to these kids," Dick said, his posture radiating disappointment. Tim could barely meet his eyes.

You shouldn't have to. I know better.

"You've told me enough about the centers you used to volunteer at for me to get an idea of what kind of kids you're used to dealing with, but just because our kids aren't from the poorest parts of the city doesn't mean they don't have problems. Abuse and neglect don't give a crap about the poverty line, and kids with nice clothes and shoes that fit can still have hard lives. Every single child who comes here deserves our best."

Tim flushed with shame as he remembered his thoughts when he'd first come to the center, how close he had come to writing these kids off. He'd only been volunteering for three weeks, but he already knew how special this place could be. He'd seen it a dozen times, how a kid could be out on the sidewalk looking like they had cement blocks tied to their shoulders, but the moment they came through the doors, that invisible weight evaporated. Tim had felt something similar himself too. The past weeks with Julius reminded him why he'd gone to college in the first place.

"I know," he said quietly. "I didn't mean... I'm sorry."

Dick kept up the stern glare for a while longer before letting out a loud sigh and sinking back in his chair.

"Do you have any idea what you even said to him that made him think to steal a car and take off with his girlfriend?" Dick asked, sounding curious instead of accusing.

"I have no idea," Tim said. "The only thing I can think of is when I told him about moving here from New York to put some distance between me and my family, but I was talking about going to *college.* I never said anything about running away. He never even said anything about *wanting* to run away. I knew he was upset about not being able to see his girlfriend, but I swear if he'd even hinted he was going to do this, I would have tried to talk him out of it."

"Well," Dick said, "I guess I can't exactly stay mad at you for something you don't even know you did. Just *try* to be careful in the future, okay? And not just because it looks bad to have cops showing up to ask questions about our volunteers inspiring teenagers to commit felonies."

If Tim had been standing, he would have collapsed with relief.

He's not kicking me out.

"Okay. I promise."

They sat together for the next few minutes with only the sound of the air-conditioning system kicking on to break the silence.

"Do you think Julius will be okay?" Tim asked suddenly.

"I'm sure the cops will find him," Dick said immediately as if he'd been waiting for the question. "If he doesn't come back on his own. Running away with a girl gets a lot less romantic when you're fourteen years old with twenty dollars to your name."

"God, I hope so." Tim didn't think he needed to say more. He was sure Dick knew as well as he did all the ways kids could earn money on the streets if they were desperate enough or thought they were desperate enough.

"Why don't you go home?" Dick suggested. "It's been a pretty stressful day, and I doubt hanging around here with nothing to do is doing anything good for you."

Tim's kneejerk reaction was to refuse to go anywhere until he heard something about Julius, but he knew how unrealistic that was. Even if the cops found him and took him home that night, they weren't exactly going to call the center and tell them.

"Yeah, okay. You'll call me if you hear anything, right?"

"It'll be the first thing I do after I find out."

"Thanks, Dick."

"You're welcome. Now get out of here and get some sleep."

Tim did so, and three days later Dick called to tell him Julius and his girlfriend had been picked up in Cedar Rapids, of all places, after they'd tried to book a hotel room with the girlfriend's laughably bad fake ID. Julius's father wasn't pressing charges for the theft, but he did send Julius to stay with some extended family out on a farm in Nebraska, probably hoping some hard labor would be a more effective punishment than getting thrown in juvie. Which, while the news was a great relief to Tim, meant he was out another Little Brother.

"Are you sure you want to try another one so soon?" Dick's tinny voice came through Tim's phone. The connection sucked—cell-phone-to-cell-phone calls always sounded awful on his phone—but the bad quality did nothing to disguise Dick's obvious concern. "You could take a break. There might even be some slots open with some of the younger kids in a few weeks."

"No." Tim gripped his phone so tightly he wouldn't have been surprised to hear the screen crack. "No, I don't want to wait. I...I'll do better, I promise."

If I don't do this now, I'll be right back where I was last month, and I have no idea if I'll be able to drag myself out of it again. Please don't take this away from me.

"It's not about you doing better," Dick said. "We always make volunteers wait a week or two before moving onto another Little Brother or Sister when they've spent a lot of time with their last one. It's for the kids as much as the volunteers. It doesn't do anybody any good for new kids to be judged against the old ones."

"I wouldn't do that! I can separate Julius from whoever I get next. Honestly, I'd kinda like to forget about what happened anyway, you know?" he added with a weak chuckle.

It wasn't even a lie, not really. Tim would *love* to forget about his screwup with Julius, but he knew he'd be obsessing over it for a while. Something he'd have to keep from Dick if he didn't want to go back to empty nights of drinking cough syrup and ignoring his mother's calls.

A loud burst of static came through the phone, and Tim assumed it was one of Dick's loud, heaving sighs.

"All right," he said. "I'm taking you at your word here. Don't make me regret it."

"I promise I won't."

Another burst of static. "We've got a new kid coming in tomorrow; never been to a center before, and he's kinda nervous about it. His name's Connor, and his dad is a friend of my ex-wife, so if anything happens with him, I'm gonna be hearing about it until the sun explodes. Are you absolutely sure you can handle this?"

Tim didn't even bristle—too much—at Dick's sharp tone. Talking with or about his ex-wife was pretty much the only thing that could consistently drag his usually cheerful boss into a surly mood. As much as he'd been brought up not to believe in divorce, he couldn't help thinking this was one marriage better off dead.

"I'm sure," Tim said, nodding even though Dick couldn't see through the phone. "I can do this. No problem."

God, if you're there, please don't let me be lying.

Chapter Five

It ended up being a few more days before Spencer could get a free afternoon. Days he spent making the lives of all the idiots stupid enough to get detention with him a living hell. When he wasn't dealing with detentions, he could be found obsessively checking his phone to make sure the Spaces Open hadn't been changed to a Lost Your Chance, Loser. It hadn't, and when the impossible happened and the entire freshman population of Laurence Tureaud High managed to get through an entire day without being assholes, Spencer snatched Connor up the second he got home and marched him downtown.

Spencer had never been to a youth center before, but he'd be lying if he said he wasn't a little bit disappointed when they got there. Sure, it seemed just as nice as the pictures on the website, but with a name like the Michael Crichton Memorial Youth Center he'd kind of been hoping for a little bit of branding. It wasn't like he was expecting a giant, animatronic T-Rex in the lobby or anything, but maybe a *Jurassic Park* logo on the doors, or even just a few prints from some of the guy's movies on the wall would have been pretty cool.

Instead, the center was just a building that looked like a slightly cleaner version of the school he taught at but with no lockers, a staff that actually seemed like they wanted to be there, and a very nice receptionist who seemed pleasantly surprised Spencer had actually come in with Connor. There was a bit of a wait as she gathered up a few forms they usually had the kids take home for him to sign, but after the paperwork was taken care of, they were directed to the center's cafeteria to wait for Connor's new Big Brother to show up. They didn't even have to talk to Dick, which was a relief. There were few things more uncomfortable than trying to make small talk with the ex-husband of his only friend for five hundred miles.

It seemed a bit weird, though, to be meeting this guy in a cafeteria instead of an office or something, especially when they actually got there and saw how crowded it was. The room was about the same size as the lunchroom back at school, only with smaller tables, and instead of a kitchen, it sported a small bar-like area in the back covered with shrink-wrapped sandwiches on small paper plates laid out for the taking. Spencer held back a grimace and tried not to think too hard about how long they might have been sitting there.

"You want a sandwich?" he asked.

Please say no.

Connor shook his head, but Spencer's relief died a second later when he noticed how tense his kid was.

"Hey, you okay?"

Two teenagers, a white boy and a black girl, who both seemed to be about sixteen, walked by laughing loudly, and Connor took a hurried step closer to Spencer.

"Not really," he said quietly. "Can we go, please?"

"What's wrong?"

Connor's eyes darted around the room. "I just wanna go home."

After the other night's panic attack, Spencer's first instinct was to bundle his kid up and run out of the building and away from whatever was causing him so much distress. It was an instinct he fought. One of the hardest lessons he'd had to learn as a parent was doing what his kid wanted wasn't always what was best for him. Which, in hindsight, seemed kind of obvious, but he'd had to learn that lesson at the same time as he'd been railing against how unfair it was that his parents wouldn't do everything *he* wanted. He hadn't been able to believe he knew better than Connor without also admitting his parents might know better than him, and it took him a lot longer than it should have for him to be okay with putting his kid through uncomfortable situations that would benefit him in the long run.

"We're not going anywhere unless you give me a reason," he said.

Connor made a frustrated noise. "There's too many people here, okay? And I don't know any of them, and it's freaking me out."

Ah, social anxiety; my ancient nemesis, we meet again.

Spencer squeezed his shoulder. "I know it's nerve-wracking, but you don't need to talk to any of them. We're only here to talk to—" *Oh God, I forgot his name.* "—one person, and that's it. That's not so bad, right?"

"Don't talk to me like I'm five," Connor snapped.

Signs of life. That's encouraging.

"Are you sure?" Spencer tilted his head. "Because it seems to be helping. If you want, you could sit in my lap until—" *It started with a T, didn't it?* "—your new friend gets here, and I can read you a story. I promise I'll do my best to give the characters different voices," he added, singsonging the last few words.

Connor's cheeks flushed red.

Shit, I said that a little loud, didn't I?

Spencer winced. "Sorry. But this isn't really as bad as it seems. There's only, what, maybe two dozen people here? You eat lunch with, like, three times as many people every day—"

"I don't."

Spencer frowned. "Don't what?"

"I don't eat lunch in the cafeteria," Connor mumbled.

"You don't?" Connor shook his head. "Then...where do you eat?"

"The library."

"There are rules against that, you know." Not that Spencer wanted to lecture him. If anything, he was impressed. Mrs. Brown was the most uptight, humorless bitch of a librarian Spencer had ever met. He'd always been under the impression that she had a wooden stake and some matches ready for anyone who might even think about walking past her library with food.

Connor mumbled something Spencer didn't catch.

"What was that?"

"I said, Mrs. Brown likes me," Connor said petulantly. "She says I remind her of her dog."

Do. Not. Laugh.

"Oh." Spencer cleared his throat and turned his thoughts to something more important. *I really underestimated how much trouble he was having with school if he has to hide in the library to eat.* He couldn't help wondering, though, if the problem was just the crowd of kids. Spencer knew better than most how easy it was to get bullied in a packed lunchroom with lots of background noise and minimal supervision. He almost pushed—if the kids who were bullying his son *did* share a lunch period with him, it would be so much easier to track them down— but managed to hold off at the last second. An interrogation was the last thing Connor needed right then. But he made sure to tuck the idea away for another day. "Well. Okay then. This might not be a library, but it's still much less crowded than the cafeteria. Do you think you could try sticking it out? For a PS4 and a new TV?"

Connor hesitated, glancing around the room, nervousness radiating off his tiny frame in waves. "You promise you're not gonna make me talk to anyone?"

"When have I *ever* made you talk to anyone you didn't want to?"

Connor opened his mouth, but whatever he was about to say died on his tongue when Spencer raised an eyebrow. *Damn right you're not saying anything. One of the reasons we're here is because I indulge your shyness. No, fuck indulging, I cultivated that shit. If I'm gonna feel guilty, there's no way you're gonna pretend the thing I'm feeling guilty about isn't true so you can bitch at me.*

"Fine..."

"Good." Spencer gave his shoulder one more squeeze before gently leading him farther into the lunchroom. "Let's go find a table and wait for—" *Tony, maybe?* "—this guy to show up, okay?"

They managed to find a free table in a corner far away from both the doors and the sandwich bar. It was round, with five plastic school chairs pushed all the way under the Formica tabletop. Connor pulled out the chair closest to the wall and threw himself into it. Spencer took the seat nearest to him much more sedately but made a show of having trouble scooting his chair over until they were right next to each other. Connor didn't crack a smile or roll his eyes at his antics (which was a wonderful word Spencer wished he could use more often), but that was okay. He wasn't bouncing his leg or drumming his fingers on the table, which probably meant he wasn't in any danger of bolting no matter what Spencer did.

Of course, after all that, *Spencer* ended up being the one who got all the weird looks—from both the kids and the staff. Not that he was complaining exactly. As much as he usually hated to be stared at, he was happy to divert attention away from his kid. He crossed his arms and met every questioning glance with his best flat, unimpressed teacher stare, smirking to himself when no one could meet his eyes for more than a few seconds.

It took about ten minutes, but eventually the curious looks and raised eyebrows tapered off as the kids got their food and met up with who Spencer assumed were their Big Brothers or Sisters. He took the opportunity to study how the kids and adults interacted and found, to his pleasant surprise, the write-ups he'd read seemed to be true. No one seemed like they were in therapy. They talked and laughed, hair was ruffled, napkins were thrown, and heads were bowed in what seemed like deep, serious conversation. If it weren't for the fact that he knew he was at a youth center, Spencer would have assumed everyone here was talking with a friend, or maybe even an actual relative. Tension he hadn't known he was carrying around eased from his shoulders.

This is exactly what Connor needs.

"How long are we gonna sit here?" Connor asked under his breath.

"Patience, kid," Spencer murmured back. "We got here early, so that means we wait."

"That was a rhetorical question."

"No, it wasn't. Don't lie." Spencer smiled briefly. "Good word usage though."

Whatever Connor might have said in return was cut off as a shadow fell across their table.

"Hi," said the man who belonged to the shadow. "My name's Tim. You must be Connor, right?"

His voice was low and smooth, neither young nor old, with a pleasant cheerfulness that stopped just short of being cloying. He spared a slightly perplexed glance for Spencer before turning all his attention toward the kid. Spencer took the opportunity to quickly size him up.

He was tall, about six feet or so Spencer would guess, with wavy light-brown hair longer on the top than on the sides—though thankfully not an undercut—and artfully tousled into gentle fluffy waves. His chocolate-brown eyes were clear, friendly, and set above circles so dark Spencer assumed he was either still in college or had a baby of his own at home. The thin, navy-blue T-shirt he wore was tight enough in the shoulders and arms to show off a little bit of muscle, but otherwise, his build seemed pretty average. His lightly tanned face was handsome, in a nonthreatening, boy-next-door-kind of way, and when he smiled at Connor, the expression seemed genuine. If Spencer had been the kind of person to base his opinion of someone off appearance alone, he would have liked him on the spot. As it was, all Spencer felt was a minor sense of self-consciousness at the way the guy kept side-eyeing his dark-green cardigan and gray *ThunderCats* T-shirt.

"Yeah, that's Connor," Spencer said when it became obvious the kid wasn't going to say anything. "And I'm Spencer."

He held out his hand. Tim took it without hesitation, giving a squeeze that was firm but, Spencer noted, not crushing. Not that he was expecting a "see how strong I am, person I just met" handshake, but it was nice to have a small bit of confirmation that the guy who didn't look like a douchebag was, in fact, not a douchebag.

"Nice to meet you," Tim said. He took a seat across from them—winning a few more points in Spencer's book for not crowding Connor—and glanced back and forth between them, a small frown forming on his brow. Spencer waited patiently for the inevitable. "Are you...Connor's brother?"

Spencer smiled as Connor let out a disgusted huff. "Nope. I'm his father."

To his credit, Tim's widening eyes seemed to be his only physical reaction, which was a nice change of pace from how this conversation usually went. Most people tended to be either disbelieving or slightly horrified when they found out Spencer had a fourteen-year-old son, especially since, when he was mostly clean shaven like now, Spencer looked a *lot* younger than his actual age.

"Oh." Spencer could practically see all the questions Tim wanted to ask lit up like bright neon signs behind his eyes; to his further credit, he didn't ask a single one. Instead, his smile came back, a bit brighter than before. "Then it's really great that you came with Connor. Most parents don't really bother."

Spencer felt his eyes narrowing slightly as his natural paranoia started poking at the back of his mind. Tim was perfect, exactly what Spencer had hoped for when he started to seriously consider the program, and Spencer had always been incredibly suspicious of perfection.

"It's not a bother at all," Spencer said, letting a bit of warning slip into his voice. "Gotta make sure you're good enough to hang around with my kid. And that you're not too interested in how he 'hangs around,' if you get my meaning."

"Oh my God, Dad," Connor groaned.

"Don't 'oh my God, Dad' me," Spencer said. "One of those papers I signed was to let you leave the center with him. If you think I'm not at least gonna ask if he's gonna molest you the second I'm out the door, you're crazy."

"He's not a pedophile!"

Spencer raised an eyebrow. "How do you know?"

"I'm...really not," Tim said, sounding torn between being insulted and bemused.

"Well of course *you'd* say that," Spencer said. "What kind of pedophile would actually admit to being a pedophile?"

Tim blinked. "Are you saying me denying I'm a pedophile means I'm a pedophile?"

"I'm *saying* I have no idea who you are, and I basically just signed my son over to you."

Sudden, irrational terror started clawing at Spencer's chest the moment the words were out of his mouth.

Oh my God, I totally just did that! I signed my kid over to a complete stranger. Holy shit. I didn't even make sure I knew his name. *He's not a dog or some twitchy freshman; I should have asked questions! What the hell is wrong with me?*

"I can assure you I *don't* molest people. Especially not kids."

And now Tim *did* sound insulted. Spencer knew he was probably in the middle of one of his bigger fuckups in recent memory, but he couldn't get himself to shut up. He was completely freaked-out by how much thought he *didn't* put into this. What if Tim really *was* a molester? How would Spencer even know? Was he being a giant asshole right now, insulting the hell out of a guy who seemed perfectly nice because he was a paranoid piece of shit? Or could he sense something lurking beneath the surface of Perfect Tim?

Fuck, I have no fucking idea. But now I can't stop worrying about this guy raping my kid.

"Can you prove that?" He hadn't even realized he was going to say anything until the words were already out of his mouth. Tim's lips pinched together, and Spencer felt a surge of satisfaction laced with something he refused to admit was the beginnings of shame.

"The center does extensive background checks," Tim said. "Which was clearly mentioned in the forms you signed."

Was it? Spencer tried to think back, but, honestly, he'd kind of skimmed. He'd been more focused on getting Connor away from the front door, so he'd have more of a chance to catch up to him if he tried to run.

"You read the forms before you signed them, didn't you?"

The warmth that had laced his voice when he'd first introduced himself was completely gone now. In fact, Spencer was pretty sure he heard the barest hint of derision.

"Of course I did," he lied. Indignation swelled inside him even though he knew he was probably in the wrong here. "But background checks only prove that you haven't been caught."

"Dad, stop."

"Look," Tim said, scowling. "It's obvious you're not comfortable leaving your son with a stranger, or at least you're not comfortable leaving him with me. And that's fine." Even through his panic and the beginnings of embarrassment, Spencer got the impression Tim was the one lying now. "You can request another Big Brother for your son any time you want. But everyone here went through the *exact* same vetting process I did, so they're all just as likely to be serial child rapists as I am."

*

If Dick ever finds out I said that, I'm definitely getting fired.

It was a fleeting thought, one quickly drowned out by a few dozen other thoughts that all seemed to revolve around punching Spencer in the face. It took every bit of self-control Tim had to keep from showing how close he was to snapping. Being called a pedophile by some guy he'd just met, a guy he'd actually been admiring not even five minutes ago for actually taking the time out of his day to bring his son down instead of making him walk alone like so many other parents, was the icing on the shit cake that was the last few months of his life.

Spencer's eyes widened in surprise. "So, you're admitting it!"

Tim clenched his hands under the table. This guy was utterly unbelievable.

"Dad, *please* stop."

And that right there made him even angrier. The man's son was obviously embarrassed by the way his father was acting, and Spencer didn't even notice. Or if he did notice, he didn't care.

"Maybe you should come back another day." It killed Tim to say it, especially since this was the *second* time in as many minutes. "You can request another volunteer on your way out."

God, he really was going to go zero for three, and in record time too. *No, this can't count. I barely even talked to Connor; no way is this one my fault. I'll just tell Dick what happened, and that will be that. I'm not going to beat myself up over some paranoid, asshole parent.*

Tim shook his head. As far as he was concerned, he was done. He didn't even care if Spencer suddenly realized what an ass he was being and apologized; Tim was going to get up and walk out and go home and wash this whole experience away with a few swigs of NyQuil.

"*No*," Connor snapped, stopping Tim before he could do more than slide his chair back. "You're not gonna drag me back here tomorrow. We had a deal, Dad."

"Our deal had nothing to do with you getting molested."

"I'm not getting molested!"

Tim held back a wince as a few people at the surrounding tables turned to stare at them. Nothing happening here was his fault, and he refused to be embarrassed, not for himself or anyone else. Spencer seemed to notice the stares too and met each one with a glare that made quite a few of them quickly turn away. Connor must have noticed the staring as well, but his reaction was much different than Spencer's.

"Forget it," he mumbled, shrinking in on himself. "Let's just go."

Connor started to stand up, and against his better judgment, Tim reached out to stop him. It was instinct, to try to stop a kid who seemed ready to run away. However, considering the "discussion" going on, reaching for Connor was probably the worst thing he could have done. Thankfully, Spencer was too busy pulling Connor back down himself to notice.

"Wait," Spencer said. Connor struggled, but even Tim could tell it was halfhearted at best, and after a few seconds he stopped. Spencer let go of his wrist immediately, but only to put his arm around Connor's shoulder. He didn't squeeze or use his weight to push his son down the way Tim had seen so many parents do. The arm was obviously supposed to be a comfort, and even though he doubted Connor would admit it, Tim could see it was working.

Dammit, why can't he be a terrible father?

Good dads were one of Tim's biggest weaknesses, and he could already feel his anger fading.

"I'm sorry, kid. I didn't mean to embarrass you."

Connor shrugged. "Whatever."

"I'll leave, okay?" Connor looked vaguely alarmed. Spencer smiled weakly. "Just for a bit. Stay here and...try to have a nice afternoon. I'll come get you later like we talked about, and we'll go get your new TV. How does that sound?"

Connor glanced at the ground, his eyes flickering up toward Tim every few seconds. Without meaning to, Tim gave him a reassuring smile, the same one he always gave when he was trying to convince kids to come out of their shell.

You should stop this here. It already blew up in your face once; do you really want to risk it blowing up again?

"Okay," Connor said finally.

Too late now.

"Okay," Spencer said. "Good."

He gave his son a one-armed hug, then turned his hazel eyes back toward Tim. "Can I talk to you for a second? Alone?"

Connor didn't seem too happy when he heard that, but Spencer somehow sensed his distress and gave him another squeeze without breaking eye contact. Tim wasn't exactly thrilled either, but he'd already encouraged Connor to stay with that smile. Freezing his dad out would send mixed messages. Possibly even set up a father/son conflict in the future if Connor and Tim managed to hit it off as program siblings.

"Okay," Tim said, keeping his voice even. "We can step out in the hall if you want."

Spencer glanced at Connor. "Maybe just a little closer to the door."

Somewhere Connor can still see us. That has to be on purpose.

"That should work."

Spencer gave Connor one last hug before standing up. Tim got up as well and was mildly surprised when Spencer passively let him lead the way to a relatively private stretch of wall about fifteen feet away. He was more surprised by the other man's size. Tim had to have at least six inches on him, and at just over six feet, he wasn't very tall himself. It felt very strange to be talking to an adult who was smaller than many of the teenagers he'd spent time with recently.

"If you're trying to figure out how to apologize, don't bother," Tim said, keeping his voice down. The last thing he needed was for one of the other volunteers to overhear what was most likely going to be an argument and mention it to Dick. Getting into fights with parents was definitely against the rules. "We don't have to like each other for Connor to get the full benefit of the program. All I ask is that if you have a problem with me, take it up with *me*. In private. Children shouldn't have to see their parents arguing with people right in front of them."

Spencer grimaced. "I think I probably deserved that."

Tim stayed silent. Any agreement he made would sound too waspish—and too much like his mother—for his comfort.

"Just like you deserve an apology, whether you want one or not," Spencer continued. "So, I'm sorry I kind of called you a pedophile."

"'Kind of'?"

Spencer glared up at him for a second before closing his eyes and taking a deep breath. "Okay. I'm sorry I *very much* called you a pedophile. I just...I didn't really think about what it would be like to leave Connor with someone I didn't know. I've never done that before, and it all kind of hit me at once, you know?"

"I don't, actually. It can't be much different than letting him go over to a friend's house unless you ask all his friend's parents if they're going to molest him."

So much for not being waspish.

Spencer crossed his arms. "Maybe I would have if he ever had any friends."

Tim frowned. "He doesn't have friends?"

"Apparently not." Spencer sighed. "It's part of the reason why we're here. I was hoping that being around someone who isn't me would help him open up to people his own age. You might not have noticed with the way he was bitching me out, but Connor is a really shy kid. Even worse than I was at his age, which is saying something. He's being harassed in school too, and I just found out he's scared of crowds, and I have no idea what to do about *any* of that and—" He cut himself off with a sharp shake of his head. "And I'm not here so I can complain to you. Sorry."

Tim hated how every word Spencer spoke dug another hook of sympathy into his heart. He really was just a dad trying to do the best he could by his kid, and considering he was here and the words "wife" or "mother" hadn't crossed his lips yet, Tim probably wouldn't have been reaching to assume he was a single dad either.

"It's not a bad thing to unload on someone," Tim said, completely against his better judgment. "But you're right that I'm here for Connor before anyone else."

"And that's good," Spencer said with a small smile. "He needs that. And definitely from someone who isn't his father."

"Then I don't think we need to waste any more time talking about what happened today," Tim said. "We'll just chalk it up to nerves and put it behind us, okay?"

Which was Tim's attempt at salving his pride by not having to actually say the words "I forgive you," but it was a mostly empty gesture as most pride-saving gestures tended to be. Even if he didn't say the words out loud, Tim was well aware he'd pretty much forgiven Spencer the second he saw how much he cared about his son.

"That sounds great." Spencer smiled up at him, tossing a few black curls out of his eyes. A moment later, the smile dimmed. "Oh, uh, one more thing you probably need to know. It doesn't happen a lot, but sometimes Connor has short mild panic attacks. They're not that bad, but you should know how to deal—"

"I know how to handle panic attacks," Tim assured him.

"Good. And, um, I wasn't trying to tell you how to do your job, or anything," he said, wincing. "Or assuming I knew more about it than you did. Because it pisses me off when people do that to me, and I'd hate it if anything I said came off like I was doing that, so...yeah."

Tim nearly smiled. *He's almost kind of awkwardly cute when he's not accusing me of wanting to rape children.*

"Don't worry about it. I know what you meant, Mister..." And now Tim was the one feeling awkward. *I don't know his last name, do I?*

"Kent," Spencer supplied. "Spencer Kent. I...probably should have said that earlier."

This time, Tim did smile. It was small, but he still couldn't help feeling like he was being a pushover. Tim was terrible at holding grudges, even when it was in his best interest—it was part of the reason Rudy lasted as long as he did.

"We both probably should have. Tim Ellis, by the way." *Kent. Spencer and Connor Kent. Why do those names sound familiar?* A moment later it clicked. "*Connor Kent.* Did you name your son after *Superboy*?"

Spencer seemed surprised for a moment and then laughed. "You know, I think you're actually the first person who's ever picked up on that."

"You mean I was right? You really named your son after a comic book character?"

That was...kind of adorable.

"I was fourteen," Spencer said wryly. "It was either a comic character or Darth Vader."

Tim's breath caught in his throat.

Fourteen? He had Spencer when he was fourteen?

He knew Spencer had to have been a young dad, but he hadn't guessed *that* young. Suddenly, he very badly wanted to ask what had happened, but once again, his professionalism held him back. He wasn't here to satisfy his curiosity. He was here to be a friend to Connor, who they'd already left alone long enough.

Still, he couldn't hold back *all* his questions.

"Why not Clark?" Tim asked. "Then he'd be Superman."

"And make him go through school with the name Clark Kent?" Spencer raised an eyebrow. "I might be an asshole, but I'm not a monster."

Tim very quickly decided there was no good way he could respond to that. "So, when were you planning on picking Connor up?" he asked instead.

"Is it okay to leave him here for two hours?"

"I'm free all afternoon," Tim said, somewhat surprised. After his earlier outburst, he'd expected Spencer wouldn't want Connor here longer than it took to walk down the block to get a cup of coffee. "That seems a bit long for a first meeting though. Are you sure he's gonna be okay with that?"

"I've got a shit ton of grading to get through, and I'd really like to get my work done before we have the fight I'm pretty sure we're gonna have about the whole pedo thing." Spencer raked his fingers through his curls. "And, honestly, it'll probably take at least that long for you to get him to do more than grunt or stare at the table."

Grading? This guy's a teacher?

"That's good to know, but it's not what I asked." Tim tried not to be disappointed Spencer didn't even consider how his son would feel being left here with a stranger for two hours. "I asked if *Connor* would be okay with that."

Spencer stared at him for the longest time before shaking his head and letting out a self-deprecating laugh.

"What?"

"Oh nothing, just realizing the guy I called a child rapist is actually a really good fucking person," he said, sounding more than a little disgusted. "Fuck."

"I thought we were putting that behind us?" Tim didn't even care if he was being a pushover anymore. Seeing those big hazel eyes swimming with regret felt like getting socked in the stomach, and he needed to get this conversation back into the realm of professionalism before he forgot which of the Kent men he was supposed to be comforting. "Part of putting it behind us means not beating yourself up over it."

Spencer shook his head again. "If you're trying to make me feel like shit, you're doing a great job."

"I'm—"

"That was a joke," Spencer added quickly. "And yeah, Connor will be fine with being here for two hours. We talked about it before we left."

"Oh. Okay. That's good." Tim nodded, falling back into his responsible caregiver persona with a sense of relief he hoped to God didn't show on his face. "But if Connor wants to come back after today, we should probably work out a schedule. I'm free most afternoons, but I'm not always here."

"We can talk about that if the kid wants to come back," Spencer said, not sounding too optimistic about the prospect. He sighed, opened his mouth, then paused and let out a little laugh. "I was about to ask if I need to drop him off every time, but since everyone seems so surprised that I'm here, I guess that'd be a no."

Tim felt his lips twitch. "You really didn't read any of those papers, did you? Everything about the program is written down right there."

"Right." Spencer flushed ever so slightly. "I have copies in my back pocket..."

"Maybe you should read them."

"I'm thinking probably, yeah." He snorted. "All right. It's definitely time to go before I embarrass myself or the kid even more." He chewed his bottom lip for a moment, and then added, "Just...he's a really good kid, okay? Don't hold me against him."

"I don't judge *any* of the kids who come here, Mr. Kent," Tim said. "And I'm not about to start because of something someone else did."

If he hadn't already been accused of being a child molester, Tim might have been insulted by how relieved Spencer looked.

"Right. So...I guess I'll see you in a few hours, then." He hesitated and then held out his hand.

After a short hesitation of his own, Tim shook it. Spencer's skin was incredibly smooth with a slight slickness to it that could only come from recently applied hand lotion. It was something Tim had noticed when they'd shook hands earlier too. They let go, and Spencer made his way back to Connor. He leaned down, said something, and then gave him a quick hug, which Connor shrugged off violently. Spencer took it in stride, ruffling his son's hair before saying something else and walking toward the door and Tim.

"Good luck with the kid," he said as he passed. Tim watched him leave and then turned to Connor. The boy still sat at the table, his head down as he picked at the seam in his jeans. His hand stilled when Tim sat down across from him, but otherwise he didn't acknowledge Tim at all.

"Hey," Tim said, as casually as he could. He smiled even though he was sure Connor wouldn't glance up long enough to see it.

Connor made a noise that might have been a mumbled word, but Tim wouldn't have put money on it. *Spencer wasn't lying about the shyness, then.* But that was okay. Tim had dealt with plenty of shy kids in his life, and he was always good at getting them to open up. A sudden surge of confidence welled up in his chest.

Nothing but grunts for two hours, huh? Just watch me, Spencer Kent. I'll have him talking in half that.

"So—"

"I'm sorry about my dad," Connor muttered.

Tim blinked.

That was easy.

"You really don't need to apologize for him."

Connor scoffed quietly. "Not like *he's* gonna say sorry."

Tim pursed his lips. Center policy said not to badmouth any of the children's parents in front of them no matter what, and Tim had always extended that to not saying anything about their parents at all unless he was asked a specific question; even then, he kept his answers as nonjudgmental as possible. He didn't know the parents personally, and it wasn't his place to put himself between family members. Unfortunately, making a noncommittal noise and gently shifting the conversation was a lot harder when he'd actually talked to one of the parents. Undoubtedly, Spencer was an asshole; the guy even admitted it himself. The problem was, from what Tim could tell, he was also a father who really cared about his son. Despite his better judgment, Tim couldn't help wanting to try fixing their relationship.

"Actually, he already apologized before he left."

"Bullshit." Connor glanced up at him through dark curls with eyes the exact same shade of hazel as his father's. In fact, aside from his slightly darker skin tone and what seemed to be a bit of Asian heritage, everything about him was the spitting image of Spencer. "Apologizing would mean admitting he was wrong, and he never does that about anything big. Especially not to strangers."

"He did to me," Tim said with a shrug. Judging by Connor's expression, he clearly didn't believe him. "Do you think I'm lying?"

"Probably."

"But why would I?"

"Because he told you to?" Connor's tone heavily implied Tim was an idiot for asking. "He hired you to talk to me, so that basically means he's your boss, right?"

"It doesn't work like that. This is a nonpr—"

"Nonprofit volunteer thing, yeah, I know. But you still have to do what he says, or he can get you fired."

Tim chuckled. "Neither one of you read those papers, did you? That's not at *all* how this works. Yeah, he signed you up for the program, but he has no say in anything I do. He can pull you out, refuse to bring you back, request someone else be your Big Brother—but he can't get me fired. I'm not here for him. I'm here for *you*. So, I have no reason at all to lie to you."

"Doesn't mean you won't."

"Of course it does. I know it sounds stupid because we're not related and we just met, but I'm *your* Big Brother. There are a lot of things that can mean, but honestly? All it really means to me is I'm here to hang out with you and talk with you—or just sit here without saying anything if that's what you want. This is all about you. Whatever you want. But no matter what that is, personally, I'm hoping we can be friends. And maybe you'd disagree, but I don't believe in lying to people I'm trying to be friends with."

As he spoke, the belligerent gleam in Connor's eyes slowly faded. It was replaced with an emotion Tim couldn't identify before Connor's gaze lowered back to the table. By the time Tim finished speaking, Connor had hunched in on himself and appeared to be even more uncomfortable than he'd been during Spencer's outburst.

"I don't believe you."

"Why not?"

"No one wants to be friends with me."

Tim's heart broke a little. If there was one part of volunteering with kids he hated, it was this. The words were always different—"I have no friends," "my mom left," "my dad won't look at me"—but the tone never changed. Absolute resignation. A too-old, world-weary acceptance that they would never have love or companionship.

"Well, I do."

The words weren't enough, no matter how much Tim wished they were, but he'd always been good at following his words up with action. He only hoped Connor stuck around long enough for him to try.

Connor crossed his arms over his chest in a way he probably thought made him appear tough. To Tim, it seemed more like he was hugging himself.

"Why?"

Tim hesitated, the usual stock answers about every person being unique and worthy of friendship or love sticking in his throat. They seemed so disingenuous. Especially since, even though Tim believed those words wholeheartedly, if he said them this time, he'd be lying.

The "right" answers don't seem to be working out for you so far. And you did promise you wouldn't lie.

Tim took a deep breath. "Honestly? Because I've been having a shitty few months, and I could really use a friend right now."

Connor glanced up. "So...*you're* the one who needs a therapist?"

Tim barked out a surprised laugh. "Probably," he admitted. Connor ducked his head, but not before Tim saw his lips twitch. "Mostly though, I just need someone to talk to who isn't my boss or trying to guilt me into coming home for Christmas."

"Your boss is guilting you into coming home for Christmas?"

"No." *If anything, she'd be trying to get me to spend Christmas with* her *family.* "That would be my mom."

"She's already talking about Christmas? It's still September!"

"*Thank* you!" Tim said a little bit louder than he'd meant to. White-hot vindication surged through his veins, and he had to fight to keep from slapping the table like some kind of eighteenth-century politician arguing a bill in front of Congress. "I don't suppose you'd be willing to say that over the phone?"

Connor flushed slightly, but he laughed too, so Tim counted it as a win. "No way."

"All right," Tim said, exaggerating his disappointment with a dramatic sigh. "I guess I'll just put on a fake voice and pretend to be you."

Connor snorted. "Don't you have other friends who can tell her she's crazy?"

"Not anymore."

Connor chewed his lip for a moment. "What happened?"

As if that isn't the loaded question to end all loaded questions. Oh well, no sense holding back now, not when he's opening up so nicely.

"My ex got them all in the breakup."

"She took all your *friends*?"

"He," Tim corrected automatically. He mentally cringed and waited for a reaction, but Connor didn't even seem to notice. He was too busy looking appalled. Tim relaxed. "And he didn't really take them; they were his to begin with."

"That's still crappy. If someone's your friend, they shouldn't stop being your friend just because you break up with their other friend," Connor said with the knowledgeable air of someone who had zero experience with what they were talking about, yet was sure they were 100 percent correct.

"It's a bit more complicated than that," Tim said, hiding a smile. "And they were kind of awful, so I wasn't really sorry to see them go."

"Then why were you friends with them?"

"That's the question, isn't it?" Tim hoped his smile didn't come off as strained as it felt.

"That's not an answer."

Tim shifted in his seat, suddenly feeling incredibly defensive. "I thought you were supposed to be shy?"

"You're not as scary as everyone else." Connor crossed his arms. "Now, are you gonna answer me or not?"

Tim almost said no. There were about a dozen guidelines he could hide behind to keep from having to answer; a dozen ways he could slip past the scary probing words of the tiny teenage boy sitting in front of him. He'd probably be destroying any chance of building any kind of trust between them, but wasn't that better than having to face the one question he'd been refusing to think about ever since he'd decided to leave Rudy?

No. You've already faced it. You just don't want to think about what it says about you.

"Sometimes..." He licked his suddenly too-dry lips. "Sometimes it's easier to go along with things you know are wrong when the people doing them make you feel like you matter. And it's even easier when you're in love with one of them."

"Your boyfriend was one of the awful people?"

Tim snorted. "He was their king."

Connor made a face. "Then why did you date him?"

Thankfully, this one had a much easier answer. "Because he wasn't all bad, at first." Connor seemed less than impressed, and Tim couldn't help smiling despite the raw gaping wound he was prodding. "Relationships are probably the furthest thing in the world from black and white. If someone gets you to fall in love with them..." He stopped. Saying it like that implied more than a few things that weren't true. As manipulative as Rudy could be, he was also strangely honest. The Rudy Tim had fallen for wasn't very different from the Rudy he hoped he never saw again: sexy and charming and toxic in equal, uninhibited measures. The only thing that changed was Rudy's decision to focus the worst parts of his personality on Tim, instead of the best. "When you fall in love with someone," he corrected, "it's really easy to ignore things about them that, in hindsight, are pretty big red flags."

"Ugh." Connor made a harsh gagging noise. "Relationships are stupid."

"They're not all bad," Tim said, his words threaded with amusement. At Connor's skeptical expression he laughed. "You'll see one day."

Connor glanced away. For several minutes he said nothing. Then, just as Tim was about to get worried, Connor asked quietly, "Was being with him better than being alone?"

"Sometimes."

Connor glanced up. "Do you still wish you were with him?"

Tim swallowed heavily. "Sometimes," he said softly.

Connor nodded slowly as if he'd expected Tim's answer. "You're alone now though."

"Yep," Tim said. "I'm alone now."

They fell silent then. Connor studying Tim with a piercing gaze that had no place on a fourteen-year-old boy, and Tim trying not to squirm as he felt like every decision he'd ever made was being silently judged.

"Okay," Connor said. "We can be friends."

Tim tilted his head and smiled, though he wasn't quite sure if he was more pleased or relieved. "Just like that?"

Connor shrugged and glanced away self-consciously. "Yeah? We don't need, like, a contract to sign in blood or anything, do we?"

Tim snorted. "No, I don't think that's necessary."

"Yeah, okay. So...yeah. I mean, you don't have to. If you changed your mind or whatever, that's fine..."

"I didn't change my mind," Tim said. "I'd still very much like to be friends with you."

"Cool." Connor lowered his head, but not before Tim could see another small flush starting to spread across his cheeks and nose. "So, what now?"

Tim leaned forward, resting his arms on the table. "Whatever you want."

Connor let out a tiny, frustrated growl. "I already told you I don't have friends. I have no idea what they do together."

"You have to have at least seen people doing stuff with their friends though, right?" Tim asked. "Stuff you maybe wanted to do but never had anyone to do it with?"

"I'm only ever around my dad and people at school," Connor said, staring up at him flatly. "That kinda limits our options to bitching about students or talking about how cool it was to get drunk and throw up last weekend."

Tim laughed. "Then we're kind of screwed. Neither one of us have students, and center policy forbids me from encouraging underage drinking."

"Good. Drunks are stupid."

"I suppose we'll just have to settle for having a conversation."

"About what? You're like twenty years older than me."

Ouch.

Tim could have pointed out that they'd already been having a conversation, but instead he smiled. He might have been more outgoing at fourteen than Connor seemed to be, but he was introverted enough to have a pretty good idea of how Connor liked to spend his free time.

"Do you like to read?"

Connor's whole face lit up.

*

Of all the things Spencer might have expected to see when he came back two hours later, Tim and his son furiously discussing *The Silmarillion* wasn't even on the list.

"It's not even a real novel! It's a textbook, and I read enough of those in college. If I'm gonna read something for fun, it needs to actually be *fun* to read."

"But it explains the *entire Lord of the Rings backstory*! You're missing out on so much by ignoring it." Connor vibrated in his seat. "And it's not a *textbook*. It's a collection of short stories and poems."

"It's a textbook," Tim said flatly.

"No, it's not!"

"Well, it sure reads like one."

"You have no appreciation for classic literature!"

"*Classic literature*? It's a handbook for nerds. I might as well read a *Dungeons and Dragons* rulebook."

"Agh! You're such a...a...a uncultured basic *bitch*!"

"Woah! Hey!" Spencer rushed over, not really sure which one of them he should be glaring at. "What the hell's going on here?"

"Oh, hey, Dad." Connor mood switched from barely contained indignation to mild surprise so fast it nearly gave Spencer whiplash. "Has it been two hours already?"

"Yes," Spencer said slowly.

"Huh. Doesn't seem like it."

"I guess time flies when you're fighting with the guy who's supposed to be looking out for you." Spencer had meant to be stern and fatherly, but he was pretty sure he sounded as confused as he felt.

"We're not *fighting*," Connor said, his voice thick with unvarnished teenage exasperation. "We're having a *conversation*."

"You called him a bitch."

"A very passionate conversation." Connor flashed small grin. "And I called him a *basic* bitch; it's totally different."

"He's right," Tim said. "About the conversation, at least. We weren't really fighting. It was actually a lot of fun."

"*See*? We weren't fighting. Even though we totally could have been because Tim has a really shitty taste in books."

"Connor!" Spencer snapped.

"Oh, come on, Dad. He thinks *Jurassic Park* is better than *Sphere*."

Tim threw up his hands. "*Jurassic Park* is a *classic*."

"So is *Sphere*!"

"I've always kind of liked *State of Fear*," Spencer put in, before quickly shaking his head. He was here to pick up his kid, not debate Michael Crichton's entire library. Even if the setting was incredibly appropriate. "Never mind. Are you ready to go?"

Connor nodded. "Yep." He pushed himself out of his chair. "Bye, Tim!"

"See you around, Connor," Tim said with a wave and a smile. Without another word Connor started walking away, leaving a bemused Spencer behind.

"He's a good kid," Tim said.

"I know." If there was one thing Spencer never doubted, it was Connor's inherent amazingness. "And, uh, you got him talking. Which is impressive, even if he *was* calling you names... I'm sorry about that, by the way."

Tim smiled. "I'm a big boy, Mr. Kent. I've been called worse things."

Spencer winced but accepted the barb he probably deserved. *So much for letting it go though.*

"You should probably go catch up with him before he gets lost."

Spencer felt strangely disappointed by the obvious dismissal. "Right. Well. It was...nice meeting you."

It was a bit of childish spitefulness, ending his farewell with a pleasantry instead of a nice neutral "goodbye," but he wanted to put Tim on the spot and maybe make him sweat about how to respond. Would he lie and return the sentiment or struggle to find a polite way to avoid returning it without completely shutting him down? The moment the words were out of his mouth, however, he lost his spite and his courage. Instead of waiting for a response, Spencer turned on his heel and took off after Connor. The kid hadn't gone too far past the doorway, so he jogged lightly to catch up with him.

"So…" Spencer said after nearly a minute of silently walking through the halls of the youth center. "How was it?"

Connor shrugged. "Fine, I guess."

Spencer sighed silently. He'd been more than shocked to see Tim and Connor interacting at all, let alone having a literary debate. He still wasn't entirely sure they hadn't been fighting, but he'd hoped the fact they'd been talking was a sign Connor might be enjoying himself. Maybe even enough to keep coming voluntarily. Spencer and Tim might have gotten off on the wrongest foot in the history of wrong feet, but the man seemed good for Connor. Spencer would have happily suffered through the inevitable awkwardness and strained conversation of potential future meetings if it meant keeping his son outside his shell.

"Well, I'm proud of you for trying," he said, trying not to sound too dejected. "I promise you don't have to do this again."

"Are you kidding?" Connor said incredulously. "He still thinks *The Silmarillion* sucks. I'm coming back *tomorrow*."

Chapter Six

October was easily Spencer's favorite month. The temperature finally began cooling down, layers were once again weather appropriate, everything everywhere was done up with awesome Halloween decorations, and it was far enough into the school year for Spencer to start bringing out the good assignments; the ones that made the kids think and actually had a chance at being fun to grade. *This* October, however, was particularly great, and Spencer had to lay a lot of that at the feet of Big Brother Tim.

It wouldn't be completely accurate to say Connor had *blossomed* these past few weeks since he started making regular visits to the center, but Spencer would have had to be blind not to notice the changes. His kid smiled more outside the house. He laughed along with the rest of the class without worrying about being so loud he drew attention to himself. He even raised his hand a few times to answer questions completely unprompted.

That terrified Spencer every time it happened because he *knew* how much courage it took for someone as shy as Connor to draw attention to themselves, and he dreaded having to tell his raisin he was wrong in front of the entire class. Thankfully, Connor hadn't been wrong yet, but Spencer was nothing if not pessimistic about the future.

Connor wasn't a totally changed boy though. He still refused to eat in the cafeteria, still refused to tell Spencer who was bullying him, still refused to admit whether or not he was still *being* bullied, and he hadn't made any friends at school. But that was okay. Because he had Tim now, and Spencer never thought he'd be so grateful for someone who was nosing around the edges of their little two-person family. Connor was improving in ways he never would have been able to with just Spencer in his life, and while he could have easily started to resent Tim, he was happy enough to share his son with anyone who put a smile on his face.

Although, if Spencer had to hear another sentence that started with "Yeah, but Tim said…," he might actually scream.

No, scratch that. I'm gonna scream if this goddamn box of Lucky Charms doesn't slide one inch closer to the edge of this shelf right fucking now.

Shopping day had come again, and since Spencer actually remembered to go this week, that meant he had to jump back into the never-ending battle against the idiot shelf stockers who put *everything he needed* on the top shelves. Which normally wasn't *that* bad since he'd had decades to get used to being this short. He could usually manage to balance on the rails of his shopping cart to get those extra few inches he needed. But *this* time, some self-absorbed mouth-breathing *shopper* had pushed the entire row of Lucky Charms a half foot back from the edge of the shelf, and no amount of stretching or contorting could get him close enough to even graze his fingers against the box. The cheerfully proclaimed 20% More in Every Box! written across the very top—the only part of the damn thing he could actually see—mocked him as the cheap paper pumpkins hanging from the ceiling watched his efforts with morbid fascination.

"I'm going to get you," he muttered between clenched teeth. He jumped, again, slamming his hand down on the empty space in front of the box after missing completely and barely grabbing the edge of the shelf before he could fall over. "I'm not leaving without you. So, you can just give up right now and tip over because if I have to ask for one of those old people can grabbers, I'm gonna come back here and burn this place to the fucking *grou—*"

"Do...you need some help?"

Spencer flinched and spun around, a few words about threats toward cereal not being legally actionable and, really, no one needs to call the cops or anything like that on the tip of his tongue, and found himself staring face-to-face with Tim.

Great.

He hadn't actually seen Tim since that first disastrous meeting. Shame and embarrassment had kept him firmly on the street side of the doors on the days he'd been home to walk Connor to the center—something that always got a very expressive teenage scoff from the kid. So, of course he'd run into him when he was tired and flustered and swearing at breakfast foods. Because the universe apparently likes to take "he can't possibly have a worse impression of me" as a challenge.

At least Tim seemed just as surprised to see him as Spencer.

"Oh," Tim said. "Hi."

Spencer couldn't read his tone, but he figured there would be a very quick "Oh, I need to be somewhere else now" regardless.

"Hey," he said back, fighting the urge to self-consciously rub the back of his head.

They stared at each other in silence for what had to be the longest fifteen seconds in the history of time.

"Are you...okay?"

Why isn't he making excuses and running away?

Oh. Right. Because, unlike you, he's a nice person.

Spencer grimaced and opened his mouth to answer. He'd meant to say that, yes, of course he was okay and then follow up with a no, of course he didn't need any help, but thank you for asking. What came out instead, in what even deaf—and dead—Grandpa Harold would have recognized as a whine, was "I can't reach my Lucky Charms."

It was only Spencer's utter horror—and his ingrained need to watch disasters as they unfold in front of him—that kept him from closing his eyes in utter humiliation. Which was the only reason he saw the small, amused smile pulling at Tim's lips before he managed to school his expression.

"Do you want me to get them for you?"

"Oh, fuck you," Spencer said before he could think better of it. Thankfully, that seemed to be all the permission Tim needed to burst out laughing, which meant Spencer didn't have time to feel bad before the indignation took over. "No, really, *fuck you.* When you've been trying to get the same box of cereal for twenty minutes, *then* you can laugh."

Of course, that only made Tim laugh harder.

"Sorry, sorry," Tim said, getting himself under control a split second before Spencer was about to forget everything good he'd done for Connor and sock him one right in the middle of the cereal aisle. "I don't even know why I'm laughing so much."

Spencer sighed. "You're laughing because I'm twenty-eight years old, and I can't reach the top shelf."

Tim pressed his lips together for a suspiciously long moment before he answered. "Sorry," he said again, sounding sincere. "I really can get it down for you if you want?"

Spencer did his best to ignore the embarrassment he could feel burning his face and gestured at the shelf. Tim took his gesture as the permission it had been, and in less time than it took to say, "Magically delicious!" he had the Lucky Charms off the shelf and in Spencer's cart.

"Thanks," Spencer muttered. "See you around."

He turned his cart and quickly made his escape.

And was then completely thrown when he got barely two feet down the aisle before Tim called after him. "Hey, wait!"

Spencer froze. This...was not in his mental script. Tim was supposed to be just as happy to end this encounter as Spencer. Instead, Spencer could hear him pushing his own cart closer until they were side by side.

Spencer glanced up, and they fell into another awkward, stare-y silence.

"Come here often?" Tim asked eventually. He winced, and Spencer mirrored the expression a moment later in sympathetic embarrassment before fully registering that *he* wasn't the one making this weird.

"Really?"

"In my defense, I'm a little out of practice at talking to people above the drinking age."

Spencer's first instinct, which was to ask, "So, you usually use cheesy dive-bar pickup lines on underage kids?" was, thankfully, easy to squash. Even better, Tim kept talking.

"And I didn't expect to see you here—" Tim paused. "—or ever again, actually."

Spencer felt a pang of...something at the implied rebuke. "Sorry," he said, turning away. "If I knew you were gonna be here, I would have come tomorrow."

"What?" Tim asked. "No! That's not what I—that wasn't a good thing."

Spencer glanced back at Tim, who was staring at him with an expression so blatantly sincere it had to be something he'd practiced for use on distrustful kids.

"You *wanted* to see me again?" Spencer asked.

To his credit, Tim seemed like he knew there was no good way to answer without lying. "I don't really like being avoided," Tim said after a long pause. "Especially since Connor says you're only doing it because you're embarrassed."

Spencer, predictably, felt himself flush again.

Sometimes, he really wished smacking kids around was still acceptable.

And on a parenting scale from Andrea Yates to Mrs. Cleaver, that puts me a few notches above the Dursleys.

"Please tell me you two don't sit around talking about me all day."

He'd meant it partly as a joke and partly a way to change the subject, but Tim didn't even take a breath before saying, "Among other things."

"Oh, good," Spencer muttered. "I thought you were gonna say something ominous for a second."

Tim looked amused.

"Okay then." Spencer crossed his arms. "What *do* you talk about?"

"Books and video games, mostly."

Spencer blinked. "Wait, can you even say that to me?"

Now it was Tim's turn to appear confused. "Say... what?"

"*Any* of that! Isn't it, like, illegal for you to tell me what you guys talk about?"

"I'm not Connor's therapist," Tim said patiently. "I'm his friend. I can tell anyone what we talk about."

Possibilities sprung to life in Spencer's mind.

"So, you can find out—"

"No."

"But you just said—"

"I said I'm his friend, which means I'm not spying on him or whatever you were about to ask me to do," Tim said with more than a vague air of disapproval.

"I wasn't—"

Tim raised an eyebrow, and the air of disapproval thickened into smog.

"Okay, no, you know what? You look way too much like my dad right now. Forget it."

Silence fell once again, and still, neither one of them made any move to leave. It made no sense because Tim couldn't *possibly* want to hold a conversation with him. And Spencer...

Honestly, he had no idea why he hadn't already fled.

"What do you want?" Spencer asked, trying as hard as he could to ignore the plaintive edge in his voice.

Tim seemed slightly thrown for a moment before visibly collecting himself. "I want you to be able to stand next to me for five minutes without looking like you'd rather be anywhere else."

Spencer blinked. "*Why?*"

Tim sighed. "Because whether you like it or not, I'm in Connor's life, and the last thing he needs is two of the only people he has being uncomfortable with each other.

Eventually, he'll feel the need to take sides, and trust me when I say nothing good will come from that."

Spencer could feel himself deflate. If there was a list of reasons for him to willingly put up with uncomfortable social situations, "because it's good for Connor" would be right at the top. It wouldn't be fun, and there was probably a good chance Spencer was going to either embarrass himself for a second time or screw up so bad Tim never wanted to see Connor again, but he'd try.

"Fine," he said.

"Oh." Tim seemed surprised at Spencer's easy acquiescence. "Well...good." His surprise quickly melted into a cheerful smile. "Do you have any shopping left to do?"

"I..." Spencer didn't need to pull out his list to know there were at least ten other things not crossed off under Lucky Charms, but he did anyway. Maybe everything else he needed would have taken pity on him while he struggled against the shelf and magically transported themselves into his cart and crossed themselves off his list.

Spoilers, they hadn't.

"Yeah. Why?"

"Because," Tim said, still with the cheer. It was slightly disturbing. "If we're gonna get comfortable, we should start by getting to know each other. What better way to do that than finishing up our shopping together?"

*

Tim, what the hell are you doing?

He'd lost count of how many times he'd asked himself the same question over the last fifteen minutes. Ever since the adorable little guy in skinny jeans and a cardigan cussing out a box of Lucky Charms turned out to be Spencer Kent, it was like all Tim's better judgment and reservation had taken a back seat to...something else. It wasn't that he'd been desperate to meet Spencer again. Far from it, actually. He'd been almost dreading his second hangout with Connor because he had absolutely no idea if he could deal with being around Spencer. The man was a distracting dichotomy, and the last thing he needed was to be thrown off his game again. Especially since, somehow, Dick had gotten wind of their altercation and had kind-of-but-not-really scolded him for getting into it with his ex-wife's good friend. So yeah, when Connor showed up for their second meet-up time alone, he was more than a little relieved. And when he came back *again* without Spencer, Tim had finally let himself relax and fully fall into his Big Brother role.

The problems didn't start until their fourth or fifth time hanging out together. It wasn't even anything big: just a story Connor had told about his dad in college dressing up like Princess Jasmine for Halloween to complement his six-year-old son's Aladdin. Tim had laughed at the mental image and then, without even thinking, admitted he would have loved to have seen that. He didn't mean it in a "I'd like to see a guy dressed like a Disney princess" way. Tim had always had a special place in his heart for good parents (and Spencer had been doing it since he was a teenager; how could Tim not be in complete awe of that?), and a dad willing to risk humiliating himself just to make his son happy was a moment he would have wanted to be around for. Connor had most definitely taken his statement the other way, though, which led to about ten minutes of him going on about how gross Tim was for lusting after his dad, and

Tim very clearly trying to explain that *wasn't the case at all.* He'd eventually convinced Connor, but before he could be relieved the conversation was over and done with, Connor had said something that stuck with Tim well after he'd gone home for the day.

"It's a good thing you don't like him that way because he never wants to be in the same room with you again anyway."

No matter how often that sentence rattled around in Tim's head over the next several days, he hadn't been able to figure out why it bothered him so much. At first, he thought it might be because, out of the two of them, *Tim* was the one who'd been wronged, and if anyone should be avoiding anyone, it was him. It wasn't until a week later, and a few more absently dropped bits of information about Spencer, that Tim finally realized why his chest felt tight every time he thought of the other man wanting nothing to do with him.

Despite his insulting lack of tact, Spencer Kent was exactly the kind of person Tim admired. He was protective, loyal, and above all, a great father who loved his son—the exact opposite of Rudy, Professor Carmichael, and pretty much everyone else he'd known in college. Tim had been so beaten down by the worst in people he'd been starting to think the best didn't exist outside of fiction. It might have been overly dramatic to say Connor's stories about Spencer reignited his faith in humanity. But only a little. And it *hurt* that someone like Spencer didn't even want to look at him.

Tim had been, maybe, more relieved than he should have been when Connor told him Spencer was avoiding him out of embarrassment. So, when the cute guy in the grocery store turned out to be Spencer, Tim realized *this was his chance.* His chance for what, he had no idea; all he knew was he didn't want Spencer walking away from him again. Not when there was a chance of getting to know him better.

Unfortunately, once Tim managed to get Spencer to stick around, he immediately ran out of things to say. The wheels of his shopping cart squeaked like tittering, mocking laughter as he followed an equally silent Spencer through the grocery store. Tim desperately tried to think of something to talk about.

"So, what's your favorite color?" Spencer asked suddenly.

Tim started in surprise. "What?"

"What?" Spencer hunched defensively over his cart. "You're the one who said we should get comfortable with each other. Isn't this how people break the ice or whatever?"

"No, it is," he said quickly. "I just...didn't expect you to ask that. I figured you'd ask me something about Connor if anything."

"I think I know my son better than you," Spencer snapped.

Tim blinked. "I never—"

"I know, I know!" Spencer crossed his arms on top of the cart handle, dropped his head into them, and groaned. "I'm being a huge asshole. Again. I'm sorry."

Tim chewed the inside of his cheek, a nervous habit he'd picked up during the last few months of college he'd never been able to successfully ween himself off of. He knew he should probably be insulted, but all he felt was a kind of distant ache like an overworked muscle right before it locked up.

"Is it...because of me?"

Spencer turned his head enough so one eye was visible. "Am I an asshole because of you? No. I'm an asshole because I'm an asshole."

Tim felt unaccountably relieved. "That's not what Connor says."

"Connor says I'm an asshole because of you?"

A surprised laugh forced its way out of Tim's throat. "No, he says you're not an asshole at all."

Spencer lifted his head and shot Tim a look of skepticism so sharp it could have cut glass.

"I swear to God."

Spencer shook his head. "Connor's been around me his whole life. Kid's fucking *inoculated* to my assholeness. Doesn't mean it's not there. You of all people should know that." Despite the wry humor in Spencer's voice, Tim noticed a brief flicker of sadness pass across his face. Before Tim could even be sure he saw it, Spencer pushed himself up and started walking. "Come on. Groceries aren't gonna put themselves in the cart."

Tim quickly followed, once again bringing his cart alongside Spencer, who was paying a suspicious amount of attention to his shopping list.

"Do you need anything, by the way?"

At least he's still talking.

"Eggs," Tim said.

Without slowing down Spencer angled his cart toward the eggs, picked up a carton, and handed them to Tim.

"Um. Thanks." He desperately tried to think of something else to say. "You...seem to know your way around?"

Spencer gave him an odd glance. "I've been shopping here for years, so..."

"Right." *If this is the best you can do, you deserve to have him avoid you.* "It's my first time. In this store, I mean. Not grocery shopping. I've done that a lot."

Another strange expression. This one *almost* included eye contact. Tim had no idea if that was a good thing or not. "So, what are you doing here?" Spencer grimaced. "Not that I'm saying you shouldn't be, or anything."

"My old store closed; this one was the next closest."

Which, now that Tim thought about it, probably meant they didn't live too far away from each other. *Huh.*

He wondered if Spencer would realize that too and comment, but all he did was hum and nod. "Come on, I need bread."

The next five minutes were filled with talking, which was a nice contrast to the earlier silence, but not one word passed between them that wasn't about shopping or food. Tim bit back a sigh of frustration. He could feel time slipping through his fingers like grains of sand, and even though he'd never been particularly superstitious, he had the sudden strange feeling that if he and Spencer didn't make some kind of deeper connection today, then they would never see each other again. Tim could see almost no trace in this Spencer of the man he'd met all those weeks ago, and definitely no trace at all of the man Connor spoke of and who Tim desperately wanted to know. The thought of never seeing either of them again disturbed him in a way Tim couldn't have defined if he had a gun to his head. He needed to think of *something*.

"My favorite color is maroon," Tim said, interrupting what seemed to be a stream of consciousness about the price of milk.

Spencer halted midsentence and gave him another strange glance.

"You asked what my favorite color was," Tim said, trying not to feel defensive.

"I know," Spencer said slowly. He stared at Tim for a long time before finally giving him a one-shouldered shrug. "You don't seem like the type though."

"The type to...like maroon?"

Spencer shrugged again and nodded. "Yeah. People who like maroon are supposed to be likeable and generous because of harsh experience. It's usually the favorite color of people who have been battered by life but came through stronger and more mature. You've got the likeable and generous part, but I can't imagine you being battered by life. You're...I dunno. Too...*something*. You don't have any hard edges."

Tim stopped dead in the middle of aisle six.

"*...battered by life but came through stronger and more mature.*"

"*...likeable and generous because of harsh experience.*"

Spencer's words hit him with the force of a hurricane. After college, Tim had purposefully avoided deep introspection whenever possible, but if he *had* tried forcing his feelings into easily digestible shapes—

Battered by life.... Harsh experience...

—he probably couldn't have done a better job.

Although, Spencer had been wrong about one thing. Tim had plenty of hard edges. They were just all turned inward.

I don't want to think about this. I'm not ready for...

Tim forced himself to start pushing his cart, desperately hoping Spencer hadn't noticed anything strange.

Judging by the return of the silence, it was probably too much to hope for.

"Sorry," Spencer said a moment later, grimacing. "That's probably weird to say, right?"

I feel like you just looked into my soul. Weird...isn't the word I'd pick.

"No," Tim forced himself to say. "It's okay. I..." *Have no idea how to finish that thought.* "Where did that come from though? The color thing? Did you make it up?"

Spencer cleared his throat and turned away. "Uh, no. It's uh...the internet. My friend Cass sent me a bunch of websites full of this new-age crap and...I dunno. The part about what your favorite colors say about you kinda stuck with me, I guess."

"Was your favorite color accurate?" Tim barely stopped himself before he could add a *too* to the end of that question.

Spencer huffed out a laugh and rubbed the back of his head. "Sort of."

When it became obvious he wasn't going to elaborate further, Tim asked, "So, what's *your* favorite color, then?"

Instead of answering, Spencer pulled at the fabric of his dark purple cardigan and wiggled one purple sneaker midstep.

"Purple?" Tim asked.

"Whatever gave you *that* idea?"

Spencer grimaced again, and because Tim really didn't want another apology or explanation for something he really wasn't bothered by, he steamrolled on before the other man could open his mouth.

"Is that a purple thing?"

"What?"

"When you say stuff like that. Stuff you seem to regret right away."

"You mean when I'm a tactless piece of shit? No. That's more of a brown thing, actually."

"You're not a piece of shit," Tim said, frowning.

"You don't know me," Spencer said. "And considering how I've been every single time we've talked to each other, you should probably think the exact opposite."

"Well, I don't," Tim said. "I think you're…"

Everything that could have come out of his mouth, every bit of Spencer he admired and wanted to surround himself with, all seemed to catch in his throat like a logjam. God, how could he even finish that sentence without sounding insane?

"Stop *doing* that."

Tim blinked. "What am I doing?"

"I…don't know." Spencer hesitated, then glanced around to make sure no one was listening to them. "But I can make a guess. I have no idea what the kid's been telling you about me, but you seem to have *ideas* about who I am, and it's kind of pissing me off."

"You're mad because I don't think you're a piece of shit?"

"I'm mad because you seem to think you know anything about me. You *don't*. You have no idea who I am, or what I think, or why I do or say the things I do. Every time I look at you, I can see you putting me into this box in your head that's neatly labeled with whatever you *think* I am."

Tim considered pointing out that Spencer had done the exact same thing to him not even five minutes ago—and accurate or not, he'd been basing his assumptions on what *color* Tim liked—but doing so ran the risk of turning the conversation toward subjects Tim wasn't at all ready to talk about. Before he could think of anything to say, Spencer took a deep breath.

"Look. I'm willing to get along with you for Connor's sake. That's totally a thing that should happen. But it's not gonna work if you ignore the things about me that suck and only look for the things you wanna see, okay?"

Tim thought for a moment. Hypocrisy aside, Spencer wasn't completely wrong. If they really were going to get to know each other, Tim needed to get to know *all* of Spencer.

"Okay," he said slowly, "but only if you stop apologizing and acting like I'm gonna kick you every time you say something that 'sucks.'"

"I'm not—"

"You are."

They stared at each other for a long moment. Finally, Spencer broke eye contact. "Yeah, okay. Maybe I am."

Tim smiled. "You really don't need to."

"Whatever."

"Nothing you've said was really that bad. Well, except for the first thing we said we weren't mentioning anymore, but even that was more of a wrong place wrong time—"

"Okay! You've made your point."

Spencer had never seemed more like his son than he did then, with his lips pressed together and the poutiest frown Tim had ever seen on an adult fixed on his cart. Tim felt his smile widen.

I'm enjoying myself. I'm having fun with another adult. I'd almost forgotten what it felt like.

He could see now he'd been trying too hard, earlier. Understandable, in hindsight, because almost every single interpersonal relationship he'd had for the last year had been some kind of struggle. He'd gone into this thing with Spencer expecting it to be a war. And that was the exact wrong way to start a friendship.

Friends... Yeah. That's what I want. Being friends with Spencer. Having a friend, like I said to Connor, except my age. Someone who isn't attached to a preexisting group of people. Someone who's just mine. That sounds...amazing.

Tim grinned. "You could even make eye contact with me from time to time," he said, almost laughing out loud at the sheer *joy* of teasing someone just to see them react. Of being able to act like a friend without wondering which one of the things he said was going to set Rudy off, accidentally encourage Professor Carmichael's advances, or upset his mother. "Ask me questions, share an opinion that isn't about food, or, you know, you could say *anything* that isn't about food—"

"You could go fuck yourself. That's another thing that could happen."

Then, Spencer glanced at him, then, out of the corner of his eye. Not apologetic, thank God, but...tentative. Watchful. Tim made sure his smile didn't slip so much as a millimeter.

A minute later, Spencer smiled too. It was barely anything, little more than a soft small upturn of his lips. But it was a smile Tim had caused, aimed directly at him.

Tim felt like he was watching the birth of the sun, and to his amazement, something that felt almost like happiness started to bloom inside him.

Okay. Let's see where this goes.

Chapter Seven

SPENCER: *Im reading an essay on Romeo and juliet written by a kid who cant spell tybalt, mercutio or Shakespeare. Kill me now.*

Tim snorted as he read Spencer's text and then looked around the kitchen to make sure Sarah hadn't heard. She was still hunched over the cake she was decorating, swearing for the three hundredth time since Tim had started working for her that she was never going to take a custom order ever again. Her process for cake decorating had always confused him, but even if they all started out looking like a three-year-old's imitation of a Jackson Pollock, they usually turned out great in the end. Not nearly as good as his mother's, of course, but he was sure there was some kind of complicated physics equation that could prove why that was impossible. Either way, he counted himself lucky his boss was too focused on her latest "never again" to start in with those weird glances she'd been giving him ever since he and Spencer had started texting each other.

TIM: *He's what, 14? 13? Give him a break. They're hard words to spell.*

He barely had time to sneak one last glance before his phone buzzed again.

SPENCER: *theyre names not words and THEYRE ALL WRITTEN IN THE PLAY MULTIPLE TIMES! MULTIPLE TIMES TIM.*

SPENCER: *Shakespeare is in every spellcheck ever. She HAD to have seen the red squiggle and completely ignored it. Honestly, the sheel levels of laziness are almost impressive. Im kinda tempted to give her bonus points.*

SPENCER: *maybe shes allergic to proofreading?*

SPENCER: *sheer not sheel**

SPENCER: *shut up*

"Y'all get some good news?" Sarah asked suddenly, her sharp Texas accent startling Tim so badly he almost dropped his phone.

"Huh?"

It was Sarah's turn to snort now. "You've been looking at that phone and grinning like a loon for the last five minutes. Gotta be somethin' good, right?"

The obnoxiously knowing glint in her eyes was muted by the icing smeared on her left cheek and, somehow, all over her hairnet. Tim shoved his phone in his pocket and did his best to arrange his face into a neutral expression. "It's nothing."

"Same 'nothing' you been all happy about for the last few weeks?"

"I have no idea what you're talking about."

"Uh-huh," she said, crossing her arms and looking way too much like his mother.

"Stop that," he said, suppressing a shudder. "You're weirding me out."

"And *you're* distracting me," she said.

"I'm not doing anything! Except my job," he added quickly at her sharp glance. Which wasn't even a lie, really, but at eleven in the morning, his job was mostly over. He'd already been there since four, firing up the ovens and baking the standard inventory for the day so Sarah could sleep in. Once the extra cashier who helped with the afternoon rush showed, he'd be out the door and collapsing face-first into his bed for a much-needed nap before meeting Connor at the center later.

"I can *feel* you bein' happy," she said, jabbing her finger at him.

"And my happiness is distracting?"

"Yes! You been carryin' around that big ol' gloomy raincloud for so long I was startin' to think I imagined that handsome smile of yours." Her expression softened. "Seein' it again is the definition of distraction."

Tim shifted uncomfortably. He thought he'd been doing a much better job of hiding his...moods. At least from people who weren't his mother. Even though he had four years of education telling him his feelings were completely valid and justified, he was still embarrassed that she'd noticed how unhappy he...was? Had been?

Was he actually happy?

He was certainly distracted, at least. There wasn't much time to wallow between his job and Connor and this new friendship with Spencer; a friendship that was...kind of wonderful. Spencer fit into his life in a way none of his other friends ever came close to.

They talked every day, mostly through random texts from Spencer that almost always evolved into amazingly fun conversations Tim had to physically tear himself away from. Something he knew was mutual because he had a dozen texts from Spencer yelling at Tim for distracting him from his grading or from making dinner.

They also had a standing unofficial shopping meetup every Thursday at their grocery store; something they'd both been early for last week, which had both of them slightly flustered as they teased each other about being kids excited for their "playdate." For the first time in longer than he could remember, Tim felt wanted; not as a sex object or a wall to scream at or a source of constant validation but as a *person*. He had no idea if he could be feeling true happiness or just euphoria at finally making a *connection* with someone again, but whatever it was, he really didn't want to question it—or talk about it with people who might *force* him to question it.

"I..."

Thankfully, his phone buzzed again, saving him from trying to think of something to say.

"Oh, go on then. Get back to your textin'. I gotta finish this damned cake up anyhow." She gave the confection a quick glare. "Tell your new man he's welcome to stop by any time. Anybody who can bring that smile back's got my seal of approval."

Tim's face started to burn. "He's not..."

Another buzz distracted him long enough for Sarah—who had been in the middle of ignoring his denials anyway—to cross the bakery and start working on the cake. Tim...was okay with that. He'd have to set her straight at some point, but it was probably best if he had some time to think about what he was going to tell her. He wasn't too sure he could actually explain his *completely platonic* admiration for Spencer without coming off exactly like a teenager with a crush.

SPENCER: *Okay. No bonis points.*

SPENCER: *bonus* fucking touchscreens. Why did we ever stop using keypads?*

SPENCER: *Anyway. Shes actually trying to say that romeo and mercutio are having a secret gay affair and that juliet is romeos beard because, and I quote, 'aint no straight boy that hot gonna date a 13 year old girl when he could be rolling in it with girls his own age'. I cant fucking even.*

Tim choked on a laugh.

TIM: *Maybe she handed it in as a joke?*

SPENCER: *Its gonna be real funny when I mark this down as her actual grade.*

Another buzz followed, but instead of a text, a picture popped up of a neatly typed sheet of paper absolutely *covered* with red marks and comments in the margins. Tim winced in sympathy—for the girl *and* Spencer.

SPENCER: *This is page 1 Tim. OF 3.*

SPENCER: *Seriously I give the kids Shakespeare to torture them not so they can torture me.*

SPENCER: *If I ever find the english teachers these kids had Im gonna make a citizens arrest for crimes against humanity. Any jury in the world would convict them.*

SPENCER: *Youre still taking the kid shopping for his halloween costume this afternoon right?*

The sudden subject change surprised Tim—they'd been texting and shopping buddies for just over two weeks now, and rare were the times when Spencer would leave off a complaining binge before he completely exhausted the topic—but he typed back a quick affirmative.

SPENCER: *Good. I need a fucking break after dealing with this. And a raise.*

TIM: *Well, I can give you the former, at least.*

There was a long delay before Spencer responded.

SPENCER: *You used former correctly.*

TIM: *Yes...?*

SPENCER: *Do you know what latter means?*

TIM: *Yes.*

Another long delay.

Spencer: Marry me.

Even as Tim laughed, he was very glad Sarah wasn't close enough to read over his shoulder.

*

Zip. Zip. Zip.

Tim nervously played with the zipper on his jacket as he waited for Connor, watching the autumn leaves blowing down the sidewalk through the front doors of the center. Since they were going to be leaving right away, there was no point in meeting in the cafeteria, but part of Tim longed for the familiarity of their routine. This would be the first time they'd left the center together, and even though they were just going a few blocks down to a costume store, he couldn't help feeling jumpy. He knew he was being ridiculous.

Connor was a good kid *and* he came with a signed permission slip. Spencer himself had practically begged him to take Connor shopping because he was too busy to go and didn't want Connor walking all over the city alone.

That casual caring, the way Spencer acted like he'd never even considered sending Connor off on his own, had made Tim smile even as the heavy mantle of responsibility settled onto his shoulders. Spencer trusted him to watch after his son out in the world, and Tim was painfully aware he could barely watch after himself these days. For the first time since meeting Connor, he was starting to wonder if maybe he might have bitten off more than he could chew.

Zip. Zip. Zip.

It didn't help that Connor was already fifteen minutes late.

Stop that. It's not like he's never been late before. Stop projecting your own fears onto a situation that's most likely completely benign.

He ground his palms into his eyes and tried not to think of all the ways someone could get hurt walking through the city. When he lowered his hands, he had just enough time for the spots to start clearing from his vision before a boy-sized blur shoved open the door. He quickly jumped back before it could hit him, but he wasn't quite fast enough to keep Connor from barreling headfirst into his chest.

"Ah!" Connor yelped, pressing his hand to the side of his face and stumbling back with wide eyes.

"Sorry. Didn't mean to..."

That was as far as Tim got before he got a clear look at Connor's face.

"Oh my God, Connor! What happened to you?" Tim asked. "Did you get mugged?"

Connor, who had been in the middle of wincing and turning away, jerked his head up. Tim held back a gasp. He'd only seen the black eye and the dried tear streaks, but now that Connor was staring directly at him, he could see a split lip and the remnants of dried blood on his chin.

"Yeah!" Connor said, seeming surprisingly enthusiastic for someone who'd supposedly just been robbed. "That's what happened."

Even the fierce surge of protectiveness that had risen up when Tim saw the bruising wasn't enough to get him to ignore such a blatantly terrible lie.

"Okay. Who mugged you?"

Connor's eyes widened. "Uh. A gang?"

"Uh-huh." Tim crossed his arms and forced himself to ignore the way Colin flinched. "And where did this happen?"

"The...streets..."

"Connor..."

"What?"

"I can't help you if you're going to lie to me."

To his credit, Connor knew when to give up.

"Maybe I don't want you to help me," he muttered.

Tim's still-fragile ego wailed for him to keep pushing, to barrel in and help Connor because that was *his* job. He ruthlessly pushed those thoughts aside. What Connor needed was more important than what Tim's ego wanted.

"Then what do you want?" Tim asked as calmly as he could. "Do you want someone else to help you? If you do, I can at least help you find them."

"Can you get me someone who won't tell my dad?" Connor said under his breath.

"You don't want Spencer to know?" Connor tensed. "Why not?"

"It doesn't matter."

Tim held back a sigh. He might not have been dealing with teenagers for very long, but the way Connor was stubbornly setting his jaw was almost a picture-perfect copy of the exact same expression on an eight-year-old. No matter how much he pushed, Connor wasn't going to answer. "Can you at least tell me why you wanted to lie to me about getting mugged?"

Connor said nothing. Tim decided to switch tracks.

"You know your dad's gonna see how beat up you are, right?"

"Not if you take me to buy makeup." Connor rolled his eyes impatiently at Tim's raised eyebrow. "*To cover up the damage.*"

"You put a lot of thought into this."

"I had a lot of time to think while Ju—" Connor clamped his jaw shut and turned his head away, flushing slightly.

"Drug-store makeup can't cover up that much of a black eye," Tim said, ignoring Connor's slip. "Not to mention the split lip. And even if it could, I'm not lying to your dad about this."

Connor glared up at him. "You said you were my friend!"

"I am."

"A real friend would lie to my dad for me."

Tim shook his head. "A real friend would want to make sure you're taken care of. Whether that means telling your dad or taking you to a hospital or a rape center—"

"I didn't get *raped!*" Connor cried.

"I didn't say you did." Though he could have collapsed with relief at hearing it. "I was just listing things."

"Well don't list *that*. De—he—they just..." Connor groaned in frustration. "Dad's never gonna let this go now..."

Now? Tim frowned. He'd never been slow, however, and it didn't take too long before things began to slide into place. "Did those kids who were bothering you in *school* do this?"

Even without the flinch, the way Connor refused to meet his eyes was all the answer he needed.

"Jesus Christ," Tim breathed.

"It's not that bad!"

"Not that bad? They're beating you up outside of school. That's *assault.*"

As far as Tim was concerned, it was assault when it happened *in* school too, even though schools rarely handled as such. But this definitely wasn't the time to dwell on the failings of public schools.

"No, it's not! They're just—I mean it has nothing to do with... *Please* don't tell my dad."

Connor's eyes started to tear up, and Tim could feel his heart wrenching.

"I'm sorry, Connor, but I have to."

"*Please!*"

"Even if I wanted to keep it from him—which I *don't*—center policy says I have to tell the parents when something happens to a kid I'm watching."

"But you weren't watching me when it happened!"

"Doesn't matter. You were on your way here, and more importantly, your dad has texts from me saying I'd look after you that were sent *after* he confirmed you'd already left. Even after I tell him what happened, he could still get me fired for that alone, and probably arrested too."

Which wasn't exactly true. Even if he thought Dick would be that unfair, the policy really only applied when the kids were in the presence of a center worker, and

Spencer would have to accuse *him* of beating Connor before the police would do anything. He felt bad about lying, especially when the tears started dripping down Connor's cheeks, but in this case, it was for the best. Spencer needed to know about what happened to his son, and fighting with Tim about it would only make Connor more upset in the long run.

"I can walk you home," Tim offered, as if he'd ever let Connor walk out of here alone after being attacked. "And I can be there when you talk to your dad if you're worried about how he'll react."

"Can you keep him from killing me?"

Tim thought it was much more likely he'd want to kill the kids who did this.

An image popped into Tim's head of him holding a flailing Spencer by the back of his shirt as he scrambled to get free to murder a group of faceless teenagers. Despite the situation, Tim had to press his lips together to smother a completely inappropriate laugh.

"I think that's probably the least I can do."

Connor glowered. "You better."

They made the walk home in silence, sullen on Connor's part and grim on Tim's. Even though this was the right thing to do, he wasn't looking forward to telling Spencer his son had been attacked.

Connor is Spencer's whole life. This will completely gut him.

Spencer and Connor lived in a surprisingly nice neighborhood for a single dad on a city teacher's salary. Their house appeared to be one of those two-story buildings that had been converted into duplex townhouses, complete with a small little garden cradled between two sets of stairs, the house itself, and the sidewalk. Connor led the way up the rightmost set of stairs like a man walking the last leg of *The Green Mile*. He pushed open the door and slunk inside, leaving it open for Tim to follow, which he did...

And was immediately hit with the sound of someone very loudly belting out the chorus of "Livin' on a Prayer."

"Dad hasn't heard us yet," Connor said quietly. "We can still leave."

Tim raised an eyebrow. "That's *Spencer*? Wow. He's really good."

Connor's face twisted into an expression of pure incredulous disgust.

"You are so weird," he said and then stalked off further into the house. Tim shook himself and caught up to him, gently taking his shoulder so he couldn't run off. It got him a filthy glare, but there was no way Tim was going to try to explain what happened without Connor right there so Spencer could see the damage. Spencer was definitely the type of person who would immediately jump to the worst possible conclusion if Connor wasn't right in front of him.

Tim took a moment to glance around the house. The small foyer they were standing in led into a short hallway. At the end of the hall, Tim could see what appeared to be a small kitchen along with two more halls he couldn't see down, one leading left and the other right. To the right of the hall Tim stood in, he saw a large open entryway. All along the hall were framed pictures, but instead of the usual landscapes or family portraits, each frame held a picture of a character from a movie or video game— including one of Darth Vader dressed as a Napoleon-era French general. Tim couldn't help smiling. It was exactly how he would have imagined Spencer decorating his house.

Then Connor led them through the entryway and into the living room, and interior decorating became the absolute last thing on Tim's mind.

The room itself seemed kind of narrow with a large flat-screen TV bolted to the far wall above an entertainment center packed full of video-game consoles and overflowing with tangled wires. On top of the entertainment center sat a display case filled with what seemed to be replica *Harry Potter* wands. Across from the TV, next to the entryway, there sat a black leather couch flanked by two recliners; one, a black leather as well, and the other one a deep-purple velvet. And right in the center of the room, singing into a PS4 *Rock Band* microphone with a cheap plastic *Rock Band* guitar slung over his shoulder, stood a Spencer Tim had never seen before.

He wore a pair of flannel pajamas, which was so different from his usual tight jeans and grandpa sweaters and at least three sizes too big. His hair, usually somewhat tamed by product, was floating around his head like soft, fluffy feathers. The scruffy, nearly full beard was also a surprise since the most Tim had ever seen before was five-o'clock stubble. It somehow made Spencer seem even younger than he usually did; like a boy who had tried growing it out in a desperate attempt to seem mature, rather than a man six years older than Tim with a son and an actual career. He looked...utterly adorable in a way Tim wasn't at all prepared for, and he had the sudden, almost irresistible urge to coo and hug him.

"Dad."

Spencer stopped singing and paused the game. "What are you doing..."

His gaze passed right over Connor and landed on Tim. He froze and then let out a tiny shriek and quickly started pushing his hair down. "Why didn't you tell me you brought him home?" he hissed. "I haven't showered in like two days..."

And then he noticed his son.

"Oh my God! What happened to you?" He immediately forgot about his hair and rushed over to Connor, pulling him into a hug before pushing him back and frantically examining the injuries on his face. "Are you okay? Did you get mugged?"

"Yes," Connor said.

"*No*," Tim said at the exact same time.

Spencer glanced back and forth between the two of them. Tim tensed, fully expecting Spencer to believe his son over someone he'd wanted nothing to do with until two weeks ago. After a long moment, Spencer gripped Connor's shoulders tightly for a second and sighed.

"Okay. Another talk about lying in the future. Great." He turned to Tim. "What happened?"

"Wait—" Connor started.

"He said the boys who were picking on him in school attacked him."

Spencer's entire body stiffened.

"I never said that," Connor said quickly.

"Names."

"Dad—"

"*Names*, Connor." Spencer leaned down so they were eye to eye. "*Now*."

"Please..."

Spencer didn't so much as blink, and Tim could see the exact moment Connor gave up.

"Dean and Julie Henderson," he muttered, roughly palming the tears away from his eyes.

Spencer blinked. "Dean and *Julie*—"

"Yeah, Dad. *Julie.*" He shoved Spencer's hands off his shoulders and moved away. "I'm getting beat up by a *girl.* Happy?"

"Not at all." Spencer frowned. "Is that why you never fought back? Because you were being beat up by a girl?"

"You can't *hit girls.*"

"Well, that's bullshit." Connor gaped at him, and even Tim had to raise an eyebrow. "Okay, I mean, yeah you can't go around hitting girls—or *anyone*—just because you want to, but if one of them attacks you? Damn right you hit her back. The most important thing is that you protect yourself if you can. I'm not gonna be mad at you if you hit someone in self-defense. Just get away and come back here, and we'll sort it out, okay?"

Connor stood stock still, not saying anything. Spencer sighed.

"I'm *not* mad at you. And I don't think you're weak or anything because you're getting bullied by a girl. I know the Hendersons. I had Julie in fifth period a few years ago, and she's fucking jacked even compared to some of the *boys* in school. And her brother's always been...off. I don't blame you for being scared of them." His expression hardened. "But you don't have to be anymore."

Spencer straightened up and turned to Tim.

"Can you stay with him while I call the cops? They'll probably want to talk to you too since—"

"No! You can't call the cops!"

"Con, they attacked you outside of school. I can most definitely call the cops, and that's exactly what I'm gonna do."

"They didn't attack me! I..." Connor wrapped his arms around his waist and lowered his head. "I hit him first."

Spencer started at him in disbelief. "You hit him *first*?"

Connor swallowed and nodded.

"*Why?*"

Connor flinched.

Spencer sighed again and softened his voice. "Sorry. I just want to know what happened. I won't yell...unless you, like, walked up to them in the streets and started swinging away. If you did that, we're gonna have a *long* talk about assault and battery and why you wouldn't last a day in juvie."

Tim frowned. That last part was a little insensitive, but he kept his thoughts to himself when all Connor did was sniff loudly and wipe his eyes with the back of his sleeve.

"I didn't," he said. "I didn't even know they were there until they stopped in front of me."

"Okay, good," Spencer said. "What happened next? Did one of them make a move like they were going to hurt you?"

"No. They just started saying the same shit they always say in school, and I can deal with it in school because it's like five minutes at most between classes, but they wouldn't *stop*, and no one was saying anything, and I got so *mad...*"

"So, you hit him." Spencer's face turned grim. "*Him*, right? Dean?"

Connor nodded. "Yeah. I hit him, and then he hit me back, and then *she* hit me. Then I fell down, and they both kicked me and left."

"They *kicked* you?" Spencer immediately reached for Connor, who quickly stepped back. "Stay still, I need to make sure your ribs aren't broken."

Connor shot a quick panicked glance at Tim. "They're not!"

"You don't know—"

"I think," Tim said, interrupting, "that if he's moving around as well as he is, his ribs probably aren't even bruised. You can wait until I leave before checking him over."

He almost smiled at the exaggerated expression of relief that came over Connor's face and silently begged Spencer not to make his son lift his shirt while Tim was there. He'd spent enough summers helping with swimming lessons at the YMCA to recognize the signs of a body-shy teenager.

Spencer pressed his lips together tightly but nodded. "All right. But the second Tim leaves I'm making sure you're not hurt. Either that or I'm taking you to the hospital," he added, steamrolling over Connor's half-voiced objection.

"Fine," Connor said sullenly. "And...you're not gonna call the cops?"

"No," he said, sounding even more sulky than Connor. "Not if you threw the first punch. Unless Tim's willing to lie and say he saw the whole thing, and they attacked first..."

He glanced questioningly at Tim, but before Tim could even think to respond, Spencer shook his head.

"Never mind. That's unfair, sorry."

Relief flooded Tim. He had no idea how he was going to say no—or if he even wanted to. Spencer and Connor had been the only bright spots in his life these past few weeks, and he'd already lost a relationship and his future because there was only so far he was willing to compromise his morals. Would he be willing to lose them too? He didn't know, and he was very glad he didn't have to find out.

"Can I go to my room then?" Connor asked.

Spencer's hands clenched tightly, and Tim got the idea the last thing he wanted to do was let Connor out of his sight. Yet, when he answered, his voice was calm, if subdued.

"Yeah," he said, "go on."

Connor glanced warily at Tim like he expected him to disagree and make him stay.

"I'll talk to you later, okay?" Tim said, flashing his best reassuring smile.

Connor barely finished nodding before taking off toward the nearby stairs. He got maybe two steps before Spencer broke, running after him and pulling him into a backward hug.

"Dad!" He struggled to get away, but it seemed to be mostly out of habit instead of an actual desire not to be touched. Spencer squeezed him tighter, burying his face in the soft curls on his son's head.

"I love you, kid," he said so softly Tim barely heard.

There was a long silence, and then, "I love you too."

Spencer's arms tightened again, and then he let him go. Connor ran out of the room. They both listened to the sounds of sneakers clomping up the stairs. His room must have been right at the top because almost the moment the noise stopped, Tim heard a door closing just quiet enough not to be a slam. The moment it closed, Spencer collapsed on the couch before resting his arms heavily on his legs and letting his hands dangle limply between his thighs.

Tim shifted in place, suddenly uncomfortable now that Connor wasn't there as a barrier between them. Should he say something? Spencer was obviously upset.

Should he try to comfort him? Tim's instinct was to sit next to him and put his arm around his shoulder, but that seemed like it could go wrong in more ways than he could bear to count. Would Spencer even *want* comforting? The more insidious thought, that this was all *Tim's fault* for not watching after Connor the way he promised, kept him paralyzed and silent. If Spencer wanted to yell at him, he would stand there and take it and know he deserved every second of it.

Which was why, when Spencer finally spoke, Tim was half-convinced he was having a wishful hallucination.

"Thank you."

Tim stared. "What?"

Spencer glanced up, a rueful expression on his face, like he knew exactly what Tim had been thinking. "For making sure he got home safe, I mean. It's just... Thank you."

"Oh. Right. Uh. You're welcome."

"We're articulate today, aren't we?" Even though Spencer's tone was teasing, his smile was nowhere to be seen. He stared up at Tim, half his face bathed in light from the paused game. He seemed tired and haggard. The circles under his eyes were so dark they had to have been building up way before Connor came home with a bloody face.

I completely forgot he's been grading papers all weekend. I was supposed to be giving him a break, and all I did was bring him his beat-up son.

"Can you sit down or something?" Spencer asked, dropping his head. "I feel like I'm about to be lectured by my dad with you standing over me like that."

"Sorry." Tim sat down next to him on the couch and only then wondered if that was okay. Was he sitting too close? Did Spencer want him to sit in the recliner off to the side instead?

Why are you being weird about this?

"Is it wrong that I kinda really wanna drive around the city until I see those little shits and run them down?" Spencer asked.

Tim blinked. "I...you have a car?"

Spencer let out a surprised laugh. "Really?"

"What?" Tim said, feeling slightly defensive—and more than slightly embarrassed by his inane question. Why was being alone with Spencer short-circuiting his brain like this today? Was it because they were in his house? Was it because of what happened to Connor?

"Let me guess—" Spencer tilted his head and peered up at him with a small, shadow of a smile. "—you're a lifelong Chicagoan, and you don't need no cah when there's public transpahtashin'?" he asked, finishing the last part of his sentence with what Tim assumed was supposed to be a Chicago accent.

The tiny Mary Ellis that lived inside his head let out an indignant gasp, and he responded without thinking. "I'm from New York, actually." Then, because he wasn't his mother and didn't really care when people didn't immediately recognize him as a New Yorker, admitted, "But yeah. I've never known anyone outside of college who owned a car."

Spencer sat up straight. "You lived in New York?"

"Yes..."

"Like, the city?"

Tim nodded. "Queens."

Spencer laughed again. "I grew up in Putnam Valley."

"Seriously?"

"Yeah." Spencer shook his head in disbelief. "That's so weird. We lived like an hour away from each other when we were kids and then met at a youth center in Chicago."

An odd, bubbly tightness spread throughout Tim's chest. "Yeah..."

"So, why did you move out here? Was it because you hated living there? Because I went to Manhattan once, and it was fucking *awful*."

"I wanted to get away from my mom." Spencer burst out laughing. Tim winced. "I mean..."

"No, no way. That was *way* too honest. You don't get to take it back. I wouldn't believe anything you tried to say anyway."

Tim huffed but couldn't quite hold back the smile tugging at the corners of his lips. He knew what Spencer was doing, latching onto pointless small talk to keep from thinking about Connor, but part of Tim relished the opportunity to learn more about him. "Fine. Why did *you* leave, then?"

Spencer's laughter trailed off. "College." He hesitated, then added, "And...Connor."

"You moved here because of Connor?"

"No, I moved *here* for my job. I went to Ohio State for college, and by the time I graduated, my parents had moved and were living with Connor in Columbus full-time...but yeah. I originally went so far away because I wanted to get away from him."

Tim gaped at him. "You *left* Connor behind?" That sounded *nothing* like the Spencer he knew. *That* Spencer lived for Connor; it was one of the things Tim liked the most about him.

Spencer smiled weakly. "Connor was born when I was fourteen. My parents helped out a *lot*, but I was still a teenager with a kid going to school with people who already hated me for being small, dorky, and gay. Getting away from it all, going to college, and pretending I was any other stupid kid just starting to grow up? That was like a fucking *paradise* to me back then, and I was weak, so I jumped at the chance."

Tim felt like he'd run all out into a brick wall. *Spencer's gay?*

Spencer snorted. "Go on and ask."

Tim didn't waste any time. "You're *gay*?"

"*What*?"

"What?"

"*That's* what you're asking?"

"You just said I could..."

"No—I mean, yeah, but...that's not what I expected..." He shook his head again. "People usually want to ask about how Connor was born."

"Through...childbirth?" Tim said before he could stop himself. He mentally groaned and fought the urge to pound his head against the wall.

"Seriously?"

"Sorry. I'm...sorry. I just...didn't expect you to be gay," he finished lamely.

Spencer's eyes turned flinty. "Do you have a *problem* with that?"

"No!" Tim exclaimed, his eyes wide. "Of course not. I...I'm gay too."

Spencer stilled. "Oh."

The atmosphere in the room suddenly changed, though Tim couldn't even begin to describe how. Maybe they'd both made assumptions about each other, and they just needed a minute to brush those assumptions away and slot new information into place.

And speaking of new information...

"Can I still ask about Connor?"

"Yes," Spencer said in a strange tone Tim couldn't interpret. His eyes were doing this *flickery* thing, almost like he was constantly forcing himself to look right at Tim. "Um, are you *going* to...?"

Oh, yeah. I've been staring at him for a while, haven't I?

Tim felt his face start to burn, and he really hoped he wasn't blushing too visibly.

"Uh." Tim cleared his throat. "So...how did Connor get born?"

Spencer studied him for a long moment. Then, ever so slightly, the corner of his mouth curled up.

"Childbirth."

Tim couldn't do anything but laugh. "Seriously?"

Spencer grinned. "Yep. Well, childbirth preceded by thirteen-year-old me getting drunk on spiked punch at a school dance and having sex with an equally drunk girl named Becky Ling in an attempt to prove that everyone at school was wrong, and I wasn't the least bit gay at all."

"Ser—" No, he didn't want Spencer to think he was joking this time. "Really?"

"Yep," he said, popping the *P* a little. "I'd probably feel bad about using her like that if I wasn't almost 100 percent sure she'd just been using me to take a dive into the deep end of the teenage-rebellion pool. That and the aforementioned drunkenness."

At Tim's questioning glance, he added, "Her parents were *really* strict and *very* stereotypically Chinese. I'm pretty sure if she was sober, she might have tried dating me, or some other non-Chinese boy, instead of...you know, jumping one. She seemed to sober up pretty fast once she realized what we'd done though." He let out a humorless laugh. "Both of us did, really."

Tim had no idea what to think.

"Wow. That..."

"Sucks? Yeah, I thought so too. Mostly because it drove home just how incredibly gay I actually was, which meant everyone who made fun of me and pushed me into lockers and everything had been right all along, and that...well. At the time, I was pretty sure that was the worst thing that could ever happen." He smiled wryly. "Imagine my surprise when Mom and Dad Ling showed up at my parent's door two months later screaming in Mandarin and demanding a paternity test."

"No way."

"Oh, yes.

"God." Tim couldn't suppress a shiver as he pictured the same situation, but with *his* mother on the other side of the door, and before he could even consider whether or not it was too invasive for their new friendship, asked, "What did your parents do?"

Spencer's lips twitched. "They locked the door and called the cops."

"They didn't yell at you?"

"Not at me, no. The poor cop got an earful when he wouldn't arrest Becky's parents."

"Really?" At Spencer's nod, Tim shook his head. "My mom would have *killed* me if I got someone pregnant in high school."

"Middle school, actually."

"*Middle school?*"

"Yep. One of the last eighth-grade dances." Spencer seemed oddly delighted, and Tim could only guess what his face must look like to get such a reaction. "To be fair though, I probably *would* have gotten a lot of shit if Becky's dad hadn't lost *his* the second he saw me and dragged me out the door by my arm. I think they thought I was being kidnapped, and I guess finding out I was a teenage dad to be wasn't so bad after fighting off the weird angry Chinese man who grabbed their son. Me throwing up all over myself when I realized what was going on probably helped too. So did the cop showing up and everything. By the time we were alone again, we were all just exhausted."

*

Kind of like Spencer was now, honestly. He was grimy and unbathed, and he'd been up since eight thirty correcting essays, and he'd gotten through *maybe* forty minutes of badly needed Spencer Time before his son showed up with a tenderized face, so, yeah, exhausted was definitely a word that described him right now. He chose to blame his exhaustion for why he'd told Tim all this...stuff when he usually liked to avoid even thinking about it. It was just exhaustion, stress, and maybe a little bit about the way Tim's face kept doing that thing where he looked like an old, scandalized Victorian matron.

And maybe a lot to do with how it's so much better to remember that day and the months that followed than thinking about Connor upstairs with a bruised face and a split fucking lip. Because I really just don't want to deal with that right now.

Tim frowned. For a moment, Spencer thought it was because he'd somehow read his mind and realized what an awful human being he was. "He grabbed you?"

Right. Mind reading isn't real.

Spencer nodded. "Almost tore my arm right out of the socket."

"And your parents didn't do anything?"

"They called the cops, remember?"

Tim scowled and shook his head. "No, I mean...if someone grabbed my son, I'd...I don't know. I really don't like the idea of some guy yanking you around like that. Or any child, really."

Spencer felt...warm. *That's oddly touching.*

"I think the fact that I'd knocked up his thirteen-year-old daughter is a pretty good mitigating circumstance."

"Don't defend him," Tim snapped, startling Spencer. He'd meant it mostly as a joke because this conversation had already gotten heavier than he'd like, but Tim seemed legitimately angry. "What he did to you and what you said he was like with his daughter, that's child abuse. There's *no* excuse for that."

Spencer stared at Tim. Despite his best efforts, this was far from the first time he'd told this story, and generally people just give him judgmental glares or break up with him—Cass being the notable exception. No one had ever gotten mad on *his* behalf, though, and Spencer...honestly had no idea what to do with that.

"Sorry," Tim said a moment later, sighing softly. "I don't really react well to kids getting abused, especially when adults try to make excuses for it. It's sort of an ingrained reaction. I didn't mean to yell at you."

Spencer waved his apology away. "You're not exactly wrong." He hesitated. He could stop here, change the subject, and let the conversation die, but for the second time in his life, he actually *wanted* to tell someone the full story. Maybe it was because of Tim's honest and open face, or his expression when he'd been angry *for* Spencer. Or maybe he couldn't force himself to ignore what happened to Connor; what *could* have happened if he'd fallen down into traffic, or if he'd hit his head too hard on the concrete sidewalk. Or maybe it was because this wasn't even the closest he'd ever come to losing his son.

Whatever the reason, he found himself talking almost before he realized he'd decided to open his mouth.

"He *was* an abusive father. And you're right, there's no excuse for a lot of the things he did. But I can't hate him because without him I wouldn't have Connor."

Spencer's eyes were focused somewhere around the vicinity of Tim's chest, so he saw the way he inhaled sharply. Whether Tim had any idea of what he was about to say, if he thought something different, or if he was just taking a breath to speak, Spencer didn't know or really care.

"Becky and her mom both wanted to get rid of the baby," he said quietly. Even after all these years, the words still sat in his throat like a cancerous mass. "That's how they said it too, 'get rid of it.' Like he was an area rug the dog peed on too many times."

It was Spencer's worst memory, sitting next to Becky in the kitchen of his old house while she glared at him with teary-eyed *loathing*, saying she hated him, hated the *thing* inside her, and wanted to get rid of it and pretend this never happened. He remembered hearing her mother's raised voice coming through the walls saying almost the exact same thing, burning away the numbness that had spread through him when he realized why Becky's parents were there, leaving behind nothing but desperate longing and ice-cold horror. He'd never thought about having kids, mostly because he was thirteen years old, but at that moment all he wanted was to hold his baby. Spencer had almost thrown up again when he realized he had absolutely no say in whether or not he ever would.

"Her dad wouldn't let her though. He said it was evil and wrong and—God, I don't even know if he was right. Maybe he wasn't. But I *don't care.* I would have strapped her down to a table for nine months and *ripped* Connor out of her womb myself if that was the only way I could have had him. I will *never* not be anything but grateful to her dad for what he did, no matter how disgusting he might be as a person."

Spencer's entire body was coiled like a spring, waiting for the judgment and condemnation. He was ready to jump down Tim's throat, yell at him, throw him out, get that two- or three-second *satisfaction* of having the permission of the righteous to be as shitty and cruel as he wanted in defending himself. He'd been here once before, with his second and final boyfriend, back in college.

His first relationship had ended because he'd kept Connor a secret, so he'd decided to start his newest with total honesty. He'd bared himself to someone in the hopes it would bring them closer and ended up being very politely—Mitchell was *always* calm and collected, part of what had attracted Spencer in the first place—informed he was a terrible person. Becky's father had no right to demand his daughter keep an unwanted pregnancy, and Spencer had no right to be happy she was forced to give birth to his son. He'd said Spencer was *wrong* for wanting Connor when Becky didn't. That it was selfish and cruel to try to raise a child on his own without a mother just because he wanted to. It was an attitude he'd encountered more than once in his life where single fathers are held to a very different set of standards than other nontraditional families. It was something he'd been conditioned to expect.

Spencer was still braced for castigation when he felt the couch dip as Tim moved closer to him. He jumped when he felt a hand being hesitantly placed on his shoulder. It was only when he glanced over, startled, and saw a vaguely Tim-shaped blur that he realized his eyes had started to tear up.

"I'm grateful too," Tim whispered like he was letting Spencer in on some terrible secret. Spencer bristled, ready to lash out, to tell him *nothing* about being grateful for Connor should be a secret and that it should be *shouted* from the fucking *rooftops*, when Tim's words finally registered in his slightly soggy brain.

"What?"

"Connor's a great kid," Tim said at a more normal volume. "I know I haven't known him that long and obviously nothing I feel about him is anything close to what you do...but I like him. He's my friend. And I think the world would be a little less wonderful if he wasn't in it."

A strangled, almost feline yowl deep inside his throat choked Spencer, and the tears finally started to pour down his cheeks. The hand on his shoulder tensed for a moment and then slowly lifted. Spencer didn't like that at all and started to protest, but then it came back down on his other shoulder as a solid, comforting arm wrapped around him, and he'd been on the other side of this kind of thing enough times with Connor to know the proper response.

He buried his face in Tim's shirt and cried.

He cried for himself because Tim *understood*, but mostly he cried for Connor. Connor, who was joy and light and life and frustration and fear and anger and sarcasm and laughter and a million other indefinable *things* so many people never bothered to learn. He cried because so many people would rather he never existed because they couldn't see him as anything other than a moral point to make where Tim just saw *Connor*.

He cried because, sometimes, there's nothing else a person can do.

Spencer had no idea how much time passed, but eventually he came back to himself the same way Hemingway described Mike Campbell going bankrupt—gradually and then suddenly.

The first thing he saw when he opened his eyes was a soaked T-shirt. The first thing he felt was the firm chest underneath it.

"Shit," he said, his face *burning*. He wrenched away, pushing Tim's arms—*that's a plural, when did he start hugging me?*—off and curling up as far as he could get on the end of the couch, wiping at his eyes. He absolutely refused to so much as glance in Tim's direction.

Oh my God, what the hell is wrong with me? I ruined his shirt. No, worse than that, I cried all over him like a fucking three-year-old.

Spencer hadn't been this embarrassed since high school.

"I should probably go..."

He glanced up without meaning to just in time to see Tim's tight smile and the tail end of something that seemed an awful lot like hurt pass across his face. *Does he think I was pushing him away?* Something inside Spencer clenched, and before Tim could do more than shift next to him, he grabbed his wrist.

"I..." He swallowed and stared at where his fingers were wrapped around Tim's arm. Tim was wearing a jacket, so it wasn't even like they were touching skin to skin, but part of him still felt...weird. Like he was crossing some kind of line he hadn't been aware even existed. "Could...you stay?"

Tim didn't say anything at first, and Spencer had to fight to keep from squirming.

Does he want to leave? Was I imagining that reluctance? Is he trying to figure out how to get the hell away from me? Am I—

"You want me to stay?"

He sounded surprised. Not in a bad way, though, more of a "I thought you wanted *me* gone" kind of way. The relief Spencer felt was disproportionate, to say the least. Of course, since Spencer was Spencer and couldn't actually *express* himself because *feelings*, what he ended up saying was "Did I fucking stutter?"

And maybe God or Odin or the universe decided Spencer was due a break because for some reason, Tim *smiled*. And this time, Spencer could see nothing tight or pained about it.

"Okay," Tim said softly. "I'll stay."

Chapter Eight

It was an hour later, and Tim still sat next to him. They'd both migrated a bit; Spencer leaning against the couch's arm facing Tim with his legs tucked under him, Tim's arm stretched out across the back of the couch, his body angled toward Spencer. They weren't close enough to touch, which totally wasn't even a problem because Spencer had an issue with clinginess. Specifically, *being clingy*. It wasn't him. And the fact that he couldn't stop thinking about how being wrapped up in Tim's arms felt was disturbing on levels he didn't even want to think about. Especially since he *really* wanted to find out what those arms felt like when he wasn't having an emotional breakdown.

So, yes. Distance was good.

And so was the turn their conversation had just taken.

"You had to deal with *parents*?"

"Yes?"

"Huh. I didn't think that was a thing. You seemed really surprised to see *me*, at least."

"It's not really common," Tim said. "Which is sad. But sometimes parents would come by, back when I was mostly helping with the younger kids at my old center. Usually, when they wanted to yell at us."

"Really?" Spencer asked, delighted. He leaned forward eagerly. "What's the weirdest thing they ever yelled at you about?"

Tim cocked his head, a tiny bit of hair sliding off his forehead in a way that should not have been as distracting as it was. "Um..."

"Come on," Spencer prodded. "It's fun. Me and my friend Cass do it all the time."

"Do what?"

"Compare weird parent stuff and like, you know, rank them to see who has to deal with the worst crap." Spencer made a show of puffing out his chest. "I'll have you know I'm *undefeated* in parental weirdness."

Tim chuckled. "And that's something to be proud of?"

"Hell *yes*, it is." Spencer summoned up his best indignant glower, but a smile broke through when Tim laughed again. "Oh, fuck off. Just tell me so I can defend my crown."

"Okay," Tim said. "But normally, I'd say the weirdest thing was that thing we said we weren't talking about anymore—"

"That wasn't *weird*. That was *rude and stupid*. Totally doesn't count," Spencer said, waving his hand. "It's gotta be something..."

Tim cocked an eyebrow. "Weird?"

"Yeah!"

Tim shook his head, but Spencer didn't miss the way he smiled down at the couch.

"All right, then." Tim paused thoughtfully. "This one time I got screamed at for letting a little girl color a picture."

"Really?"

Tim nodded. "Yeah, it was a picture of a jack-o'-lantern, which apparently meant I was teaching her to be a Satanist."

"No fucking way," Spencer said, laughing.

"Oh yes. Her father came in the very next day to tell us off for our unholy ways. He went on for about thirty minutes too, right in front of his daughter and everything. When he was done, I had no idea who was more embarrassed, me, my old director, or the poor little six-year-old girl." Tim's lips twitched. "The best part was when the daughter came back the next week and apologized for her father because 'he was born in a different time.'"

"That did *not* happen."

Tim placed his hand over his heart, and God, how did Spencer never even suspect this man was gay? "I swear it's 100 percent true."

Spencer finally got himself under control and wiped his eyes. "Oh, my God. Okay. You might actually have me beat."

"Yeah?" Tim seemed pleased with himself. "What's yours then?"

Spencer thought for a moment. "Okay. So, a few years ago I had this kid in my third-period class named Curtis. He was...probably the *worst* student I've ever had. I mean, *really* fucking bad. Like, he'd turn in *links to Wikipedia* as his book reports, bad."

Tim raised a very skeptical eyebrow.

"Oh, fuck you with that look." Spencer threw a throw pillow at him. Tim caught it, laughing, and hugged it to his chest. "I have every single thing he ever turned in saved on my laptop, I can go get it right now, and *then you'll know*. Dealing with this kid is like dealing with knowledge of Cthulhu's existence. It slowly drives you insane until you're screaming into the fucking void of your own madness as the Great Old Ones rise to ravage the Earth."

Tim rolled his eyes, but Spencer was pretty sure he wasn't imagining how utterly charmed he seemed to be. His stomach did sort of a funny little flip-squirm thing. *What the hell was that?* "I think there was supposed to be a story about a parent in here somewhere?"

Spencer shook himself and wet his suddenly dry lips. "I'm *getting to it*. The setup is important."

"This needs backstory?"

"Yes. Now shut up." Spencer cleared his throat as obnoxiously as he could, and Tim *grinned. No, seriously, what the* hell *is that?* "Um."

Spencer completely drew a blank on what he'd wanted to say. Which, well. Kind of completely understandable. How could anyone be expected to do something like *have higher brain function* when they were being stared at like they were some kind of cross between a pile of puppies and a winning lottery ticket?

"You were talking about Curtis and Lovecraftian horrors?" Tim prompted gently right as the silence began to get uncomfortable.

"Ah, yeah." Spencer willed himself not to flush. He was pretty sure it didn't work. "Right. So, terrible student, Wikipedia links, plans to burn down whatever middle school that keeps producing these people dancing through my head. Anyway, one day he comes into class and actually turns in his homework. After I was done checking that reality hadn't imploded, I looked down and noticed he'd signed it as Lebron James—don't interrupt!"

Tim slowly closed his mouth.

"Which, okay, kind of weird, but whatever. Except he kept doing it. Every assignment he did had Lebron James written right at the top. But then it gets worse because *then* he starts refusing to answer anyone who calls him

Curtis because he wants to be called Lebron because he claimed he got his name *legally changed*. I refused, of course, because he's full of shit and once you start calling one kid Lebron then you need to start calling everyone else Tom Cruise or Sephiroth or Lord Sparklestar, Destroyer of Worlds, and before you know it the very fabric of our republic is unraveling right before your eyes."

"That's all it takes to unravel the...republic?"

"Hush. But yes. Because we are a republic and not a democracy and republics are *fragile*. So, I did the only thing I could. I gave him detention and sent him to the principal. As it turns out, the detention was a big mistake because the next day his mother storms into the school demanding to see me, and I get dragged out of class by a flustered office aide and have to listen to this woman wearing more perfume than the entire city of Paris scream at me."

"She yelled at you for not calling him Lebron James?"

"No! Not even that. She yelled at me for *not believing that he'd legally changed his name*. She went on this huge tirade about how her son wasn't a liar, and how disrespectful it was that I just assumed he was lying about his name change, and this is why children turn to drugs and gangs, and teachers need to respect their students no matter who they are and on and on and on. So, when I can finally get a word in, I ask, 'So did he really get his name legally changed?' Without even the slightest hint of shame, she says, 'Of course not. Curtis is a family name!'"

Tim laughed. "So, what happened?"

"Nothing. The principal eventually got her to leave and told me to either call the kid whatever he wanted or ignore him for the rest of the year because he didn't want to deal with this crap again."

"I can't picture you going along with that."

"Oh, I went along with it. It was my second year, and I didn't have tenure yet. What else could I do? I ignored the kid, complained to Cass, and then bumped his grade up at the end of the year so he'd pass, and I wouldn't have to deal with him again."

"Is that...legal?"

Spencer shrugged and then spread his arms. "Do I look like a lawyer?"

And that was when it happened.

Tim's eyes flickered. Nothing more. Just a small glance up and down Spencer's body. Most likely a completely unconscious action because Spencer had basically invited him to give him a once over. Nothing even remotely meaningful or suggestive about it.

Or there wasn't until Tim finished his perusal, met Spencer's eyes again, and froze like he'd just been caught doing something he wasn't supposed to.

Was he checking me out?

The second he had the thought, Spencer wanted to smack himself. *Of course he isn't, you idiot. Don't do the thing where just because you're gay and he's gay, you assume everything he does is because he wants to fuck you.* Spencer *hated* that attitude, hated the general arrogance and shallowness he'd encountered during his brief time testing the waters of the so-called gay community in his younger years. He'd always swore he would never be like those people: the ones who sneered at his clothes because they were comfortable instead of fashionable, or who saw his height and his youthful face and assumed he was just another slutty brain-dead twink. Yet, here he was, doing the same damn crap to the only male friend he'd had since college.

Stop. You're gonna drive him away because you're misinterpreting shit. You somehow managed to get away with crying on his chest without things getting weird; if you start overanalyzing everything he does looking for hints of attraction that will never *be there because you are unappealing, then you might as well just end this friendship now because you're just going to ruin it like you ruin everything else.*

Spencer nodded firmly at his mental pep talk and then made a point of meeting Tim's eyes so he could say something funny and clever to completely defuse the situation and make everything normal again.

He has really nice eyes though.

The only thing that kept the sheer horror Spencer felt toward himself at manageable levels was the small bit of red he could see beginning to stain Tim's cheeks. And that was all it took; just one small easily misconstrued hint that what he was feeling could, in some alternate universe, possibly, just ever so slightly, be returned. In no time at all, the air between them grew heavy and thick, but no magic joke or self-deprecating comment came to mind to cut through it. It hadn't been so long that Spencer had forgotten what it felt like when a crush started forming. He'd probably rather use a more adult term, but the *feeling* was unmistakable, no matter what it was called. Like a long-unused switch had been flipped somewhere deep inside, Spencer went from *This Is Tim, My Completely Normal Friend Who I Am In No Way Attracted To* to *Oh...Hi* in less time than it took to blink. Before he could stop himself, he'd already started cataloging the things he liked about Tim with new crush-tinted glasses.

His eyes are so warm, and his smile is gorgeous. He likes to read. He's great with Connor. He's patient with me. He rolls with my bullshit and doesn't care when I text him a hundred times a day. Buying groceries together is one of the highlights of my week. He's never judged me, at least not since he's gotten to know me. He held me when I didn't even know I needed it, and I think he's probably the only reason I'm not losing my mind about what happened to my kid today. Holy fucking shit. How did I never realize how perfect he is?

"Dad?"

The bright, shiny new-car smell of his feelings, the sudden *awareness* of all things Tim, the half-formed, panic-tinged thoughts of *how are you ever gonna hide this so he doesn't find out and reject the fuck out of you,* everything came screeching to a halt as reality came crashing back in.

It took much longer than it should have for Spencer to be able to tear his eyes away from Tim, but when he did, he saw his battered son standing in the entryway to the living room, dressed in faded-green pajama pants and one of Spencer's old Power Rangers T-shirts with his arms wrapped tightly around his waist.

Spencer hadn't felt so out of his depth as a parent since Connor was born. His kid had been upstairs for over an hour, beat up and probably crying, and what had he been doing? Trading funny stories and forming a crush. Jesus Christ, he was the worst dad ever.

"Hey, kid," Spencer said. Guilt shot through him at the way Connor's eyes widened when he took a few steps into the room and saw Tim sitting on the couch.

"What are you doing here?"

If Spencer had asked that, it would have come out rude and defensive, but the kid didn't sound anything but confused and curious and...

Spencer had no idea how to explain why Tim was still here.

"I was just talking to your dad a bit," Tim said with an easy smile. Spencer tensed, but instead of taking it badly and getting upset that he'd basically been ignored, like *Spencer* would have, Connor visibly relaxed.

"Oh," he said, glancing back and forth between them. He shifted in place, and bad parent or not, Spencer knew that meant he wanted to say something but was embarrassed to bring it up.

"It's getting kind of late. I should probably get going," Tim said, giving Spencer a quick, knowing smile. For a moment, he thought Tim had found out about his crush, but before he could panic, he realized he'd probably just read Connor the way Spencer had and decided to give them time alone.

Spencer almost choked on the surge of affection that welled up inside him.

Tim got up and walked over to Connor, giving him a short one-armed bro hug. Which looked more than a little hilarious with how much he had to bend over to do it.

"Maybe we could try getting a costume after school tomorrow?" he asked.

Connor blinked, glanced at Spencer, and then shrugged. "Maybe."

Tim grinned and ruffled Connor's hair. *That* got a reaction, and Connor scowled as he tried to get his curls back in some kid of order. It was such a *normal* thing for Connor to do, and Spencer could have kissed Tim for being so great with him.

Thankfully, he was still too worried about his son to blush. Much.

"Text me later, okay?" Tim asked. It took Spencer a second to realize he was talking to *him*. "About costume shopping?"

"Oh, right. Yeah. Sure."

Tim smiled. "See you later then, guys."

And before Spencer could do more than echo his goodbye, Tim left. A moment later, he heard the front door open and close. Leaving him alone with Connor.

"Hey, kid," Spencer said softly. "You wanna take a seat?"

Connor didn't even nod, just walked over and sat down *exactly* where Tim had been sitting and wrapped his arms around his knees. *Nope, not thinking about Tim now. Time to forget your stupid, doomed crush and focus on your son.*

"Are you gonna tell people?" Connor asked after a short silence.

Spencer held back a sigh. He wasn't looking forward to this conversation at *all*. "You know I have to."

"But *why*?"

"Because I can't teach class and worry about you at the same time."

Connor's jaw dropped. "You're going to make my life hell because of your *job*?"

The kid seemed so *insulted,* and Spencer had to bite the inside of his mouth to keep from letting out a totally inappropriate laugh.

"No, I'm going to *protect you* because I'm your dad, and I love you, and *that's* my job."

"So, yes then." Connor scowled and crossed his arms.

Spencer couldn't hold back an eye roll—kid was way too much of a smart ass for his own good—but he managed to otherwise ignore the comment. "It's either I tell the principal what's been going on, or I follow you around and walk you to and from every single one of your classes *including* lunch, which we'll be eating together in my classroom."

"That's not fair!"

"No. What's not fair is that my son got punched in the face, and I can't call the cops on the people who did it because technically *he* started it. I've kept quiet for this long because you begged me to, and you swore it wasn't that bad and said you could handle it."

"I can!" Spencer raised an eyebrow. "Well, I *was*," Connor said, pouting.

"No, kid. 'Handling it' and 'suppressing how bad it makes me feel until I snap and hit someone' are two different things. We tried it your way." *And I never should have. Jesus Christ I'm a terrible parent.* "Now, we're doing it mine."

"Even if I get pulled out of your class, and you get in trouble?"

Spencer didn't so much as blink. "Even if."

"Even if it means they beat me up *every day* because you got them in trouble?"

"If they do that, I'll keep sending them to the principal until they get expelled." Spencer made sure to stare Connor right in the eye, so he knew how serious he was. "No matter what I have to do, you're going to feel safe at school. Understand?"

"I'm safe now," Connor insisted. Spencer didn't even try to hide his disbelief. "No, really! They're not gonna punch me in school because they know they can get in trouble. They never hit me before, and they're not gonna start now."

"Really?"

"Yes!"

Spencer sighed. "What's the rule about lying?"

"I'm not lying!"

"The rule, Connor."

"I know what it is."

"Then tell me."

"Ugh! Fine. As long as I don't lie, I won't get in trouble for things."

"Too *much* trouble," Spencer corrected. "Now the second part, come on."

"And if I get caught lying, I'll get grounded for twice as long," Connor recited, sounding bored. "But I'm not lying."

"You said, and I quote—"

Connor groaned.

"—*and I quote*, 'I'm *getting beat up* by a girl, are you happy?' *Getting beat up*, Con. Meaning it's an ongoing process. That doesn't really fill me with a lot of confidence about you being safe."

"Oh my God. Did you ever think that maybe I said it wrong? Can you maybe stop being an English teacher for five goddamn *seconds*? I—"

"Hey! Watch your language," Spencer scolded. "I'm a *literature* teacher, not an *English* teacher."

Connor made a noise like a strangled cat. "You're an *asshole*!"

"That's it, go to your room." Spencer internally cringed at how TV dad he sounded. "And keep your door open and your video games *off*."

"Fine!" Connor jumped up off the couch and started to stomp out of the room.

"Wait! Get back here."

In true teenage-drama-queen fashion, Connor stomped back over mumbling under his breath about people who can't make up their fucking minds. Spencer stood up and crossed his arms.

"Shirt off."

"*What?*"

"I told you I was checking you over after Tim left. I might have let it go, but now that you're *lying* to me, I need to make sure you're not hiding any other injuries."

Connor gaped at him. Spencer knew what he was doing could, from a certain point of view, be considered mildly unfair. He didn't give a shit. On the best of days, he hated being lied to, and he hated fighting with Connor, and this was definitely not the best of days. If he couldn't be the cool, fun parent, then he was damn sure going to be the overprotective one. It wasn't like there was anyone else to fill the role.

An image of Tim standing in this very living room and refusing to let him lie to Spencer popped into his head. He ruthlessly pushed it away.

"*Now.*"

Connor started to shake, from anger or frustration or humiliation Spencer didn't know, and pulled his shirt off in jerky movements before throwing it on the ground.

Spencer's breath hitched.

The entire left side of his son's skinny little chest was completely black and blue. Spencer's hand shook as he reached out and gently touched Connor's ribs. His son flinched, and Spencer didn't know whether he wanted to cry or punch the wall.

"Does that hurt?" he asked quietly.

"Of course it hurts," Connor snapped, looking at everything in the room *but* Spencer. "And I'm gonna be like this *every day* if you—"

"Take a deep breath," Spencer said, cutting him off. He'd heard it all before. "Does it hurt any more when you breathe?"

"No."

Spencer nodded. "Okay. Good. Your ribs are probably fine then."

I have no idea how. Jesus Christ, he's so skinny. There's not even a tiny bit of fat or muscle to protect his bones.

Connor had his shirt back on almost before Spencer had finished speaking.

"I told you."

"Room," Spencer said. "Door open. No TV."

"I heard you the first time." Connor glared, and Spencer had to fight not to cringe at the utter *loathing* in his eyes. As he stomped out of the room for a second time, he said, just loudly enough for Spencer to hear, "I can't believe I'm getting grounded for getting beat up."

Anger roared to life inside Spencer.

"You're grounded because you're a lying little smart-ass!" Spencer screamed after him. Instead of answering, Connor ran up the stairs and kicked his door so hard Spencer swore he heard the wood splinter. He had to grab the edge of the entryway to keep from running up after him and yelling some more, maybe even taking a book out of his own days of hormone-fueled rage and putting a few holes in the wall. It would feel good—*so* good, *better* than good, nothing felt better than letting his anger have free rein—but he'd never lost his temper with Connor, not like that; not to the point where he needed to be cruel to keep from feeling like he was being eaten alive by bile and spite. He took several deep breaths and forced himself to sit down on the couch. The late-afternoon sun shone in a bright halo around the edges of the room-darkening curtains, and Spencer had to blink several times to make sure he was actually seeing it. Surely it couldn't still be light out? It felt like years had passed since Tim had brought Connor home, not less than two hours.

"Shit," he said to no one in particular. He'd meant it to be bitter and scathing and everything he couldn't be around Connor, but the voice echoing off his narrow living-room walls only sounded sad and defeated and old.

Spencer dropped his head into his hands and wished with everything he was that Tim hadn't left. He'd risk his stupid crush being found out a thousand times over if he could have just a little longer to hide in his arms.

Long silent minutes passed until his muffled text tone—the sound of a lightsaber igniting—broke him out of his increasingly morose thoughts. He fished around between his couch cushions until he found his phone. His lock screen was a picture of Connor from the previous summer when they took a trip to Washington DC and spent a whole week exploring one Smithsonian museum a day. The kid was crouched in front of the Apollo 11 command module, grinning up into the camera so wide his delicate, almond-shaped eyes were almost completely shut.

Spencer's heart lurched, and he quickly unlocked his phone.

In his inbox was a single text from Tim.

> TIM: *Hey, how did everything go? Is Connor okay?*

Spencer stared down at his phone until long after it relocked itself. Hours later, when the sunlight seeping around his curtains faded until it was overtaken by the dim glow of the streetlights, he still had no idea how to answer.

Chapter Nine

Tim barely had enough time to take his finger off the Kent's doorbell before the front door flew open, and a tiny Spider-Man raced past him and stomped down the steps.

"Come on," Spider-Man barked as he came to a stop on the sidewalk. He crossed his arms, causing the large Halloween-themed bag in his hand to bounce off his hip, and refused to so much as glance back at the house. Tim held back a sigh and turned toward the still-open door, completely unsurprised to see Spencer standing just inside, staring right past Tim. His eyes were pinched with stress at the corners, and his hair stuck up wildly, like he'd been running his fingers through it constantly. He looked...worn.

"Still not talking to you?" Tim asked.

Spencer snorted. "Oh, he's talking. Getting more grounded every time he opens his mouth, but he's talking."

Tim smiled sympathetically even though he hadn't really expected anything different.

The last few days after Connor had gotten attacked hadn't been the best for either of the Kent men. Spencer was still seething over the school administration refusing to do anything about the assault because it hadn't happened on school grounds, or the bullying because there were no witnesses, and Connor refused to talk about it. Connor was still pissed Spencer had even reported it in the first place and *infuriated* that he'd started following Connor around and refused to let him out of his sight when they weren't at home. They'd had some pretty epic fights in the days leading up to Halloween—Tim hadn't been there for them, but he had about a hundred texts from both Connor and Spencer complaining about each one—and Tim was pretty sure the only reason Spencer was letting him take Connor out trick-or-treating like they'd been planning was because they might actually end up killing each other if they stayed locked in the House of Tension, as Spencer called it, for another night.

Tim couldn't help being depressed by the whole situation. Spencer and Connor had a great relationship, and Tim's heart broke to see it fracturing right in front of him. It was also *really* frustrating because both of them were stubborn *asses* and absolutely refused to back down. Tim wished he'd known them longer, that he was closer to them because as much as he desperately wanted to force them to sit down and *talk* to each other without it devolving into a screaming match, he knew it wasn't his place.

Spencer shook his head and made a small, frustrated noise.

"Ugh, whatever. I've been bitching at you all week, and I'm kind of just done for right now." He took a deep breath and then finally turned to Tim. And blinked. "Uh, are you wearing argyle? And zombie makeup?"

Tim could hear Connor shifting impatiently behind him. Part of him wanted to hurry away so he could be a good friend and give Connor at least a few hours of fun, but a much bigger part was painfully aware this was the first time he'd seen Spencer since he'd brought Connor home after being attacked, and he'd missed his other older friend more than he'd like to think about.

"Yeah," he said somewhat sheepishly. This was probably the least flattering outfit he'd ever worn, and he was suddenly a little embarrassed Spencer was seeing him in it. "Pleated pants too."

He stretched out one of his legs and gave it a little shake. Spencer's eyes darted down and then almost immediately snapped back up. A small flush spread across his face, which Tim realized must have been freshly shaven because he'd never seen him so smooth before.

Tim had the sudden inexplicable urge to run his fingers along Spencer's jaw.

"Ah." Spencer cleared his throat. "And after all the shit you give me about my grandpa sweaters."

"I like your grandpa sweaters though," Tim admitted. "They're cute."

Spencer's eyes widened as his flush quickly spread down his neck.

Why the hell did I say that?

"Sorry."

"'S fine!" Spencer's voice cracked, slightly. He cleared his throat again. "Uh, is...costume? Is that your costume?"

"Um, yeah," Tim said slowly. He felt like he was missing something. "I'm Uncle Ben."

Spencer blinked, then snorted so hard his eyes started to water. "Shit." He quickly wiped them. "Zombie Uncle Ben taking Spider-Man trick-or-treating. That is wrong and awesome, and I love it."

"Better than Superboy?" Tim asked, only slightly teasing. One of the things he'd learned while taking Connor shopping was Spencer had dressed him up as nineties Superboy every Halloween until he was twelve, which was adorable, and Spencer had texted him dozens of pictures to prove it. He'd never really gotten over

Connor refusing to put the spandex and leather jacket back on.

"I wouldn't go that far," Spencer said automatically. He chewed his lip for a moment and then said, "Okay, maybe I would."

Tim laughed.

"Can we go now?" Connor called. A quick glance showed he still had his back turned, but his arms were still crossed, and his hip was cocked, and he was actually tapping his foot.

That's so cute...

"Sickening, isn't it?" Spencer asked with a knowing gleam in his eyes. "Like looking at four sleepy puppies kind of adorable. I have no idea how he doesn't have an army of senior girls all fighting over who gets to make him their honorary Little Brother."

"Well—"

"Tim!" Connor snapped.

"Aaand that would be why. You should...probably get going," Spencer said. He shifted in place and chewed his lip again—*the son has nothing on the father*—and nodded. "Yeah. Um. Back by ten, okay? And don't take him too far past—well. You know what to do. I texted you like fifty times...but if he gets sick or hurt, call me. And if you think he might be about to apologize, call me, and put me on speaker. And don't let him eat any candy before you get back. He has weird reactions to some of it, and you don't want to be stuck without a bathroom, especially since he won't mention how bad he's feeling until grossness starts spewing out one end or the other—"

"Spencer." Tim smiled, placing his hand on his friend's shoulder in what he hoped came off as a comforting gesture. "We'll be fine."

For some reason, Spencer flushed again, and this time Tim had to tighten his grip to keep from seeing if those cheeks felt as warm as they appeared.

This is not good.

"I-I know." Spencer nodded and then cleared his throat again and took a step back right as Tim let him go. "Thanks again for doing this."

"You don't need to thank me," Tim said, his voice strangely soft. "I wanted to."

Spencer swallowed visibly and glanced away. "Cool. Have fun!" he called down to Connor.

Connor gave him the finger.

"Right." Spencer gave Tim a tight-lipped smile. "You better get going before he starts consuming the souls of the innocent."

And with that, he stepped fully inside and closed the door.

Tim stared at it for a long moment before shaking his head and making his way down to Connor.

"Okay," he said, giving Connor his best carefree smile. "Ready?"

Connor nodded stiffly before taking off down the sidewalk.

"Okay," Tim muttered to himself and then followed.

*

It took twenty minutes or so, the bright sun of Halloween fun breaking through the storm clouds surrounding Connor in the form of jittery excitement and hard-won laughter, but eventually the tension between them evaporated, and they fell into a pretty good rhythm. Tim had always liked planning his trick-or-treating out in advance so he could hit the maximum number of houses as quickly as possible, and he was pleasantly surprised to see Connor shared his philosophy. Even better, he actually knew the area: which houses gave out the most candy, which ones were stingy to anyone over the age of six, and which houses were well meaning but awful and gave out fruit or toothpaste.

As Connor's dad might say, they cleaned the fuck up.

Tim had almost forgotten how awesome Halloween could be. Aside from his freshman year, he'd always been too busy in college to bother dressing up or following his roommate around to parties. Even when he'd been with Rudy and kind of inherited his group of friends by default, they'd never really been big into Halloween. Somehow, over the years, the simple joys of wearing a costume and gorging himself on candy had been lost, and it didn't take long before his enthusiasm stopped being solely about Connor having fun and started being about *Tim* having fun too.

Maybe too much fun because it took him a lot longer than it should have to notice Connor had gotten sullen again.

"I haven't seen this much Pez since I was in high school," Tim said, staring down into the bag he'd somehow ended up holding—probably because the thing was so full it was about a tenth of Connor's body weight—in exchange for a small share of their haul. "I changed my mind; I want the grape ones, not the Snickers."

Connor grunted.

"Grape Pez is the best," Tim went on. "If I could only eat one thing for the rest of my life, right now I'd pick grape Pez. I'd completely regret it within two days, but I'd still pick it."

"Hm."

The back of Tim's tongue began to get that bitter-sour feeling he got whenever he really wanted some candy, and he started to reach into the bag only to pause before his fingers could even graze the sugary goodness. He'd tried this about seven other times since they'd been out, and every time Connor had smacked his hand away and yelled at him for being a candy thief. Tim had a brief irrational spike of panic thinking he'd lost Connor at some point and hadn't noticed, but a quick glance showed Connor still right beside him, staring at the ground and hugging himself around the waist, exactly like he had the night Tim brought him home.

"Hey, you wanna take a break before we hit the rest of the houses?" Tim asked as casually as he could.

"No."

"Well, I do." He smiled to take the edge off his words, but Connor was too focused on the sidewalk to notice. "Come on, there's a bench over there. Let's sit down for a bit."

Connor didn't say anything, but when Tim took a seat and placed the bag on the ground between his legs, he sat right next to him on the cold metal. Tim noted the thin material of his Spider-Man costume and grimaced, but if Connor was feeling the cold at all, he wasn't showing it. He just sat back so his legs were dangling off the bench and stared at his knees.

"Pretty good haul this year, huh?" Tim asked. Connor didn't say anything, but Tim hadn't really expected him to. "Do you guys usually get this much?"

A small flinch when he'd said "you guys." *So, this is definitely about Spencer, then. Not like I expected any different but still good to know.*

At least, maybe Tim would get the chance to talk to one of them about this whole stupid cold war they had going on. He'd just have to be *very* careful about how he brought the subject up. If he said the wrong thing, he was sure Connor would just clam up and maybe even demand to be taken home. Tim would need to use every conversation skill he had to subtly coax Connor into—

"What did Dad want?"

Or not.

"Back at the house." Even with the mask on Tim could tell he was glaring. "You were talking to him forever. What did he want?"

"He—"

"Did he tell you to 'talk sense' into me or something? Is that why you're doing this?"

Tim blinked. "If you mean why am I taking you trick-or-treating, it's because I want to. I wanted to before you and your dad started fighting."

"Yeah, and he's been keeping me locked in the house since then."

"I know."

"And he wouldn't let me out just to go trick-or-treating. There's no way he trusts you enough to 'look after me' or whatever." Tim's heart sank. "So, he wouldn't let me out unless he thought you were going to make me forgive him."

It took a lot of effort, but Tim pushed aside his own feelings—*he's wrong anyway. Of course, Spencer trusts me. Even if he hasn't actually said the words, he wouldn't let me spend so much time with Connor if he didn't. Right?*—and focused on what Connor was saying. All his instincts were telling him to say whatever he needed to get Connor to calm down, but those instincts were honed over years of dealing with emotionally troubled preteens. Connor was older, and smart to boot, and maybe this time a judicious bit of truth telling would be for the best. It seemed to work well enough for them this far anyway.

"You really wanna know why he let you come out tonight?"

Connor nodded, and Tim had to hold back a smile. No matter what Connor thought about how much Spencer trusted Tim, *he* obviously trusted Tim enough not to ask if he was going to tell the truth.

"Then take that mask off. Please?" he added when Connor seemed like he might be about to protest.

After a short hesitation, Connor pulled off the Spider-Man mask. His hair stuck up in every direction like he'd been struck by lightning, but he didn't even bother trying to straighten it out.

"So?"

Tim took a breath. "Okay, honestly? He wanted you out of the house so you could both have a break from each other. All he told me was to make sure you had fun."

"*What*?"

"He—"

"A *break* from each other? We could have had a *million* breaks from each other if he'd stop following me around like I'm on suicide watch!"

"That's not exactly what he's doing—"

"I *know*! I was being—"

"But I completely agree."

Whatever Connor had been about to say died on his lips. His jaw dropped, and he stared at Tim like he'd never seen him before. "What did you say?"

Connor's words were guarded like Tim's words were a treasured toy that might be snatched out of his hands by a cruel babysitter at any moment.

"Your dad's being a bit unreasonable," Tim said, shrugging. "Keeping you locked up together twenty-four seven isn't doing either of you any good."

Connor stared at Tim like he was the *Second Coming*.

"That's exactly what I said! Dad said I had no idea what I was talking about, and that he'd rather sew us together than see me get punched in the face again. *Then* he started talking about the best *way* to sew us together, and it's *impossible* to have a rational conversation with him when he refuses to take anything seriously. It's so childish."

Tim quickly covered up his amusement. "Well, as your center-approved Big Brother, I'm not really supposed to offer my opinion here." *Please God, don't let this backfire on me at some point.* "But...as your friend? Yeah, he's definitely being childish."

"*Thank you!*" Connor threw his hands in the air and sagged back onto the bench, which made this the only time Tim had ever seen someone calm down by getting worked up. It was kind of fascinating to watch. "No one *ever* agrees with me."

"Ever?" Tim couldn't help asking.

Thankfully, Connor either didn't hear the irony in his voice or chose to ignore it.

"Yes! Grandma and Grandpa keep saying I should listen to Dad. *Dad* keeps saying I should listen to Dad, and...I don't have anyone else. Except you. And you agree with *me*," he said, glancing up at Tim through his eyelashes with eyes that seemed to sparkle under the nearby streetlights.

Tim's heart *ached*. He knew exactly how Connor felt. He'd been there before. Maybe not this young, but he knew what it was like to feel lost and alone and locked in a battle with the people who'd always had his back. For Tim, it had been his parents he'd been fighting with. They'd both wanted him to stay in New York for college, but Tim had wanted to be on his own. He'd wanted to get away from his mom's stifling expectations. And in Tim's house, going up against his mom almost always meant being at odds with his dad too.

By the time the allure of college and casual dating had worn off, he'd felt just as alone as Connor did now. The only difference was Tim hadn't had anyone like himself to turn to. Instead, he'd floundered through short-lived relationships until he'd latched onto a mentor who abused his trust and a boyfriend whose idea of love was twisted and selfish. Tim thought he'd been getting better over the last few weeks. He'd thought the long days and longer nights of reliving the worst months of his life were behind him. But even now, when his life was objectively better in every way and Connor was counting on him to be present and supportive, Tim couldn't help slipping into the past. For just a moment, Connor, the bench, the street, and the buildings all faded away, and he was back in his old dorm with Rudy smiling softly and telling him it wouldn't be so bad to take Professor Carmichael up on his offer.

"Come on, it's not like it's something you hate doing. You're good at it. It's not cheating if I give you permission. Go blow his mind, baby."

"You withdrew your application? What the hell, Tim? What are we gonna do now? Am I supposed to sit around while you get some white-trash minimum-wage job? Did you even think about me? Or is a little bit of selflessness too much to ask?"

"No, honey, fuck you. I can't believe I wasted almost a year of my life on a fucking baker."

Tim shook his head, and the present snapped back into focus. He glanced down at Connor, who hadn't seemed to notice his slip, and swallowed heavily.

Stop it. Rudy is gone and you're never going to see him again. Your present is Connor and Spencer. It's Dick and Sarah and your customers at the bakery. It's Mom and Dad who you're finally on good terms with again, even if Mom hasn't gotten any easier to handle. And despite all the shit Rudy put you through, in the end you left him. Remember the look on his face when he realized you were breaking up with him. Focus on that if you have to think about him. Nothing else.

Tim cleared his throat and summoned his best smile for Connor. "Yeah. Well, this time I do, anyway."

"Dude, you agree with me *now*. I thought..." Connor wrung his hands together and glanced down toward the bench.

Tim let his smile slip. It didn't matter how much of himself he could see in Connor. All that mattered was Connor finding someone better to hold on to when he was vulnerable than Tim had.

His Rudy issues could wait. Right now, it was time to put those four years of college-psychology courses to good use.

"You thought I'd side with your dad because you're not used to anyone but him being in your corner, right?"

"That sounds really stupid," Connor said as he started picking at the chipped paint on the bench.

"But it's not wrong."

Connor shrugged. "Maybe."

"But now you know that *I'm* in your corner too," Tim said very deliberately, not phrasing it as a question. Still, he wasn't very surprised when he got one in return.

"Are you?"

Connor's question was serious, for all that he refused to make eye contact, so Tim made sure his response was equally serious.

"*Always.*"

To his surprise, Connor snorted. "Stupid *Harry Potter*," he muttered.

"*Harry Potter*?"

Connor shook his head. "Nothing. Never mind." He chewed his lip for a moment. "What if you're not though? Dad..."

He trailed off, but Tim didn't need to hear the words to know what he was going to say.

"Just because you guys are fighting right now doesn't mean he's not on your side." Connor shot him probably the most incredulous look he'd ever received. Tim bit back a smile. "I know you won't want to hear this, but this whole thing is happening *because* he's trying to be on your side. You two are just disagreeing on what 'your side' is."

Connor made a face. "That sounds fake. And you didn't answer my question."

Tim held back a sigh. "If I'm ever not, then your dad will be. And if he's not, then your grandparents will be."

"And when they're not? Because that's kind of all I have."

"Then you'll have a shitty few days," Tim said bluntly. "You'll fight with all of us, and it'll suck, but it won't last forever."

"That's such condescending crap." Connor scowled. "'It'll suck, but it won't last forever.' You're completely invalidating my feelings."

Tim winced. *You're invalidating my feelings* had pretty much been Rudy's catchphrase. He'd always sounded like a whiny little kid when he said it, but since Connor actually *was* a kid, Tim couldn't really hold a bit of childishness against him.

"I'm really not," he said as calmly as he could. "The only reason this fight seems so bad is because you're not used to fighting with your dad. Eventually, it'll get easier."

"But I don't *want* to fight with him all the time!"

"No one's saying you're going to."

"You just said it'll 'get easier.' That means we're gonna have to fight more."

"Yeah, but not all the time."

"I don't want to fight at *all*." Connor hugged himself and glanced away again. "I just want things to go back to the way they were."

Tim had to grab the bench to keep from pulling Connor into a hug. "You know that's impossible though, right?" he asked gently. "Things have already changed between you guys, and they're going to keep changing. That's just part of growing up and getting older."

"Jesus Christ with the guidance counselor shit," Connor grumbled. "I *know* all that, okay? I'm not some stupid kid who needs to be told that *things change when you grow up*."

Tim decided not to get annoyed at the whiny, mocking voice Connor put on when he repeated what he'd said. They were wading into uncharted waters in their friendship, and to be honest, Tim had no idea where the line between friend and Big Brother was anymore. And that wasn't even accounting for how close he and Spencer had become. The whole situation had gotten complicated and confusing. The only thing Tim knew for sure was there was almost nothing he wouldn't do to make them both happy.

And if this isn't the worst time to have that revelation, I don't know what is.

"I never said you were," Tim said, as patiently as he could.

"You implied it."

This time, Tim couldn't stop from rolling his eyes. Luckily, Connor wasn't looking. They sat in silence for a few minutes, Tim having no idea what to say and Connor seeming perfectly content to stare at the sidewalk and sulk.

"Did you fight with your parents a lot?" Connor asked suddenly. A surprised laugh forced its way out of Tim's throat. Twin spots of red painted Connor's cheeks. "What? You just said everyone fights with their parents. It's not a stupid question."

"I'm not laughing at you, I swear," Tim said. "It's just the *way* you asked. Did I, like it's a thing that doesn't happen anymore."

"So...that's a yes?"

Tim hesitated. Was this another line he couldn't see? *You said you were going to tell him the truth...*

"Not...fights, exactly. At least, my mother wouldn't call them fights. We have a series of 'extended disagreements' that get brought up every single time we talk until I give in and do what she wants."

Connor glanced up at him. "Seriously?"

Tim nodded. Connor took a moment to think that over, a small frown etched on his forehead.

"That's the most passive-aggressive thing I've ever heard."

Tim laughed again. "God, what I wouldn't give for her to hear you say that."

Connor's lips twitched. "She wouldn't get the full effect without meeting Dad though."

"Oh God," Tim coughed. "Don't say that."

"Why not? It's true. Sometimes I think he majored in passive-aggression in college."

"Because I have about twenty things I wanna say, and I'm not supposed to encourage my Little Brother to rag on his dad."

"Oh, come on! You can't just say something like that and then not follow through! What things?"

"No. Way."

"I'm not gonna tell on you. And it's not like you're not already breaking the rules by taking me out after seven for like an hour and a half." Tim must have looked as surprised as he felt, because Connor snorted. "Like I wouldn't look up what you're allowed to do with me the second I decided to come back. I needed to be sure you couldn't force me to, like, open up about my feelings or whatever."

I don't think he's ever looked more like Spencer. Tim was so thrown he almost forgot to answer.

"I have a permission slip," he said. "For Halloween. I don't have one that lets me encourage you to hate your dad more."

The slightly teasing smile hovering at the corners of Connor's lips evaporated.

"I don't hate him," he said. Then he blinked. "Shit. I really *don't* hate him."

"And that's a...bad thing?"

"It makes it a lot harder to stay mad at him," Connor grumbled. Tim might have chuckled, but Connor seemed so put out he doubted it would be taken well. Besides, he actually had something useful to contribute now.

"Well, you know your dad doesn't hate you either, right?"

"Yeah…"

"So, it's probably just as hard for him to stay mad at you," Tim said. "Sort of pointless for two people who don't want to be mad at each other to keep finding reasons to *be* mad at each other, don't you think?"

"But he's still wrong though!"

"Yes, he is," Tim agreed. "But you're a little bit wrong too."

Connor's face twisted into an expression of utter betrayal. "But you said—"

"Sometimes," Tim cut in, "people can be wrong *and* right in a fight. I understand why you didn't want to go to the principal, but not going after you got attacked in the streets was a bit reckless. Even if you hit first," he added when Connor opened his mouth to argue. "They kicked you when you were down, Connor. That goes *way* beyond self-defense or high-school bullying. People who can do that and just walk away have the potential to be dangerous, and as stifling as your dad is being, he's only doing it because he knows that as much as I do, and he's scared of having anything happen to you."

"I can take care of myself."

Oh my God…

Tim took a deep breath. "Okay. Even putting aside the fact that you already got beat up by these kids once, you look like you weigh about as much as a wet shoe—"

"I'm ninety-five pounds!"

Tim paused. "You know that's still almost twenty pounds underweight for your age, right?"

"Almost."

That's it, I'm feeding him more from now on.

"Whatever you weigh, you don't have the size or the muscle to fight back against people bigger than you. Of course your dad's going to worry about you."

"You're not sounding like you're on my side right now."

"God." Tim huffed out a disbelieving laugh and shook his head. "I can't believe I ever doubted you were his son."

"What the hell is that supposed to mean?" Connor asked, frowning.

"Nothing. Look," Tim added when Connor started to speak, "do you want me to talk to him for you?"

So much for not putting myself in the middle of this.

Whatever Connor was about to say seemed to be forgotten the second the words were out of Tim's mouth.

"You'd do that?" he asked, wide-eyed.

Tim didn't give himself the luxury of hesitating. If he was going to do this, he was going all in.

"Yeah. But you know you're gonna have to compromise with him, right?"

Connor's expression suddenly became mutinous. "Why?"

"Do you want to give in, tell him he's right, and agree to let him do whatever he wants?"

"No!"

"Exactly. And neither does he." Tim stared him in the eye. "You two are both way too stubborn to give in fully. So. Compromise."

"But he's wrong!"

"And so are you."

"But he's actually *doing* something. All I'm doing is *not* doing something." Connor scowled. "He's *more* wrong."

Tim wanted to bang his head against a *wall.*

Okay. This obviously isn't working. Time to try something new.

"Even if you think he's more wrong," Tim said slowly after a minute of quick thinking, "agreeing to a compromise would make your position stronger."

"What does that mean?"

"You'll have the moral high ground," Tim said. "If you say you want to work something out, and he says no, then he's the one who looks unreasonable."

"He's already being unreasonable."

"More unreasonable, then."

Tim had a brief moment where he thought Connor might be seeing through the thick fog of utter *bullshit* he was blowing at him, but after taking a moment to think, Connor cocked his head.

"He won't see it that way."

Of course not because none of this is true, and I'm going to Hell for lying to you.

"Yes, he will," Tim said quickly. "Because he's smart. Right now, he thinks *he* has the high ground; that's why he's not giving in. Once we can show him he's being unreasonable in one way, he'll be more open to seeing how he's doing the same thing in another."

Connor frowned. "And...you're gonna tell him? That he's being unreasonable?"

"If you tell him you want to compromise, yes." *Because I won't need to tell him anything after that. Spencer will jump at the chance to make up with you, and there's no way he won't be open to figuring out a different way to keep you safe as long as I can be there to keep you two from starting another fight.*

Tim held his breath as he waited for Connor's response. Thankfully, he didn't have to wait long.

"Okay. Let's do it."

Chapter Ten

Tim collapsed onto Spencer's couch and let out a moan of exhausted relief.

Two hours. That's how long Spencer and Connor had taken to come to an agreement. *Two goddamn hours* to agree to the simple compromise of giving Connor back his freedom in exchange for a promise to go to the principal if anyone got physical with him again. Two hours of pride and suspicion and shouting and both refusing to admit any fault and Tim literally having to grab them and shove them back down into their chairs at different times so they couldn't run off in a huff. He had never in his *life* met two people who absolutely refused to admit they could possibly be in the wrong more than Spencer and Connor. It was so bad that, by the time they'd finally stopped fighting, Tim was 100 percent sure the easy apologies he'd gotten from Spencer back when they'd first met had to be concrete proof of God's existence because there was no earthly way Spencer would admit he was wrong so many times without some kind of divine intervention.

If he'd known what he was getting into, he never would have...

Tim sighed, unable to even finish the thought. As satisfying as indulging in some childish complaining would be, he'd made a promise after Rudy that he wouldn't lie to himself anymore. Instead, he pushed away all the negativity of the last few hours, closed his eyes, and focused on the soul-deep sense of accomplishment and peace that had flowed through him when they finally stopped fighting. On the memory of a pair of arms tentatively reaching out. On the way a slight figure still dressed as Spider-Man had eagerly accepted the uncertain offering. On the tears that had fallen down both their cheeks as they finally let go of their *stupid* fight and forgave each other.

Tim wanted to live in that memory for at *least* the next ten minutes. He deserved that much.

And it seemed like God agreed with him because he was able to get *fifteen* minutes of complete peace before he felt the couch dip as someone sat down next to him. Whoever was there didn't say anything, but when Tim cracked open an eye, he wasn't at all surprised to see Spencer. He was tucked into the corner where the back of the couch met the armrest, his own arms wrapped around his legs and his chin resting on his knees. Except for the tips of his fingers, the oversized gray sweater he was wearing swallowed his hands.

Tim had seen *smiling babies* that were less adorable.

"Hey," Spencer said. His voice was soft, barely more than a whisper like he was afraid anything more would be enough to shatter Tim's peace. Or maybe Tim was just projecting. Either way, his own reply was equally gentle.

"Hey." Tim let his other eye fall open. "Where's Connor?"

"Upstairs. Changing." Spencer's lips quirked into a wry smile. "He is Spider-Man no more."

Tim snorted at the reference to the famous comic title and then picked at his own sweater. "I should probably do the same."

He was grateful he'd already washed all the makeup off. That stuff seriously started to itch after a few hours.

"You don't have to," Spencer said quickly. Tim stilled at the strangely insistent tone and then cocked his head as Spencer's cheeks darkened in the dim light. He buried his face in his knees and groaned.

"I mean," Spencer said, his voice slightly muffled, "you'd have to leave for that, right? And you should totally stay. For dinner."

For some reason, Spencer's head shot up with a panicked expression on his face.

"A thank-you dinner. With Connor. And...me. Because. You know." He swallowed roughly before continuing, his voice regaining its earlier softness. "We'd still be fighting if it wasn't for you. So...thank you."

"You don't need to thank me." Tim fought the urge to start squirming under Spencer's grateful gaze. It was an odd feeling for him since he'd never really had a problem accepting gratitude before. "I mostly did it because you two being stubborn jerks was grating on my last nerve."

Tim froze. He had no idea which was worse, actually saying that out loud or sounding almost exactly like his mother when he did. To his relief, Spencer didn't seem to be remotely offended.

"Well, shit. Now I *definitely* have to make you dinner."

"You really don't need to do anything for me," Tim said quickly. "And I shouldn't have said that. It was rude. I'm sorry."

"Apology accepted. Just like *you* should accept *my* thanks and eat with us." Spencer's grin started to fade when Tim didn't respond right away. "Unless you don't want to, I mean. Which you probably don't. Shit. You've been dealing with our shit all day, so more of us is probably the last thing you want."

"Spencer—"

"No! No, it's fine. I totally get it. We'll just get you a card or something. Maybe a cake—no, you're a baker, you can probably make way better cake than Walmart. A fruit basket?"

"*Spencer.*" Tim reached over and squeezed his leg. Spencer stopped, and Tim smiled. "I'd love to stay for dinner."

Spencer's muscles tensed beneath his hand, and Tim felt like he'd tripped into a river of white-hot mortification when he realized just how high up on Spencer's thigh he'd grabbed him. The sleep pants under his hand were so thin he could feel the warmth of Spencer's skin and a few rough small hairs poking him through the fabric.

Tim snatched his hand back, apologies spilling from his lips, only to halt when Spencer grabbed his wrist. His eyes were wide as he stared up at Tim, his mouth slightly open like he was about to speak, but any words he might have said never passed his lips. Spencer's breathing became heavy, and Tim felt his own chest tighten at the way Spencer stared at him. Tim flashed back to the last time they'd been on this couch together. Spencer's hand around the exact same wrist, his shirt soaked with Spencer's tears. His face started to warm, and he wondered if he'd end up with his arms around Spencer tonight too.

"I..." Spencer started.

The soft dim light from the only lamp in the room fell across Spencer's face, creating shadows that filled in for the stubble Tim was so used to seeing on his cheeks and deepened the nearly invisible laugh lines around his mouth. They made him seem somehow younger and older at the same time, and Tim was almost 100 percent sure he'd never seen anything so charming in his life. A heavy warmth wrapped itself around him like a blanket fresh from the dryer had somehow bypassed his skin entirely and came to rest directly on his heart.

"What?" Tim asked. If he hadn't been so focused on Spencer's face, he probably would have been taken aback at the rasp he heard in his voice.

Spencer licked his lips, and even though his throat was hidden behind his knees, Tim could still clearly see him swallow nervously.

"Um." Spencer chewed his bottom lip. "I..."

Tim leaned closer. "Yeah?"

"I..." Spencer cleared his throat. "I don't know if I have any food..."

A small high-pitched laugh bubbled out of Tim's mouth, and suddenly the strange mood was broken. Spencer let go of his wrist and wrapped his arms around his knees again. Tim slowly took his hand back, fighting the urge to touch the skin where Spencer's fingers had just been.

"We have candy," Tim found himself saying.

Spencer snorted and rubbed his hands roughly over his shins. Tim wondered why the motion bothered him so much. A heartbeat later he realized it was because he didn't know if it was a nervous gesture, or if Spencer was trying to wipe all traces of Tim's skin from his palm.

What the hell is wrong with me?

"Connor would love that," Spencer said. He sounded completely normal like they hadn't just been in the middle of some kind of moment, but the redness in his cheeks and the way he absolutely refused to look at Tim suggested he was very much aware of it. "Less so when all his teeth fall out and he has to be the only kid in school with dentures, but candy dinner would definitely win some short-term points."

"Did you say candy dinner?" Connor asked, popping his head around the doorway. His shoulder and left arm were the only visible parts of his body, but Tim could see he'd changed out of his costume and into a brown T-shirt.

Spencer jerked violently and clutched his chest. "Jesus Christ! Make some fucking noise or something. And no, we're *not* having candy for dinner."

Spencer twisted around as he spoke, actually having to stare *up* at Connor since the couch was so low to the ground. For a moment, Tim felt like he'd fallen into an alternate universe where Connor was the parent, and he'd just caught Tim and his son on the couch doing something inappropriate. He squirmed in place until Connor responded, breaking the illusion.

"Why not?" he asked, pouting.

"Because that's a question you even have to ask."

Connor raised an eyebrow and stepped fully into the room, revealing the design on his shirt—a picture of Bigfoot with the words *I Believe* written under it—and the blue and black plaid pajama pants he was wearing.

"You let me eat Nutella for dinner."

"*Lunch*. And it was *one time*. And you're not supposed to tell people I did that," he added, shooting a nervous glance at Tim like his entire opinion of Spencer was based on whether or not he let his son eat a Nutella meal. The whole thing, the way Spencer and Connor interacted, the warmth that spread through Tim at being included—however peripherally—felt so achingly familiar despite the fact they'd rarely all spent time together. Joining in on the banter felt like slipping into an old, comfortable sweater.

"How much Nutella?" Tim asked.

"A spoonful," Spencer said.

"The whole thing," Connor said at the same time.

"Judas!" Spencer accused, though even facing away Tim didn't miss the tiny smile tugging at his lips.

"I have no idea what that means."

Spencer let out the most overly dramatic sigh Tim had ever heard. "I suppose 'tis the bane of all teachers of the literary arts to be saddled with uncultured sons who—"

"Oh my God, stop!" Connor covered his ears and backed out of the room. "Fine. No candy. Just stop talking. God, you're so embarrassing."

"Who," Spencer continued, getting louder as Connor quickly stomped down the hall, "knows not even the most *basic of references to famous betrayers! Woe betide me! My own flesh and blood*, and he's gone."

Tim chuckled, and Spencer gave him a quick grin before standing up in a single fluid motion. He hesitated then, his grin fading into something more uncertain and apprehensive. His expression cleared almost immediately, and if this had been any normal night, Tim might have been able to convince himself he'd imagined it altogether.

"Come on," Spencer said, turning away. "Let's see if we've got anything to eat."

Tim followed him slowly, his thoughts churning a mile a minute. Those thoughts finally settled down while Spencer was bent over searching through the fridge. Which meant Spencer's ass stretching out a pair of tight sleep pants while he muttered darkly about potatoes would forever be the backdrop to Tim realizing he was a little bit head over heels for him.

Tim was less startled by this revelation than he probably should have been. His breath barely even caught as he realized what all the strange little moments he kept feeling actually meant. Part of him wanted to panic and another part wanted to run, but they were very quickly overridden by the rest of him that just sort of settled. Like a large part of himself had been in a state of constant upheaval, and only now could it finally start to get back to normal. None of this made any sense to Tim—surely he would have noticed if he was that out of sorts, right?—but he couldn't deny he was more relieved than anything else. As much as he might have sworn off romance after Rudy, he knew himself enough to know he'd fall for someone else eventually. When he let himself think about it, it was only long enough to send up a barely voiced prayer that his next crush would be something he could handle: someone who wasn't as bad as Rudy. Like a low-ranking Mafia member or a refugee from one of those hate churches that protest funerals. Having his heart settle on Spencer was like opening the squishy present on Christmas morning and, instead of socks, finding it filled with lottery tickets.

He wasn't quite sure if he'd win anything yet, but he couldn't deny being kind of eager to find out.

They did have stuff to eat, as it turned out. Spencer's freezer was filled with almost nothing but steak, and while Spencer cooked three of them up on the grill out back, Tim and Connor hung out in the kitchen until dinner was ready.

"How does your dad have fifteen steaks but no pizza?"

"Don't even get me *started*."

The meal, when it was ready, started off slowly with Spencer and Connor tiptoeing around each other like wary animals as if they hadn't just been joking around less than a half hour ago. Thankfully, it didn't take long until the conversation became less stilted, and they fell back into their usual patterns.

"We who are about to die, salute you," Connor muttered, poking his slightly burnt strip steak with a fork. Spencer gave his hair a yank. "Ow!"

Their easy, casual banter sort of set the tone for the rest of the evening, much to Tim's surprise. This was the most domestic situation he'd ever been in with both Spencer and Connor, and he found himself completely fascinated by the way he could see all the different facets of their relationship at the same time. They spoke in inside jokes and references like friends. They bickered like siblings. Spencer took care of Connor like a father, and Connor sought out that care like a son. Sitting in the small Kent Family kitchen around an even smaller kitchen table, Tim saw the entirety of Spencer and Connor; not in glimpses and snatches but in all its intoxicating fullness. It felt like gazing into a living version of a Norman Rockwell painting, updated for the modern age, and he couldn't help holding the memories of his own family over the living picture in front of him. His mother, while supportive and caring, had never really understood Tim or his needs, and she rarely understood his sense of humor. His dad had always been a little distant, more interested in his job and his own life than Tim's. He wasn't neglectful, and Tim knew his dad loved him, but there'd always been a wall between them, and the only thing that changed from day to day was whether that wall was made of cellophane or brick. As much as he loved his parents, he'd never been as close to them as Connor was to Spencer.

Tim might have been envious, new revelations aside, except he knew both of them now. Connor was his friend and...charge, he guessed would be a good word. Not Little Brother, with its implications that the only thing tying them together was a voluntary program at a youth center, and definitely not *little brother* with the capital letters removed and a whole different relationship implied. It made Tim more than a little uncomfortable to think of being related to Connor that way even if only as a label or a way of explaining their relationship to other people. *Oh, he's like my little brother*, he could say, ruffling Connor's hair and getting the same annoyed glare the boy turned on Spencer when he did something similar. But Tim wanted something different. He wanted what they already had. Friendship, with an added layer of responsibility placed on his shoulders by Spencer's trust. Spencer was his friend too: as close to him as anyone ever had been with an added layer of something deeper. Something that had been there for a while, hovering in the background of their friendship and flitting out every now and then like a hummingbird trying to grab Tim's attention. Something terrifying and thrilling all at once. Even better, they both treated *Tim* like a friend. It would have been so easy for them to fall into their normal dynamic and leave Tim on the outside looking in, but they each made an effort, separately and together, to pull Tim into their orbit and keep him there.

Tim felt like he *belonged* with them. Like he was wanted.

He hadn't felt this way in a very, very long time.

*

"Of *course* it's a Christmas movie!" Spencer said, continuing the argument he and Connor had been having ever since they all finished dinner. "I can't even believe I have to say that to my own *son* of all people."

"Oh my God, the melodrama." Connor rolled his eyes. "Just because a movie happens *on* Christmas doesn't mean it's a *Christmas* movie!"

"Yes, it does!"

"No, it doesn't!" Connor looked mortally offended. Tim had to hide a smile behind his glass of cream soda. Connor always threw everything he had into any argument he was a part of, no matter how silly. It was completely adorable. "That's...ugh! So, do you think *Gremlins* is a Christmas movie then?"

"*Gremlins* is a Christmas *classic.*"

"I can't believe you. I thought people who graduated college were supposed to be smart."

"That was your first mistake," Spencer said easily. "Your second was assuming I was going to let this Christmas *blasphemy* slide in my own home."

"You're the worst..."

"*Also,*" Spencer went on, "just being set on Christmas isn't the only reason why either of them are Christmas movies. They both incorporate aspects of traditional—"

"Oh my *God.*"

"*Of traditional Christmas movie themes,* while at the same time updating and adapting those themes for the genre change in question—action and comedy-horror respectively."

"This should be good."

"It will be," Spencer agreed. "*Gremlins* is actually nearly a thematic equivalent to *It's a Wonderful Life* where the protagonist makes a potentially life-altering mistake, in this case intending to commit suicide compared to feeding the mogwai after midnight, and then, through a personal struggle—seeing how the world would be if he never existed compared to having to save the town from the gremlins—they both come to realize their lives aren't as bad as they once thought and learn to appreciate what they have. Classic Christmas movie moral."

"I can't believe this is happening."

"And *Die Hard*," Spencer continued, obviously warming up to the subject, "is basically a shot-for-shot re-imagining of *How the Grinch Stole Christmas*. Except, instead of his heart growing three sizes, Alan Rickman gets thrown out a window and falls thirty stories to his death."

Tim imagined the silence that fell over the kitchen then was only slightly louder than the aftermath of a nuclear holocaust. *And speaking of nuclear...* Connor's face had turned a shade of dark red Tim had never seen on a person before. He braced himself for the explosion.

Then Spencer's lips twitched, and Connor let out the loudest groan Tim had ever heard.

"You are *such* an asshole!"

Spencer burst out laughing. "You're so easy!"

"I *hate* you."

"No, you don't, kid." Spencer's laughter dimmed into a fond smile. "You said it yourself."

"I was obviously lying," Connor grumbled.

"Nah, you're pretty bad at that. I would have noticed."

Connor muttered something under his breath but didn't seem too interested in protesting any further. "At least you're not really trying to convince me *Die Hard* is a Christmas movie."

"Oh, no, it totally is," Spencer said. "It's just not the Grinch. It's its own unique take on the Christmas genre."

Connor turned to Tim, a pleading expression on his face.

"*Please* tell me you don't agree with this—" He flailed his hands around as he struggled to think of a word. "*This—*"

"Of course he does," Spencer said before Tim could answer. "Tim is *smart.*"

"Tim has *taste* and *common sense*, which means he can't agree with you."

"Tim can also answer the question himself," Tim put in, amused.

"Yeah, *Dad.* Let Tim answer."

"Yeah, *son.* Let him answer."

They both turned identical expressions of expectation toward Tim. Or, almost identical. The expression on Connor's face made him resemble an eager puppy, completely precious and in desperate need of being petted. The one on Spencer's face...well. Tim couldn't actually say how his expression was any different, but it made Tim's chest tighten and his stomach flip. He ignored the feelings—he didn't really need the confirmation at this point, but it was still nice—and gave Spencer his best apologetic smile.

"Sorry," he said, "there's no way *Die Hard* is a Christmas movie."

"Yes!" Connor punched the air. "I *told you.*"

Spencer quickly smothered a smile before putting on the most overly exaggerated expression of shock Tim had ever seen.

"I invite you into my *home*, I cook you *food* that I bought with the fruit of my *labor*, and this is how you repay me? With treachery?" He shook his head. "This must be exactly how Han felt when Lando turned him over to Darth Vader."

Tim didn't even try to hide his smile. "Wasn't Lando the one who invited Han to dinner, though?"

"*Exactly. How. Han. Felt*," Spencer said, nodding once as he finished.

"That makes no sense," Connor said. He went to take a drink, saw there was nothing left in his glass but ice, and then shrugged and started eating a half-melted ice cube.

"*That* makes no sense," Spencer said, pointing at Connor's glass with a shudder. "My teeth are aching just watching you."

Connor grinned and then very loudly crunched his ice.

"Ugh."

"Eating ice is actually really bad for your teeth," Tim said.

"So is candy," Connor said. "And yet..." He pointed at the medium-sized ziplock bag on the table next to Tim, filled with his portion of the Halloween haul; all grape Pez, of course.

"Candy isn't gross," Spencer said, reaching over and grabbing the glass out of his son's hand before he could fish out another cube.

"Hey!"

"Go on," he said. "You've got a whole bag full of candy in the other room. Take it up to your room and put yourself into a sugar coma."

Connor gave him a suspicious glance but didn't waste any time getting out of his chair and scrambling away. Even then, Tim found himself basking in the family atmosphere that filled the air in their narrow house when they weren't fighting.

It was an atmosphere that subtly changed once Tim realized he was now alone with Spencer. And from the way Spencer began fidgeting with his utensils, he must have felt the change too.

"So, uh." Spencer cleared his throat. "I should clean this up."

He gathered up his dishes, then Connor's, and put them in the sink. Tim picked his own up and followed. When Spencer turned away from the sink, he seemed surprised to see Tim standing right behind him.

"Hi," he said.

"Hello," Tim replied.

Spencer stared up at him for almost a full minute. Tim barely let himself breathe, worried even that much noise would send Spencer running. The last thing he wanted was for things to get awkward between them. Not after the wonderful night they'd been having.

"Hey..." Spencer said breathlessly.

Tim smothered a laugh. "The sink is behind you," he said instead, gesturing with his dirty plate.

Spencer very slowly closed his eyes and groaned out loud. If he'd been watching, he would have seen Tim smiling fondly down at him. The Tim of a year ago would have been certain he was reading the signals correctly. That Tim would have stepped a little closer and brushed past Spencer just slow enough so he'd know it was deliberate to test the waters. Only recently had Tim learned to be hesitant and unsure of himself, and he was both grateful and resentful of that as he carefully stepped around Spencer and put his plate and glass in the sink.

When Tim turned around, Spencer had disappeared. Tim let out a small, disappointed sigh.

What are you doing?

He shook his head, partly in disgust and partly in amusement, before walking back over to the table and gathering up his bag of candy. He fully expected Spencer to pop back in and usher him out the door, so he was surprised when he left the kitchen and found him standing down the hall in the entryway to the living room.

Their eyes met for barely a second, but Tim didn't need eye contact to feel the way the air between them had changed. Spencer ran his fingers nervously through his messy curls and took a deep breath.

"Are you leaving?"

Tim froze.

"You don't have to," Spencer continued quietly, very carefully not making eye contact. "If you don't want to. You could...stay for a bit."

The words were almost an exact mirror to those Spencer had spoken the last time Tim was here, but the emotion he detected in every line of his body, the way that emotion seemed to charge the space between them with *meaning,* was unmistakably different. Tim had no idea what to do. The smart thing, the *responsible* thing, would be to leave. To thank Spencer for dinner, shake his hand, and walk out the door. He'd go back to his tiny apartment, sit on his lumpy secondhand couch, and eat his candy alone. It might even be comforting. A taste of the old familiarity he'd settled into before meeting Spencer. Maybe he'd even down some NyQuil, something he only now realized he hadn't done in weeks, for old-time's sake. No thinking, no *feeling,* no trying to figure out what the hell he was going to do about the fact that when he saw Spencer, slightly flushed and timid, so very obviously putting himself out there in a way Tim couldn't pretend to misunderstand, all he wanted to do was kiss him.

And *there* was the terror he'd been expecting earlier. Except, maybe terror was the wrong word. Apprehension, maybe, mixed with a generous helping of good old-fashioned guilt. Staying was the most irresponsible thing he could do. He wasn't fully over Rudy, that was painfully obvious given what had happened earlier when he was out with Connor, and this wasn't just some guy he'd met in class or at a coffee shop. Spencer was a twenty-eight-year-old man with a teenage son who Tim was supposed to be helping—*counseling,* really, for all that the center tried to avoid the word whenever possible. No matter what Tim's feelings were, no matter how many times he'd woken up with half-remembered dreams of how Spencer felt in his arms, or the way he could see whatever confidence Spencer had gathered crumbling to dust with each second Tim didn't say anything, it would be beyond stupid to consider staying.

Tim had never been happier to do something stupid.

"Do you have any movies?"

"That's okay, I'll see...you..." Spencer trailed off. "Oh."

Oh.

Now Tim's confidence began to waver.

"*Should* I leave?"

Spencer shook himself. "No. No! I. Um." He licked his lips and then let out a short laugh. "No. Definitely not."

"Good."

Spencer pressed his lips together like he was trying not to smile. "Good."

Their eyes met, and for the first time that night, Spencer held his gaze.

"So! Movies. You said movies, didn't you? Which is great. Really great. Movies are awesome. And, you know, not vague. Like, um. Because I wasn't... Hmm. I'm not a...I mean, I don't... Oh God I haven't had this conversation since I was nineteen and—" Spencer closed his mouth with a loud *click* and started wringing his hands. "Don't say any of that," he said, his voice so quiet Tim wondered if he even knew he was talking out loud. "That's so creepy and presumptuous; *don't be that guy.*"

Tim smiled. He had no idea what it said about him, but watching Spencer have a minor meltdown over this gave him a sense of peace about his decision to stay. Neither one of them had any idea what they were doing here. They were both floundering in uncharted waters.

Perfect.

"Do you want to pick something out?" Tim asked, only somewhat surprised at how steady his voice was. "Not *Die Hard*," he added quickly before Spencer could answer.

"What's wrong with *Die Hard*?" Spencer asked. It was clearly an automatic response out of his mouth almost before Tim had finished speaking. Tim smothered a laugh as he realized there was only one way to answer.

"I don't really feel like watching a Christmas movie right now."

Spencer stared at Tim like *he* was Christmas.

"Fuck," he said softly. "I..." He shook his head and laughed. "Never mind. Okay. But our non-Christmas DVD collection is pretty much exclusively anime, BBC shows, and Harrison Ford movies, so you might regret limiting your choices."

The way he smirked and cocked an eyebrow was so *Spencer*, and Tim had to fight not to start grinning like an idiot.

Uncharted waters or not, he's still the same guy who sent me fifty-seven pictures of the same We Rate Dogs tweet because I teased him for accidentally sending it twice. Which means I don't have to be anything other than Tim.

"Maybe I should pick."

"If you insist." Spencer's serene smile barely got its legs under it before being swept aside by a slightly worried frown. "Anything other than *Kingdom of the Crystal Skull!*"

Which pretty much guaranteed they wouldn't be watching anything else.

They sat together on the couch, Spencer curled up in the corner and, after a moment of hesitation, Tim sitting just close enough for their legs to touch. Spencer gave the spot where his knee pressed against Tim's thigh a soft smile before clearing his throat and starting the movie. Night had fully fallen, leaving the living room in pitch darkness, the only light coming from the TV or sneaking in the entryway from the kitchen down the hall. The dim lighting created an intimate atmosphere despite the candy wrappers all over the floor, and the lump in the corner suspiciously resembling dirty laundry.

Tim smiled to himself, enjoying the tense anticipatory feeling that always came with new relationships. Not that this was a *relationship*. Not yet. Tim hadn't jumped the gun so badly since he'd first started dating, and he wasn't about to start again now. This wasn't even a date really. It was more like a feeling out process. A way to find out if what they were feeling would be enough to push them beyond friendship and into something more. The idea should have scared Tim, but no matter how much he poked and prodded his feelings and no matter how many doomsday scenarios he thought up, it was impossible to be anything other than excited. For the first time since Rudy, he could picture someone else filling the empty hole in his future.

They managed to last almost ten minutes before Spencer started ripping the movie apart.

"Gunpowder didn't have any metal in nineteen fifty-seven. It wouldn't be attracted to magnetic aliens."

"If you pull off the bottom of a shotgun shell, there's gunpowder, not pellets."

"Jesus Christ, those soldiers have *metal guns*. They should be sticking to the box with the *magnetic alien* they're carrying."

"Oh, my God. I'm not even getting into everything that's wrong with that fucking refrigerator."

There wasn't much that could drive Tim to violence. Talking during a movie? Never failed to make him want to punch somebody in the *throat*.

So, of course, he found it completely charming when Spencer did it.

He even broke his own movie rules and started talking back. Not just about the movie, which was pretty close to sacrilege already, but about their personal lives as well, and somewhere between when "I can't believe you made me watch this" turned into "shut up, this is the best part," Tim learned more about Spencer in softly murmured conversation than he had during their entire friendship. Everything from his favorite movie ("*Empire Strikes Back*, of course. How is this even a question?") to his favorite childhood memory ("My mom hired someone to dress up as a Ninja Turtle for my fifth birthday. I was the coolest kid in kindergarten for like a week."). How he could afford his house ("My parents bought it for us.

Single guy with a kid on a teacher's salary living in the city? No way I'd be this far away from murder central without help.") to even his utter indifference to bacon ("I mean, yeah, it's tasty, but I don't see why people get so crazy about it. Did you know they sell bacon-scented soap? It's insane. Now, if we're talking about dinosaur-shaped chicken nuggets, on the other hand...").

In turn, Tim shared parts of himself he'd almost never spoken of. Not because they were too personal or he was keeping some great secret, but because before Spencer, no one had really cared enough to ask. Most of his early relationships were, he was embarrassed to admit, mostly physical; they were more about making out after school and seeing how far he could get before his parents got home than any kind of big emotional commitment. His attitude toward relationships hadn't changed much during his first year of college when most of the gay freshmen were exploring their sexuality for the first time, and Tim's high-school experience-born confidence and easygoing personality drew more than his fair share of admirers. Not that he was a slut about it even back then, and he was always, *always* safe on the rare occasions his "dates" moved past mutual blowjobs and into full-on sex, but it had still been easier than it probably should have to get someone into bed. Even when he'd finally started dating for real, most of the guys he ended up with weren't big on long personal conversations—not about *Tim,* at least. Something Tim had realized recently he was ashamed of more than his early sexcapades was, even before Rudy, he tended to end up in relationships with people who took a lot more than they gave emotionally. Having someone he liked showing interest in the little bits of his life was a brand-new experience, and it was just as exhilarating as the first time he'd ever kissed another boy.

So, he told Spencer all about his favorite teacher. *You mean besides you? No, don't say that. You can't pull off a line like that right now.* ("Third grade, Mrs. Jergensen. She used to bring in mountains of cupcakes every time someone in class had a birthday. I didn't realize until years later that she was buying them all from my mom."). His *least* favorite movie ("*Black Hawk Down.* The most boring two hours and twenty minutes of my life. All they do is run and yell and shoot. For the whole movie."), and his first and only experience at a concert ("It was for some local band I went to see with a few people from high school. They were playing in this tiny little all-ages club, and I inhaled so much secondhand pot smoke I was almost floating home. I got about two steps in our apartment and threw up all over the carpet. My mom grounded me for two months and made me clean it up with a toothbrush. Since then I've never really had any desire to give live music another try.").

Things eventually quieted between them, their soft conversation trailing off into a few whispered sentences here and there, until it finally stopped altogether right around the time Shia started swinging through the Amazon on computer-generated vines. Tim found himself getting caught up in the movie despite how silly it was. He'd spent his childhood watching *Indiana Jones.* It was one of the few movie franchises he and his dad both liked, and he still fondly remembered when they'd gone together to see a midnight showing of *Crystal Skull* when it came out. He didn't have many father-son-bonding memories, so he'd always have a soft spot for the movie, no matter how dumb parts of it were. And despite all the complaining, he was happy he could share it with Spencer too.

It wasn't until the credits started rolling and he began searching for the remote that he realized Spencer had fallen asleep.

He'd moved closer during the movie, curling toward Tim now instead of tucked away in the corner of the couch. His head wasn't *quite* resting on Tim's shoulder, but there couldn't be more than three inches between them. Spencer's curls were a mess, sticking up wildly in the back where they were smushed up against the couch. His breath came in the long, loud drags of the deeply asleep, punctuated every few seconds with tiny, hardly audible snores. His lips barely parted, and his face so soft and relaxed he seemed almost too young.

Tim had never really been attracted to cute. He'd always liked guys who were confident and assertive; cute too often tended to be timid as well. Tim's type leaned more toward tall and willowy with sharp features and easy self-assured grins. They were usually the kind of guys who had no problem telling Tim what they wanted. Tim liked that. He liked not having to guess. He liked knowing exactly what someone needed, and he liked being the one who could provide it.

So, he had absolutely no idea why Spencer, at his most adorable, was the single most attractive thing he'd ever seen.

It wasn't just his cuteness that Tim was drawn to either. It was everything about Spencer that shouldn't make sense. It was the way he seemed to flit back and forth between desperately needing to be taken care of and being almost painfully self-reliant. It was the way crippling shyness could turn into caustic sass in the blink of an eye. It was the way he could have absolutely no confidence in himself, yet still act and know exactly what to do when Connor needed him. It was the way Tim could so easily see Spencer turning that same level of caring toward him. It was the way he knew, on some level, Spencer would never try to take more than Tim could give.

"When did all this happen?" Tim murmured to himself.

He regretted speaking a moment later when Spencer jerked awake with a loud snort.

"Wha'?" Spencer slurred, blinking rapidly and staring at the tail end of the movie's credits in sleepy confusion.

"You fell asleep," Tim said quietly.

"I did?"

"Yep."

Spencer blinked again and then rubbed his eyes with the palm of his hand. "Huh." He seemed like he might have been about to say something else, but before he could, he turned his head toward Tim and suddenly stilled. It took Tim a few seconds to realize he was staring at his shoulder, a faint blush of his cheeks barely visible in the light from the TV.

"Um." Spencer swallowed. "I'm sorry if I fell asleep on you."

"You didn't." Tim hesitated and then, feeling bold, added, "But I wouldn't have minded if you had."

"Shit," Spencer whispered, rubbing his cheeks.

"What?"

"Oh God, nothing," Spencer said with a laugh. "That was just...really fucking suave."

"You think?" Tim asked, smiling slightly.

"Yeah." Spencer flashed a smile of his own and shook his head. "This is so weird."

"Is it?"

"*No.* And that's *why* it's weird. Because it should be, you know? Do you... Oh, God, I'm gonna sound so fucking high school when I ask this, but you do...*like* me, right?"

"Yes," Tim answered. He didn't even bother trying to hide how charmed he was by the way Spencer asked.

"Right," Spencer said, his blush deepening. "Okay. Good. Um. I like you too. But that's why it's so weird, you know? I wasn't even gonna say anything because I haven't dated since the iPhone came out, and you're about a million years younger than me and so far out of what my league was when I still *had* a league I figured the best reaction I'd get is if all you did was laugh at me."

"You don't really think that, do you?" Tim asked, frowning.

"Think what? I mean, yes. But, what specifically?"

"That I'm out of your league?"

"Of course." Spencer said it like it was the most obvious thing in the world, and Tim's frown deepened.

"I'm not anything special."

Sure, Tim was decent looking, and he knew what kinds of clothes and hairstyles went well with his body and face, but there were a million guys who were a lot more attractive than him. Single dad or not, Tim would be surprised if he was the hottest guy who had ever shown interest in Spencer.

"You like kids," Spencer said flatly. "You like *my* kid. You like my *jokes.* You don't get annoyed when I text you all day. You went out of your way to get me and Connor to stop fighting. You don't hold it against me when I say something stupid and insulting. Jesus Christ, Tim, I could keep going if you want?"

"No, please don't." Tim glanced away, part of him feeling more than a bit guilty he'd assumed Spencer was being shallow and talking about his appearance. The rest of him was too busy being awed at the things Spencer saw in him. Too often Tim looked at himself and saw nothing but his failures and flaws. It was beyond nice to know with certainty that someone—that *Spencer*—saw more. "That's...not all there is to me though."

"Of course not. But that's shit I'll find out later. That's what dating is for. Or so I've been led to believe." Spencer's lips twitched. "I can't even believe I just said that, but that's my *whole point*. All of...*this*—" He gestured between them. "—should be really weird or feel forced or *something*. But it's not. I feel..." He let out a small laugh. "This is going to sound so lame, but I feel *right*. You know?"

Tim nodded slowly. Tonight *had* felt less...fraught, he supposed would be a good word, than he might have expected. Aside from a bit of awkwardness in the beginning, he couldn't remember the last time he'd felt so comfortable with another person.

"Yeah," Spencer went on. "Definitely not what I was expecting when I asked you to stay. So...I guess what I'm *trying* to say is, I have absolutely no idea what to do now."

A thought popped into Tim's head then. One that was reckless and brash and a whole bunch of other things Tim hadn't been in a long time. Common sense told him to ignore the thought, but Tim wasn't listening. He was too giddy, riding high on the endless possibilities that seemed to stretch out in front of him and too weak with relief at reconnecting with a part of who he *had been* before life and bad relationships ground him down into who he *was*. So, instead, he acted on his thought.

And kissed Spencer.

The kiss lasted a second, maybe two, but it was the first time in almost half a year Tim had had any kind of intimate contact with another person, and even if Spencer had been exaggerating about how long he'd been single, he could tell Spencer's dry spell had lasted much longer than his. When he pulled back, Spencer stayed completely still, staring at Tim, his wide eyes shining with awe and confusion and bright vulnerability.

"That's what we can do now," Tim said, his voice soft.

"Um." Spencer licked his lips. It was only when he started to repeat the action that his cheeks began to flush again. "I meant...you know, like 'where do we go from here.' Like do we...go on a date or...what do we do *tomorrow*. Not...you know, literally right now." He cleared his throat and glanced away. Then, quietly, he said, "But that was nice too."

This time, Tim didn't even think. "Can I do it again?"

Spencer nodded rapidly.

Tim grinned.

Their second kiss was slower than the first, enough for Tim to perfectly catalog every single new sensation. Spencer's lips were plump but chapped. He kissed hesitantly, closed mouthed like someone who had never been kissed before, and for some reason, that set Tim's blood on *fire*. Without thinking he gave in to the temptation he'd been fighting all day and touched Spencer's face, his fingertips trailing slowly down impossibly soft cheeks and gently caressing the slightly rougher skin of his jaw where tiny hints of stubble were just starting to grow back. He reveled in the differing sensations and deepened their kiss, mildly surprised when Spencer met him eagerly, opening his mouth the moment Tim's tongue brushed lightly across his lips.

They made out like teenagers for what seemed like forever. Tim never tried to take things any further even though he was so turned on a stiff breeze *outside* would have been enough to fully complete the teenage experience and make him come in his pants. It would have felt wrong to do more than kiss. For all his eagerness, Spencer still felt like a tightly coiled spring against Tim's chest. His hands clutched at Tim's shoulders desperately, like he was scared what might happen if he let go.

Tim wanted more. *God* did he want more. He couldn't remember the last time he'd been aroused enough to even think about jerking off. His brain seemed to be making up for lost time by painting vivid pictures of all the *filthy* things he could do to Spencer, or on Spencer, or *in* Spencer. But the last thing he wanted was to pressure Spencer into doing anything he wasn't ready for. It was a miracle they hadn't already ruined their friendship, and he wasn't going to be responsible for ruining the fragile thing their friendship had only barely begun evolving into.

Eventually their kisses slowed and then stopped altogether. Spencer panted heavily into Tim's mouth, and when he pulled back, Spencer actually whined before dropping his forehead onto Tim's chest.

"Fuck me..." Spencer breathed out.

Tim stilled. Then, after a long moment, so did Spencer.

Is he...?

"That was a figure of speech," Spencer said slowly.

"Got it," Tim said.

They relaxed simultaneously.

"Where did you learn to kiss?" Spencer asked a few minutes later, turning his head so his cheek was resting right over Tim's heart. He wondered if Spencer could hear how rapidly it was beating.

"School."

Spencer laughed. "What kind of school did *you* go to?"

"New York public schools," Tim answered, only partially focusing on the conversation, such as it was.

Spencer let out a long breath. "Yeah. Me too."

Tim wondered at the small thread of sadness he could hear in his voice before remembering everything Spencer had told him about his time in school.

They all hated him because they thought he was gay. He probably would have killed to go to a school where he could find guys who would talk to him, let alone kiss him.

Tim pulled Spencer closer. It was definitely time to move onto a different topic.

"So...you mentioned dating?"

"Timothy Ellis," Spencer said playfully, leaning back to meet Tim's gaze, "are you asking me on a *date*?"

Tim took a deep mental breath and forced himself not to think about all the ways this could go horribly wrong. "Yes, Spencer Kent, I believe I am."

Spencer glanced down, which gave Tim a great view of the bridge of his nose as it turned bright red.

"Awesome," he said, sending a shy little grin toward the couch.

And just like that, Tim had a date with Spencer.

Chapter Eleven

Spencer Kent spent the day after Halloween in a state of mild panic.

Of course, the term *mild* was kind of relative, he thought as he stared at himself in the mirror that morning, wondering where in the fucking *hell* the almost smooth dude who'd been wearing his face the night before had run off to. Mild sauce, for example. Some people find it pretty bland. However, to someone who hasn't eaten anything spicy in almost a *decade*, mild could end up burning the shit out of their mouth like Vesuvius burned Herculaneum, sending them running for the nearest carton of milk in a desperate attempt to save their tongue while it could still relay the sensation of taste.

Sadly, Spencer didn't drink milk. So, all he could do was panic.

Mildly.

He finished brushing his teeth and getting dressed—utterly ignoring his hair because he'd learned long ago to pick his battles—without giving in to his panic, but the moment he'd done up the last button on his cardigan and his hands no longer had anything occupying their attention, his phone appeared in them like magic, and he began frantically checking through his texts.

Okay. Nothing from Tim. That's...good?

No texts meant no cancellation, which Spencer would have totally understood considering what he'd done last night after Tim had asked him out; and it didn't matter if Tim really needed that list of foods Spencer didn't eat and activities that would make him throw up to stave off potential *date disaster*. He'd still felt simultaneously like a parent leaving his kid with a babysitter for the first time *and* the kid who was entrusting his very survival to someone he'd never been in this situation with before. Except, usually, the parent and the kid didn't both want to make out with the babysitter…

I wouldn't blame them for wanting to though. Tim is soooo good at kissing.

Spencer let himself daydream about Tim's lips for around a minute before he grabbed his phone and keys and made his way into the kitchen. Connor was already there, eating a bowl of cereal and following Spencer with his eyes like piercing bullets of judgment and suspicion.

"*What?*" Spencer snapped as he spun around and crossed his arms.

"Why are you acting so weird?" Connor asked around a half-chewed mouthful.

"I don't know. I'm not. Eat your corn flakes and shut up."

"These are Fruit Loops."

"That's exactly what I'm talking about!" Spencer screamed, his voice echoing around the tiny kitchen.

"Okay…" Connor gently swallowed his food. "I'm gonna go to school now," he said slowly, standing up and watching Spencer warily as he backed out of the room. A moment later, Spencer heard the front door close.

Spencer pinched the bridge of his nose.

Stop. Being. Crazy. Having a date with Tim is a good thing. I've been lowkey crushing on him for days, which makes this the fastest crush-to-getting-a-date turnaround I've ever had. I should be happy, not freaking out.

Which was true. Hell, Tim hadn't even seemed bothered by *the list*, which he probably should have been since it was a pretty big hint about how high-maintenance Spencer could be. All he'd done was smile fondly, give Spencer another one of those slow kisses, and promise to do his best. Well, Spencer was 90 percent sure that's what he said; his brain was kinda muddled for a few minutes after the kissing.

He sighed and then shook himself out of his thoughts. Biting his lip, he unlocked his phone again and checked his last texts to Tim.

> SPENCER: *Sorry Im so weird. If you wanna pull out ill totally understand*

> SPENCER: **BACK OUT I meant back out*

> SPENCER: *because pull out can be sexual and I swear to god im not coming onto you*

> SPENCER: *oh god*

> SPENCER: *brb drowning myself*

> SPENCER: *didn't really*

> SPENCER: *its too cold to get wet*

> SPENCER: *just realized its three in the morning and you're probably sleeping lol*

> SPENCER: *but really if you changed your mind about dating me ill understand*

And that was it. Spencer cringed as he read that over. Fuck, he was such a nuisance, sending a text barrage in the middle of the night. But Tim did say he usually got up around four to open the bakery...

And today is his day off, isn't it? Which means he'll be sleeping in and he probably hasn't even gotten the texts yet.

Spencer groaned out loud, wishing he could unsend unread texts like he could with emails back in the AOL days. Jesus, he was so embarrassing. He thunked his head on the kitchen table.

"I am such an idiot..."

Thunk. Thunk. Thunk.

Whether it was the self-punishment, which Spencer always found strangely cathartic, or the realization that a sleeping Tim probably wasn't ignoring him or second-guessing their tentatively scheduled date, he found himself finally calming down. Or at least enough to start thinking about other things.

Like why the hell had Connor gone to school so early? A quick check of the kitchen clock gave him his answer.

He didn't. I'm just super fucking late.

And now he had something non-Tim related to panic about.

All was well.

*

Nobody noticed he'd been late.

Not the principal, not any of the other teachers, and not even the kids in his first period class when he walked in fifteen minutes after the bell. Spencer had no idea how to feel about that. He considered giving them another surprise quiz to salve his ego a bit and give him more time to check his phone, but honestly, he was getting as tired of grading them as the kids were of taking them. Reading through a chapter in class gave him just as much free time to be an obsessive mess, so he scrapped his lesson plan for the day and told the kids to get their books out.

By the time his second period ended, he'd fallen completely back into the rhythms of teaching. It was surprisingly comforting.

Fifteen minutes into Spencer's third period class there came a brief knock, followed by the door opening, and Cass poking her head in the room.

"Got some hot gossip," she said in her usual laconic drawl.

The entire class turned, as one singular amorphous mass that couldn't care less about learning, to stare at her.

"If it's about Shakespeare being gay, I'm not allowed to teach that."

That got a few chuckles from some of the kids and a dry smirk from Cass.

"Hallway. Five minutes. You're gonna wanna hear this," she finished in a singsong tone before slipping back out and closing the door behind her.

The amorphous mass turned its attention back to him.

"You're not gonna leave us to gossip with Mrs. Baker, are you?" asked Kelly Slater, who, sadly, was not the famous pro surfer/Baywatch star and instead one of the bigger—well, if they were in Britain she'd probably be called a "swot," but here in America Spencer stuck with the term "insufferable know-it-all." (It was the paradox of Spencer's life that he constantly complained about how little his students cared about learning while also being unable to stand most of the ones who did.)

"Of course not," he answered, getting more than a few disappointed looks. "That would be incredibly unprofessional."

Kelly gave him a sharp nod.

"But what I *am* going to do," he continued, "is take a short bathroom break for the next—" He thought for a moment. "—five to eight minutes. While I'm gone, I'm going to need someone to look after the class. Any volunteers?"

Seven hands shot up, including Kelly's even though she seemed like she wanted to demand he stay behind, and Spencer nodded to himself.

Okay, that's seven out of the running. Who's left?

He took a quick glance around, trying to find a student who was at least semi-responsible. Eventually he decided on Derry Smith mostly because as a popular jock, who was nice to pretty much everyone *and* took his studies somewhat seriously, he shattered a lot of Spencer's preconceived notions, and he always thought the world could do with more of that.

"Derry," he said, ignoring the disgruntled looks the hand-raisers were giving him. "Come on up. Keep everyone reading out loud from the chapter we're on, and call on someone new every two paragraphs or so. Can you handle that?"

Derry stood slowly, seeming unsure for a split second before nodding. "Sure, Mr. Kent."

"That's what I like to hear." Spencer made his way toward the door, stopping just before he was within reaching distance of the doorknob and turning back to the class. He glanced around, making sure to meet the eyes of every single person in the room before speaking. "While I'm gone, I expect you to act as if I've never left. You will sit and you will work, and you will treat Derry with the same respect I expect you to give to *all* of your teachers. And if I come back and you guys are doing *anything* but sitting quietly or reading out loud, you'll all be doing long-form essays for the rest of your natural *lives*."

It was times like this Spencer *really* liked his reputation as an unfair bastard because it was more than a little satisfying to see how quickly everyone's heads snapped back to their books. One or two even shuddered. He allowed himself a small smirk and then spared a moment to lock eyes with Derry, silently promising him a fate much worse than endless essay writing if he should lose control of Spencer's classroom. Derry nervously licked his lips and then called on the first student with a mostly steady voice. Spencer waited a moment until the reading started and then left the room.

He saw Cass waiting fifteen feet down the hall.

"Okay, I ditched my responsibilities. What's up?"

She wasted little time getting straight to the point. "Benjamin Rasputin quit this morning."

Spencer's jaw dropped. "Benji *quit*?"

Cass nodded.

"No way. That's..." Spencer struggled to find the words. Shit, no wonder nobody noticed he'd been late. "Are you sure it was Benji? The same guy who chained himself to the front doors the last time Principal Corbin brought up retirement? The guy who showed me The Spot in his classroom he picked out to drop dead on? That Benji Rasputin?"

"The one and only. Burst into the office during the morning announcements, threw his shoe through the window on Corbin's door, and quit."

"What the fuck..." Spencer shook his head. "Come in late *one time* and you miss shit like this. Did he say why?"

"No," she said, pursing her lips in displeasure. "But the rumor is his son won the Powerball and he's moving the whole family to Bermuda."

"Why Bermuda?"

"Because it's hot," she deadpanned. "I don't know. It's just a rumor. The other one going around is that old Rasputin found out about a terrorist plot to blow up the school, and he's leaving before it can happen. But no one really believes that one. If anything, he'd stand in his Spot and count down the seconds."

"Out loud probably, just to see the reaction."

"Yep. But none of that's why I pulled you out of class."

"Then why did you?"

Cass rolled her eyes. "Benjamin Rasputin isn't teaching here anymore. You *know* what that means."

It took Spencer a moment, but once the shock over hearing about Benji started to fade a bit, he realized he did know exactly what she was talking about.

"The room…"

Cass smirked. "Exactly."

Spencer's heart skipped a beat because Mr. Rasputin, aside from being batshit insane and having *the* most badass teacher name ever, was the man who, up until this morning apparently, had a stranglehold on Room 210.

210 was a cosmic anomaly, a place in the universe where the very forces of creation itself weaved together to give life to an array of miracles only witnessed once or twice in a geologic age. In the winter, it was just warm enough to be comfortable without being so stiflingly hot it lulled students and teachers alike to sleep. In the summer it received exactly 16.4 percent more chilled air from the school's ancient AC system (in the early eighties 210 held a science class that did the calculations), making it the only place besides the basement locker room that was actually tolerable during the sweltering months of May and June. It was also one of the few rooms on the eastern side of the somewhat narrow school, which meant it was

one of the only rooms whose every window faced the boring brick wall of the neighboring building, making it nearly impossible for kids to be distracted by staring outside. The room was spacious, comfortable year-round, and just being there brought a teacher's student average up at least five percentage points. In short, 210 was the Holy Grail of LT High. A room every teacher desperately wanted, whose owner was the most hated and envied person in the entire school. It was also right in the middle of the part of the building reserved solely for ninth-grade teachers and their classes.

And now it was up for grabs.

"Jesus Christ," he breathed. "It's gonna be a bloodbath."

"Mmhmm."

Spencer narrowed his eyes suspiciously. "You're enjoying this."

"A little," she admitted, smirking. *Of course she is. Her class is always in the cooking lab. She gets to sit back and watch the rest of us tear each other apart.* "But I haven't even gotten to the best part."

"Oh, God," groaned Spencer. "You're being cryptic. *Why* are you being cryptic?"

"Because."

"I hate you."

"You'll be loving me in a second."

"I really don't think I will," Spencer said and then, without a trace of shame, asked, "Why?"

"Because," she said, drawing the word out for several syllables. *God*, Spencer needed new friends. "I know who the frontrunners are."

Spencer blinked. "There are already *frontrunners*?" He shook his head. "Of course there are. Corbin's been trying to get rid of Benji for years; why wouldn't he have his replacement all picked out? Who are they?"

To his surprise, Cass answered plainly. "Steph McConnell—"

Spencer grimaced. *Dear Lord, how many poor freshman boys is she gonna go through if she's in a room that gets cold enough to make her nipples hard?*

"—and you."

"*What*?" Spencer gaped, then shook his head. "No, that can't be right. I'm the newest teacher here. I still get stuck with *detention duty* for fuck's sake. Why the hell would I be even close to the front of the line?"

"You've got the highest test scores out of all the ninth-grade teachers and the lowest cut rate in the whole school," she said. "Plus, ninth-grade detentions are the lowest in the school since you took over. Principals eat that stuff up."

"So, I'm being rewarded because I make my kids terrified of me?"

"Pretty much."

"Huh." *Being a hard-ass actually works. Who knew? Aside from dads in the fifties, I guess.* Spencer shook his head again. "How do you know all this anyway?"

"Corbin."

"He *told* you?"

"Of course, not," Cass said. "But he did get a shoe thrown through his door. Hard to have private phone conversations when half your door is a giant hole covered with construction paper."

Spencer had to laugh. "You were eavesdropping?"

"I was using the photocopier," she said with a shrug. "If he didn't want me to tell everyone what I heard, he should have waited until I left."

Ah.

Cass had a long and storied feud with the main office photocopier. She'd never told him why she hated the thing so much—it always worked fine for him—but she usually ended up in a pissy mood when she was forced to deal with it. Eavesdropping on Corbin would have been a welcome distraction.

"Well—" He froze as he realized exactly what she'd said. "Wait...you told *everyone*?"

She smirked again.

"You evil *bitch*," Spencer said, half pissed beyond belief and half in awe.

"Gotta have my fun somehow," she said. "And if I have to suffer, so does everyone else."

"Christ, out of all the bad habits you could pick up from me... You do realize Steph might try to kill me if 210's on the line, right?" She nodded. He huffed. "I hate you. And how the hell are *you* suffering, anyway?"

"You ever been in a room with thirteen ovens on all day?"

"No."

"Exactly." She nodded. "There's a reason I haven't worn anything but extra-strength men's deodorant for the last twenty years. And I'm still swimming in sweat by the end of the day."

Spencer scrunched up his face. "That's so gross."

"Try living it."

"I'd rather not."

The conversation lulled then, which gave Spencer a whole lot of free time to think up all the ways the various personality disorders that masqueraded as teachers in this school could tear him apart.

"Are you *sure* you heard right?" he asked. "Corbin really said me and Steph were at the top of the list?"

"Yep."

Spencer mewled quietly.

Cass sighed. "Oh relax. I didn't actually tell everyone, you big drama queen."

"Really?" he asked, perking up.

She shrugged. "Who would I tell besides you?"

"Lots of people," he answered immediately. "Everyone likes you."

"But I don't like everyone."

The implication—that she *did* like Spencer enough to come tell him even if she did fuck with him a bit first—was strangely touching.

"Aw, Cass..." He smiled. "I love you too."

"Yeah, yeah." She seemed less smirky than she had a minute ago, despite her dismissive words, so Spencer was pretty sure they were having a moment. "You know it won't stay secret for long though, right? Nothing does in this school."

Moment over, I guess.

"Kill me now."

She snorted. "If it's bothering you so much, you could always tell Corbin you don't want the room."

Spencer inhaled sharply and stared at her in utter disbelief. "Of *course*, I want it. It's *210*."

Even more important, it was *validation*. Spencer was young, and some of his teaching methods—teaching students *how* to think instead of *what* to think, refusing to coddle the "gifted" kids or ignore the lazy ones—had gotten him more than a bit of scorn and ridicule over the years. He and Corbin butted heads more than once about his refusal to teach to standardized tests since he got tenure, so to hear that his kids had the best marks in the grade, and Corbin wasn't ignoring it? Spencer would have fought for room in a janitor's closet if it was a physical representation of being proven *right*. Room 210 would be his metaphorical "suck it" to the rest of the faculty, and everyone whoever doubted him would see him teaching inside it for the rest of his career and know they'd been completely wrong.

He just wished the whole thing could have stayed a secret until *after* he'd been given his room. Teachers were vicious when something like the perfect classroom was on the line, and he really wasn't looking forward to his colleagues coming after him like he was sitting on the Iron Throne.

"Well, there you go," she said without an ounce of sympathy for his impending hardships.

"I wouldn't take pleasure in *your* suffering," he said petulantly.

"Yes, you would. You get way too happy when you tell me what you do to your students, you sadist."

"They're *students*," Spencer said, rolling his eyes. "It's their job to suffer. And all teachers are at least a little bit sadistic. Nonelective teachers, at least," he added at Cass's raised eyebrow. "You think we give homework because we want to make their lives *easier*?"

"I think you people give homework because you're lazy, and you can't teach them what they need to know during class."

First-Year-Teacher Spencer would have been completely offended by that, but Safely Tenured Spencer only shrugged. "That too. But we don't get tips or bonuses for kids getting good grades, so we have to make do with the way the light leaves their eyes when they realize you've just given them their third hour of pointless busywork for the weekend." He closed his eyes and shivered slightly. "Oh yeah. That's the good shit."

When he opened them, he saw Cass watching him with an odd expression on her face. "I have no idea how serious you're being right now."

Spencer grinned.

Cass rolled her eyes, and Spencer took the opportunity to pull his phone out and check how long they'd been talking. Only seven minutes.

His phone buzzed in his hand, the short-short-long pattern he'd set for texts from Tim's number during school hours, and he almost dropped it in shock. He fumbled, feeling like something out of an old Chevy Chase movie as he tried to keep it in his hands, and then opened the message before he could start to freak out about what it might say.

> TIM: *Of course I haven't changed my mind. I wouldn't have kissed you if I didn't want to date you. :)*

While he was reading, another message came in.

> TIM: *Your texting is adorable, by the way.*

> TIM: *Just like you.*

Holy.

Shit.

Spencer could feel his insides turn to goo.

"Are you okay?"

"Totally fine." He winced at the amount of squeak in his voice. He cleared his throat and tried again. "I'm...super."

Cass studied him for a long moment, then narrowed her eyes suspiciously. "Did you just swoon?"

"No!" He tried to glare, but he could still see Tim's text in his peripheral vision, and he was pretty sure the goofy blushy grin on his face canceled it out. Her mouth started to open, but he quickly cut her off. "I have to get back to class! Can't talk now. Sorry. Bye!"

As he scurried down the hall, he knew he'd only given himself a temporary reprieve. *Fuck it. All my reprieves are temporary. I can deal. Later. Way later.* He paused and collected himself before going back into his classroom. The last thing he needed was to look like he'd just been swooning out in the hall with Ms. Baker. When he was ready, he slipped inside with his phone still clutched in his hand. He winced when he pulled the door closed a little too hard behind him. The fourth row front, who he was almost sure was named Kyle, stumbled over his reading at the noise and then snapped his head around to stare at him. Just like everyone else.

Spencer put his hands behind his back, hiding his phone from view. It didn't do much. Tim's texts were burned into his retinas. Luckily, being the sole focus of his students was enough to get his head back in the game.

"Thanks, Derry," he said, pleased with how normal he sounded. "You did a good job. Take a seat and get out your book."

Derry calmly did so, which was impressive—the calmness. Spencer would have to keep him in mind for stuff like this in the future. Spencer went back to his desk and sat in his own chair. Once he'd gotten the kids reading again, he promptly ignored whatever the hell they were saying and took his phone back out. After rereading the texts Tim sent him about fifty times, he concluded no, there was absolutely no way he could be misinterpreting them. Tim was flirting. Blatantly.

Spencer covered his mouth to hide his smile. For once, he didn't overthink things. He unlocked his phone and went with what felt natural.

SPENCER: *Oh my god you asshole im in class right now. Stop making me swoon.*

Tim responded right away, and Spencer hid another smile at the thought of him nervously checking his phone, wondering how Spencer might respond.

TIM: *I made you swoon? :)*

SPENCER: *Yes! Right in front of cass too. Shes gonna ask me a million questions later.*

There was a short pause this time, and Spencer used the break in messages to call on someone else to read.

TIM: *Is that okay?*

SPENCER: *That cass saw? Yeah it's fine. She doesnt usually tease. Much.*

TIM: *That I made you swoon, I mean.*

SPENCER: *Of course its ok.*

He chewed his lower lip as he debated whether he should say more. In the end, he decided holding shit back had a good chance of sabotaging this thing before it could really get started.

SPENCER: *I kinda like it honestly.*

SPENCER: *Really like it, actually. I haven't felt like this in years.*

TIM: *Like what?*

Spencer stared at that text for a long time, wondering why it was almost always seemingly simple questions that had the potential to tear him apart. He almost didn't answer. The middle of class was the last place he wanted to leave himself raw and exposed, but he so badly wanted to open up to Tim. Spencer had spent so long convincing himself having Connor and being the way he was meant he could never have any kind of huge all-encompassing *connection* with another person. Yet, he could feel one trying to form right now; a wispy fragile thing like tendrils of smoke reaching toward each other from neighboring campfires. He wanted to grab those tendrils and pull them close, to tie the ends together and shove them so deep inside himself no one would ever be able to dig them out again. That kind of need was scary, exhilarating, and new, and he wondered if there was ever a time he could have avoided being here with Tim or if they had always been hurtling full force toward moments like this since that first day in the center.

> SPENCER: *Happy. Wanted. Needed. Desirable, maybe. Like I'm normal. Like I can have normal things and want normal things. Like im worth something to someone besides Connor or my parents. Like having a kid doesn't mean that's the only thing im allowed to have. Take your pick, or add in any sappy overwrought shit you want, because chances are im feeking that too.*

Spencer's face *burned* as he read over what he'd sent. *Jesus Fucking Christ, I can't even bare my soul without typos.*

> SPENCER: **feeling*

Spencer made a mental note to save up for a new phone. Preferably one where the autocorrect *corrected* things.

It took Tim longer than usual to respond, and while Spencer waited, hoping to any god that might be listening he hadn't just made a complete idiot out of himself, the bell rang. By the time he got his class dismissed and the new one set up reading, his phone had buzzed several times.

TIM: *That's very sad.*

TIM: *You're an amazing person Spencer.*

TIM: *You should be happy all the time.*

TIM: *I would say you should feel wanted and desired all the time too, but I'm just selfish enough to want you all to myself. ;)*

TIM: *Sorry. You're being serious and I'm giving you terrible lines. I meant what I said in the first three texts though.*

TIM: *Are you there?*

There were no more texts. Thank God, too, because Spencer was pretty sure he was already as red as his marking pen. He had no idea what to say though. Their conversation had taken a sharp left into a field of feelings and meaning, and even though he was the one who'd taken it there, he was starting to feel a little *too* open.

SPENCER: *I'm here. Sorry, had to at least pretend to be a teacher for a minute.*

TIM: *That's okay. :)*

Spencer tapped his finger on his desk, getting an irritated glare from one of the girls closest to him. He glared right back and called on her to be the next one to read. The moment she started, the phone buzzed again.

TIM: *You didn't mention anything else I said though. Did I go too far?*

TIM: *I do that sometimes. Jump into things too quickly. If I did, you can tell me to back off. I won't mind :)*

Spencer sighed.

SPENCER: *Goddammit, why are you so perfect?*

TIM: *:) But you're deflecting. I did go too far, didn't I?*

SPENCER: *No. Its my fault. Im the one who went all deep first.*

He typed out "Thank you for what you said. It was very nice of you" and then immediately deleted it.

Jesus Christ, that sounds my mom's forcing me to write a thank-you card.

He took a deep breath. *Come on, it won't kill you to give him something genuine here.*

SPENCER: *Im blushing like crazy, by the way. Actually im so red im pretty sure my students think im about to explode on them for their horrible mispronunciation again, so it's not like I didnt like it. I just think we should save the super serious stuff until, you know, maybe AFTER we've had our first date?*

Maybe by then Spencer would be less of a bipolar mess.

TIM: *Lol. Fair enough. :)*

TIM: *So, safe pre-date question: How's your day been so far?*

Spencer smiled to himself, relieved that Tim wasn't insulted. Even better? He actually had something to talk about.

SPENCER: *More like GREAT pre date question. You're not gonna believe the shit that happened today.*

Chapter Twelve

Spencer wiped condensation off the mirror for the fifth time in the last ten minutes and then grimaced when that somehow didn't change what he was seeing. Same dull eyes with...yep, the faint dark circles were still there. Same damp curly hair that he couldn't blow-dry without turning it into a puffy, tangled mess. He rubbed his cheeks, annoyed at the roughness he could feel on his jawline even though he'd just showered, shaved, and slathered moisturizer all over himself; thankfully his face *looked* smooth. Against his better judgment, he stepped back so most of his naked body could be seen in the mirror.

He poked his belly, thankful beyond words it still didn't jiggle; he hadn't let himself go *that* much, at least. Not that he'd ever had a great stomach, even when he was a teenager. He'd always had a bit of paunch to him, mostly invisible unless he went topless or wore a tight shirt, but something he was always painfully aware of, especially since he'd been surrounded by rail-thin teenagers for most of his life. He turned to the side, sucked it in, let it out, and made a face. If nothing else it looked better smooth, just like the rest of his body. Not that he was planning on letting anyone *see* his body, of course. Spencer Kent was no first-date slut, but he'd already be going into this date thing with near zero confidence; shaving everything from the neck down so he at least *felt* sexy wasn't that big of a deal aside from how long it took.

While he was sideways, he figured he might as well check out his ass. Not too bad, he thought, twisting a bit. Bit of a curve, proportionate to the rest of his body, no visible sag. Not the greatest ass, but with the right pair of jeans it could be something. He gave some thought to flexing his arms, but he knew better than to push when he was ahead. His arms and legs had always been skinny, and all the *nothing* he'd been doing in the gym hadn't magically changed that.

Spencer turned back to face the mirror head on and sighed.

So, we're going with layers, then.

Which left only one question.

What the fuck does somebody wear on a date these days?

Twenty minutes later he'd decided on black boxer briefs and a pair of white ankle socks before he got stuck.

"Shitshitshit," he hissed under his breath as he checked the clock again. He only had fifteen minutes until Tim got here for their mystery date, and there was no way he'd answer the door practically naked. He needed *clothes*, goddammit! The problem was, he didn't really have any "date" clothes. Just drawer after drawer of skinny jeans, sweatpants, pajamas, sweaters, T-shirts, and a few frumpy collared button-ups he sometimes wore for work. And even though Tim had assured him he didn't need to dress up fancy for wherever they were going, he still wanted to come off like he'd tried. He was getting desperate, but he couldn't *choose,* so that only left him with one option.

"Connor! Come here for a minute!"

Stomping footsteps came closer to his open door. "What do you—ah!" Connor covered his eyes. "Why are you naked!?"

"I'm not *naked*," he said, snapping the waistband on his boxers for emphasis. "I need your help picking out an outfit for my date."

"It's close enough..." Connor stilled and then peeked through his fingers. "Did you say 'date'?"

Spencer nodded slowly. "Yes... I told you about it on..."

Oh. No, I didn't.

"Goddammit," he muttered, pinching the bridge of his nose.

"You really have a *date*?" Connor asked, sounding more than a little lost.

"Yeah."

"But...you never date."

"Well, I am now," he snapped and then sighed again and ran his fingers through his hair. "Sorry."

Connor barely seemed to hear him. "Who are you dating?" He wrung his hands together. "Please tell me it's not someone at school. That would be so gross."

Spencer's lips twitched. "I dunno about that," he said before his better judgment could kick in. "Principal Corbin's only about thirty years older than me. And the burst capillaries on his face are kinda fetching in the right light."

"Oh my God..."

Connor's face twisted into his best I-Can't-Believe-We're-Related grimace, and Spencer didn't even try to stop himself.

"There are some studies that show attraction is genetic, you know. I'm not gonna have to fight you for him, am I?"

"What is *wrong* with you?"

"I'm just saying."

"Ew." Connor shuddered. "You're gross. Why are you so gross?"

"Revenge for when you were a baby and threw up on me, and I had to see your shit every day, probably."

"Dad!" Connor's face burst into a furious blush, and without another word he spun on his heels and stalked toward the door.

"Wait!" Spencer called. Connor cringed, but, to Spencer's surprise, he actually stopped.

"What?" he said, refusing to turn around.

"I need your help."

Connor glanced over his shoulder with his brow creased. "With...what?"

Spencer rubbed the back of his head. "What do people wear on dates?"

"Why are you asking *me*?"

"Do you see anyone else around here?"

"I've never dated anyone!"

"Good." *And if I have any say in it, you never will.* "You go to school though. And you hang around young people all the time. Kids talk about personal shit way too loud when they're in groups, so you had to have heard something."

"Something about what you should wear on a date?"

"Turn around before you strain your neck." Connor rolled his eyes but did so. "And something about what *anyone* wears on dates. I haven't been on a date since you were five."

And he'd worn ripped jeans and a hoodie, neither of which he had now, so he didn't exactly have an old standby to fall back on.

"Well, I don't know!" Connor glanced away. "Can you put a shirt on please?"

Spencer grinned. "Great! Which one?"

"I don't—ugh! Something that doesn't have a picture on it."

"But that only leaves my work shirts..."

"Then wear those. Just...put something on. This is really weird. And I don't wanna think about why you don't have body hair anymore."

Now Spencer began to flush. He hurried into his closet and pulled out the first button-up he saw. It was white, so he paired it with a navy V-neck sweater, half remembering something about layers needing to be in contrasting colors to look good.

"Are jeans okay?"

"I guess... Where are you going?"

"Dunno," he said, rooting through his jeans pile for something that wasn't too wrinkled. "He said it was a surprise."

Spencer smiled briefly at the less-than-impressed noise that came from the doorway. Connor had never been a fan of surprises for some reason Spencer had never been able to figure out.

"What's his name?"

"It's Tim," Spencer answered absently.

"*Tim*?"

"Yeah."

"*Tim* Tim?"

"Yep." He paused and then poked his head out of the closet. "Is that a problem?"

Connor's face scrunched up like he'd bitten into a lemon that was filled with other, even more bitter lemons. "He's my friend."

"He's my friend too," Spencer said, his calm voice a complete contrast to the panicky refrain of *please don't have a problem with this, please don't have a problem with this* running through his head at the speed of light.

"You're going on a date with my friend."

Spencer debated for half a second, then decided that this conversation was too important to rush through half-naked. He dropped the clothes he'd picked out on the floor and pulled on the first oversized sleep shirt he saw. It was ratty, but it came down almost to his knees so he figured he'd covered up enough that Connor wouldn't complain when he hugged him. Which is exactly what he did when he left the closet. Connor didn't struggle, but he also didn't hug back.

"Yes," Spencer said, pulling back and staring his son in the eye. "I'm going on a date with Tim, who's your friend and mine, and I really, *really* want him to be more."

"Why?"

A small, slightly strained, slightly giddy laugh forced its way out of Spencer's throat. "Fuck if I know, kid. I just...really like him. He makes me feel...happy."

Which was, apparently, the wrong thing to say. Not just because it was incredibly embarrassing but because of the stricken expression on Connor's face after he said it.

"Connor...?"

Connor chewed his lip. "I don't make you happy?"

"*No.* Nonono, that's not..." He bit back a frustrated sigh. This dating thing had been so much easier when Connor was five and two hundred miles away. "Hey, look at me."

Connor shook his head, a move much more reminiscent of that long-gone five-year-old than the teenager he'd become. Spencer had to physically shake himself to keep from drowning in the sudden wave of bittersweet nostalgia that came over him.

"Hey," he repeated softly, gently lifting Connor's head by the chin. The watery shimmer in his kid's eyes nearly broke his heart. "You have *never* made me anything but insanely happy, okay? You've been the best thing about my life since the day you were born. The people in the hospital nursery didn't even have to tell me which one was you because I knew the second I saw your scrunched-up little face. You looked exactly the same as every other little wrinkly, malformed raisin, but I already loved you so much that I knew you were *my* raisin. And nothing's changed, okay?"

Connor's brow furrowed. "I..." He shook his head. "Then why do you need Tim to be happy?"

Spencer sighed and just barely stopped himself from saying *because men have needs,* which was a sentence that had never solved anything in the entire history of spoken language. "It's a different kind of happiness."

"That sounds like bullshit."

"It's really not," Spencer said, smothering the fond smile that wanted to spring to life at the familiar sass. "It's..." He sighed again and then shrugged and gave his son a half smile. "I'm lonely, kid. Tim makes me feel like I don't need to be."

Connor raised an eyebrow. "You have more friends than I do."

"It's a different kind of loneliness."

"Oh my God, you're talking about sex."

"No!" Spencer's face started to burn. "I'm talking about..." *God, this is so hard.* "Haven't you ever had a crush?"

Connor blinked. "No."

"Really?"

Connor nodded. Spencer's shoulder's slumped, even as the *dadness* inside him did a tiny little jig at not having to deal with *that* particular bit of puberty right now. "Then this is harder to explain, but...okay. You know how sometimes you feel like I don't love you, and I'm going to leave you, and you'll be all alone forever?" Connor grimaced, but nodded again. "Okay. Well, part of me feels that bad all the time. And it sucks, but I can ignore it because I have you, and I have Aunt Cass and your grandparents, and we've got a pretty decent life going, you know? But...when I'm with Tim, that feeling goes away. I feel like...I feel like I can want more. Like I *deserve* more. And even though our life is great, and I love it, and I love you, and I wouldn't change anything if it meant I had to lose any of what we have, Tim makes me feel like I can have all that and more and, God, kid, I want that. I want it so bad. I want to have you and Tim, and I want..." He broke off and swallowed roughly.

I want us all to be a family. That's what he wanted to say, but he couldn't. Not out loud, and not to Connor, who was already dealing with so much. Especially not when whatever was going on with him and Tim was still so new with every potential in the world for disaster.

"I want you to be okay with that." He brushed Connor's curls away from his forehead, smiling slightly when they sprang right back into place just like his own. "*Are* you okay with it?"

Please say yes. If you say no, I can't do this, and I want to do it so fucking bad.

Instead of answering, Connor hugged him so hard Spencer had to struggle to breathe as he returned the hug just as tightly. They stayed that way for a while, Spencer bathing in the feeling of holding his little family in his arms even as he hoped that, one day, there could be another set of arms surrounding them both. Eventually, Connor started to pull away, and even though it was the last thing Spencer wanted, he let him go. Connor stared at him for a long moment, seeming small and fragile in a way Spencer had never seen on him before, before pressing his lips together and standing up straight.

"You should probably get dressed," he said. Spencer politely ignored the way his voice wasn't quite steady.

Spencer decided that was probably as much approval as he could hope for right then. "What?" he asked, spreading his arms and showing off his—*dear God, I thought I threw this out*—threadbare Buffy and Angel T-shirt, the one with the huge ancient mystery stain right on David Boreanaz's face. "Not good enough to go out in?"

Connor's lips twitched. "Not unless you're going to Walmart."

Spencer snorted. "We might be, for all I know."

Although the odds of Tim being classier than that were pretty high, so back into the closet he went. He shucked the shirt and went back to his search. After a short deliberation, he pulled on a pair of tight jeans, wiggling a bit to get them on all the way, and then picked up the shirt he'd dropped earlier and buttoned it up, taking a second to savor the unmistakably sensual feeling of fabric sliding across freshly shaven skin before slipping the sweater on. After running his fingers through his mostly dry hair a few times, he slid into his favorite pair of purple Converse, stepped out of the closet, and spread his arms again.

"So? Do I look okay?"

Connor studied him critically, but before he could say anything, the doorbell rang.

"Shit!" hissed Spencer. "I'm not ready. Go answer the door, please?"

Connor paled slightly, but dutifully turned on his heel and left. Spencer didn't have any more time to hope that Connor was going to be okay with him dating Tim. He barely had enough time to run into the bathroom, quickly brush his teeth, style his hair as best he could, and give himself a quick spritz with the first body spray he saw, which happened to be strawberry. Spencer gave himself one last glance in the mirror, not finding anything too horrible about his appearance, aside from everything he usually hated about himself. He took a deep breath and glared at his reflection.

Please don't screw this up.

Back in his bedroom, he picked his black thigh-length wool coat up off the floor and put it on, taking a moment to smooth the slightly wrinkled fabric out before grabbing his keys, wallet, and phone and heading toward the front door.

"Hey, sorry I'm..." Spencer stopped dead in the middle of the hall.

Oh. My. God.

Spencer had read a *lot* of classic literary romance in his life, an unavoidable side effect of studying to be a literature teacher. He'd never enjoyed them. They were too melodramatic, with stupid people doing stupid things because of emotions they couldn't coherently explain. He'd read a thousand first meetings between destined "true loves." A thousand overwrought, angst-ridden internal monologues. A thousand different paragraphs-long descriptions of how this or that character was *ruined* or *devastated* merely by glancing at the person they claimed to love. It always came off as incredibly childish to him, like an (admittedly well-written) entry in some tween girl's diary about how *super*-hot her boyfriend was and how they were going to be together *forever* and get *married* and have a million kids and blah blah blah. The kinds of things that happened in romance novels never happened with real adults, something he'd argued loudly—and constantly—with the people in his college classes and more than one of his literature professors.

Apparently, he owed them all a huge fucking apology.

Because he'd always known Tim was attractive, but Tim dressed up for a date—no, Tim dressed up for a date with *Spencer*—was on a whole different level. His hair had been teased back off his forehead, held in place with some kind of product that made it look like the softest thing ever. He wore dark, fitted jeans—*fitted jeans!*—that clung to his thighs in a way that had to be illegal in at least a few states, along with a thick white cable-knit sweater that contrasted beautifully with his slightly tanned skin.

Overall, Tim looked...kind of devastating.

Fitted jeans and a sweater. I might actually die right here in the fucking hallway.

Tim seemed slightly confused by something, and Connor was nowhere to be seen, but the moment he saw Spencer, his eyes brightened and a smile bloomed on his face that fit a hundred different clichés Spencer would never admit to knowing off the top of his head.

"Hi," Tim said. It would have sounded inane coming from anyone else, but Spencer was so fucking *gone* that a stupid greeting made him flush and duck his head. The small part of him that could think something other than *Guh!* really hoped this wasn't going to be a thing for the whole night.

"Hey..."

Spencer glanced up in time to see the tail end of Tim checking him out.

"You look amazing."

"Yeah." Spencer flushed even harder. "I mean..."

Tim smiled again. Smiled with lips that had, the last time they'd seen each other, been *kissing Spencer.*

"*Yeah...*"

He had no idea how long he stood there like a moron waiting for his brain to reboot, but enough time passed for Tim to start nervously rubbing his hands over the tops of his thighs.

"So...are you ready to go?"

Spencer tore his eyes away from everything below Tim's waist and focused on his face.

"Uh, yeah." He cleared his throat and ran down his incredibly out-of-date predate checklist, trying to think of anything he was forgetting. *I shaved, showered, I don't have homework anymore...* "Fourteen's good for not having a babysitter, right?"

Tim laughed. "I'm sure Connor will be fine."

Fuck, I hope so. He shook off his worries about Connor as best he could.

"Probably. Not like he has any friends to have wild, boozy sex parties with," Spencer said.

"I don't think he'd be the type even if he had friends."

"Like father, like son."

Tim let out an obviously fake sigh. "Damn, now I need to change the whole date around."

Spencer laughed. "I dunno, hot stuff, for you I could probably make an—oh my God, no, I can't even finish, holy shit."

"'Hot stuff'?"

"Shut *up.*"

They shared a grin, which devolved into snickering when they both jumped as someone blew their horn right outside the house.

"Come on," Tim said. "I think the cabbie's getting impatient."

A joke about city people and their public transportation died on Spencer's lips as Tim held his hand out to him. He stared down at it, unable to describe the feeling that came over him as anything other than *warm.*

"Is something wrong?" Tim asked, his smile starting to fade.

Spencer shook his head. "No. It's..." He shrugged and glanced up at Tim. "I've...never held hands in public before."

Tim's hand started to drop. "We don't—"

Spencer grabbed him, twining their fingers together almost without thought like it was something they'd done a thousand times before.

"No," he said quietly, "we really do."

He squeezed Tim's hand.

"Spencer..."

"Come on," Spencer said, ignoring the tightening in his chest and trying not to think of how pathetically grateful he was that Tim was willing to touch him—*claim* him, if only as his date for the night—in front of other people; even if "other people" in this case meant a single impatient cabbie. "We've got a mystery date to get to, right?"

Without waiting for Tim to answer, he opened the door and pulled him outside.

*

They held hands for the whole cab ride.

Tim never thought something so simple would be anything to take note of. He'd held hands on dates all the time; in restaurants, in malls, on the street, and it had been a long time since he gave such a simple touch any special thought.

The same was obviously not true for Spencer.

Despite being the one who'd dragged Tim out of his house and into the waiting cab, he couldn't stop giving the cabbie nervous glances every minute or so. The last thing Tim wanted to do was make him uncomfortable, especially since he knew this date was going to be weird enough on its own, but every time he started to pull his hand away, Spencer tightened his grip, smiled thinly, and gave his arm a violent little yank.

It was strangely sweet, but also a little heartbreaking. It wasn't the nineties anymore; it wasn't even the first decade of the twenty-first century. Holding hands with a date, even if that date was another guy, shouldn't be something anyone had to stress about. The way Spencer so obviously wanted the contact even though it scared him made Tim want to punch every single person Spencer had gone to school with. He wasn't sure what he wanted to do with any of Spencer's old boyfriends, but it would be more violent than a punch. Spencer had only vaguely mentioned his dating history, mostly in offhand comments, but Tim knew enough. Spencer had been in at least one relationship before, and Tim had no idea how anyone could be with him and not want to shower him with affection, to draw out more of those blushes and shy smiles, to bask in the feeling of being the focus of Spencer's full, unguarded attention.

There was a slight possibility Tim was more than a little bit besotted, but he couldn't help it. Spencer hit every single one of his protective, caring instincts, and even though he promised himself he would be cautious this time, it would take a much stronger man than Tim had ever been to resist falling for Spencer. He was also sure that, once Spencer finally started to relax and get used to it, he would take to being loved like a flower to the sun.

And this is not something I should be thinking about on our first date.

Especially not when there was still plenty of time for Spencer to hate where he was taking him.

"So, we're in the cab now," Spencer said, his voice just low enough for Tim to realize he was trying to keep the cabbie from overhearing. "Do I get to know where we're going, yet?"

"It's a surprise," Tim said, hoping he was doing a good job at hiding his nervousness. Spencer made a face, and he laughed. "Not a fan?"

"Of surprises?" Spencer raised an eyebrow. "Hell no, I *love* surprises. It's the waiting for them part I suck at."

"I'll keep that in mind for Christmas," Tim said, unable to resist teasing even though he wasn't sure how Spencer would react to the assumption that they'd still be together at Christmas.

"Oh God, I used to be such a little *shit* before Christmas," Spencer said with a soft laugh. "I could barely get to sleep I was so excited, so I pretty much just kept my parents awake and miserable half the night. Hiding all the cookies and soda in the house was the only way to get me to sleep before three in the morning."

Tim laughed. "I wish I could have seen that."

"I don't. It's gonna be hard enough..." He glanced down and mumbled the rest.

"Sorry, I didn't get that last part."

Spencer sighed, glanced at the cabbie again, then lifted his head. "I said it's gonna be hard enough trying to convince you I'm worth dating. Last thing I need is you having been there when I was a stupid little kid."

"I already think you're worth dating," Tim said, giving Spencer's hand a gentle squeeze.

"You think I'm worth *a* date," Spencer corrected. A second later he crinkled his nose and then muttered under his breath, chastising himself about how "pathetic it is to say shit like that on a first date."

A fond smile tugged at Tim's lips, and he happily went about fixing the misconception.

"I already think you're *worth dating*," Tim repeated. "I don't date casually. Not..." Now it was Tim's turn to trail off with a grimace. Going into his Rudy issues on their first date would be a much bigger faux pas than anything Spencer might have done so far. The cab suddenly took a sharp turn, and he used the momentum as an excuse to lean his head closer to Spencer's.

"I wouldn't have asked you out if all I wanted was one date," Tim murmured. "I want a whole lot more than that."

Spencer bowed his head again, but this time Tim could see a small, pleased smile. "Yeah?"

Tim moved closer, his eyes drawn to Spencer's lips. As sweet as his smiles were, Tim wanted to kiss this one right off his face. "Yeah," he said, the word little more than a breath. Spencer glanced up at him, and whatever he saw in Tim's expression brought a light flush to his cheeks even as he tilted his head up, inviting another kiss.

"You've a good one there, my friend!" The cabbie's voice, thick with an Eastern European accent, boomed through the cab, making both Tim and Spencer jump in their seats. After a moment Spencer froze, then, very carefully, turned to the front of the cab.

"Thanks...?" he said.

Which was apparently all the permission the cabbie needed to burst into a loud, gesture-heavy monologue in semi-broken English about how happy it made him to see "young love" blossoming in the city, and he didn't even mind that it was "the homosexual love," not like his "bastard cousin Yuri," who, along with a whole load of faults the cabbie was all too eager to list off, was apparently a "massive homophobia."

Thankfully, it wasn't too long before they reached their destination. When they stopped, Tim pulled out some cash and paid, but before they could get out, the cabbie glanced over his shoulder and gave him a wink and a big, enthusiastic thumbs-up. He couldn't quite decide if it was sweet or weird, but he gave the man a slightly strained smile anyway before Spencer dragged him out of the cab. They both stood on the street corner and watched as the cabbie pulled away and disappeared into traffic.

"So," Spencer said after a minute of silence, "assuming cousin Yuri doesn't leave his 'paid whore wife' passed out at his 'garbage slum house' to come out and stab us to death for being the 'best of young, homosexual passion,' where are we headed?"

Tim let out a short laugh and took a moment to enjoy the relaxed, unconcerned way Spencer was holding his hand in the middle of the crowded street.

Guess cousin Yuri is good for a distraction, at least.

"Turn around," Tim said, pushing away his disappointment at not getting to kiss Spencer again. He really, *really* wanted to though, and he hoped he wasn't about to crash and burn before their night could even get started.

Spencer glanced at him out of the corner of his eye, then turned to study the building behind them. It was on the small side, only two stories tall and just narrow enough to make it seem like it was slightly squashed between the bigger structures surrounding it, but what the building lacked in size it more than made up for in sheer neon gaudiness.

"Madam Sarkisian's Wax Museum?" Spencer asked, reading the brightly lit sign on the awning that covered half the sidewalk. He seemed honestly curious, not annoyed or insulted, and Tim's nervousness dialed back a few notches.

"Well, there's no food," Tim said, earning a snort from Spencer. "And there's a special exhibit going on now that I thought you'd like."

"Yeah?" Spencer asked with a small, playful smile. "What kind of exhibit?"

Tim couldn't hold back a grin at how well Spencer was taking this.

"It's called Differences in Interpretation," he said. "What they do is they pick well-known books that got turned into movies or TV shows and they make different statues, some of how the main characters looked in the adaptations, and some that are made based on how the characters are described in the book. They have little write-ups too about why certain changes were made and stuff like that." Tim let out a quick laugh. "You've complained enough about the *Harry Potter* movies mangling the books, so when I heard about this, I thought of you and..." He shrugged, starting to feel a little awkward with the way Spencer kept staring at him. "Yeah."

Tim tried not to squirm as he waited for Spencer's reaction. Thankfully, he didn't have to wait long at all.

"That," Spencer said, "sounds like the coolest fucking thing *ever*."

"Yeah?" Tim asked.

Spencer nodded rapidly. "Fuck yeah." He hesitated, flushed, then stood up on his toes and gave Tim a quick kiss. It was nothing near what he'd been imagining back in the cab, but the fact that Spencer initiated it, and in public no less, sent a bolt of heat straight through his stomach. "Way better than dinner and a movie."

Once again Spencer's timid boldness gave Tim the best possible kind of whiplash, and without thinking, he leaned down to give Spencer a kiss of his own. His lips were much softer than they'd been the other night, tasting of vanilla lip balm and mint toothpaste. He'd only meant to return the quick peck, but once their lips were touching, he couldn't help himself. He pulled Spencer close, deepening the kiss and feeling himself flush when Spencer let out a surprised squeak that turned into a brief, throaty moan.

"We're kissing in the middle of the street," Spencer muttered against Tim's lips a minute later.

"Does it bother you?"

"Yes."

As soon as the word left his mouth, his lips were back on Tim's. Tim grinned into the kiss.

For the first time in a long while, he felt like he'd finally done something *right*.

Chapter Thirteen

Wax museums were fucking *awesome.*

Okay, so maybe Spencer's sample size was a little less than scientific, what with this being the first wax museum he'd ever been to and all, but if any of the other wax museums around the country were half as cool as this one, he'd happily stand by his statement. The level of detail in the statues was amazing, and to someone like Spencer, who could be a bit of a snob when it came to realistic computer graphics, seeing a pile of wax shaped into a photo-realistic statue of an actual person was incredibly satisfying. Even better were the statues based off the book descriptions, because they were all, without fail, utterly *perfect.* Thin, knobby-kneed Harry Potter. Twelve-year-old Jonas from *The Giver*, who stood as a sharp and much-welcomed contrast to the aged-up abomination from the movie. Beautiful elves and hairy-footed hobbits. They even had an entire wall filled with various Mr. Darcys, including one that was blood spattered and fighting off zombies.

But the best part of the night, by far, had been Tim.

In the brief snippets of time between worrying about when the 210 drama would start and obsessing over all the ways tonight could go wrong, Spencer had come to the conclusion that the best he could hope for was a date that wasn't too awkward and didn't ruin their friendship. Tim tolerated him, so Spencer didn't have to worry about hiding too many of his flaws, but that was all it was—*tolerance*. All Spencer's life people had *put up* with him or *dealt* with him; no one had ever really *wanted* him.

But Tim did. He made his desire obvious with every soft smile and eager touch.

More than that, he made their date *fun*. He didn't just take Spencer to a cool exhibit and let him amuse himself, even if Spencer totally would have been okay with that. He dragged Spencer around to things *he* wanted to see; he started heated debates about which books or movies were better that somehow never crossed the line into actual fights; he took about a million pictures on his phone, pushing a blushing Spencer in front of the camera and making him pose with all the wax characters.

He held Spencer's hand calmly, never flinching or turning away no matter how many people side-eyed them. He didn't put up a single complaint when Spencer got lost in his excitement and started dragging *him* around. He smiled with genuine pleasure when Spencer finally took out his phone and demanded pictures of his own. He guided Spencer with gentle touches on the back or the shoulder, sat next to him on benches when they wanted to take a break, and leaned close whenever they stopped to talk in a way no one could mistake for anything other than intimate. It seemed so natural to Tim, this going out with another man and making it obvious they were there *together* thing. So natural that, throughout the night, Spencer started to relax inch by inch, until he finally felt comfortable enough to not just lose himself in the moment like he had in front of the museum, but to let that moment stretch on; to let one moment become two moments, then four, then eight, until without even realizing it Spencer was resting his head against Tim's shoulder and cuddling his arm as they stared up at a giant John Travolta dressed as Terl from *Battlefield Earth*.

Turns out, there were things in the world that were way more embarrassing than holding hands with another guy.

They spent just over two hours in the museum, and by the time they were done, Spencer was beyond starving. Still, he had enough social graces to make sure Tim didn't have anything else planned before hailing another cab and giving the cabbie the address for one of his favorite restaurants. In a sudden bout of glorious payback, he refused to tell Tim where they were going. Tim pouted, which was so unfair, his all-American, boy-next-door face melting through Spencer's willpower like a welding torch. Luckily, the ride didn't take long, and the cab stopped before Spencer could cave.

It was totally worth it to see the dumbfounded expression on Tim's face.

"A *restaurant?*"

Spencer burst out laughing. "Jesus, you look like I took you to an open grave."

Tim blinked, but recovered quickly. "I'm the one with fifty texts telling me not to take you out to eat anywhere."

"It wasn't *fifty*." *At least I hope not.* "And all I said was I didn't want you *picking* anyplace to eat. I love eating out. It's just I eat like, five different things, and I'm *really* picky about how I like them made." He shrugged, trying to hold down his self-consciousness as much as he could. "Taking me out for dinner is pretty much a surefire way to have me ruin a date."

"You did give me a list."

Spencer groaned. "Don't remind me."

Tim grinned and took his hand again. "It was a very cute list."

"I feel like my manly pride should make me hate being called cute."

"But you don't hate it."

"But I don't hate it," Spencer said with a sigh.

"Good." Tim leaned in so close Spencer thought he was going to be kissed again. "Because you're completely adorable."

Spencer flushed. "Shut up. How the hell are you smooth? It's not fair. At all."

Tim looked pleased. "You still think I'm smooth?"

"Oh, please. Like you don't know how fucking—" He flapped his hand wildly at the entirety of Tim."—smooth you are."

Tim glanced down bashfully, making himself seem more like a puppy than any guy his size should be able to pull off. Spencer had to clench his free hand to keep from petting him. "Thank you."

The way he spoke sounded slightly off, almost like he was surprised that Spencer said something nice about him. Spencer frowned. *Am I really that bad at this dating thing that he thinks I'm not totally into him?*

This was something he'd definitely have to fix.

"Really, I mean it. You're as smooth as sharkskin. It's kind of..." *Say hot. You wanna say hot, so just say it.* "Cool."

You fucking loser.

Tim laughed, but instead of being mocking—which Spencer totally would have deserved after that terrible attempt at flirting—his laughter sounded fond.

"You know sharkskin is actually very rough, right?"

Spencer blinked. "No, it's not."

"It is."

"It can't be. I've touched sharks before, and they were really smooth."

"You touched a smooth shark?"

"Well...okay, maybe it was a manta ray, but they look like they have the same kinda skin, you know? And the ray was really smooth, so..."

Tim burst out laughing again.

"Jesus Christ," Spencer muttered. "Next time I'll get a fucking marine biology degree before going on a date with you."

"No, you won't," Tim said, tugging him closer. "I'm not waiting four years for another date."

Spencer's eyes widened.

"What?" Tim asked softly. "Did you really think I wouldn't want to go out with you again? Even though I told you I wanted more than one date in the cab?"

"I have no idea what you're thinking," Spencer said, perhaps a bit more honestly than he'd meant to.

"Is that a problem?"

Spencer snorted. "Give me enough time and I can turn it into one."

"Let's not do that, then."

He leaned down and kissed Spencer. *Holy shit.* This kiss was *nothing* like the kiss he still wasn't sure how he'd found the balls to initiate in front of Madam Sarkisian's. That kiss had been sweet and tender, a reassurance and a promise that Spencer would do his best to be better. It wasn't even like their hot-yet-slightly-embarrassing make-out session on Halloween. *This* kiss was an assault on the senses: a battering ram, complete with an army for storming the castle in the form of a wet, impossibly smooth tongue. Spencer had no idea if he was kissing back—fuck, he had no idea if he even knew *how* to kiss back, and not just because it had been forever and a day since he'd done anything like this.

Jesus fucking *Christ*, Tim could kiss.

"So, is it a problem yet?" Tim asked when he pulled back from the kiss—and Spencer was going to need to call whatever *that* was something new because whatever Tim just did to him was orders of magnitude higher than any kiss he'd ever had before. It was a good thing Tim's other arm had snaked around his waist while they were better-than-kissing, because Spencer's knees were weak, and who knew that was even a thing that really happened?

"Um." Spencer licked his lips. Tim hadn't tasted any different than the inside of Spencer's own mouth, but Spencer still imagined he could lick off the faint aftertaste of the other man. "I don't think I know what words mean right now."

Tim's grin held more than a hint of smugness. "Good."

He better-than-kissed Spencer again. Spencer moaned and closed his eyes.

I could do this forever.

It was a strange thought. Aside from a healthy relationship with his right hand and a few sporadically used toys, he'd never been a very carnal person, and he'd definitely never had a kiss affect him like this. Even on the few occasions when he'd had sex, Spencer hadn't felt half the way Tim's mostly innocent advances made him feel. Of course, that could just be because Spencer's only real sexual experiences were with another teenage college freshman who had been just as much a virgin as Spencer at the time, but something deep inside told him different. That even if Spencer had a different guy every day for the past ten years, none of them would have come close to setting him on fire the way Tim could.

Any other guy would have been a mile marker on the highway; Tim was the destination.

It scared the hell out of him. He hadn't felt this much this fast for anyone since the first day he'd held Connor in his arms, and this was completely different. It was so easy to lose himself in Tim, to forget everything but how it felt to be touched and kissed. Spencer *really* wished he hadn't written so many essays trashing classic literary romance as unrealistic because it might have been a little less embarrassing to find out he was completely wrong all these years if there weren't so much documented evidence...

When Tim finally pulled away again, Spencer's swirling thoughts—and stomach—stilled. He glanced up into Tim's face, so open and honest and practically glowing with affection, and said the first thing that popped into his head.

"Are you sure sharks aren't smooth?"

Tim threw back his head and laughed. "Come on," he said, squeezing Spencer's hand. "Let's go eat."

Thankfully the restaurant wasn't anything fancy, and even though it was dinner time on the weekend, they only had to wait about ten minutes for a table. Spencer was still half lost back in their kiss and all the *feelings* that kept exploding in his chest, which turned out to be a lucky break because he was too distracted to be nervous about the dreaded First Date Dinner Conversation. Talk flowed easily between them, a lot like it had during *Crystal Skull*, except with a slightly different tint to what they talked about. By silent agreement they hadn't really spoken about anything too meaningful on Halloween. That night had been about spending time together and seeing if they could fit themselves into the new shape their relationship was twisting into. Tonight was a *date*, and dates needed to go a little further.

"Why did you become a teacher?"

Which was...fair, Spencer grudgingly admitted. He chewed his lip for a moment, trying to decide between total honesty and toning himself down so "first date" didn't become "last date" too. The food came before he could decide, and while they were thanking the waiter and getting their napkins and knives and shit in order, he decided to throw caution to the wind and go with honesty. He'd already slipped a bunch of times tonight anyway, and Tim hadn't batted an eyelash. He was either really good at hiding his disdain, or he actually *liked* Spencer's Spencerness.

He took a bite, moaned quietly—it was only baked chicken, but goddammit it was fucking *delicious* baked chicken—then swallowed and answered.

"Because journalism is fucking bullshit."

Tim choked on the soda he'd been drinking. Luckily, it didn't dribble down his chin or get all over his shirt, and he recovered quickly.

"Sorry," Spencer said. "I didn't think you'd find that funny."

Tim shook his head. "No, it's okay. It was just unexpected." A moment passed. "So, journalism is bullshit?"

"Yeah." Spencer took a sip of his water. "I took journalism courses my whole first semester of college, mostly because all the assholes I went to school with were always held up as these like paragons of what a person is supposed to be. You know, all 'he's such a *good* boy' and 'oh that Kevin, what a *trip* he is' while he's interrupting class with his stupid jokes, shit like that. I hated it so much, and I always had these fantasies about exposing them to all the teachers who thought they were so fucking perfect. Like 'yeah, Kevin's such a little jokester, isn't he? Here's a video of him shoving me into a dirty urinal and calling me a fag. What a scamp.'"

Tim reached across the table and touched his hand. "Spencer…"

"It's fine." Spencer smiled quickly and pulled his hand back. The last thing he wanted was to be pitied for shit that happened more than a decade ago. "So that's what I thought journalism was, you know? Exposing corruption and scumbags and making them face public ridicule and all that. Except, as it turns out, along with a whole bunch of *really* boring research and actually *writing* articles—which is a whole other nightmare—no one's really interested in exposing anything that doesn't back up the worldview they've already decided on." He ate another piece of his chicken. "I did this project once where we had to take a controversial issue and write an article supporting or opposing one side of it, and I apparently picked the side the professor didn't agree with because he went off on me in front of the whole class. Said I was an idiot and the only place I'd ever be able to get a job as a journalist was on a 'crazy conspiracy blog.' Totally turned me off the whole thing. The idea of having to write what someone told me even if I disagreed with it was just…no. I think I'd rather shoot myself."

He shot Tim another smile to show he was joking, mostly because his mom always took him way too seriously when he said things like that.

"So, you went from journalism to teaching?"

"Sort of." Spencer smirked. "This whole thing happened a month or so into the semester, and I couldn't just switch or drop classes without wasting all my parents' money, so I stayed around and did every single project and report we had on subjects I knew would piss him off."

Tim snorted and shook his head. Spencer grinned.

"And it worked too! The guy had no fucking chill at all. He never caught on that I was just messing with him either. Not even when I handed in a practice article on how George W. Bush would have been completely justified in retroactively awarding himself the Medal of Honor for his military service in the National Guard after he got elected president."

Tim coughed. "Jesus…"

"I know! To this day I still have no idea what the worst part of that was for him: that he had to read it or that the old hippy had to actually defend the military when he was tearing it apart in front of the class."

Tim chuckled. "Did they think you were being serious?"

"The other students?" Tim nodded. Spencer shrugged. "Probably not. Either way they obviously never said anything to him. Personally, I like to think I wasn't the only one appalled by the way he taught his class. The only other option is that everyone there was as stupid as he was, and that would just be depressing."

Spencer took a drink, marveling about how easy it was to talk to Tim. He usually hated being the center of attention unless he was teaching, and he doubly hated talking about himself, but with Tim the words wouldn't stop. Spencer didn't really want them to. He *wanted* to share himself with Tim—or, at least stories about his life, he corrected with a small flush. Sharing *himself* was not a first-date activity, no matter how much certain parts of his body were loudly campaigning for a rule change.

"Anyway, after he took great delight in informing me that I failed his class, and I took even greater delight in giving him an apoplexy by telling him it didn't matter because I was switching majors anyway, I ended up deciding to give teaching a try. Because if *he* could be a tenured professor, then teaching couldn't be *that* hard. Plus, I really liked the idea of being a more successful teacher than he was."

"So...you decided to become a teacher out of spite?"

Spencer laughed. "Yes. Well, no. Well, *maybe.* Partially. And mostly I picked literature because I liked to read and thought it would be easy." He scoffed. "Shows what I knew."

"I'd always wondered about that, actually," Tim said. "Everyone always likes to bring out the 'those who can't do, teach' quote, but teaching always seemed really hard to me."

"Eh." Spencer waggled his hand. "The *teaching* itself isn't really hard once you've got your lesson plans all sorted out. The first year where you're settling in and figuring out what you need to do is the worst. But, like, taking the classes and getting the degree? That shit is *hard.* And, dear *God,* the Shakespeare. You know what the worst part of being a literature teacher is? *You can never escape Shakespeare."* He took a bite, and around a mouthful of food added, "I'll take Hemingway's simplicity over Shakespeare's flowery poetics any day." He swallowed. "It's so much easier to analyze someone's writing when they don't actually say anything."

Tim laughed, not even a little put off by Spencer's awful table manners—something that *definitely* wouldn't have been true in reverse. "You know, for a literature teacher you really seem to hate classic lit."

"Not at all. I *love* classic lit; gimme some Lovecraft or Robert Howard and I'm *set.* I just hate the crap they make us teach. Especially Shakespeare. And Steinbeck, but mostly Shakespeare. *Especially Romeo and Juliet.* I have no patience for stupid characters. *Hamlet* is okay though. I usually have them read it at the end of the year so we can watch *Lion King* when we're done. Kind of an apology for putting up with me for ten months."

"*The Lion King*?"

"Hell, yeah. That shit's basically *Hamlet* anyway. Usually the principal gets pissy about showing movies, but as long as I make them do a write-up about the thematic similarities between the film and the play, he lets me do it. It's pretty much the only thing they let me teach that I actually enjoy."

Tim cocked his head, studying Spencer with a kind of passive intensity, if such a thing could exist. Spencer would have almost said it seemed like Tim was hanging on his every word, if he thought he was being even remotely interesting. "You don't get to choose what you teach?"

Spencer grimaced. "I can to a point, but not really. It's all state standards and teaching to pass tests instead of teaching kids how to think. I take every inch of wiggle room I have, but at the end of the day there are still too many hard guidelines I have to follow. It's like a microcosm of college. All 'that's too controversial,' or 'that doesn't teach the right values,' or, my personal favorite, 'isn't that author *problematic*?' Like a little bit of Orwell or Bradbury or, God forbid, Rand is going to melt kids' brains or turn them into raging anarchists or something. You should have seen the looks I got when I wanted to put *Animal Farm* back on the summer reading list. Like I'd just walked in with shit smeared on my face and asked for a kiss. Part of me wished I'd waited until I got tenure and brought in a copy of *Mein Kampf,* just to see if anyone actually took a swing at me."

"You have a copy of *Mein Kampf*?" Tim asked, frowning and thankfully not commenting on Spencer talking about covering himself with shit while they were eating dinner. *It's amazing I don't have more people begging to date me, truly.*

"Of course not. But even if I did, so what? What's so bad about reading something from a different viewpoint? Especially something I don't agree with?" Spencer made a token effort to cut his rant off there for the sake of first-date harmony, but Tim had hit on a subject he felt *very* strongly about, and he would have had a better chance of putting the moon in a dress and marrying it in Vegas. "How the hell are people supposed to confront abhorrent ideas if they don't learn about what those ideas actually are? Sticking your head in the sand and pretending they don't exist is stupid, and trying to make it a punishable offense to mention them just makes them mysterious and appealing and turns them into forbidden fruit. Every idea should be placed under a harsh light, so there are no shadows and no hidden corners, and then let people decide for themselves what to believe."

"But what about dangerous ideas?" Tim asked.

"No such thing. *Ideas* aren't dangerous; it's what we do with ideas that are dangerous. And if I've learned anything from being a parent, it's that you can't just tell someone 'this is bad' and have them listen. You have to tell them *why* it's bad and, sometimes, let them do it anyway and figure it out for themselves."

"I don't know...I don't really think kids are mature enough to...I don't even know what the word is. Not 'think critically.'"

"Please, most *adults* can't think critically."

Tim snorted. "Still, it's not the word I want to use."

"Fine. Parse, maybe?"

"Maybe."

"Look," Spencer said, gesturing with a particularly salty french fry, "I'm not saying we should make fourteen-year-olds read, like, *The Anarchist's Cookbook* or something, but a little intellectual diversity can go a long way to teaching them *how* to think. And maybe high school isn't even the right place for what I want. But college? God, I almost wish we were living in the sixties or seventies just to see a college atmosphere where debate and thought was encouraged by students instead of stifled. It was bad enough back when I was in college, but the shit I read about now is just depressing. It breaks my heart to think of how horribly unprepared most of these kids are to encounter the real world." The only reason he had enough self-control to stop there was because he could hear his voice rising with every sentence. *Social philosophy on the first date. Way to keep things light and fun, you idiot.* He shook his head. "Sorry, I didn't mean to go into a whole thing."

"No, don't apologize." Tim hesitated. "It's...nice to see you so passionate. Honestly, I'm not even sure if I disagree. It's not something I ever thought about. All the problems I had with my teachers weren't really about what they taught..." He cleared his throat. "I'm curious though...you never really said why you became a teacher, and it seems like you hate it just as much as journalism. Actually, it seems like you have a lot of problems with the whole concept of teaching."

Spencer snorted. "Have you ever seen something that was so obviously broken, and it drives you crazy every time you see it, and you try to tell people, but nobody who can do anything about it believes you until all you wanna do is either smash the shit out of it so you never have to look at it or fix it yourself?"

Tim glanced away. "Yes."

"There you go." Spencer spread his hands. "Turns out it's a lot easier to be a teacher who teaches right than it is to destroy the entire American public education system."

Tim huffed out a laugh. "I'll take your word on it."

They shared a small grin.

Silence fell between them after that as Tim went back to eating, but it was a surprisingly comfortable silence considering the heaviness of what they'd been talking about. Spencer watched Tim as he ate, swooning slightly over his table manners and the way he used his napkin instead of just letting food get everywhere until he finished eating. Few things grossed Spencer out more than a messy eater, and seeing Tim wiping his face and chewing with his mouth closed very nearly turned him on.

"So," Spencer said a few minutes later, "can I ask you something now?"

Tim smiled, though there was a nervous edge to it Spencer wasn't used to seeing. "Sure."

Spencer chewed the inside of his mouth as he tried to work up the courage to ask about something that had been weighing on his mind for a while. "Does it bother you that I'm old?" he blurted out.

This time, Tim choked on his food.

"Shit," Spencer said, wringing his hands together, "sorry! Sorry!"

"S'okay," Tim coughed out.

"Take a drink," Spencer said even though Tim was already gulping down half his soda. "Are you okay? Do you need to go to the bathroom? Should I smack your back?"

Tim cleared his throat after downing half his glass and raised an eyebrow. Spencer's cheeks started to burn.

"Sorry," Spencer said again, wincing. "Dad mode."

Tim shook his head, smiling, if still a bit red from the coughing. "Don't worry, it's cute."

Spencer stuck out his tongue.

"I thought you liked when I called you cute," Tim teased.

"That was thirty minutes ago. Things change fast around here."

"I could have made a joke about calling you 'Daddy' instead."

"Ha! I'm like half your size. If anyone's calling anyone 'Daddy,' it should be me." Tim's eyes widened at the exact same moment Spencer's brain caught up with his mouth. "Oh my God. Jesus fuck, just...please ignore me."

Miracle of miracles, Tim did exactly that. "So...you, uh, asked about our age difference?"

Spencer grimaced. "You don't need to answer. Actually—"

"No, I want to." Tim shifted in his chair. *That can't be good body language.* "It...does bother me, but not in the way you think," he added quickly, no doubt correctly interpreting the expression of panic on Spencer's face.

"Okay," Spencer said, mostly to himself. Tonight had been going so good, so of course there had to be *something* to bring him down. But that was okay. He could deal. Tim had put up with so much from him already and hadn't so much as flinched. Spencer could handle Tim having a problem with his age.

Tim sighed and then reached across the table and took Spencer's hand. "I knew you'd take that the wrong way."

"There's a right way to take it?"

"Spencer..."

Spencer shook his head and gave Tim's hand a squeeze. "Sorry."

"Nothing to be sorry for," Tim said, lacing their fingers together. It was a bit awkward holding hands across a table, but even this small bit of contact soothed something inside Spencer.

"Okay," he said, squaring his shoulders. "Hit me."

Tim's smile was as fond as it was brief. "It has *nothing* to do with your age," he said, giving Spencer's fingers a reassuring squeeze. "You're only six years older than me; that's *not* old."

Spencer disagreed—he was, after all, way closer to thirty than Tim—but he didn't protest out loud. Something about the way Tim spoke, the slight hesitations and the inconsistent eye contact, told him, for whatever reason, this wasn't easy for Tim to talk about. It was even more obvious because Tim had been nothing but smooth and sure of himself all night so far, and the last thing Spencer wanted to do was make this about his own insecurities when it seemed like Tim might be having some of his own.

"It's..." Tim grimaced. "This is going to make me sound like such a child, but I'm kind of jealous of how put together your life is. You're only six years older than me, but you're raising a son, and you have a stable career you're really good at. You're pretty much exactly where I wanted to be when I got out of college."

"You wanted to have a teenage son when you got out of college?"

Tim let out an exasperated sigh. "You know what I mean."

Spencer bit back any other comments he could have made. Now wasn't the time for sarcasm. "Okay, but...you know my life isn't perfect, right? You've *been* there for a few of the less than nice bits. There's no reason to be jealous."

The very thought of someone like Tim being jealous of a human mess like Spencer was even more confusing than algebra.

"And," he added when Tim didn't say anything, "at the risk of sounding even older than I am, you're, what, twenty-two? You probably just got out of college. Almost no one gets a career right out of college. Fuck, it took me over a year to get hired once I got my degree, and even longer to get tenure." He gave Tim another squeeze. "There's nothing wrong with not having your life together at twenty-two."

Tim frowned. Several times he opened his mouth like he was going to speak, but each time he closed it again without saying anything. Spencer's insides twisted, exactly like they did when Connor was distressed, and every inch of Spencer's being yearned to *fix everything*.

"And maybe what you wanted to do in college isn't what you want to do anymore, and that's okay too," he said, warming up to this whole comforting thing. Of course, he was basically just parroting the speech his mom gave him when he started talking about switching majors from journalism, but it had worked on him so maybe it would help now too. "What *did* you go to college for anyway? I don't think I ever asked."

"I want to be a child psychologist."

"That sounds fucking *perfect* for you. Uh. Unless you really don't wanna do it anymore, then I'm sure there's something even *more* perfect—"

Tim cut him off with a short laugh. "No, I definitely still want to do it..." He glanced down and gave the table an awed little smile. "I...still want to do it. And you're right. It is perfect for me..."

"Awesome." Spencer grinned. "So, what's the problem?"

"You know," Tim said softly, "I have absolutely no idea."

*

The rest of their dinner passed in a daze for Tim, which was ironic, because for the first time in months he felt like he was finally thinking clearly. All because of an offhanded comment from the amazing, beautiful man sitting across from him. So *what* if Professor Carmichael was a scumbag? Who cared if Rudy didn't want to be with him unless he was making money? What did it matter if Carmichael *had* slandered him to every professor he knew who ran a doctorate program? There were other schools, other professors who had never even *heard* of Edward Carmichael. Tim had his bachelor's. He'd *earned* his degree, through years of hard work and sleepless nights and endless hours of second guesses and fears of not being good enough. Nothing was stopping him from going to another school and trying again. He might not even have to go too far away from Chicago. Which...well.

He smiled down at Spencer walking next to him on the sidewalk.

There were very good reasons to want to stay in Chicago.

The restaurant Spencer had taken them to was close enough to his house to walk back, and that's exactly what they decided to do. Tim was grateful. Not only because it gave him time to process, to get used to having motivation and *drive* again, but because he was nowhere near ready to say good night. He wanted to wring out every possible moment with this wonderful man who'd given him back a part of himself he'd thought was gone forever with nothing more than an awkward, utterly endearing attempt to be supportive. He wanted to hold Spencer's hand and take in the sights and sounds of a city that felt more like home than New York ever had without his senses dulled by apathy and self-pity.

Most of all, he wanted to revel in being young and happy and completely, irredeemably in love.

"You haven't stopped smiling since we left the restaurant," Spencer said when they were about halfway back to his house, if Tim judged the distance correctly.

"Is that a problem?" he asked, almost laughing when he felt his smile widen all on its own.

"You smiling? Never." Spencer started to smile back but must have realized what he'd said because his face erupted into one of his adorable blushes, and he coughed slightly. "Um. Just, you know, noteworthy. I don't think I've ever seen you look so happy before."

That's because I love you.

Thankfully, he wasn't so far gone he said that out loud. This definitely wasn't the right time for love confessions, no matter how much Tim wanted to tell literally every single person who passed them on the sidewalk, and maybe a few of the people in the cars too. Spencer deserved a perfect moment with flowers and candles and every romantic cliché in the world. He deserved to hear those words for the first time from Tim in a way that would leave no doubt he was nothing less than 100 percent serious.

At the very least, he deserved a second date.

"I'm having a great night."

Spencer tilted his head and glanced up, the light from the nearby streetlamp gleaming in his eyes. "Yeah?"

Tim swung their hands between them as they walked. "Best night ever."

Spencer laughed but didn't try to dispute it, which Tim had half expected. Instead, he studied Tim for a long moment. "Hey, can I ask you something?"

"Sure."

"How tall are you?" Now it was Tim's turn to laugh. Spencer huffed, but Tim could see he was fighting to keep from smiling. "What? It's a legit question, and it's been bothering me for weeks."

"My height has been bothering you for weeks?"

"Yes! You're usually so..." He flattened his free hand and held it several inches above his own head. "But tonight, you're all..." He raised the hand up a bit. "But I swear to God I've seen you"—he lowered it so it was an inch or so below where he originally had it—"like this too. It's driving me crazy."

Tim grinned. "I'm six foot one," he said. "All the time. But sometimes, like tonight, I wear dress shoes, which have a bit of lift in the back, and that brings me up here." He placed his own free hand on top of his head. "And sometimes I just wear sneakers, which don't have as much lift, and I'm here." He held his hand in front of the top of his forehead. "And then there are times when I take my shoes completely off," he said, lowering his hand another quarter inch or so, "which brings me right about here."

Spencer dropped his hand and narrowed his eyes. "You're making fun of me, aren't you?"

"Not at all, I swear." Then, when Spencer raised an eyebrow, he added, "I might be teasing you a bit though."

"Hmm." Spencer studied him for a moment. "You should take your shoes off more often. You're way too tall."

An idea popped into Tim's head, and he stopped dead in the middle of the sidewalk. There weren't many people around, but the few who were close behind them gave him dirty looks before picking up the pace and striding by.

"Wha—" Was as far as Spencer got before Tim started slipping out of his shoes. "I didn't mean now!" he said, his words trailing off into a laugh when Tim dropped down about an inch. "Holy shit, you weren't lying."

"Nope," Tim said, picking the shoes up with his free hand. "Never."

They were facing each other now, and while Tim had always been terrible at eyeballing measurements, he figured Spencer couldn't be any taller than five six or five seven with the way the slightly fluffy hair on the top of his head barely came up to Tim's nose even with the shoes gone.

"Okay, so, another insecurity question coming," Spencer said, chewing his lip briefly. "This doesn't bother you, right? That I'm so..." He held his flattened hand up to the top of Tim's head, then lowered it to the top of his own.

Tim frowned. "Why would it?"

Spencer shrugged. "It happens. We don't exactly live in a part of the world where guys my size are common. It's weird, right?"

"Spencer," Tim said softly, "there's nothing weird about your height." Spencer shot him a skeptical look, and Tim held back a sigh. "Do you really think I care how tall you are? At *all*?"

"Lots of guys do."

For a moment, all Tim could feel was a seething disgust toward every single person who had ever told Spencer he was anything less than perfect.

"A lot of guys are idiots," Tim said bluntly. It got a small chuckle out of Spencer, which made him want to smile, but he could see Spencer still wasn't completely convinced. "Do you have a problem with *my* height?"

Spencer winced. "Not...as such." Tim blinked, and Spencer quickly rushed to clarify. "It's not that I'm not attracted to you! Because, and I'm so going to regret saying this in a few minutes, that's *definitely* not the case. You're...*whoa*. Like, the ideal guy, you know? Over six feet, nice shoulders, great smile, confident but not up his own ass." He smiled ruefully. "You're basically every standard I've ever been compared against, and there's a small part of me that kinda wants to hate you."

Tim tried to keep how much Spencer's words had hurt from showing. "And the rest of you?"

Spencer's eyes suddenly widened like a deer in the headlights. *So much for not pressuring him about feelings.* "The rest of me," he said slowly, "wants to climb you like a fucking tree and make a nest in your hair. Which makes even less sense to me than it probably does to you, but there you go."

Tim blinked again. "That's...probably the sweetest thing anyone's ever said to me."

"You're fucking kidding me."

"No," Tim said unable to fight the smile pulling at his lips. "No one's ever wanted to make a nest with me before."

Spencer studied him for a long moment, probably trying to decide if he was being teased or not. Judging by the return of the blush, he must have decided he wasn't.

Which was good, because Tim had never been more serious in his life.

"Well...I do." Spencer cleared his throat. "I mean, it's not like I'm saying we should move in together or anything but"—he met Tim's eyes and took a deep breath—"I want a whole more than just a date too."

Tim could live inside those words forever. "Good."

"And you're sure you're okay with that? Being my— Trying for—" He shook his head. "God, I have no idea what to call you when I'm nearly thirty."

"I think we're still young enough that 'boyfriends' would be fine," Tim said, amused and charmed in equal measure.

"Oh, thank God."

"Hm?"

Spencer's blush deepened as he shrugged. "No, nothing, I just hate calling the person I'm with a 'lover,' or anything like that. Lover implies sex, boyfriend implies an emotional connection. I can't say 'Oh, hi, this is Insert Name Here, my lover' without thinking it sounds like 'Hi, this is Whoever, the guy who's fucking me.'"

"What about 'partner'?"

"Ew. Way too clinical. I'm not practicing law with somebody. I'd much rather have a boyfriend."

"Well," Tim said, smiling, "I'm more than happy to be your boyfriend."

Spencer didn't return the smile. Instead, his expression turned completely serious, bordering on solemn. "And you're really okay with that? Really? You know being my boyfriend means Connor's going to be an even bigger part of your life, right? I don't know—I mean, I think he might be too old for another 'dad,' but if this works out, you know that's basically what you're gonna be. Is...is that too much?"

Suddenly, Tim felt like an idiot. He'd been so worried about not turning things too serious too fast he'd forgotten how different this relationship was going to be to any he'd been in before. Spencer was a father, which meant he couldn't do anything *but* take dating seriously. And if he'd already agreed to date Tim, then he must already have strong feelings for him.

Still, that didn't mean they couldn't take things slow. He was pretty positive slow was the only speed Spencer had, and Tim still had more than a few Rudy-shaped hang-ups rattling around in his head. He wasn't quite ready to lay his heart out on the line yet, no matter how many Sure Thing signals Spencer was giving off. For right now, the *L* word was better left off the table.

Even if Spencer was giving him everything he'd ever wanted.

"It's not too much at all," he said.

"Are you sure?" Spencer asked. "Because if it is, you gotta tell me now. Tonight's been perfect, but I think we can still walk away and just be friends without fucking us up too much. But if we do this again, and it's anything like this?" He let out a long breath. "At the risk of sounding creepy and possessive, I don't think I'd ever be able to let you go."

Tim smiled. "I like the sound of that."

"Really? Even though I have a moody teenage kid?"

So that's his biggest hang-up.

"Spencer." Tim let go of his hand and cupped his face, savoring the contrast of the slight roughness of his jaw and the downy smoothness of his cheek. "I want both of you."

Then he kissed him.

Tim only meant to give him a quick kiss; a reassurance, a way to connect Spencer's moment of doubt with every other kiss they'd shared that night, so he'd know nothing had changed. Problem was, he'd somehow forgotten how addicting Spencer's lips were. One second turned into two, then four, then more, then tongues got involved and it would take a stronger man than Tim to keep counting with Spencer panting into his open mouth. Somewhere in the back of his mind he knew they were making out on a sidewalk in the middle of the city while he was holding his shoes. The rest of him, however, only acknowledged the back of his mind long enough to revel in the fact that Spencer had once again kissed him in public with total abandon.

When they finally parted, Spencer stared up at him with large glistening eyes.

"Tim." Spencer licked his lips. "God, please tell me you want us in different ways."

The moment the words were out, Spencer's eyes widened, and he slapped his hand over his mouth. He dropped his head on Tim's chest with a groan.

"I didn't say that out loud, did I?" he asked, his voice muffled by his hands.

Tim laughed. Apparently, at some point between "Hi, nice to meet you" and "Oh crap, I love him," accusations of being a pedophile went from enraging to cute. Good to know.

"You did," Tim said, dropping a kiss on top of Spencer's head just because he could.

"Kill me now."

"I'd rather kiss you."

Spencer pulled back and stared up at Tim. His cheeks were burning red, and his brows were pinched together.

Tim couldn't resist seeing if placing a kiss on his forehead would smooth them out.

It did.

"You know what," Spencer said a moment later, "I'm not even gonna question it."

He yanked Tim down for another kiss.

This time, Tim didn't even bother starting a count.

Chapter Fourteen

SPENCER: *kids on his way. He should be there in 15 minutes or so. If hes late, fall FBI*

SPENCER: **call*

SPENCER: *also. HEADS UP. He is wearing his new wonder woman t shirt and hes really sensitive about it*

SPENCER: *make fun of him all day long so he gets over that shit*

SPENCER: *kidding! Please don't make fun of my son for wearing a wonder woman shirt*

SPENCER: *make fun of him for wearing a wonder woman MOVIE shirt*

SPENCER: *kidding again. Were a dc movie family. You need to get with the program because we are RIDE OR DIE tim*

So you hate Kingdom of the Crystal Skull but you like Dawn of Justice?

SPENCER: *ride*

SPENCER: *or*

SPENCER: *DIEEEEEEEEEE*

SPENCER: *can you tell im bored out of my fucking mind yet?*

Tim snorted for the fifth time since Spencer's text spree started, drawing another strange glance from the center's receptionist.

TIM: *No grading this weekend?*

SPENCER: *I wish. Why do you think im so bored?*

Tim smiled fondly.

A week had passed since their date had ended with a simple kiss on Spencer's front porch, making it the most chaste first date Tim had ever been on. Not that he minded. He would have been more than happy to trade every orgasm he'd ever had for one of Spencer's kisses. Especially the shy ones. But even more especially, the really desperate, aggressive ones Tim got when Spencer forgot to be self-conscious and lost himself in the moment. Tim was addicted to being the thing that made Spencer lose control.

SPENCER: *Also*

SPENCER: *HUSH YOUR MOUTH dawn of justice is an underrated GEM.*

TIM: *If you say so.*

SPENCER: *quick, pick a movie that you like that you think i hate*

SPENCER: *dont question me just do it*

TIM: *I don't know what's more impressive, that you knew what I was going to say or that you typed all that out before I could type "why?" And the Doctor Who movie.*

SPENCER: *Great!*

SPENCER: *wait, really? you like the doctor who movie?*

Tim smirked to himself.

TIM: *It's an underrated gem.*

SPENCER: *if I didnt hate emojis id be giving you like a million poop emojis right now*

SPENCER: *Actually, no. thats perfect. Thats our next date. Youre coming over here tomorrow and were gonna watch dawn of justice and the doctor who movie back to back and see which one is better.*

Tim grinned.

TIM: *Our next date, huh? Aren't you gonna ask? Or are you deciding for both of us?*

SPENCER: *ive decided*

SPENCER: *is that okay?*

Tim laughed.

TIM: *It's perfect.*

Suddenly, the center's front doors slammed open, letting in a burst of cold air that was followed very quickly by Connor. His nose and cheeks were reddened by the cold front that had moved in the night before, and even though he wore a thick jacket, he still had his arms wrapped around himself trying to keep warm. He spotted Tim before the doors started to close and froze. They stared at each other, and Connor hunched in on himself before scowling down at the floor.

"Hey, Connor," Tim said, greeting him with a smile.

Connor didn't say anything, and Tim's smile slipped. His phone buzzed again, but Tim barely glanced at the new text before firing off a quick *"Connor's here talk later."* He knew Spencer wouldn't mind. Center time had always been Tim and Connor time, and even before they'd started dating, Spencer had respected and encouraged it. Connor was usually eager to hang out with him too, which was sweet and kind of sad. He was pretty desperate for friendship, and Tim knew he enjoyed the fact that a guy Tim's age liked him and wanted to be his friend. Right now though, Connor seemed like he'd rather be anywhere else.

He wondered if this was what Spencer meant when he said Connor had been acting "weird" all week.

"You want to get something to eat?"

Connor grunted.

Okay then.

"Hey, is everything all right?"

Connor nodded and then shrugged. Tim held back from prying. He knew how important privacy was to Connor and, even though the receptionist was the only other person around, sound tended to carry in the entrance area.

"Come on," he said. "Let's get further inside and warm up a bit; then we can talk."

Surprisingly, Connor followed him without complaint. Tim debated heading to the cafeteria, but it was close to lunchtime and there would be too much of a crowd for Connor to feel comfortable. Instead, he led his friend to a nearby empty office, opening the door before turning to face him.

"Do you—" He barely got those two words out before Connor walked past him and dragged him in. Connor tried to close the door, but Tim stopped him and kept it open halfway. He'd be in enough trouble if he got caught with a kid in someone's office; he didn't need to close the door and make it seem like they were trying to hide what they were doing. Connor barely seemed to notice. He was too busy pacing back and forth, chewing on his thumbnail.

"Are you really dating my dad?" Connor asked, spinning around and shooting him a challenging glare like he was daring Tim to admit it. Or maybe he was daring him to deny it, Tim couldn't tell. Either way, the question wasn't what Tim had been expecting, although if he thought about it, he probably should have.

"I am," he answered.

Connor stared up at him. "Why?" he asked plaintively.

Tim held back a frown. Spencer had told him, a few days after their date, about Connor's reaction to finding out they were dating, but he'd made it seem like Connor was okay with it. Was he wrong? Or was he trying to keep how Connor really felt from Tim? Was *this* why Connor hadn't been to the center since last week?

"Because I care about him."

"That's not an answer. I want *reasons.*"

Tim raised his eyebrows. "You want details about my relationship with your dad?"

"Not like—" Connor snapped his mouth shut and glared. "You're teasing me, aren't you?"

"Not on purpose, I swear."

Connor kept the glare up for another few seconds before deflating and letting out a long, breathy sigh. "Whatever."

"Connor—"

"Is that why you're friends with me?" His voice was quiet, but his eyes were wide, and his breath came rapidly, his narrow chest rising and falling like he'd just run a marathon. "Because you wanted my dad?"

"What?" Tim stared at him in shock. Was *that* what he thought? "Of *course not*."

"Then why *are* you friends with me?" Connor crossed his arms. "And if you're *my* friend, why are you dating *my* dad?"

Tim pulled on every bit of self-control he had to keep his expression neutral. He was terrified his relationship with Spencer would be more than Connor could handle. That the very idea of them being together was about to drive his brand-new boyfriend's son into a panic attack. Tim may not have dated anyone with a child before, but if there was one universal rule of going out with a single parent who cared about their kids, it was that the relationship was doomed if the kids didn't approve. He had to fight down a rising panic of his own that this might be one of those situations. Tim had known too many kids who suffered because their parent started dating someone they hated, and he never wanted to be the cause of something similar himself. If Connor had a problem with them being together, Tim would end the relationship himself even if Spencer wouldn't, no matter how much his heart was already breaking at the thought.

"I'm—" Tim cleared his throat when the word came out rough. "I'm friends with you because I *like* you."

"It's your job to like me."

"You know that's not true," Tim said patiently.

"I don't know anything!" Connor ran his fingers through his hair in a gesture so painfully *Spencer* Tim had to dig his fingernails into the palm of his hands to keep from pulling him into a hug. "You told me you were friends with me because you didn't have anyone else, and now you've got my *dad,* and you don't need me anymore, so the only reason you're even here is because of *him.*"

Tim's head was spinning at how quickly Connor jumped from one insecurity to another.

"Connor." He sighed. "Can you please look at me when I say this?"

Surprisingly, Connor did so, forcing himself to take long, deep breaths. His eyes were bright with frustrated tears he seemed to be holding back from spilling down his cheeks with nothing but sheer force of will as he visibly struggled to keep himself together.

Tim was so impressed by the inner strength he was witnessing he almost forgot to start speaking.

"My relationship with your dad has *nothing* to do with our friendship. I *like* hanging out with you. I liked it before I liked your dad, and I still like it now that I... Now that I love him." Tim was breaking all kinds of relationship rules here, telling Spencer's son before he told Spencer himself, but he didn't want to hold anything back. Connor deserved to know how Tim felt as much as Spencer did. "And even if me and Spencer break up one day, I'll *still* be your friend. Nothing will ever change that."

It kind of stunned Tim how well he and Connor got along. No matter what he said when they first met, he never expected to be such good friends with someone who was barely into their teen years. Connor was mature for his age though, in certain ways, and he was smart and quick, and Tim could talk to him for hours about nearly anything and never once feel like he'd been talking to a child. In a lot of ways, Connor was probably his *best* friend, and not just because he was the only real friend he still had who wasn't also his boss. Connor, and Spencer too, had gotten in deep underneath Tim's skin, burrowing down beneath his defenses and settling into the places in his heart marked *family*. And he so desperately wanted them to stay there.

But this wasn't about Tim. This was about what Connor needed. And right now, Connor needed a friend more than he needed family.

Connor blinked, then violently wiped his eyes right as the tears started to spill over. "What if I'm the reason you break up?" he asked, his voice small.

Tim slowly reached out and placed his hands on Connor's shoulders, giving him every opportunity to back away. He didn't. "*Nothing.*"

"Do you promise?"

Years of psychology courses and a lifetime of experience told Tim this was an impossible and, more importantly, *irresponsible* promise to make. He didn't even hesitate. "I promise. We'll always be friends. No matter what."

Connor went stock still for a moment, and then Tim felt the tension drain out of him. He sniffled and knuckled away the last of his tears, and Tim couldn't resist anymore. *To hell with it.* Tim had already broken almost all his other rules for Connor; what was one more? He pulled Connor into a hug, almost completely melting when Connor threw his arms around his waist and hugged him back tightly.

A fierce swell of nearly blinding love burst to life inside Tim. It made him want to shield Connor from the world at the same time as he wanted to see him go out and conquer it. Was this how Spencer felt every day? Was this what it felt like to be a parent? Tim had no idea, but he allowed himself to hope, even if only for a few minutes, that he might find out some day.

The hug didn't last long, and when Connor pulled away, he looked completely mortified, but he didn't seem to be upset anymore. It was one of the things Tim admired about him, his resilience, his ability to bounce back from things in a way Tim had never been able to do. Of course, now that the crisis had passed, Tim was painfully aware they were alone in somebody's office, and his imagination had no trouble at all painting vivid pictures of exactly how much trouble Tim would be in if they got caught. Thankfully, Connor jumped at the suggestion that they go out to eat at a nearby diner, and by the time they'd walked there and got their food, things were back to normal between them. Mostly.

"So, if you're dating my dad, isn't it kinda weird that I'm still your 'Little Brother'?"

Tim winced. "It's...not the best terminology, no."

Connor snorted. "Yeah, but that's not what I asked. I asked if it was weird."

"Maybe a little," Tim admitted. "But it helps that I never really thought of you as a brother."

"Really?"

Tim studied Connor as surreptitiously as possible for any signs he was hurt or insulted, but he didn't seem to be anything other than genuinely curious. "Yep. It never really felt right, you know? Besides, friends are way better than siblings. You're stuck with siblings no matter what, but you can choose your friends." He bit into a fry and grinned. "And I definitely choose you, Pikachu."

"Ugh." Connor's exaggerated gagging noise was slightly offset by the faint blush staining his cheeks.

"You've definitely been spending too much time with my dad."

Tim laughed. "What about you?"

"Have I been spending too much time with my dad?"

"No, smart-ass." Tim threw a fry at Connor. It bounced off his shoulder and landed on the counter in front of him where it was scooped up and shoved into Connor's smirking mouth. "I mean, is it weird? Me and your dad."

"Definitely," Connor said, thankfully after swallowing. And maybe some of Tim's sudden dread showed on his face, because Connor quickly added, "But not a bad weird, I guess. More like a…'I'm gonna have to get used to it' weird." He seemed thoughtful for a moment before he grimaced and nodded. "Yeah, definitely gonna have to get used to it." He shuddered. "Ugh, I wish brain bleach was real…"

"Do I even want to know what you just thought about?"

Connor rapidly shook his head. "*I* don't even wanna know what I just thought about."

Tim chuckled, and they ate quietly for a few minutes. Eventually, Connor broke the silence.

"So…are you gonna get a new one?"

"A new one?"

"A new Little Brother."

"Connor," Tim said, turning on his stool and giving Connor's knee a reassuring squeeze, "I told you I'm not—"

"No, I know. I don't mean like, you're gonna replace me or anything. But I don't have to come here to be your friend, and if you're gonna be—" He stuck out his tongue. "—*doing stuff* with my dad, you'll probably be around a lot, right?"

Tim cleared his throat. "Probably, yes." *I hope so.*

"So, there's no point in me being your Little Brother anymore."

Tim held back another wince. He knew where Connor was coming from, but hearing it put so bluntly still seemed wrong. "I guess. Are you—do you wanna drop out of the program?"

Connor shrugged. "I don't really care. I mean, I only came here to get the PS4 in my room." He flashed a small grin at Tim. "But...you're, you know, cool and stuff. And I like spending time with you. It doesn't really matter where we do it."

Tim held back a snort at Connor's attempt to be unaffected and cool as if he hadn't been crying in Tim's arms about the possibility of them not being friends less than an hour ago. But that was fine. If that's what Connor wanted—even if that was *all* Connor wanted—then Tim was happy to provide. "I can see that. And coming over more will give me a chance to kick your ass in *Mario Kart.*"

"You *wish.*" Connor shoved him, which only unbalanced Connor on his stool. Tim grabbed him to keep him from falling, politely ignoring the embarrassed flush on his cheeks as he resettled himself and continued like nothing had happened. "But don't you need this? Or... whatever?"

Despite the lack of eloquence, Tim knew what he was getting at. He'd told Connor a very heavily edited version of his college debacle and what followed during one of their afternoons together. To be honest, he was kind of surprised Connor had been paying enough attention to remember it.

"Actually..." He hesitated. This really was something he wanted to talk about with Spencer first...but what the hell. He'd already started setting a pattern for telling things to Connor before anyone else. Why break it now? "I'm probably gonna go back to school and work on finishing my degree."

Connor seemed surprised. "Really?"

"Yeah. So, with all the work and going to classes and everything, I wouldn't have time to volunteer anyway."

"That's cool. The going back to school thing, I mean."

"Yeah." Tim smiled. "But, uh, can you kinda keep it a secret for a bit? I wanna tell your dad myself."

Connor smirked. "Maybe after you tell *him* you love him?"

Tim flushed. "Exactly."

More silence, more eating. Or Tim ate, at least. Connor mostly sat there and picked at a seam in his jacket. Tim pretended he didn't notice. He felt pretty sure he knew what Connor was working up to asking. "Do you...really love my dad?"

"Yes," Tim answered immediately.

Connor seemed to think about Tim's answer for a moment, then nodded. Then he made a face. "Okay, but...*why*?"

The question sounded different, this time. More teasing, like a kid ragging on his friend for doing something gross instead of someone trying to make sense of something he didn't understand. Still, Tim answered honestly. "Because he makes me happy."

He had no idea why Connor burst out laughing.

Chapter Fifteen

59...58...57...56...

Spencer leaned in and chewed his bottom lip as he watched the numbers tick down. His chest pressed up against the top of the oven, and he could feel the heat bleeding through the ceramic and insulated metal. His shirt had become plastered to his body with sweat born from warmth and worry.

This was it. His last chance. His final opportunity.

45...44....43....42....

His eyes flickered off to the side, landing on the smoke alarm he'd discarded on the kitchen table. The device lay silent, now, its guts long since torn out, but he knew better than to take his eyes off it for too long.

36...35...34...33...

Somewhere behind him, he heard the shifting of clothing as his progeny watched on with bated breath. He could easily picture eyes so much like his own boring through him with the steady, unshakable pressure of a hydraulic press as the mantle of responsibility on his shoulders grew ever harder to bear.

17...16...15...14...

So close now. He gripped the edges of the counter until his fingers went numb as he took a deep, steadying breath. The smell of charred flesh from the carcasses next to him invaded his senses, reminding him of his previous failures. Bile rose in his throat. If this didn't work, if he failed once again, the bitter tang of humiliation and defeat would be nothing in the face of the knowledge that he'd destroyed the hopes and dreams of an entire family.

5...4...3...2...1

Beep-beep-beep-beep.

He pushed himself away from the counter and pulled the oven open.

Inside was a turkey, perfectly golden and glistening with succulent juices. He slipped on an oven mitt, pulled the pan out, and set it on the counter. Now came the moment of reckoning. With shaking hands, he cut into the breast.

"Dad...?"

Spencer closed his eyes and nearly collapsed in relief. "It's perfect."

Connor let out an exasperated breath. "Thank *God*. Can I go now, or are you gonna have another nervous breakdown?"

Spencer glared over his shoulder. "I didn't have a *nervous breakdown*."

"I came down to see why the fire alarm was going off, and you were on the floor crying surrounded by burnt turkeys."

"I wasn't *crying*."

Connor raised an eyebrow. "You were *sobbing*. I thought you were dying or something."

Spencer scowled. The only thing dying was his bank account and his sanity. "Let's see you run out at ten in the morning on Thanksgiving to try and find more turkeys because you burnt the *three* you bought and see how well you handle it."

"I wouldn't have burnt any of them."

"*I wouldn't have burnt any of them*," Spencer mocked in a slurred, high-pitched voice. "Then why didn't you cook them?"

"Because you didn't ask me, and you started cooking them when I was asleep!" Connor snapped. "I don't get why we couldn't just have Baskin-Robbins like we do every year. Tim wouldn't have minded."

"Awah!" Spencer squawked, drawing himself up to his full (if unimpressive) height in righteous indignation. "That's—no!"

"It's not like he's gonna suddenly hate you if you can't cook for him."

"That's not the point!" Although now that *someone* had said it aloud, it was kind of exactly the point. "It's embarrassing to have takeout on Thanksgiving."

"We literally do that every year."

"It's different when there's someone new."

Connor crossed his arms. "So, I'm not worth the effort of cooking, but Tim is?"

"Yes! No." Spencer bit his lip again. "It's...*we're* not worth the effort of cooking. But Tim is."

Yeah, that sounded right.

"You're being stupid. And weird."

"Ha! I can't *wait* for you to bring your first girlfriend or whatever over for the holidays. Then we'll see how ridiculous and *weird* and okay with giving them takeout you are."

Connor flushed. "If dating makes you this crazy, then I'm never dating anyone!"

"Good!"

They stayed frozen, glaring at each other from opposite ends of the kitchen, for a painfully long moment before Connor glanced away and sighed. "Seriously though...you're okay now, right?"

Spencer stole another look at his turkey. His golden, succulent, *perfect* turkey. "Yeah. Yeah, I'm fine now." He rubbed his warm cheeks and tried to pretend they were flushed from the oven's heat. "Sorry for worrying you."

"It's okay," Connor said with a shrug. He hesitated, then asked, "You...need any help?"

Spencer winced, suddenly drawn back into the dark minutes of yesterhour when Connor had asked that very same question, and he'd responded by screaming incoherently and throwing a box of stuffing at him. It was far from Spencer's proudest moment, but in his defense, he'd probably been legally insane for most of the morning-slash-early-afternoon. "Um. No. I think I've got the rest." All he had to do was keep the turkey warm, fix the cranberry sauce, microwave the gravy for Connor, cook up some pork because he vaguely remembered his mom doing that every year, boil the corn, and not burn the house down. Totally doable. "If you could take the garbage out though, that would be great." He kicked the open heavy-duty bag next to him, scowling at the ruined turkeys inside it. "Hopefully this place won't smell like burnt meat by the time Tim shows up," he muttered.

"Sure." Connor made a face as he tied the bag up and tried to lift it. "Ugh. This is so heavy."

"It smells like death too," Spencer said helpfully.

While Connor grumbled and dragged the garbage bag out of the kitchen, Spencer unstuck his black turtleneck from his chest. He had the vague thought that ovens probably weren't supposed to let out enough heat to glue people to their clothes. Maybe that's why he'd ruined so many turkeys? Because it let out too much heat and he'd ended up overcooking them to try to make up for them not being done enough? That wouldn't explain why this one cooked fine though...unless him hovering over the oven so much kept enough of the heat in, maybe...

No. That would be stupid and improbable.

Okay, enough of that. Corn time.

He filled up a pot and dumped a few ears of corn inside. And...that was all he had.

Shit. I should have looked up how to do this while the turkeys were burning.

Still, how difficult could cooking corn be? He took out his phone and searched "how long do you boil corn?"

"'How long you boil corn depends on your taste,'" he read aloud. "Well, fuck. That would be great if I actually liked corn." He continued reading silently until he reached the end of the short article. "Okay, so it's either one to two minutes for warm and crisp or three to ten for warm and soft. Good thing three to ten isn't horribly vague or anything..."

Footsteps from down the hall entered the kitchen and came to a stop behind him.

"Oh good, you're back," Spencer said without turning around. He held up a stalk—*ear, they're called ears*—of corn and gave it a little shake. "Do you think Tim would like this hard or soft?"

Of course, since he asked weirdly, it was pretty much a cosmic rule Connor wouldn't be the one standing behind him.

"There are so many ways I can go with this," Tim said.

Spencer sighed, accepting his fate—and the fact that he was destined to blush *forever* around his boyfriend—and glanced back. Tim looked unfairly great in a crisp maroon button-down and black slacks; a sharp and elegant contrast to Film School Hipster Spencer with his thin black turtleneck, black skinny jeans, and bare feet.

Tim leaned casually against the entryway with his arms crossed and an amused smirk on his lips.

"Jesus Christ, of course you look more edible than the food," Spencer muttered. Tim laughed. Spencer groaned. "I need to fucking sew my mouth shut…"

Tim pushed off the wall and walked over to him. Soft fingertips scraped their way across the light stubble on Spencer's jawline from his neck to his chin and back again. "But if your mouth is sewn shut, I can't do this." He leaned in.

"I haven't shaved since five thirty this morning," Spencer murmured in apology.

"I like it."

The barest hint of pressure under his chin had Spencer tilting his head up.

"You like that my beard grows like a Chia Pe—mmph!"

The kiss was short, but the tongue-to-kiss-time ratio was ridiculous, and Spencer was a little breathless and more than a little turned on by the time Tim pulled back. Spencer blinked as Tim plucked the corn out of his hand.

"Hard or soft, a simple ear of corn could never taste better than you."

Spencer stared in disbelief. "How the fuck can you still be smooth when you're holding *corn*?"

"You thought that was smooth?"

"Uh, yeah. Super smooth. What else…" Spencer's eyes widened. "Oh. My. God. *Please* tell me you said that with the corn, so I'd call you *corny*."

"If I did, you didn't live up to your end."

Spencer nearly moaned. How the hell did he get so lucky? "I don't know what's better, your kisses or the fact that you give me *puns*. With *props*. How the fuck can one person be so awesome?"

Tim laughed again, though Spencer didn't miss the slight flush to his cheeks. "It's a talent." He gave Spencer another quick kiss.

"Stop that," Spencer snapped before pushing up for a kiss of his own. "I'm gonna ruin dinner if you keep distracting me."

Tim peered over his shoulder. "You're not cooking anything right now though."

"Trust me, I'll find a way." Spencer summoned up the willpower to step away from Tim. "What are you doing here anyway? You said you were gonna show up at—" Spencer sent a quick, panicked glance toward the clock; nope, Spencer still had time. "—five. You"—he poked Tim in the chest—"are *early*."

Tim grinned sheepishly. "Yeah. I...forgot."

"You forgot I told you eight times to come at five?"

"I'm used to eating a lot earlier on Thanksgiving," he said, shrugging. He tilted his head and held up the ear of corn again. "I could help?"

Tim looked so bashful and boyish and just uncertain enough to be heartbreakingly adorable and—*No! Self. Control. If you start kissing him now, you're never gonna get this dinner ready.*

"Can you boil corn and make pork?" Tim nodded. Spencer smiled. "Then you're hired."

Tim smiled back and got to work. He was, of course, much better at the whole cooking thing than Spencer, which was a relief, but it also kind of made him feel a little inadequate. Ever since he realized Tim was going to be alone on Thanksgiving, he'd wanted to give him the holiday and everything that came with it. Food, family, embarrassing moments brought on by too much wine— Tim deserved it all. It was an old instinct, ingrained deep inside Spencer by societal expectations and even deeper by ancient, out-of-date hunter/gatherer instincts. He wanted to bring down a bison with a single arrow and cook the meat over an open fire. He wanted to raid the neighboring village, kill their warriors, and steal their bountiful crops. He wanted to *provide for his fucking man.*

"Do you have any butter?"

Spencer froze.

"Spencer?"

"*Shit.*"

It was probably a good thing Tim didn't really need to be provided for.

Luckily, it didn't take long for Spencer to get over it because, in the end, it *was* just outdated instincts and pressure from society. And who the hell wanted to provide when it was so much easier to *assist.*

"Where's your mixing bowl?"

"Right here."

"Knives?"

"Got 'em!"

"Can you put this in the microwave for five minutes?"

"Sure."

"Stand still for a sec?"

"Oka—mmph!"

Spencer hated to think in clichés—though he'd been slowly getting used to it recently—but he and Tim fell into making dinner together like they'd been doing it for years. They flowed around each other in the tiny kitchen like choreographed dancers, Tim taking charge and directing while Spencer followed those directions and somehow managed not to screw anything up. Spencer had barely skimmed the surface of what it meant to be in a relationship with someone, but he didn't think they were this easy for most people. Especially when they hadn't even been together for a month.

The ease continued once dinner was on the table, and Connor had been summoned out of the depths of his room. This wasn't the first time Tim had been over for dinner since they started dating, so Spencer hadn't really been too worried about him and Connor getting along. Still, this was their first Thanksgiving together—Spencer's first *ever* holiday with a boyfriend. He couldn't help that his heart did a warm flippy thing when they talked and laughed and passed the food around like they'd been doing it together their whole lives.

Like a family.

So yeah, Thanksgiving dinner ended up being a huge hit. Connor was—more or less—comfortable with Tim and Spencer being obviously couple-y; Tim was relaxed and happy, and not even a tense phone call from his mother halfway through dinner could spoil his mood for long. For the first time in Spencer's life, he *got* why his mom had always insisted on big family get-togethers even though they almost always started off with yelling and tears. Spencer would cry over burnt turkeys any day if, at the end, he got to spend time with his two favorite people; if he could see them laugh and tease each other and smile and *fit* in each other's empty spaces the way family should. At one point, Spencer almost couldn't *breathe* because of the sudden onslaught of *holy shit this is everything I ever wanted.*

The feeling stayed all throughout dinner and well into dessert—which had been provided by Tim's boss, Sarah, who Spencer had met the week before when he went to surprise Tim at work during a day off at school. She was nice—*incredibly* Texan, but nice. Although she did seem to be under the impression they'd been dating for a lot longer than three weeks. Amazing baker, though, even if Tim claimed her cupcakes weren't half as good as his mother's. Which made Spencer glad his boyfriend was being weird about even telling his mom they were dating because if he tasted anything better than these cupcakes, he'd end up inhaling them so fast he'd need to get his stomach pumped. As it was, he ate so much he was barely able to roll himself out of the kitchen and onto the couch with Tim after Connor had his fill of family time and disappeared up to his room to play video games for the rest of the night.

It was different than what he expected, what happened after Connor left. Spencer had meant to groan and hold his stomach and make jokes about how he was never going to eat anything again, and Tim had better like fat guys because there was no chance he was going to be able to hang onto what little figure he had if Tim kept bringing home irresistible desserts. Spencer didn't even get the beginnings of the first word out of his mouth. The moment Connor left, the atmosphere in the living room changed, like a plug had been removed from the bottom of a bottle. The room got smaller, the space between them sucked away into the ether until there was nothing left but stillness and silence and the gentle press of hair and skin as they curled up on the couch. The only contact between them were the two inches of forehead pressing together as they laid their heads against the backrest. They'd had moments like this before. In the backs of cabs and in movie theaters and even on this very couch a time or two. This moment felt different though. At least to Spencer. He imagined this is how his parents must have felt after their own holiday dinners when their relatives went home, and Spencer left to play his own video games, and the chaos of the day faded away until nothing remained but the satisfaction of having given their family something special.

It was a feeling Spencer could lose himself in. One he wanted again and again with Tim and with Connor for the rest of his life.

Conversation, when it happened, came in fits and starts. A "Did you get tomorrow off?" here, and a "Did you finish your grading?" there. Tim going back to school came up, again, as it tended to do, and Spencer ground his teeth together, as he also tended to do, when he thought of *why* Tim hadn't already finished; a conversation they'd had a week or so ago, and one that still got Spencer's blood boiling when he thought of it. He cooled himself off by thinking of Tim's stunned face after getting off the phone with the doctor whose grad program he was currently signed up for; apparently, Tim's Professor Dickhead never bothered following through with his threat to blacklist Tim, mostly because he already had a well-known reputation around the Illinois psychiatric community as an unprofessional lecher. There wasn't a single credible professor in the state who would take his word on anything. Not only that, Tim's new teacher at Illinois State was so appalled by what happened to Tim he'd accepted him on the spot and promised to bring the issue to the attention of the dean of CSU, who he'd gotten to know a bit through various academic get-togethers over the years. With any luck, Professor Asshole would soon be Professor Unemployed.

"So, I talked to Dr. Payton again the other day," Tim was saying. "I think I might actually be able to do this."

The wonder and awe in Tim's voice made Spencer's heart clench. "I know you can."

Tim smiled. "Thanks. But—"

"Fuck buts." Tim quirked an eyebrow. Spencer rolled his eyes. "You know what I mean. You're gonna be awesome. Best psychology doctoral student since whoever the most famous one of those is."

Tim laughed softly and lightly stroked Spencer's cheek with the backs of his fingers. "Thank you. That means a lot."

Spencer knew because they'd already had that conversation too. The one where Tim confessed how directionless and alone he'd felt after graduating college when he thought he had nothing in front of him but endless weeks and months of the same life he'd left behind in New York, except this time with no one to come home to at the end of the day, and how meeting Spencer and Connor had changed everything for the better.

Spencer had immediately turned into a sloppy, teary, emotional mess. Tim had kissed him anyway. What a fucking keeper.

"What about you?" Tim asked. "Any news on your new room?"

"It's not mine yet," Spencer said quickly.

"It will be though," Tim said, with all the confidence Spencer had just shown in *him* but could never have in himself.

"Cass hasn't heard anything recently; he could have changed his mind. And even if he hasn't yet, no one's switching rooms until next year, so he's still got a lot of time."

And that wasn't even mentioning all the crap he'd have to deal with from his jealous colleagues when it finally came out he was one of the frontrunners. Although, maybe the resentment had already started, if the dirty glares he'd gotten from a few of them the day before Thanksgiving break were any indication.

He made a mental note to check for buttered floors or suspiciously landmine-shaped lumps in his desk chair on Monday.

"You'll get it," Tim said. "You deserve it."

Spencer snorted. "If only we all got what we deserved."

"I think you did." Tim pulled his head back just enough so they could meet each other's eyes and smiled again. This one was small but bright and more than a little bit teasing. "Don't you?"

Spencer's lips twitched. "Maybe."

"*Maybe*?" Tim sighed. "I guess I'll just have to convince you."

Spencer was still trying not to grin when Tim pressed his lips to Spencer's.

Their kiss started out the way all their kisses did, slow but deep, building and building. This time, though, something changed. Maybe it was the angle of Tim's lips, or the faint aftertaste of wine on his tongue, the first taste of alcohol Spencer had had in fifteen years. Or maybe it was the night itself, the creeping sense of *family,* and *I want this,* and *please don't let this ever go away* covering the two of them like a blanket. Whatever it was, their kiss changed from something familiar into something new. Something a little bit rougher, a little bit needier—a little bit *more*. Where before Spencer or Tim would have pulled back, they found themselves racing forward. Fingertips traced cheeks and jaws, then trailed lower over necks and shoulders. Spencer gripped Tim's bicep and shuddered as he felt Tim's hand slide over the back of his shirt, high at first, then lower and lower and lower...

"Oh God."

"What?" Tim murmured against his lips.

"You're—oh!" Spencer's breath hitched as Tim's fingers slipped under the hem of his shirt. He'd forgotten what it felt like, having fingers on his skin. "Shit."

"Something wrong?"

"Nonono," Spencer moaned. Fuck, he was harder than he'd ever been in his life. "Touchmetouchmetouchme."

"Okay." Tim slid his hand into Spencer's shirt, his fingers hot against Spencer's skin. He stroked Spencer's back, up and down, tracing his spine with soft fingertips, lifting Spencer's shirt higher and higher with each caress. "God, you're so smooth."

Spencer let out a noise that was closer to a giggle than he'd like to admit. "Gillette knows their shit."

"You shave?"

"Mmm." Spencer licked Tim's lips. "Have to." He gasped when Tim licked his tongue back, then moaned when he sucked it into his mouth. *This is the filthiest fucking kissing ever. I love it.* "Look like a carpet otherwise."

Tim pulled back, his eyes glazed like...well, like one of the fifty or so donuts Spencer had eaten earlier, and didn't *that* just make him feel sexy... "Do you—" Tim cleared his throat. "—do you shave...everywhere?"

"From the neck down," Spencer said, flushing slightly. *Oh God, is that a problem? Is he one of those body-hair guys?* He might have asked, but from the way Tim closed his eyes and groaned, he thought he might have his answer already.

"Fuck. I need. God, I need to..."

"Yeah." Spencer nodded, though he had no idea what he was agreeing to. He'd be okay with anything if it got Tim's lips back on him. "Do it."

Tim surged forward and, yep, there were the lips. Spencer opened his mouth the moment he felt Tim's tongue. *I could do this forever…*

And he might have, too, if the feeling of fingers tracing their way across his stomach hadn't snapped him right out of his lust-induced haze.

"Ah! Um. No—" He pushed Tim's hand off his belly and yanked his shirt down.

Tim stilled, his expression concerned. "What? Is this too much?"

"No! You just…you don't need to touch…there."

"You don't like it?"

Spencer grimaced. "I'd rather get a little farther before you get totally turned off by my fat."

"Are you kidding right now?"

Well, at least he's not trying to tell me I'm not fat. That's…something, I guess. "No?"

Tim studied him for a long moment, then sighed. "Spencer, there is nothing about you that turns me off." His eyes flickered down toward his own lap. Spencer followed his gaze without thinking and— *Oh, that's a pretty big hard-on filling out those pants.*

"I think you're hot," Tim went on. Spencer scoffed. "You *are.* And since I'm not you, that means my opinion is worth twice as much."

"That makes no sense."

Tim ignored him. "And *this.*" He gave Spencer's belly a quick caress ending with a gentle squeeze. "This is really sexy to me."

"You're fucking kidding me."

Tim raised an eyebrow. "Do you need me to pull it out and show you how hard I am for you?"

Spencer...stopped. Just...fucking *stopped*. "Oh, my God. Yes, please."

Tim's lips quirked. "Yeah?"

Spencer nodded rapidly. Safe to say, his lust was making a roaring comeback. "Fuck yes." Shit, who cared if Tim had been lying about finding his pudgy stomach hot? Spencer hadn't seen anyone else's dick in the flesh in like ten years. Not even his many insecurities could stand up against a decade of desperation. "Wait, no, *shit*. We're still in the living room."

"Upstairs?"

"Ye-es!" Spencer's voice caught as Tim lightly ran his hand across the erection filling out Spencer's suddenly way-too-tight jeans. *Fuck, he's gonna kill me.* "Now. Right now, or I don't care how traumatized Connor might get. You're gonna come all over me right fucking here."

Tim's pupils were blown as he stared at Spencer in what could only be described as *shock and awe*. They both stilled, breathing heavily and staring into each other's eyes...and then the moment broke, and they scrambled off the couch and all but ran to the stairs.

"Shh!" Spencer grabbed Tim, stopping him before he could start to gallop up. "Kid's room is right at the top. We need to be quiet, or he'll come out." Tim stifled a laugh. "What?"

"Nothing," Tim said, clearing his throat. "I just got this image of you as Elmer Fudd going, 'Be vewy, vewy qwiet,' and sneaking past Connor's room on your tiptoes."

"Elmer Fudd? Really?" Spencer raised an eyebrow, then shook his head. "And people say I'm the old one."

"No one says that but you."

"Doesn't make it untrue."

"Do you want to argue? Or do you want me to come on you?"

Spencer bit back a groan as, somehow, his cock got even harder. "Shit. Okay. Yeah. Just...ah, fuck it. Be very, very, quiet," he deadpanned.

It was a goddamn miracle Tim's hysterical, barely muffled giggling didn't give them away.

*

Somewhere in the back of Tim's mind there was a very vivid picture of exactly what it would look like if Connor opened his door and saw him with his hands down Spencer's pants.

Thankfully, it was easy to ignore.

They'd barely gone three feet past Connor's room before Tim's hands were back on Spencer's body. *God*, that body though. He'd never been with anyone as soft and rounded as Spencer before. He'd never even known that was something he'd be into until he had his hands under Spencer's shirt. Slender waists and tight abs had *nothing* on the gently curved, slightly squishy roundness Spencer hid under those sweaters. And the fact that he shaved too—which was definitely something Tim knew he liked—pretty much made Spencer the hottest person in the world. His earlier plans of taking it slow and going at Spencer's pace were completely and utterly shattered. It was blind luck Spencer seemed to be on the exact same page.

"Fuck," Spencer said, hissing slightly when Tim pushed him up against the wall and kissed him. Spencer kissed like a wet dream; hard and rough, with teeth and tongue and lips used in equal measure, but his mouth was always willing to yield when Tim asserted any kind of control. In fact, Spencer seemed to get off on that more than anything else. He wasn't subby about it either, which Tim appreciated. As much as he loved teasing his partners during sex, he'd never really gone in for the whole Dom thing. He'd tried the whole Master and slave thing before, once, and the experience had left him feeling like he was trying to act out a play he hadn't read the script for. This was different. This was more like Spencer desperately wanted to be pleasured. Like he took the most pleasure in *being* pleasured, instead of seeking it out himself. And while Daddies and Masters and all that might not be Tim's kink, being *needed* definitely was.

"We need to get to your room," Tim said as he nibbled on Spencer's jaw. "I need to see you naked."

"Ah! Oh, God." Spencer gripped Tim's shoulders tight. "Room. Lights. *Fuck.*"

Tim grinned against the smooth-rough skin of Spencer's face and ran his fingers over Spencer's shirt-covered nipple again.

"What was that?" Tim asked.

"*Guh.*"

Tim laughed. "Is this one yours?"

"Yeah. Probably." Even as he was talking, his fingers were fumbling with the doorknob. Tim had just enough time to notice Spencer's room shared a wall with Connor's before the door opened and Spencer was dragging him inside. "Oh good, it *is* mine."

Tim closed the door behind them, remembering at the last second not to slam it. Spencer reached past him and locked it. When he made to pull back, Tim grabbed his wrist and pulled him close. Spencer was breathing heavily, his chest rising and falling against Tim's own as he peered up at him with eyes filled with lust and need and the slightest edge of uncertainty.

"I need to see you naked," Tim said again, solemnly this time with none of the ragged desire that was pooled in his stomach. He ran his free hand up and down Spencer's side, then gave his shirt a gentle tug upward. "Can I take this off?"

"Um." Spencer stared, wide-eyed. "I—can I—maybe—um. The lights? I should turn them off. First."

"You don't have to," Tim said, keeping his voice as soft and even as possible. He desperately wanted to be able to see his boyfriend's body, but if Spencer really wanted the lights off, then Tim wouldn't press. Tim had never pressured someone into doing something they didn't want to, and he wasn't going to start with the man he loved.

"I feel like I do."

"Do you *want* the light off?"

Spencer said nothing. Tim held his breath. Finally, Spencer glanced away and shook his head.

That was all the permission Tim needed.

"Then let's get this off."

Instead of ripping Spencer's shirt off and exposing all that pale baby-soft skin, Tim lifted up his own shirt and pulled it over his head. Spencer's eyes darkened as they ran up and down his body, and Tim held back a smile. He'd never been quite as fit as he'd wanted, but since he and Spencer got together, he'd been trying to work some basic exercise back into his day. As a result, his arms and chest were a little harder, a little more defined than they'd been in years. His stomach was still flat, even if the abs he'd had as a young teenager were long gone, and he felt a surge of satisfaction at the way Spencer's gaze lingered on his torso. It was quickly drowned out by a much more powerful surge of lust when Spencer tentatively brushed the skin of Tim's stomach with his fingers. Spencer chewed his lip, then began lightly tugging on the wispy hairs of the small brown treasure trail that started just below Tim's belly button. Tim shuddered at the unexpected sensations, and Spencer grinned.

"Your turn," Tim whispered.

The grin slipped a bit, but Spencer nodded. "Yeah. Okay then." He ripped his shirt off the way most people would rip off a bandage and tossed it aside. He stared up at Tim, a challenging gleam in his eye, like he was daring him to be turned off.

Nothing could be further from the truth.

Spencer's body was small with narrow shoulders and a flat chest with two small pink nipples that stuck out about half an inch. Tim nearly whimpered out loud. He'd always had a thing for nipples, and he started to salivate at the possibility of getting them in his mouth. Spencer's stomach was as sexy as he'd imagined: a gentle, protruding curve with just the slightest bit of visible softness. Tim groaned and unconsciously squeezed his cock through his pants.

"You're beautiful," he said.

Spencer's eyes were glued to Tim's crotch. "Okay," he said faintly, "I believe you. I mean, you know, *you too*, but..." He shook his head and let out a short, breathy laugh. "I feel hot when you look at me." He groaned and covered his face. "God, who says shit like that?"

Tim answered by pulling Spencer's hands down and kissing him, smirking mentally when his boyfriend melted into his arms. *Physical affection is the best way to get Spencer out of his head, good to know.*

As they made out, Spencer walked backward, grabbing Tim by the belt and pulling him along. They both groaned when their bare chests touched for the first time, but even that wasn't nearly enough. Tim hadn't been touched in so long—hadn't expected to be for a while yet and for months before getting with Spencer had pretty much resigned himself to a life of celibacy. Being here, in Spencer's bedroom, with a topless Spencer grabbing at his pants, was almost more temptation than his good-boy impulses could handle.

"Naked," he rasped, "now."

Spencer nodded rapidly, then pushed Tim away. Tim blinked in confusion, but before he could say anything, Spencer had his own pants undone, peeling them off so fast it had to be some kind of record for removing skinny jeans. Tim moaned when he saw Spencer's smooth, slender legs for the first time and the—*dear God*—tiny, tight black briefs just barely keeping him decent. Spencer flushed slightly when he saw the way Tim was devouring him with his eyes, and Tim almost came. He'd never been with anyone who blushed so beautifully, and with Spencer a thin bit of fabric away from being naked, even a tiny bit of pink on his cheeks was deadly.

Then, when he thought he couldn't possibly be more aroused, Spencer glanced up at him and flashed a wicked smile before turning around and *stretching*. Tiny, barely visible muscles clenched in his shoulders as he raised his hands above his head and stood on the balls of his feet. Tim's eyes devoured every inch of exposed skin, pulled tight and displayed just for him. Spencer must have had some kind of sixth sense for where Tim was looking because the moment his gaze dipped toward Spencer's fabric-covered ass, he tightened up and gave his hips a little shake.

"Fuck..."

Spencer glanced over his shoulder, his expression surprised and more than a little pleased. "You like?"

Tim couldn't even speak. The delicate swell of Spencer's ass held all his attention. He couldn't resist anymore. He reached out and grabbed it, moaning softly as he gave the cheeks a squeeze. They were a little on the small side, but they had just the right amount of spongy give to drive Tim crazy. Spencer let out a surprised yelp and fell forward, only to be caught around the waist by Tim's arm and pulled back tight against his chest. They both let out low groans when Tim's diamond-hard cock pressed right into the center of Spencer's crack.

"Okay, forget coming on me," Spencer said, breathlessly. "I need—"

Tim drove his hips forward.

"Ah! Yeah, that."

Tim bit his lip, hard; the pain was the only thing keeping him from finishing in his pants right there. "Are you sure?"

"Yes!"

Showing surprising strength, Spencer pushed Tim's arm away before spinning around and dragging him down into another kiss. They stumbled backward, Spencer's hands tangled in Tim's hair as Tim fought to open his pants. He eventually got it and even managed to kick them and his boxers off without tripping. Spencer didn't seem to notice his newly naked state at first, at least not until Tim's dripping cock brushed against his stomach.

"Oh my God," Spencer moaned, pulling away from Tim's mouth and staring down. The moment he saw it, his eyes widened. "Holy shit!"

"What?"

Spencer stared incredulously. "What do you mean, *what*? That thing is huge!"

Tim couldn't help it; he preened—even though, if he were being honest, his length was pretty average, *maybe* slightly above. He was thicker than most, though, and that definitely made him seem larger.

"It's not that big," Tim demurred.

Spencer raised an eyebrow. "I'd hate to see what you think is big, then. Jesus. Now there's no way I'm getting naked in front of you."

That broke Tim out of his self-satisfied mood. "What? Why?"

"Really? Why do you think?" Spencer gestured between the two of them. "You're all..." He held his hands apart like he was showing someone the size of the last fish he caught. "*This*. And I'm all..." He grimaced and lowered his hands, not even attempting to mime out a comparison. "Let's just say everything's proportional, okay?"

Ohhh.

"You know I don't care, right?" Tim glanced at Spencer's brief-covered cock which, despite everything, hadn't lost a bit of hardness. "Besides, those little things you're wearing don't leave a lot to the imagination, and from what I can see you're plenty big enough for me."

Spencer flushed, and Tim decided to grab the bull by the horns, as it were, before he could fall further into self-deprecation.

"Yep," Tim said as he gave Spencer's cock a tight squeeze. "Definitely not too small."

The high-pitched keen that tore out of Spencer's throat was a thing of beauty. Spencer was so *responsive*. And this was still through a layer of fabric. What would Spencer sound like when it was finally skin on skin?

Let's find out.

Tim tugged at the waistband of Spencer's briefs. "Can I?" He gave Spencer's length another caress. "Please?"

Spencer pressed his lips together and nodded rapidly. Tim wasted no time. He lifted the waistband over Spencer's cock, very carefully not touching it at all as it was exposed. Spencer was about an inch or two shorter than he was, and much thinner. Like he'd been promised, there wasn't a single hair to be seen, and Tim wanted nothing more than to drop to his knees, bury his face in Spencer's crotch, and rub against all his soft-looking skin.

So, he did.

Spencer jumped in surprise, then moaned when Tim rubbed his smooth cheek over equally smooth skin. He took a deep breath, inhaling the unmistakable musty scent of male, mixed with a very light floral aroma Tim assumed was body lotion. It was intoxicating. Tim had always loved the way men smelled between their legs, and Spencer's smell was just the right balance between earthy and sweet.

"Shit," Spencer said, breathlessly. "Are you...I'm gonna...oh God..."

Tim allowed himself a single smug grin at the stream of nonsense pouring out of Spencer's mouth.

If this is driving him crazy, I wonder how he'll react when I...

Tim tilted his head and gave the side of Spencer's shaft a long, slow lick.

Spencer's reaction didn't disappoint.

"*Oh my God!*" Spencer's whole body tensed, his hands shooting to Tim's head and grabbing his hair tight. Tim winced at the slight pain, but it wasn't nearly enough to take the edge off the pleasure he felt at seeing Spencer come nearly undone from a simple lick.

"You are so sensitive," Tim said, awed.

"Fuck," Spencer said as his body, incongruously, relaxed. "You'd be sensitive too if you just had someone's mouth on your dick for the first time."

Startled, Tim pulled back enough to see Spencer's face. His hair was a mess like he'd been abusing *it* before his hands found their way to Tim's, and his bottom lip was bitten almost raw. "No one's ever...?"

The light flush on Spencer's cheeks deepened. "No?"

Tim stared at him in disbelief. *What kind of idiots did Spencer date? How could anyone get him naked and not want to put their mouth on him? Or...maybe I made too many assumptions...*

"Have you..." Tim hesitated, but there was really no delicate way to ask so he plowed on. "Have you ever been with a guy before?"

"Yes!" Spencer practically shouted, his entire body radiating indignant embarrassment.

"Sorry," Tim said. "You're just...perfect. And I can't believe anyone could get you like this and resist..." Instead of finishing his sentence verbally, Tim gave Spencer another slow lick. Spencer moaned loudly, and his fingers twitched in Tim's hair.

"That is *so*—mmm, yeah." Spencer shook himself and fixed Tim with a *look*. "I'm not a virgin though. I'm *twenty-eight*. I've been with men." He winced. "Well, *man*, I guess. College boyfriend. Only one that lasted long enough for me to trust with...you know..."

By the time Spencer finished speaking, his voice had trailed off into an embarrassed mumble. *You sure know how to set the mood, Tim...*

"You know I wouldn't care, right?" Tim asked, running his hands up and down Spencer's smooth legs.

Spencer shuddered under his touch. "If you'd never been with anyone or if you'd been with a hundred guys. I'd still find you hot, and I'd still want to get my hands—" He gave the backs of Spencer's thighs a squeeze. "—and my *mouth*—" Tim's lips grazed Spencer's weeping, flared head, getting a taste of the sweetest precome he'd ever encountered. "—all over you."

He suckled lightly on the tip of Spencer's cock, needing more of that superb sweetness. A sharp bolt of pain tore through his head as Spencer's hands tightened to the point where Tim would be shocked if he hadn't torn a bit of hair off. Not even the thought of having his hair ripped out was enough to dim Tim's arousal.

"You're wrong about one thing though," Tim said, staring up into Spencer's lust-blown eyes.

"W-what?"

"You might have been with a guy, but you've never been with a man. Because no man on Earth could see what I'm seeing and not want to do *this*."

A slow, dark grin spread across Tim's lips right before he swallowed Spencer's cock in one smooth motion.

*

Spencer's entire world contracted until there was nothing left but hot, wet *suction*. Was this how it always felt being on the other side of a blowjob? Because if it was, holy shit, now he understood sex in a way he never had before. No wonder Sebastian always got so excited when Spencer wanted to blow him. This was...well. Spencer's brain was a bit too overwhelmed with *oh fuck his tongue,* so it wasn't really up to searching through adjectives, but later on the only word that would come to mind would be *sublime.* Not quite as good as being fucked through an orgasm—

although it had been so long his memories might be exaggerating how amazing that felt—but still light-years better than the last time he'd tried putting himself inside another person, which happened to be Becky.

Tim licked and sucked, his hands running lightly over Spencer's too-sensitive skin, touching, caressing, and every once in a while *scratching* with his fingernails. Spencer was totally overloaded with sensations, and in an embarrassingly short amount of time, he was on the edge of what was sure to be an absolutely mind-blowing orgasm.

"T-Tim! Gonna—"

That was all the warning he could get out before his abdomen tightened and—

Tim stopped.

Tim stopped.

Worse, Tim stopped, then grabbed the base of Spencer's cock to make sure he couldn't come.

The sound Spencer made in protest was barely recognizable as human.

"*Why?*" Spencer whined, dragging the word out several syllables longer than it had any right to be and only peripherally aware he was sounding way too much like his kid.

Tim grinned, the low lighting in the room creating shadows that gave his face a sinister cast. "Oh, you wanted me to keep going?"

Or maybe his innate evil was just showing through.

"You're—ah!"

Tim gave Spencer's cock a long, slow lick; the smooth, wet muscle slid up his shaft like silk. It felt *so* good, and Spencer's grip on Tim's hair tightened as he let out a long moan. Once he reached the tip, though, Tim stopped *again* and pulled away. He did this for a while, teasing Spencer to the brink, driving him crazy with lust and need and pulling back right when he was *finally* about to release. It was torture. Pure, unambiguous, Geneva-Convention-level torture.

Spencer had never felt so much pleasure in his *life*.

Tim played his body like a familiar instrument, somehow knowing instinctively exactly what spots on Spencer to touch and pinch and scratch, exactly how much pressure and suction to use to pull the most embarrassing, feral noises out of Spencer's throat. It seemed like his hands were everywhere except, maddeningly enough, anywhere between Spencer's tightly clenched cheeks. Despite Tim totally ignoring his favorite erogenous zone, eventually Spencer's legs became so weak he had to let go of Tim's hair and brace himself against the edge of the bed to keep from collapsing. His pleasure crested and waned, growing higher and higher only to pull back like the super wave at the end of *The Abyss* the moment before it would have come crashing down. After a while, he didn't even care he wasn't being allowed to finish. He lived for the *build*, for the slow pressure that came closer and closer to being unbearable, then danced across the line with blithe disregard, sending him into a realm of permanent, agonizing bliss.

Tim was obviously some kind of sadistic genius, because it seemed like no sooner had Spencer learned to love the feeling of constantly being on the edge, Tim gently flicked his tongue into the slit in Spencer's head, let go of the base, and ever so gently grazed his fingertips over the smooth, sensitive skin just behind Spencer's balls.

Spencer had just enough sense left to cover his mouth with his hands before he screamed and came down Tim's throat.

He didn't even realize he'd collapsed back onto the bed until he felt the mattress dip as Tim lay down next to him and pulled him over to rest against his chest. Those skilled, gentle, *evil* fingers brushed damp hair away from Spencer's sweat-slicked forehead as he slowly came back to himself.

"*Fuck*," Spencer said breathlessly.

Tim made a small humming noise. "Good?"

"If you wanna wait five minutes for my brain to start working again, I can go through my mental thesaurus and think of something better, but for now..." Spencer sighed happily and nuzzled Tim's firm chest. "Yeah, good."

They stayed cuddled together for a few minutes; Spencer floated along on a post-sex high while Tim ran his fingers through his hair and, every so often, over his shoulder and arm as well. Spencer shivered pleasantly at the light touches.

"Has it been five minutes yet?"

Spencer blinked as Tim's words brought him out of his sleepy almost-doze. "Dude, did you just ask me to tell time?"

Tim snorted. "'Dude'?"

"Shut up," he said, feeling his cheeks start to burn. "I'm not that old—holy shit, you're still hard!"

Distantly, he heard Tim laughing, but it didn't really register. He was too busy staring down at Tim's stiff, slightly leaking cock in growing mortification.

I just came and left him hanging. Oh my God, I'm the worst.

Before Spencer could think, he reached out and grabbed it. A surge of satisfaction shot through him when Tim's laughter stuttered, but it was short-lived and quickly replaced by *holy crap I'm holding someone's cock again* and *fuuuuck this thing is thick.* He couldn't even get his fingers to touch.

Move or...something! Don't just sit here holding it.

Spencer slowly began jerking Tim off. Tim let out a low moan.

"That feels so good."

Heat pooled in Spencer's groin at Tim's words, and absently he wondered if he'd developed a praise kink sometime in the last ten years or so. He'd never had one before; hell, he'd never been into dirty talk before, and *that's* definitely changed. He felt his face heat up as he replayed some of the things he'd said earlier—*come all over me? Who says shit like that?*—but even though it was embarrassing, remembering only added to his arousal.

Spencer had never been bold in bed. He'd always been too scared, too shy to ask for what he wanted, content to fumble around and be led like the blushing, hormone-crazed virgin he'd been. Age hadn't given him much in the way of experience, but maybe his teenage hormones evening out had been enough to give him some measure of confidence. Or maybe it was because he was doing this with Tim, who went out of his way to make sure Spencer knew how attractive he found him. Who was calm and patient and the hottest fucking thing *ever.* Who tore Spencer apart and didn't even bother putting him back together because things were a hell of a lot more fun to play with when they were in pieces. Who, with just a few words and a lot of touching, made Spencer feel *sexy* for the first time in his life.

I could ask for anything I want, and he wouldn't laugh at me.

He had no idea where the thought came from, or even if it was true, but that didn't matter. It *felt* true. And if there was anything Tim had taught him tonight, it was that feelings had power.

Though, even with all the tantalizing possibilities in front of him, there was still only one thing Spencer wanted.

"I need you inside me."

Tim shuddered. "Yes," he hissed. "We need lube and—" Spencer couldn't resist rubbing the sensitive skin under Tim's head. "—ah! Oh my...condoms! *Now.*"

As tempting as it was to get some payback for earlier, there was no way Spencer had that kind of self-control. He let go of Tim—prompting a surprisingly cute whine from the man—and crawled across his bed to rummage through the nightstand. "Got the lube!" He tossed the small bottle toward Tim.

"Condoms?"

Spencer made a face. "If I have any, they're packed away with my college shit."

Tim froze. "You don't have any?"

"Why would I?" Spencer asked, feeling slightly defensive. "Do *you* have any?"

"No..."

"Well, there you go." Spencer started to lean back and begin what would no doubt be a very shameless display filled with spread legs and probably more than a little begging, only to realize he might have jumped from point *B* to *D* while Tim was still very firmly stuck on *C*. "Do we...need them?"

Tim's face twisted into an expression of...well. Horror might have been an understatement. "I..."

"I'm clean," Spencer said, flushing slightly. "They made me get a full physical before I started teaching with blood work and drug testing and everything, and it all came back negative. I obviously haven't been having bareback sex parties all these years, so..." He trailed off with a forced laugh. "I'd be fine giving them a skip."

Biggest. Understatement. Ever.

"I've...never had sex without one," Tim said slowly like he was still unsure if they were even having this conversation.

"Oh." Spencer chewed his lip. "First time for everything?" he asked hopefully.

"Spencer..."

"Sorry," Spencer muttered, trying to hide the crushing disappointment settling in on his chest. "But, I mean, I trust you, you know? So, if you say you're clean too, I have no reason not to believe you. and if you trust me too then..." He swallowed heavily. "Do you...not?"

"Of course, I trust you," Tim said, thankfully able to decode Spencer's ramblings. "I don't know if I can have sex without them though. That's...a pretty big thing, you know?"

Spencer made a vague noise, but otherwise stayed silent. This probably wasn't the best time to tell Tim he'd *never* used condoms and, honestly, kind of hated the idea. Sure, safe sex was important and all, but really half the enjoyment Spencer got from sex was feeling his partner come inside him. He loved the wet, sticky, *used* feeling he got between his legs after sex, the way the come dripped down his thighs when he stood up, the way he could reach down and *feel* the mess, everything. It was the one kink he had that came close to being necessary for him to enjoy sex, and the idea of possibly not getting it his first time with Tim very nearly devastated Spencer. And not in the good way.

"I'm clean too though," Tim said. "I got tested after I broke up with Rudy, and I haven't been with anyone since."

Spencer bit back the *So, what's the problem?* that wanted to come out.

"Just putting it out there, but I'd be more than okay with going bare." Spencer tried to keep his voice as neutral as possible, well aware he was skirting the line of pressuring Tim into doing something he wasn't comfortable with. "But if you're not, that's...okay too. I could just, you know, do what you did."

"I didn't say that," Tim said quickly. Judging by the expression on his face, it was probably a toss-up as to which one of them was more surprised by his words.

"Oh?"

Tim shifted so he was sitting cross-legged on the bed facing Spencer, which was...all kinds of distracting because he was still half-hard and *glistening* and—

Spencer forced his eyes up when Tim cleared his throat. He expected to see Tim giving him a knowing look, but he wasn't even watching Spencer. He cleared his throat again, then let out a little huff.

"What's wrong?" Spencer asked.

"Nothing." Tim laughed softly. "Nothing at all." He peered up at Spencer through his eyelashes, a surprisingly vulnerable gesture from someone who had been so in control a few minutes ago. "But I do have something I need to tell you."

A brick settled inside Spencer's stomach. Never in the history of spoken language had the phrases "We need to talk" or "I need to tell you something" led to anything good.

"Oh?" he asked again, his voice cracking.

"It's nothing bad," Tim said, smiling gently. "I hope, anyway. I've wanted to say it for a while, but I figured it was too soon, and I didn't want to come on too strong or move too fast or...anything. I sort of have a history of...all of that, really. The thing is, though, I've felt like this before, and I've said the words before, but I've never even considered ditching the condoms with anyone before. And when I realized I was prepared to do that with you, it seemed....kind of stupid to be okay with that and not okay with telling you how...ridiculously in love with you I am and—*mmph*!"

The second the *L* word was out of Tim's mouth, Spencer lost all control. He leaped across the small space between them and crashed into Tim, knocking him back and fucking...*slamming* their lips together. Thankfully Tim got with the program pretty quick, kissing back and slipping his tongue inside Spencer's mouth and grabbing his hair and—*fuck*, he was feeling too many things. Physical feelings and emotional feelings and things he couldn't even quantify were all swirling around inside him, stopping off in his stomach to flip it around a bit. Moving onto his heart and stopping it and swelling it and making it skip beats and all that cliched shit. Speeding up to his head and exploding into a fucking riot of colors behind his eyes. He felt completely drunk like he hadn't let himself be since that night with Becky, but this was so completely different because instead of alcohol and self-loathing, he was drunk on love. At that moment, hearing one stupid word he'd said a million times in his life about food and movies and video games and all sorts of unimportant *shit* coming out of Tim's mouth, wrapped in nerves and awe and *meaning*, Spencer felt like he could kick down the door to the universe and *own* that bitch.

"You don't need to say it back," Tim said, breathlessly, pushing Spencer away just enough to meet his eyes. "I don't expect—"

Spencer kissed his words away. "Shut the *fuck* up." He bit Tim's lip for emphasis. "Of *course*, I fucking love you. You're just so...*ugh*. I'm sharing my fucking *kid* with you. And fuck what I said before, I *want* you to be his other dad. I want him to call your parents Grandma and Grandpa, and I want you to meet my parents, and I want us all to have those awful, awkward holidays together where your dad and my dad argue politics, and my mom brings a casserole that no one eats, and your mom gets all passive-aggressive about wanting us to visit more, and we all hate it, but we go every year, and fuck, I want *years* with you. Years we can rank and say, 'This year wasn't as good as last year, but I think next year's gonna be amazing because I'll be with you,' and completely ignore that we were together *last* year too because it's a stupid schmaltzy thing couples say, and I'm warning you right now I'm probably gonna come in my *pants* the first time you do a dad joke with Connor. I'm not even kidding."

He broke off and took a deep breath and leaned down, the tips of his curls brushing against Tim's forehead. His heart began pounding again, newly restarted and energized. This was somehow the most and least eloquent he'd ever been about his feelings, and he didn't even care how much of a rambling mess he was, because *Tim loved him,* and nothing had ever made anyone else this happy in the whole of existence.

"I want *everything* with you," he said, his soft voice a complete contrast to the sheer amount of *meaning* behind his words. "And you think there's any chance I don't love you."

"I know better now," Tim said, matching Spencer's tone with wide, suspiciously shimmering eyes.

"Damn right you do," Spencer said, and then he kissed him.

It didn't take long for slow, sensual kissing to turn into touching and then into frantic grabbing and rutting. Physical pleasure mixed with a constant refrain of *lovelovelovehelovesmeIlovehimfuckfuckfuck* until Spencer could barely think. The world outside himself came in flashes. Tim's mouth on his neck. His hands grabbing the backs of Spencer's thighs. Pressing down on Tim only to blink and realize Tim was now on top of *him.* Gently probing fingers slipping between his legs—*when did they get so slick?*—teasing, touching, slipping inside—*fuck, it's been so long*—curling and sending jolts of half-forgotten pleasure through his body. One finger turning to two turning to three, and Spencer was, impossibly, hard again and *aching.* Tim's own hardness was sitting heavy on his hip, and Spencer had never needed anything so badly in his entire life.

He must have said something he couldn't remember because the next thing he knew the fingers were gone—*empty, wet, need more*—and the thick, blunt head of—*oh fuck, finally*—Tim's cock teased his entrance before slowly—*too slow, need it now, fuck it's so thick, I've never been this full*—pushing inside.

Spencer heard noises, moans, keens, and pleas for *more,* and they must have been coming at least partly from him because *more* was exactly what he got. Tim pulled out so just the tip of him was inside Spencer, then slammed home hard and—Spencer didn't even have the words. Being fucked was *the* be all, end all for sex as far as he was concerned; not even Tim's life-altering blowjob could change how much Spencer loved having a cock inside him. This, though...this wasn't just Tim fucking Spencer or Spencer being fucked. No matter how hard Tim went, or how shamelessly Spencer spread himself or wrapped himself around Tim, squeezed or scratched or bit or *was* bitten, it was also Tim making love to Spencer. He could feel it in every thrust, in the way Tim covered him with his body, protecting him and holding him close, until Spencer couldn't be sure he wasn't, in some indefinable way that went beyond anything he ever thought he could experience, inside Tim as well. Tim's eyes, hot with lust and soft with love, never left his, and Spencer couldn't look away. Tim's hands finally settled on his hips, gripping tightly and pulling Spencer to him as he drove himself inside, occasionally slipping down to cup Spencer's ass and pull him open to get that little bit deeper.

There was no room for insecurity, no room for doubt or worry or anything outside of the two of them. The whole universe contracted until nothing existed but the small opening in Spencer's body where they were connected. And when Spencer finally touched himself and came all over his stomach *again*, his internal muscles pulsed and squeezed around Tim, sending his smooth, hard rhythm into stuttering, jerky movements, and he came deep inside Spencer with a drawn out, guttural groan.

Spencer had never felt anything better in his entire life.

When the world finally settled back into something familiar again, Tim had collapsed on his back and Spencer was sprawled on top of him, his head resting on Tim's sweat-slicked chest, listening to his slowly steadying heartbeat. He closed his eyes, not even trying to keep the wide, stupid smile off his face. *That was amazing.* He clenched his hole, shivering at the wet sogginess he could feel, sweetness and raunchiness meeting in what had to be the greatest dichotomy ever.

Suddenly, a thought popped into Spencer's head, startling a laugh out of him.

"What?" Tim's voice was on the edge of sleep, not quite slurred, but Spencer was obviously the more *present* of the two of them.

"Nothing," Spencer said, letting out another huff of amusement. "Just, now that I actually said the words, I'm realizing I've been in love with you way longer than I'd like to admit."

"Mmm." Tim yawned and started playing with the hair at the back of Spencer's neck. "I've loved you since that night on the couch."

Spencer almost asked which night he was talking about, but he kind of thought finding out Tim had fallen in love with him while Spencer told the story of how he knocked up a thirteen-year-old girl would break the mood, so instead he grinned into Tim's chest. "So, basically, on the outside we were both being super responsible and not rushing anything and taking things slow, but on the inside, we were already house hunting and trying to figure out how many new siblings Connor would be okay with?"

There was a long moment of silence, followed by a "Wh-what?" from a suddenly much more awake sounding Tim. "Is that...do you want more kids?"

Spencer blinked, not at the question, which he'd kind of invited honestly, but at the tone. Confusion mixed with fear and a tiny bit of something that might have been hope. Spencer didn't know what to say, so he defaulted to the answer he always gave when someone asked him if he'd ever have another kid.

"Nah. I can't even play video games more than once because they're too damn long these days. Going through the whole kid thing again is just...no."

Then, because he apparently wasn't done proving how perfect he was, Tim said without missing a beat, "No matter how long a game is, or how many times you've played it, sometimes going back and playing it with someone else can make the whole experience new again."

Spencer stilled as a new world of possibility opened in front of him, his plans for the future rearranging themselves into new, terrifying, wonderful ideas...

He took a deep breath and let them all go.

"This seems like a conversation we should be having a year or two from now."

"Okay," Tim agreed, sounding happy and sleepy again in equal measure. Spencer wondered about the happy, considering the conversation, until he realized how causally he'd assumed they'd still be together years from now, talking about *kids*. It reeked of commitment in a way even exchanging I love yous didn't, and Spencer was...more than okay with that.

"Come on," he said. "Let's get some sleep."

"Connor will know I spent the night."

Spencer wrinkled his nose, then shrugged. "He'll have to get used to it at some point."

Nothing more was said, so Spencer closed his eyes.

*

See though, the thing was, Spencer had never actually tried sleeping with someone before, since he always left Sebastian's dorm, afterward, and went back to his own. He'd read a few romance novels though, both classics from bygone years and more modern fare, and he'd seen his share of romantic movies, so he had some idea of what it would be like.

Turns out, movies and romance novels were full of shit.

Falling asleep with someone else was uncomfortable and weird. They moved and shifted, snored and stole the covers, and it took him about three minutes to realize falling asleep on Tim's chest was never going to happen. Chests were hard and they moved and were all around a terrible substitute for a real pillow. As great—no, fuck that, as utterly *transcendent* as it was to be made love to by Tim, Spencer's first time sleeping with someone was a bit of a letdown.

But that was okay. Because morning sex?

Totally lived up to the hype.

Chapter Sixteen

Tim smiled at the office secretary as she passed over the visitor's badge, politely ignoring the pink tint to her cheeks as their fingers brushed together. He slipped the badge around his neck, gave her a wave, and slipped out of the office and into the halls of Laurence Tureaud High, unable to keep his smile from growing at the idea of walking through Spencer's school. Ridiculous? Maybe. But Tim would be lying if he said this was the stupidest thing he'd caught himself mooning about in the weeks since Thanksgiving, and he refused to be embarrassed.

I'm stupidly in love with someone who loves me back; what's there to be embarrassed about?

Okay, the morning after Thanksgiving when a bleary-eyed Connor walked into the kitchen to find Tim sipping coffee and wearing the same clothes he'd had on the night before was pretty high up on the awkward scale. Less so than when, two seconds later, Tim's sleepy brain thought it would be a good idea for him to attempt to stumble his way through the sex talk and the "I'm in love with your dad" talk at the same time. Thankfully, he'd barely gotten to "when two people love each other very much" before Spencer smoothly cut in and asked Connor what he wanted for breakfast and, oh yeah, if he heard any weird noises the night before he should probably say something now and get a new pair of noise-canceling headphones out of the deal because those kinds of sounds probably weren't going to be stopping any time soon. It was a rare moment when Spencer was the only person in a room *not* blushing or avoiding eye contact, and after the awkwardness faded, it became one of the many things Tim couldn't stop smiling over when he thought back on it.

He also loved that adding sex to their relationship hadn't changed anything. Sure, there was a new *awareness*, a sense of simmering possibility that buzzed between them whenever they spent time together. Whatever they were doing *could* lead to sex, and sometimes did, but they could still do things together and have them be more than just a prelude to getting their pants off. Being with Spencer was so different to any of Tim's previous relationships, and though he'd never say it out loud, he thanked God Spencer was old enough not to be ruled by hormones.

A short, pudgy girl crashing into him with a squeak and a softly muttered "s-sorry" before running away brought him back to the present. Not that being knocked out of his thoughts did anything to dull the soft, squishy feeling in his heart. Walking through the place where Spencer spent so much of his time, a place he'd dedicated years of his life, both in studying to get here and working to be able to stay, was fascinating. Aside from the undercuts and the manbuns many of the students were sporting, Tim could have been back in his old high school with how similar everything was, but he still took it all in with a sense of awe. These weren't just students; these were students *Spencer taught*. Those weren't just lockers; they were lockers Spencer passed every day. The appreciative glances Tim caught from a lot of the girls and a few of the boys should have made him feel uncomfortable—and, to be fair, they kind of did. He'd been in bed with people who hadn't eye-fucked him so shamelessly; when did teenagers get so...forward?—but he was too busy wondering how many similar looks Spencer had gotten over the years, how many silent crushes had sprung to life over his youthful features and sharp glances and disarming smiles—

Tim snorted and shook his head. If he'd ever doubted how utterly infatuated he was...

It was kind of crazy though, this whole thing, the way he'd been acting. He wasn't new to the *L* word. He'd said it before, when he was younger and thought every new relationship was It; he'd even felt it with Rudy, in the beginning, before everything fell apart. A small part of him worried the same thing might happen with Spencer, that he'd fallen too fast and the only way this could end was in disaster.

Tim really liked telling that part to go to hell, because his relationship with Spencer was different.

They might have only been together just under a month before they said the words, but before they'd ever broached the possibility of a relationship, they'd known each other for two and a half. First as hostile strangers, then as stories told by someone else, and finally as friends before trying for more. It had been a fast progression, maybe, but it was natural, and so different from anything he'd ever had. With Rudy, the feelings came fast and they blinded him to things he should have seen much sooner. With Spencer, he got hit with the flaws first, and only later found the diamond in the rough.

Tim made his way through the halls, dodging teens rushing to and from their lockers and stepping over the occasional dropped book or spilled backpack. It was barely noon, but they were already packing up to go home, laughing and sharing in the general giddiness that came with getting out of school early. A surge of sudden, unexpected nostalgia welled inside him. Tim had always loved half days. Both his parents worked, but his mom always made a point to get home within an hour or two after he normally got home from school, so half days were the only time he had the house to himself for an extended period. He missed that feeling, the sense of freedom and possibility unique to being a teenager and knowing you were alone for at least the next five hours. As crappy as high school could be, some days he'd kill to go back to a time when his biggest worries were about getting his homework done, or finding a boy to make out with, or hiding his report card from his mom.

He shook himself out of his thoughts with a laugh. *I sound way too much like Dad on one of his "good old days" tangents right now. I'd better find Spencer's classroom before I start complaining about the economy or how City Hall is bleeding us dry.*

It took a few minutes, but he eventually found the right room and, judging by the voices inside, he wasn't too late. Connor might have a half day because of a teacher's conference in the afternoon, but Spencer didn't, which was why Tim was here to pick up Connor. They had a whole day of fast food and binge-watching *Stranger Things* planned out—something Tim had really been looking forward to. Tim had half expected not to see his boyfriend at all until much later when the conference let out, but one of the voices was his. The other one came from an unfamiliar woman, and Tim hesitated just outside the closed door and listened. If Spencer was in there with another teacher or a parent, the last thing he wanted to do was interrupt. Especially since he was self-aware enough to realize the chances of him *not* barging in and pulling Spencer into a kiss or doing something equally satisfying and completely inappropriate for school were pretty low right then.

The last thing he expected to hear was an argument.

Or, really, the tail end of one, because he'd barely begun to try to make out what they were shouting at each other before the door was yanked open and an irate woman stalked out. It was only Tim's surprised jump back that kept her from running right into him. Instead, she pulled up in surprise, her eyes widening slightly before giving him a quick once over. She seemed youngish, maybe a little older than Spencer, and tall for a woman, almost as tall as Tim, with straight brown hair pulled into an elaborate updo and a face more handsome than pretty, with sharp features seeming to toe the line between striking and off-putting. Although, part of that could have been the way her lips were still partly twisted into a sneer. She wore a pair of tight jeans and a blouse unbuttoned just enough to suggest that modesty was something she might have heard about in passing at one point, but never bothered to ask for clarification on. She also seemed oddly familiar.

"Tim?" Spencer asked.

"Hi," Tim said, giving a small, uncertain wave.

The woman studied Tim with a raised eyebrow.

"Who are you?" she asked. There was a sharpness to her question she didn't bother trying to soften. Tim was taken aback by the unnecessary hostility.

"Um. I'm—"

"He's none of your business," Spencer cut in, glaring at the woman.

Two bright spots of angry color flared to life on her cheeks as she pressed her lips together so hard, they turned white. Tim couldn't quite help the uncharitable thought that her expression pushed her face firmly over the line into "incredibly off-putting." Instead of the blowup he half expected, though, she made a visible effort to control her reaction. After a moment, she turned away from Spencer and glanced Tim over again. Then turned back to Spencer. Then back to Tim.

It didn't take her long to conclude who Tim was to Spencer.

"*Oh.*" She scoffed. "Typical."

Spencer narrowed his eyes. "What's *that* supposed to mean?"

"Nothing," the woman said, the sharp bite in her voice making it obvious she was lying. "I just think it's great that people treat me like I'm diseased but have no problem with people like *you* teaching children."

Indignation flared up in Tim's chest. "Hey—" he started but was quickly cut off by Spencer.

"*Please* finish that thought," he said quietly. "I'm begging you, say something homophobic. I'm *dying* to see how many strikes you have left."

The woman pressed her lips together again. "They never should have let men become teachers," she said after a long moment.

"Ah, a safe prejudice," Spencer said, his voice soft and laced with disgust. "What a coward."

Without another word, the woman pushed past Tim and stalked off down the hall. When she rounded the nearest corner, Spencer let out a long, heavy breath and pinched the bridge of his nose.

"Come on in." Spencer's tired smile as he ushered Tim inside the room didn't quite reach his eyes. "Kid's not here yet."

Tim walked in and Spencer closed the door. Despite his confusion, Tim couldn't help smiling at the small Darth Vader bobblehead sitting on Spencer's desk, or the posters on the walls with quotes from *The Phoenix on the Sword*, *1984*, *Fahrenheit 451*, *Call of Cthulhu*, and a few other books or stories Tim knew Spencer loved but, for various reasons, wasn't allowed to teach. Much like the posters and figures strewn throughout his house, there wasn't really any rhyme or reason or attempt to organize anything. Instead, it seemed like Spencer's interests had exploded out of him one day and stuck to the walls.

Tim loved it.

Spencer leaned against his desk with a sigh and tugged the collar of his sweater—an olive-green pullover at least one size too big—away from his neck and rubbed his stubbly face. When his arms fell back to his sides, the sleeves covered half his hands.

"God, what a fucking day," Spencer said.

"Is everything okay?" Tim asked. He rested his hip on the desk next to Spencer and angled his body to face his boyfriend. "Who was that woman? She seemed..."

"Like a pissy drama queen?"

Tim snorted. "Something like that."

"That," Spencer said, "was Steph McConnell."

Where have I heard that name before...?

"The other teacher who might get your room?"

Spencer smirked. "Well, not anymore..."

"Oh yeah?" Tim asked. "What happened?"

"Corbin officially offered it to me today," he said, bouncing lightly on the balls of his feet.

Tim grinned. "Really?"

"Yep. You're looking at the brand-new owner of the legendary room 210."

"Oh my God!" Tim pulled him into a hug. "I'm so proud of you."

Spencer hugged him back. "It's just a room..." he mumbled into his chest. Tim could almost feel Spencer's burning cheeks through his shirt.

"Nope. You said it yourself; it's validation for your whole teaching career. I get to be proud and you get to be smug. End of story."

Now it was Spencer's turn to snort. "End of story, huh?"

"Yep," Tim said, nodding. "Sorry, I don't make the rules."

Spencer laughed, and Tim loosened his arms just enough so he could pull back and stare him in the eye. "I *am* proud of you," he said softly. "I know how much you wanted this, and I can't think of anyone who deserves it more than you."

"You're biased," Spencer said, his cheeks bright red as he tried, in vain, to hold back a smile.

"Your principal isn't. And just because I'm biased doesn't mean I'm wrong."

"Okay, okay." Spencer grinned up at him. "I'm awesome and I deserve all the rooms. Happy?"

"Almost."

"Almost?"

"Mmm hmm." Tim lowered his voice. "You deserve one more thing."

"Oh yeah?" Spencer matched Tim's tone. "What's that?"

Tim leaned down. "This."

Then he kissed him. It was hard to remember they were in a school when he was practically bursting with happiness and pride for his boyfriend, but somehow Tim managed to keep himself in check. They only made out for about a minute or two, and while hands might have wandered, they stayed firmly above the clothes.

Mostly.

"So, what did she want anyway?" Tim asked a few minutes later. They were still on Spencer's desk, though now Tim was sitting completely on top of it and Spencer was standing between his legs. "Did she really come all the way over here to yell at you for getting the room."

"And we were having such a nice moment too," Spencer said with a groan before kissing Tim's neck to let him know he was at least partly joking. "But no. She doesn't know I got the room yet. She came all the way over here to yell at me because she heard I *might* get it."

"Seriously?"

"Yup," he answered, popping the *P* a bit. Tim's face must have been showing at least some of the incredulity he was feeling, because Spencer smirked and ruffled his hair. "Your concern is adorable, but honestly this is way tamer than I was expecting. I thought I'd have to dodge tacks on my chair and buttered floors for weeks. All she did was yell a bit and stomp around like a bitchy little baby."

"Wow." Tim frowned. "That's pretty unprofessional."

Spencer burst out laughing. "Oh my *God*!"

"What? What did I say?"

Spencer shook his head, the only answer he could give while laughing so hard. It took him almost a full minute to calm down. "Sorry," he said, choking back what sounded like another giggle.

"Was I wrong?"

"Oh, fuck no, not in the least," Spencer said with a snort. "But I think 'having sex with students' is a bit more unprofessional than 'yelling at another teacher because he's getting the awesome room.'"

Tim's stomach turned to lead. "Please tell me you're joking."

"Not in the least," Spencer said, his lip curling in disgust and any sense of levity gone from his voice. "I really never told you about her?"

"No! I'd remember if you told me about a teacher who had sex with students."

"I guess that would be pretty memorable."

"She doesn't..." Tim paused, unsure if he really wanted to know.

"Tim?"

"I mean. She's a ninth-grade teacher, right? Surely, she doesn't have sex with her *own* students. Not that having sex with seniors is much better, but..."

Spencer was already shaking his head. "Seniors are way too old for her."

Tim shuddered. "Jesus Christ. How the hell does she still have a job?"

"Tenure and a damn good teacher's union."

"Seriously?"

Spencer shrugged. "It's the going theory. She's been investigated by the cops twice since I've been here, and each time they couldn't find enough evidence to arrest. Corbin can't fire teachers without a good reason, and the school board doesn't really give a shit what happens as long as test scores are good, and nothing actually goes to trial." Spencer smiled in grim sympathy at Tim's appalled expression. "Welcome to Chicago."

Tim felt ill. And she'd been standing right in *front* of him. He'd been so close to someone who...

A thought occurred to him, then, and he felt the blood drain from his face.

"How..." His voice caught, and he cleared his throat. "How do you know all this? Did...did Connor ever..."

Spencer's eyes widened. "Oh. No! No, no, not at all." Tim almost collapsed in relief. Spencer winced. "Sorry, I didn't mean to make you think... But no. Definitely not. I warned him never to be alone with her before the year even started. I only know about her because of Cass. And because she thought I was a student and hit on *me* my first day."

"Oh, thank God."

"I...guess?"

Tim startled himself by laughing. "Not about you. About Connor."

"Oh. Right. Definitely."

"Not that I like the idea of her hitting on you," Tim said with a scowl.

"It *was* pretty horrifying. Especially when I realized she thought I was a kid." Now it was Spencer's turn to shudder.

"You reported her though, right?"

"Of course."

"What happened?"

"I already told you," Spencer said sourly. "Nothing. Well, nothing except making sure I always come to school with at least a little bit of stubble so people wouldn't think I was a fucking teenager, I guess. A few days later I got to be friends with Cass, and she told me all about Steph's sordid history. A few days after that, someone told Steph I turned her in, and we've pretty much hated each other ever since."

"How the hell did she get to be the other teacher in line for your room?"

Spencer grimaced. "Apparently being a pedo sex fiend doesn't necessarily make you a bad teacher."

Tim shook his head, unable to fully wrap his mind around what he was hearing. He'd seen more than one good person completely ruined by just the *accusation* they'd behaved inappropriately with kids. Hell, even the worst youth centers he'd volunteered at—

"Oh my God," Tim said softly. "That's where I've seen her before."

"You've *met* her?"

"What? No." Tim blinked, then shook his head again. "I've seen her, though, at my last youth center. She was getting thrown out by the director, and I'm pretty sure I remember someone saying she failed her background check the week before and tried to come back anyway. I never even gave it a second thought until now..."

"Jesus," Spencer said in disgust. "Small fucking world where child molesters run all over the place and we don't get to meet each other until I'm almost thirty."

"Hey, I love how we met, and the way we got together was perfect." Tim couldn't help smiling as he thought about it. "*And* if we'd met too much earlier *you* would have been the one dating an undera—"

Spencer started gently tapping Tim's mouth with both of his hands. "Hush, you."

Tim laughed as he grabbed Spencer's hands, and, after taking a quick glance around to make sure no one was watching through the small window in the door, he gave them both a kiss. "You could make me."

"That's what I was *doing*."

Tim smiled slowly, meeting Spencer's eyes and pulling him close. "You could make me," he repeated, his voice a low, sensuous murmur.

Spencer raised an eyebrow. "Are you seriously trying to seduce me right now?"

"Are you seriously trying to say it's not working?"

"Definitely." Spencer smirked and pulled their joined hands languidly down his body and pressed them into his crotch. "See? Not even a little bit hard."

Tim's body started to burn, and for one sharp, eternal second all he could hear was the blood rushing through his veins. What had started as a joke to get Spencer's mind off Steph McConnell had suddenly turned into a *challenge*. That they were in a school, a place where Spencer *worked*, didn't matter. All that mattered was his boyfriend was practically in Tim's lap and Spencer wasn't aroused in the least. Tim's recently reawakened sexual ego needed to fix that *now*. "I'll—"

It was probably for the best when the classroom door opened before he could finish his sentence.

"Spencer, do you know—"

The woman in the doorway stopped mid-stride and stared at them, her eyes slowly widening in surprise. She stood about Spencer's height, noticeably plump, and had her light-blonde hair pulled back into a messy ponytail. More importantly, she didn't seem overly disgusted to have walked in on two guys pressed up against each other. Still, when her shock melted into a smug smirk followed by an innuendo-laden "*Oh*," Tim's protective instincts kicked in. He hadn't been able to do anything for Spencer with McConnell; there was no way he'd let another teacher get away with insulting him or their relationship. He hopped off the desk and shifted so he stood between

Spencer and this new woman, but before he could do more than start to cross his arms, Spencer slipped by him like he wasn't even there.

"I knew you were swooning," she said before Spencer could even open his mouth.

"You knew *nothing*," Spencer said, tilting his head back and looking down his nose at the woman even as his cheeks turned red.

The woman ignored Spencer and turned her attention to Tim. She gave him a slow once over, and even though he was ready to tear her apart if she tried to attack Spencer, he still squirmed under her scrutiny.

"So, you're Spencer's new beau?" she asked.

"You don't have to answer that," Spencer said quickly. "He doesn't have to answer that. And, by the way, he's my *boyfriend*. I'm not Taylor Swift and he's not the latest It Boy my agent told me to date for publicity. I don't have *beaus*."

The woman snorted, but otherwise gave no indication he'd spoken. She seemed to be waiting for Tim to answer her question. Something he had no problem doing.

"Yeah. I'm his boyfriend," he said, very pointedly leaving out the word *new*. Even though he knew Spencer hadn't dated anyone but him in a long time, the implication that he was just the latest in a line of guys pricked him the wrong way. "Who are you?"

She smiled, and despite himself Tim couldn't think of anything but a hungry shark stumbling upon an injured dolphin. "I'm the best friend," she said. "Cass Baker."

She held out her hand, and Tim shook it automatically.

"Tim Ellis," he said, frowning slightly.

This was Spencer's friend Cass? Spencer had mentioned her in passing a few times, but he'd always pictured her as being closer to Spencer's age. The real Cass seemed like she could almost be his mother.

"Oh my God," Spencer said, his eyes darting back and for the between them. "Is this a *shovel talk*? Cassandra Baker, are you about to give my boyfriend a *shovel talk* right now?"

It was the use of her full first name that had Tim connecting the dots. He was more than a little embarrassed he hadn't realized sooner.

"Are you Dick Baker's ex-wife by any chance?"

Cass raised an eyebrow. Spencer's eyes widened. "You know Dick?" she asked.

Tim nodded, not sure if he should be even more wary of her now or not. Either way, the awkward levels in the room were ticking up a few points.

"Yeah. I volunteer at his shelter. That's how I met Spencer and Connor, actually."

Spencer winced. *Shit, should I not have said that?*

"Oh." Cass smiled, and as easy as that, her whole demeanor changed. She let go of his hand. "In that case it's really nice to meet you."

It was only Tim's ingrained politeness that had him returning the sentiment. The rest of him was very confused about what just happened. And he wasn't the only one.

"Did you just approve of my boyfriend because he knows your ex-husband?" Spencer asked.

Cass nodded. "More or less."

Spencer *stared*. "Fucking straight people," he muttered.

Cass rolled her eyes. "Oh, stop that. Dick's a good judge of character. If he thinks Tim's good enough to look after the kids at his shelter, I'm sure he won't be anything but good for you and Connor." She turned a sharp glance toward Tim. "Am I right?"

"I love them both," Tim said, a bit more honestly than he had intended.

Well, I guess that's one reason why her and Dick got married in the first place. They both make it easy to open up without meaning to.

"Good." She smiled again. Her smile quickly melted into a smirk when she turned back to Spencer, however. "So, you want to admit I was right, or should I expect a thank-you letter in the mail?"

"Shut up." Spencer glowered. "And nobody uses the mail anymore, you triceratops."

"He never would have taken Connor to the center if it wasn't for me," Cass told Tim.

Tim found himself smiling. He decided he liked Cass. She obviously cared about Spencer, and she had this great deadpan way of speaking that amused the hell out of him, now that he knew she wasn't about to start any homophobic crap.

"Well then, *I'll* thank you," he said. "Anyone who had anything to do with Spencer and Connor being in my life deserves at least that."

Cass's lips quirked. "Good answer."

"So fucking smooth," Spencer muttered. He shook his head and glanced at Tim. "And don't do that. You'll just encourage her."

"Encourage me to make your life better?"

"Yes. No. I don't..." Spencer turned to Tim with an exaggerated pout on his face. "Tiiiiiim! Make her stop being mean to me."

Tim laughed. He was still laughing when the door opened again. Spencer was facing the doorway, so he saw whoever had come in first, and whoever it was had his face twisting with fury.

"Goddammit!"

Spencer's sudden shout startled Tim. His laugh choked off when he saw Connor standing in the doorway with a split lip, hunched over under the weight of his bulging backpack and holding a bloody wad of toilet paper against his nose. Tim could see more blood staining the front of his shirt through his open jacket.

"What the *hell* happened?" Spencer demanded, though it was obvious from the way he was grinding his teeth together he already had an idea of his own. Connor flinched, but didn't answer. Spencer scowled. "I said—"

"Are you okay?" Tim asked, cutting him off. Connor glanced up, obviously surprised at the softly spoken question, and Tim politely ignored the way he saw Spencer flinch out of the corner of his eye.

"M..." Connor swallowed heavily, and Tim held back a flinch of his own. *I hope that wasn't blood.* "My nose hurts..."

"Aw, kid..." Spencer said. Tim gave his wrist a squeeze before turning his full attention to Connor.

"Can I take a look?" he asked, using his best Everything Will Be Okay voice. He'd seen Connor hurt before, and he'd seen Connor miserable before, but he'd never seen him looking so young and *lost*. Tim could actually feel his heart breaking. "Just to make sure it isn't broken?"

"I should go," Cass said quietly to Spencer, her voice was low and hard. "Maybe I can catch them before they leave."

She obviously wasn't out of the loop on what was going on with Connor.

Spencer just nodded, most of his attention understandably taken up with his busted-up son. Cass gave his shoulder a quick squeeze before her eyes met Tim's. They shared a moment of silent communication, a wordless promise that they were now allies in protecting Connor and watching after Spencer. Tim nodded. Cass nodded back. Then she left.

Connor glanced away and wiped at his eyes before answering Tim, his voice barely loud enough to understand. "Okay."

Tim wasted no time moving across the room and kneeling in front of him. It scared him, how docile Connor was being, but he pushed his own feelings to the side, well aware Spencer was taking this a million times worse than Tim. With Cass gone it was up to Tim to keep them both together right now.

Gently, he took hold of the soaked through toilet paper and moved Connor's hands away from his face. He pulled the wadded-up paper away from his face a moment later, holding back a wince at the way blood hadn't stopped pouring out. *This can't have happened more than a few minutes ago. Maybe she'll actually catch them.* Thankfully, his nose didn't seem to be broken, just swollen and very, very red.

"It looks a lot worse than it is," Tim said, speaking to both of them. He carefully placed the wad back under Connor's nose. "Not broken at all."

Spencer let out a whoosh of air. Connor blinked away more tears, but, otherwise, he didn't react at all.

"Kid," Spencer said softly, coming over and kneeling down next to Tim. He hesitated for a moment, then pulled his son into a hug. Their embrace was slightly awkward, with Tim still holding the toilet paper against Connor's nose, but he stayed still and let Spencer do what he needed. "Fuck."

"Dad..." Connor's voice was muffled by Spencer's shirt as he hugged him back.

"Okay," Spencer said a minute later, pulling back and taking in his son's face. His jaw clenched, and he took a deep breath through his nose. "Okay. What happened?"

Connor's only answer was to stiffen up.

"Connor," Spencer said, his voice sharp. Connor flinched.

"Spencer," Tim said quietly, placing his free hand on his boyfriend's shoulder. He was so tense his nearly nonexistent muscles felt like corded steel. Their eyes met, and it was their turn for silent communication.

I know you're upset and feeling helpless, but please don't take this out on him; it's not his fault.

Spencer let out a breath, and Tim felt some of the tension slowly melt out of his body.

"Fine."

Now for the other half.

"Connor," Tim said, his voice still soft. "Can you please tell us who did this to you?"

He wasn't sure if it was the tone, or the way he asked instead of demanded, or, maybe, it was the way Tim and Spencer were both acting like concerned parents together for the first time, but whatever the reason, Connor deflated in the face of it.

"Dean and Julie beat me up again."

With all the blood coming out of Connor's nose, Tim would have thought it impossible for there to be enough left over for a blush, but Connor's face turned a deep, burning red the moment the words were out of his mouth. He pretended he hadn't seen and checked Connor's nose. The blood had finally slowed, so he tossed the toilet paper in the nearby trash can before handing Connor a small wad of tissues and giving him an encouraging smile.

"Did this happen at school?" Spencer asked, his voice surprisingly calm.

Connor slumped even more. "Yeah..."

"Did you throw the first punch?"

"No."

"Okay." Spencer nodded. "Kid, I am so sorry this happened to you, and I swear to God the second we're done here, you and Tim can go do whatever you were gonna do today, but I gotta ask—you remember our deal, right?"

For a second, Tim saw familiar defiance flash across Connor's face, but before he had the chance to do more than mentally cringe at the thought of being in the middle of another fight about this, Connor sighed and nodded. "I remember..."

Tim barely held back a sigh of relief.

Maybe he finally realizes how serious this is.

"All right." Spencer met Tim's eyes, another silent conversation passing between them in an instant.

I'm going to handle this my way. Will you let me?

Tim nodded grimly. *You know I will.*

"Okay," Spencer said, nodding back. "I can deal with this."

*

Tim had known from the second they'd met that Spencer was protective of his son, but seeing him in full on Papa Bear mode was more arousing than it had any right to be.

He kind of hated that he thought so, because Connor was obviously shook up by what happened and this was pretty much the least appropriate time and setting to want to tear Spencer's clothes off, but none of those truths changed the fact that he followed Spencer to Principal Corbin's office with half a hard-on filling out his jeans. One that turned into a full-on when Spencer barged in, his arm still around his son's shoulder, and demanded the principal order the Henderson siblings to the office. When Corbin tried to protest that they probably already left the school, Spencer just grabbed Connor and pushed him right in front of the principal's face, bloody tissues and all.

Five minutes later a bus monitor dropped two visibly annoyed teenagers off at the office.

For as big of a shadow as they'd cast over Connor's life—over *all* their lives—these past few months, Dean and Julie didn't really look like much in person.

Dean could have been any other fifteen-year-old boy; a bit taller than most, maybe, but he still swam in his tough guy outfit of baggy jeans, an overlarge white T-shirt that came down to his knees, and a thick camouflage jacket. A crooked Chicago Cubs snapback covering what seemed to be a blond buzzcut completed the look. The only thing noteworthy about him were his eyes. They were a startlingly clear blue, and Tim might have even called them pretty if they hadn't been glaring at Connor with palpable fury.

Julie shared her brother's coloring, though she wore her hair long and done up in a simple ponytail. She dressed in tight black jeans with a large gray sweatshirt, and even though her top was baggy enough to hide her build, Tim could tell she was unusually stocky. Not fat, but solid in a way teenage girls usually aren't. Her face was angular and, like Dean's eyes, probably would have been pretty if she weren't currently scowling.

"Mr. Henderson. Ms. Henderson," Principal Corbin said. He appeared to be in his midsixties with thinning salt-and-pepper hair, the permanently red nose of an alcoholic, and the sharp clear eyes of someone who hadn't had a drop in a while and was better off for it. His obvious disdain for the entire situation he found himself in was apparent in every line of his overweight body, and Tim wondered if it was because of Connor's bloody face or because he wanted to get on with his day and having to deal with last-minute discipline issues was holding him back. Either way, he didn't seem eager to waste any time. "Did you attack Mr. Kent?"

Both Hendersons looked at Spencer in confusion.

"The *younger* Mr. Kent," Corbin said, a hint of impatience creeping into his tone.

"We didn't do anything," Julie said. Her eyes never left Connor, though, and the threatening glare on her face was open and obvious.

"Would you like to explain why he thinks you did?"

Tim bristled at the question, but Spencer didn't so much as twitch, which surprised him.

"'Cause he's an autistic crack baby," Dean muttered just loud enough for Tim, who was closest to him, to hear. Julie elbowed her brother in the side. "Ow! What?"

"Is that what he said?" Julie asked, glaring at Connor now and pointedly ignoring her brother. "That we attacked him?"

Jesus, she's not even trying to be subtle.

To Tim, she was obviously trying to intimidate Connor into either staying quiet or saying they never hit him, but for the first time since calling the Hendersons into his office, Corbin seemed almost hesitant.

"That's what we're here to discuss, yes."

"Well, we never touched him. If anyone's saying we did, they're lying."

"Are you calling my son a liar?" Spencer asked. His tone was calm and even, but both siblings still flinched.

"He's *your* kid?" Dean asked, his voice squeaking slightly. Even Julie seemed apprehensive now.

Ah. So, Spencer's the Scary Teacher, then.

"I see your ability to comprehend the English language hasn't improved at all since last year, despite my best efforts," Spencer said, fixing Dean with a stern, predatory smirk that all but screamed *oh, so you're the weak link.*

"Mr. Kent," Corbin said, his eyes narrowed in warning.

"Maybe I *should* have sent you to summer school," Spencer went on, ignoring Corbin completely. "I'd hate to think any students left my class without getting the full benefit of my lessons." Spencer snapped his fingers. "I know! We should set up an after-school tutoring session, just you and me, just to make sure you understand *exactly* what—"

"Mr. *Kent*," Corbin snapped.

Spencer huffed. "We'll discuss this later, Dean."

"No, you won't," Corbin said. "And," he continued when Spencer opened his mouth, "we're not here to talk about anyone's academic record. If you'll recall, we're here to find out what happened to your son."

Tim leaned toward Spencer. "This isn't helping Connor," he said, as quietly and as gently as he could. He understood Spencer's frustration, his anger, his need to lash out. Tim felt all those things too, if he was being honest. He also understood Spencer would always do what was best for his son, as long as he had a reminder of what that was. Spencer didn't so much as glance in Tim's direction, but he knew by the slight slump to Spencer's shoulders that he was listening.

"*Fine.*" Spencer crossed his arms and glared at Corbin. "But we already know what happened."

"Yeah, and we didn't do it," Julie said, staring Spencer in the eye and showing none of her earlier almost-fear of him. "Look, Mr. Kent, I'm sorry your son got beat up, but it wasn't me *or* my brother that did it. I don't know why you think we did, or why he said we did, but we *didn't.*"

"Have you spoken with Connor today?" Corbin asked.

"No," Julie said, her eyes wide and earnest. "We've barely ever talked to him. The freshman hall is nowhere near any of our classes, so even if we wanted to, we wouldn't have the time."

"This didn't happen between classes," Corbin said. "According to Mr. Kent, Connor's nose was still bleeding when he walked into his classroom fifteen minutes ago. Since this is a half day, there was nowhere you or your brother needed to be."

"We had to get to the bus," Julie said. "Our parents work until dinnertime, Principal Corbin. If we miss the bus, we're stuck here. We'd never risk that." She turned toward Connor again, but this time her expression held nothing but vague sympathy. "But even if we had all the time in the world, we still wouldn't beat up some freshman we don't even know. We're not assholes."

"Language." Corbin fixed her with a stern glare.

"You said you don't have time to go to the freshman hall?" Spencer asked suddenly.

"Yeah?" Julie answered slowly.

"And that's why you couldn't have beaten up Connor, right? Because the freshman hall is too far away from your classes?"

"Right. But like I said, even if it wasn't, I wouldn't beat him up."

"Because you don't know him."

"Yeah. I mean, I don't beat people up at all."

Spencer eyed her sharply. "Then how do you know he's a freshman?"

Julie stilled. "Huh?"

"It's not a hard question, Julie," Spencer said. Despite his short stature, when Tim thought back on this moment, he would swear on a stack of Bibles Spencer had been looming over her like a gargoyle on a New York skyscraper. "If you don't know Connor and you never go by the freshman hall, how do you know my son is a freshman?"

Tim could almost see the bright, flashing panic lights going off behind Julie's eyes as she realized the trap she'd walked into. Satisfaction surged through Tim's body. Even with all his years of helping troubled youth, there wasn't a single part of him feeling the smallest bit guilty for how much he wanted to see these two get the punishment they deserved.

"Well," Julie said slowly, "look at him. He's so small; how can he not be?"

"Oh please." Spencer rolled his eyes. "Cut the bullshit."

Tim winced. Not because of the language, but because he could see from the expression on Corbin's face he was giving Julie's words serious consideration.

"Language, Mr. Kent," Corbin said.

To her credit, and Tim's dismay, Julie was quick. She'd barely glanced at the principal before realizing he was her best bet and turning on her best, innocent expression. "Principal Corbin, I swear me and Dean didn't do anything to Mr. Kent's son. If he's not a freshman, I'm sorry for assuming, but you can't blame me for thinking someone so short is a ninth grader. I don't know him, though, and I've never even *talked* to him before. And neither has Dean, right?"

After a barely noticeable hesitation, Dean shook his head. "No, never."

Corbin nodded thoughtfully.

You can't be serious...

Spencer's jaw clenched, and this time Tim was the one who nearly lashed out. This was the exact kind of thing Spencer had complained about on their first date, and Tim wasn't exactly new to it either. Bullies could be so charming and earnest when they were trying to get out of trouble. Sadly, often adults, especially school administrators, fell for it. They'd rather believe the pleasant fiction that nothing bad ever happened in their school than have to deal with the fact that kids could be evil little sociopaths when people with authority over them had their backs turned. Connor was hunched over and staring at the ground, his face was a bloody mess, and he was obviously terrified of the two other kids in the room, but even that could be explained away by someone determined enough. It wasn't fair. Connor didn't deserve this. And neither did Spencer.

After a long moment, Corbin sighed and rubbed his bulbous red nose. "Mr. Ke...*Connor*. Can you tell me what happened?"

Connor cringed and glanced up. His eyes went from Corbin to Spencer, then slowly slid over to the Hendersons even though it was obvious they were the last people he wanted to look at. He shrunk in on himself when his eyes met Julie's, and Tim knew he was about to cave. He didn't even blame him. Confronting a tormentor was terrifying.

Tim reached out and gave Connor's shoulder a gentle squeeze. "It's okay," he said.

Connor's eyes swam with shimmering tears. "I..." He trailed off and glanced away, ashamed. That was okay too. Tim didn't really need him to finish. *"I can't." "I'm scared." "I don't know what to say."* All variations on the same theme. All sentiments a strong, stubborn, independent kid like Connor should never have to say out loud in front of people who made him feel anything but.

Tim knelt so he was gazing up at Connor. Connor refused to meet his eyes, at first, but Tim was patient. Because Connor *was* strong, when it counted. And maybe he even trusted Tim, now. Trusted those words Tim had said to him on Halloween were true. Sure enough, after a few moments, Connor slowly met Tim's gaze. When he did, Tim gave him his best smile. "It's *okay*. You don't need to say anything."

Connor frowned. "But..."

"No buts. Everything's going to be okay."

Some things were more important than morals.

With one last reassuring squeeze, Tim stood up and faced Corbin.

"Connor doesn't need to say anything. I saw what happened."

*

"I saw what happened."

For Connor, the rest of the meeting passed in a daze. He'd felt drained before, emotionally. Mostly after fighting with his dad, which, secretly, almost always ended up making him a little sick to his stomach. This felt different. He wasn't really drained, though that would probably come later. This felt more like...drain*ing*. Slowly. Like a partially clogged sink after someone pulled the stopper. Everything inside him, the terror and shame and humiliation and frustration and self-loathing, it was circling the drain, slowly slowly slowly seeping down through the crud backing it up, the dirty water that made up those feelings slowly exposing a slightly stained porcelain sink as it drained. The clean, shiny whiteness breaking up the stains were mostly made up of bits of half heard conversation.

"...against the wall, hitting him..."

"...there to see the whole thing..."

"Bullshit! That's not what we did..."

"...*up*, you *idiot*..."

"...suspended for a week..."

"...apologize, Spencer, but these things..."

"...well, I'm taking the rest of the day off to be with my bloody kid so..."

And, through it all, a densely woven thread tying everything together, was one single thought.

He lied for me.

No matter how many times the thought ran through his head, it still sounded fake.

He lied for me. He lied for me. He lied for me.

A door opened. Someone led him through it. The bright sun and the cold, sharp wind hit his face at the exact same time. He took three steps and stopped, stunned, as the sink finally emptied.

"Connor?" Tim's hand on his shoulder. "Are you all right?"

Connor blinked as the world came back into focus, and slowly turned his head toward Tim. He was kneeling on the ground, eye level with Connor, and all Connor could think now was *He's getting his pants dirty. He lied for me, and now he's ruining his pants. He...he...*

"You *lied* for me?"

Connor hadn't realized he'd spoken out loud until Tim smiled at him. "Yeah, I guess I did."

He sounded...proud.

"*Why?*"

"Because I meant what I told you on Halloween," Tim said. "I'm always on your side."

Connor's breath hitched in his throat, and for a second he nearly forgot how to breathe. Except, that wasn't right at all. No, it was more like...being able to breathe properly for the first time in his life.

"A-and," he said, his voice shaking, "did Principal Corbin really suspend Dean and Julie?"

"Oh yeah." This came from his dad, who squatted down next to Tim. "And it won't be the last time either. If they ever do this to you again, they're gonna *wish* all they got was a suspension. I'll see to that."

The remaining weight on Connor's shoulders evaporated. Sure, he'd heard his dad say similar things before, but this time Connor believed him. Maybe it was because Dean and Julie had finally gotten in trouble when they always seemed so untouchable, but Connor kind of thought it might be something else. Ever since they moved out of Grandma and Grandpa's house, it had been Connor and his dad against the world. No one else had ever gotten so far inside their bubble. No one else had ever *stayed.*

Until Tim. Tim didn't hover just outside their life. Tim didn't have his own family to focus on. Tim didn't move back to Ohio. Tim didn't spend most of the year traveling around the country in an RV. Tim stayed. Tim had burrowed himself so far into their lives that Connor couldn't imagine going back to the way things were before. It would have been hard enough losing Tim when he was only his friend, but it was impossible now, when he was so much more. He'd become someone Connor could hold on to and rely on, someone he could run to when the pressure and responsibility of growing up and standing on his own became too much, someone who would always be there when he really needed it.

Or, rather, someone *else* who was like that.

Is this how it feels to have two parents?

Connor thought it might. And if it was, he wanted to grab the feeling and hold on to it forever.

"Thank you..." Connor whispered. He barely even noticed the tears flowing down his cheeks, even though he'd been totally mortified every other time he'd cried in front of someone. How could he be embarrassed when strong arms were pulling him close, protecting him, shielding him, *caring* for him? He didn't even bother trying to figure out whose arms they were.

How could that possibly matter, when the other set joined in soon after?

"I love you, kid," one of them said, softly. He thought it might have been his dad, but in the end that didn't matter either. Connor's response would have been the same no matter what.

He closed his eyes and hugged them both back as hard as he could. "I love you too."

Chapter Seventeen

As the credits for the latest episode began to roll, Tim carefully paused Netflix and took stock of the two bodies surrounding him. Connor, on his left, dead to the world, his head on Tim's shoulder and one leg slung over the arm of the couch. Spencer, on his right, curled up under his arm and, if Tim's estimate was correct, he hadn't been watching anything but Tim for at least the last half hour.

Which, coincidentally, was right about when Tim started having trouble concentrating as well.

"Is he sleeping?" Spencer whispered.

"Yeah."

"On you?"

"Yep."

Spencer let out a content little hum. "Fucking adorable."

Tim chuckled quietly. "Yeah."

"Is that okay?" Spencer asked after about a minute of contented silence.

"That he's sleeping on me?"

"Yeah." Spencer shifted against Tim's chest. "It's not too much, is it?"

Tim frowned. "Too much what?"

"You know...like, closeness, or whatever..."

"Is it too much closeness for the son of the man I love to fall asleep on my shoulder?" Tim asked, raising an eyebrow. "Shockingly, no."

Spencer sighed. "That was a stupid question, wasn't it?"

"Very."

"Sorry." Spencer wrapped his arm around Tim's waist and gave him an apologetic squeeze for emphasis. "I just...worry."

"About what?"

Spencer snorted softly. "Everything. But right now?" He chewed his lip. "I think I'm mostly worried that you're gonna get sick of us at some point."

Tim...wasn't sure how he felt about that. "Really?"

Spencer shrugged. "I guess? I mean...you lied to my principal today, and now Connor's falling asleep on you and we've barely been together for more than two months and...I don't know. Do you think this is all going a bit fast?"

"Not at all," Tim answered. He paused then, surprised at how much he meant it. Tim couldn't remember ever being this content in a relationship. Hell, he couldn't remember ever being this content, period.

Spencer sat up, his face echoing Tim's surprise. "Seriously?"

"Yeah." Tim smiled. "I'm...really happy."

"Even though we barely go on dates and you're getting sucked into dealing with my kid's parent crap? You really don't want...I dunno, more?"

Tim rolled his eyes. "Of course I want more. But I want more of what we already have." He paused to gather his thoughts. "It's...I like it. A lot. I feel like..." *Please don't let me be overstepping...* "I feel like I have a family."

Spencer inhaled sharply. "Are you sure?"

"Yes." A thought occurred then, causing Tim's heart to constrict painfully. "Is...is *that* okay?"

Spencer let out a quiet, incredulous laugh. "'Is that okay?' he asks. Of *course* it's okay. That's why this whole thing is fucking me up. Today, when you lied to Corbin for my kid? I've never felt more..." He paused. "I never felt *more* in my whole life. Maybe when I held Connor for the first time, *maybe*. I don't...fuck, I feel like I'm getting everything I ever wanted, and I'm just...dragging you along into it."

"If you are, I'm being dragged willingly." Spencer didn't laugh. Tim sighed. "Where is this coming from? We were having a nice night, right?"

"The best I've had in a while," Spencer said. "But that's the *problem*."

"It's a problem?"

"I didn't mean it like that!" Tim winced at the volume of Spencer's voice, and quickly checked to make sure Connor was still asleep. He was.

"Then how did you mean it?"

Spencer chewed his lip. "Okay, so maybe I meant it *sort of* like that. Not that I didn't love tonight," he added quickly. "But...okay, full disclosure, I know exactly how this is going to sound, but I'm terrified at how easily my life is falling into place right now. For years it's been just me and Connor, and as much as I tried to make that enough for both of us, I think I always knew there was something missing. Something we *both* needed. But I never looked for it. I pulled the blankets over my head and closed my eyes and told myself over and over that everything was fine. I never dated—fuck, I barely even made friends. Then I meet you, and suddenly it's like, 'Hey, maybe I could take a look for that thing I'm pretending I don't need over in Tim's direction,' and, *bam*, there you were. Just fucking...there for the taking. So, I reached out and took it."

"And...that's a bad thing?"

Tim had been going for wry humor, but Spencer nodded quickly, wide-eyed and serious. "Yes! How the hell is it fair that I find exactly what I need right out of the gate? People look their whole *lives* and never find someone who fits into their life the way you fit into mine. I looked for, like, ten minutes, and you were literally the first place I looked. Great for me, but..." He wrung his hands. "What about for you?"

God, how could he possibly be feeling so many things at the same time? Tim loved the picture Spencer was painting of him, but at the same time he hated being the cause of one of Spencer's seemingly random bouts of insecurity.

"Spencer..."

"Don't 'Spencer' me," he mumbled, glancing away. Tim smiled.

"*Spencer.*" Tim gently lifted his boyfriend's head. "Do you really think I'm not feeling the exact same way?"

Spencer blinked. "Yes..."

Tim rolled his eyes fondly. "You're kind of an idiot sometimes."

"I'm aware." Spencer paused. "And fuck you, by the way. I'm being serious here."

"So am I." Spencer started to speak, and Tim pressed two fingers against his lips, silencing him. "Why do you think I spend my free time volunteering with kids?" Spencer crossed his arms and shot Tim an adorable, pouty glare before biting the tips of his fingers. Grinning, Tim lowered his hand. "You can talk now."

"Oh, well now that I have *permission*..." Spencer huffed.

"You do," Tim agreed easily. "So, answer the question, please."

"I don't know. Because you like kids, probably. Or you're a secret masochist."

"Almost," Tim said. "It's because I *want* kids. Someday, with the right man. And I'm sure I don't have to tell you the odds of finding a single gay man who actually wants to have a committed, monogamous relationship, let alone one who also wants kids."

"So...you're dating me for my kid?"

Tim sighed. "Please don't pretend to misunderstand what I'm saying. It's very unattractive."

"So, now I'm—"

This time, Tim covered his mouth with his entire hand.

"I'm with you because I love you," Tim said. "You're different from every guy I've ever tried to seriously date, and that alone would be enough to get me to want you, but it's so much more than that, because..." He shrugged. "We fit. It's *easy* being with you. Even the parts that should be hard are easier than they usually would be. And maybe you found me the moment you started looking, but I found you two right after I stopped. I thought I'd be alone for the rest of my life, and now I have you and Connor and you two are the most important things in the world to me. Not to be too corny about it, but if that doesn't sound like something that's meant to be, then I don't know what is."

"Can I talk now?" Spencer asked, his voice muffled.

"Hmm," Tim said, pretending to think about it. Spencer rolled his eyes and licked his hand. Tim snorted. "I've had that tongue in my mouth," he said dryly. "Licking my hand isn't nearly as gross as you think it is."

He could *feel* Spencer's pout. Laughing, Tim removed his hand.

Spencer gave Tim a halfhearted glare, but it quickly tapered off into a thoughtful frown. "Do you really mean that?"

"Every word."

"You care about both of us?"

"*Love* both of you."

Spencer's eyes dilated. "And...we're not a burden?"

"Not in the least."

Spencer licked his lips. "Good."

If he hadn't been half expecting some move, Tim probably would have woken Connor up by jumping when Spencer grabbed his soft cock through his pants and gave it a squeeze.

"Jesus...*fuck*," Tim said, just barely keeping his voice above a whisper.

"Nah, it's more like, Spencer fuck," Spencer said, continuing to knead Tim's rapidly hardening length. "Or even better, *fuck Spencer*."

"Spencer..." Tim's voice was strained. "Connor is—"

"Asleep." Tim hissed as Spencer lightly squeezed his balls.

"But he could wake up..."

"Nope. When he falls asleep watching a movie, it takes an act of God to wake him up." Before Tim could say anything, Spencer stood up and yanked Tim further down the couch away from Connor. His head slid off Tim's shoulder and bounced on the couch cushion. Tim stared at the injured boy in horror, but Connor never moved. "See?"

Tim turned his incredulous look toward Spencer, only to come nearly face-to-face with a hard, jean-covered bulge. "How are you turned on right now?" he asked, ignoring his own more-than-half-hard cock.

Spencer grinned and gave a cute little half shrug. "You love me. You love my kid. You lied to my principal to get those little fucks in trouble. All that's...a pretty big fucking turn-on. Honestly, I probably would have jumped you in the parking lot if Connor wasn't there."

"You just told me you were worried about me lying to the principal."

Spencer smirked. "Worry and horny aren't mutually exclusive."

Tim opened his mouth, but now it was Spencer's turn to press fingers to lips. "Unless you're opening up to put something in there, it can wait." He paused. "And even if that's what you're doing, we should probably get behind a door with a lock. Kid's dead to the world, but I'd rather not test that too far, you know?"

Despite his own arousal, Tim was still unsure. Spencer's mood swing had thrown him. Did he really believe Tim? Or were these kinds of insecurities going to keep coming up in their relationship? And what if Connor woke up while they were gone? What if he needed one of them...

Spencer let out an impatient huff. "Okay, how about this," he said, leaning in. Slender fingers sensuously carded their way through Tim's hair as Spencer's lips brushed against his ear. "If you come back to my room with me," Spencer said, his voice low and husky, "I'll let you do whatever you want to me." He licked down the shell of Tim's ear and gave his lobe a quick nip before pulling back and staring Tim in the eye. "Absolutely *anything* you want."

Tim's gaze unfocused as a wealth of possibilities began to play out in his head, with one possibility in particular, something he'd been thinking about a lot lately, stuck on repeat.

Arousal: 1

Tim's sense of responsibility: 0

Standing in one fluid motion, he grabbed the front of Spencer's shirt and pulled him in close.

"Get in the bedroom."

*

Spencer blinked. Cocked his head. Blinked again.

"Spencer? Are you okay?"

"Uh..." Spencer cocked his head in the other direction, getting a slightly different angle on the scene in front of him. He blinked once more for good measure, but...nope. Nothing changed.

Tim still lay on his stomach on Spencer's bed, naked, throwing a coy smile over his shoulder with his legs slightly open and his smooth, round ass...well, *presented* probably wouldn't have been too inaccurate of a description. He'd even hitched his hips up enough to spread his cheeks open, and Spencer couldn't stop staring at the glistening—

"Is that lube?" His voice came out strained and high pitched. "Did you lube your ass while I was in the bathroom?"

Tim smirked and nodded, but as soon as he'd asked the question, Spencer knew the answer. He'd done the exact same thing to himself while he was in the bathroom, after all. He'd thought, after his offer, he'd barely get two steps out of the bathroom before Tim would grab him and do deliciously vile things to him. Never in a million years would he have expected this.

"Oh." Spencer absently chewed his lip. He couldn't deny the sight in front of him was kind of sexy. Tim had always been "hot AF," as the kids say, and his ass had never had too much trouble filling out a pair of jeans. It was nicely proportioned, fleshy and muscular in equal measures, and the top curve melted flawlessly into the lines of Tim's lightly muscled back. He even had those mouth-watering dimples at the base of his spine. Tim from the back was...kind of a work of art.

"Oh," Spencer repeated. "Um. Why?"

Tim raised an eyebrow. "What?"

Spencer was suddenly very aware of the slickness between his own cheeks, of the open, stretched feeling of his hole. Did Tim also...?

"I don't understand."

"I'm facedown on your bed, naked, and I just lubed myself up for you." Tim paused as Spencer squeaked. "What part is giving you trouble?"

"I thought—" Spencer's voice caught. He cleared his throat. "I thought you were going to...you know. Do something to me?"

"You said I could do anything I wanted." Tim rolled over a little onto his side and propped his head up with one hand. Despite everything, his erection hadn't started going down in the least.

"Yeah...to *me*."

Tim grinned. "Well, I want you to do something to me."

"Really?"

"Yes."

"Are you sure?"

"Yes."

Spencer bit his lip. He'd literally never been in this situation before. People usually took one look at him and assumed he was a bottom without even asking, which worked out well for him, since that's exactly what he was. "Oh..."

Tim's brows furrowed. "Do you...not want to?"

Slurred, drunken words from fifteen years ago reached out from the past and sunk their claws into Spencer.

"Come on...just do it. You know you want to."

He grimaced.

"I guess I'll take that as a no..."

Tim's voice sounded calm, but all Spencer could see were his flushed cheeks, his downcast eyes, the way his body subtly began curling in on itself. Spencer felt Tim's embarrassment as if it were his own. Tim had put himself out there, literally opened himself up to Spencer in a brand-new way.

And Spencer had cringed.

Fuck, I'm a terrible boyfriend. Tim isn't Becky. He can't get pregnant and leave you with a kid. He can't call you in the middle of the night and yell at you for ruining his life. You won't have to stay up until three in the morning looking up homemade abortions on the internet and praying to a God you don't really believe in that he doesn't have access to a computer.

The thing was, he was pretty sure if he said any of this out loud, Tim would understand. He'd be sympathetic and comforting and the humiliation Spencer could see radiating off his body like heat off hot desert sand would disappear like it had never been. It would be so easy...but Tim deserved better than easy. He deserved better than someone who would trot out their trauma and hide behind it like it was an all-purpose excuse. He'd be telling the truth, yeah, but sometimes the truth only made things worse in the long run.

Sometimes a half truth was the best way to go.

"It's not like that," Spencer said softly. He got on the bed and knelt next to Tim, placing a hand on his calf. "It's just...I've never..."

God, he couldn't even get the words out.

Thankfully, Tim was smart enough to know what he'd been trying to say.

"You've never topped?"

Tim's embarrassed flush all but faded as he *finally* met Spencer's eyes. Which of course made admitting it out loud pretty much impossible, so Spencer shook his head.

Tim's whole face lit up. "So, I'll be your first?"

Spencer's heart swelled. "You stupid, romantic idiot." He quickly clamped his hands over his mouth.

I said that out loud!

"*Your* stupid romantic idiot," Tim said with a wide grin. Spencer's face *burned*, and he quickly moved his hands to cover as much of it as possible. "You are the cutest thing ever."

"Shut up," Spencer mumbled, his voice slightly muffled by his hands. "There's no way I'm gonna get hard enough to fuck you if you keep being lame and embarrassing."

"So, you're gonna do it?"

Spencer's shoulders tensed. The denial he wanted to give was right there on the tip of his tongue...but he couldn't voice it. Tim sounded so happy—no, more than happy; *delighted*. Delighted because he wanted Spencer to fuck him.

How the hell was anyone supposed to resist that?

"Okay," Spencer said quietly. "Let's do this thing."

He peeked out through his fingers in time to see Tim's delight soften into an expression of absolute fondness.

Tim sat up and gently moved Spencer's hands away from his face before cupping his cheeks and pulling him in for a soft, lingering kiss.

"You're the best," Tim said. Spencer couldn't hold back a scoff. "Hey, I mean it."

"I haven't done anything yet," Spencer said. "And, you know, I've *never* done this before so, might wanna temper your expectations a bit."

"That's not what I meant." Spencer shivered as Tim lightly stroked his cheeks with his thumbs. "I've been wanting to share this with you for a while. It means a lot that you want to also."

Personally, Spencer thought "want to" was a bit too strong a term...but fuck it. Maybe topping wasn't something he'd ever choose to do on his own. Making Tim happy, though? *That* was something Spencer would never turn away from.

"All right, all right," he mumbled, unable to meet Tim's eyes for more than a second without turning into a blushy, stuttering mess. "Stop saying shit like that or I really won't be able to get hard."

"Well," Tim said, a teasing lilt slipping into his words, "we can't have that, can we?"

He pulled Spencer in for a searing kiss, fucking *plundering* his mouth with a single-minded lust for conquest the world hadn't seen since Genghis Kahn was running around China. It was hot and hard and demanding and everything Spencer loved about making out.

His cock hadn't gone from limp to boner so fast since he was a teenager.

Spencer let out a tiny whimper when Tim pulled away.

"And now you're hard," Tim said, sounding more than a little smug. He kissed Spencer's nose and gave his dick a quick squeeze. Spencer moaned.

"Fucking tease…"

Tim laughed. "Teases don't put out." He rolled over onto his stomach and glanced back over his shoulder. "And I *definitely* plan on putting out."

"Jesus…*fuck.*"

Spencer stroked himself as he stared at Tim splayed out before him like a fucking medieval feast. He couldn't believe he was about to do this. After a minute of jerking himself off, he realized he was stalling. *Come on, stop being a pussy. Just do it.* Nodding at his own pep talk, he crawled into bed on his knees, straddling one of Tim's thighs. Spencer's legs were so skinny compared to Tim's; hell, his everything was small in comparison. This must look so ridiculous, he thought, tiny Spencer trying to mount a sexy, normal-sized guy.

"Come on, Spencer," Tim said. "Touch me."

Spencer swallowed roughly, surprised to find his cock twitching at Tim's half-pleading words.

Okay, this is turning you on. Good. Focus on that. Don't think about Becky. Don't worry about how bad you're going to be at this. Tim wants you. He wants you.

Spencer licked his lips as he stared at Tim's beautifully rounded ass. And maybe the feast metaphor was a mistake, because all he could think about was how delicious that ass looked. Not even a monk would be able to resist sinking his teeth into those succulent globes.

And despite a decade of celibacy, Spencer was no monk.

Tim let out a startled yelp. Panicking, Spencer pulled back. "Sorry!"

"Did you just bite my ass?"

"I'm sorry! I won't do it anymore."

"No way," Tim said. "That was *hot*. Do it again."

Spencer's cheeks flushed. "R-really? You liked that?"

"Oh yes." Tim smiled over his shoulder. "More please?"

Fuck, I love this man.

"Whatever you want."

Spencer bit him again.

It was strange, he mused as he went to town on Tim's ass, how much his boyfriend's squirming and little moans of pain-tinged pleasure were turning him on. Spencer had always happily taken the more submissive role during sex, and when he jerked off, his fantasies always had him firmly on the bottom in every conceivable way. He never thought switching things up would be this hot.

Suddenly, he *really* wanted to fuck Tim.

Pulling back, he stared at Tim's ass for a moment, admiring the bite marks he'd left on his boyfriend's cheeks. Another surge of arousal shot through him as his cock began to leak on the back of Tim's thigh. One day he was going to have to do this before Tim got lube anywhere near that hole—eat him out properly. For now, though, the lube was exactly what he needed.

"You ready?" he asked, his voice shaking with nerves and anticipation.

"God, yes," Tim said, his face half pressed into the comforter as he hitched his hips up further. "It's been a while though. So, go slow at first, okay?"

Spencer bit back a groan, unable to tear his eyes away from Tim's pink, glistening entrance. "Maybe tell me that without spreading yourself open? I'm basically a virgin here. A really, *really* horny virgin. We're not exactly known for our restraint."

Tim chuckled. "I have faith in your self-control."

"If you say so..."

Without another word, Spencer centered himself behind Tim and lined his cock up with Tim's ass. His hands began to tremble.

This is it. I'm actually going to do it.

Slowly, Spencer pushed inside.

Holy. Shit.

"So tight—I've never felt—oh my God."

Tim's hole squeezed his cock like a satin glove as Spencer sank inside him, and it was all he could do not to thrust his whole length in. *Nothing* had ever felt this good on his cock, not sex toys, not even Tim's mouth. Even Becky had...well, to be honest, it was impossible to remember what it had felt like with Becky. Becky was a hazy, alcohol-soaked memory. Tim was hot and alive and right in front of him. And Spencer wanted him to stay there forever.

"You can move now."

Tim's words dragged Spencer out of his thoughts, and he was surprised to find himself buried to the hilt in Tim's ass.

"Wow," he said breathlessly. "This is so cool."

Tim let out a short laugh. "'Cool,' huh?"

Spencer's face started to burn. "Shut up! This is the first time I've had my dick in an ass; I can't fucking adjective right now, okay?"

A small laugh slipped out of Tim's throat, and he quickly buried his face in his arms. Spencer glared at him as his shoulders shook with muffled laughter.

"Hey!" He gave Tim's ass a smack. "Stop laughing or I won't fuck you."

Surprisingly, his threat worked. Mostly. Tim glanced back over his shoulder. His lips were pressed together suspiciously tight, but he made a little locking motion in front of his mouth and that was enough for Spencer.

"Damn right," he said with a firm nod. He smacked Tim's ass again, just because he could, then grinned. "Fuck yeah."

I'm in charge now, bitch.

He grimaced. Apparently, there was a definite upper limit to how dommy Spencer could be without feeling icky and uncomfortable. He mentally shrugged. He'd never had a problem with being a bottom, and he wasn't about to start now.

Maybe I'll be so bad at this Tim won't come and then he'll have to fuck me too.

With that happy thought in his head, Spencer pulled back for his first thrust.

Then paused.

There was...less dick than he'd been imagining.

"Are you sure I'm big enough?" he asked, wringing his hands together. "Because if I'm not, I can just get one of my dildos and—"

"Oh my *God*," Tim groaned. "Stop talking and *fuck me*."

Spencer nodded quickly. "Yeah, okay."

Then he moved his hands back to Tim's hips and started to thrust.

Fucking Tim was...different. Not really a better adjective than cool, but different was the only word that came to mind. Tim was tight, and his ass gripped Spencer's cock more forcefully than he ever thought possible. He liked it though. Not necessarily the feeling on his dick, though that was pretty fucking awesome, but the way it felt emotionally. *He* was the one giving this pleasure. Every time Tim moaned, Spencer's heart skipped a beat. With every thrust backward onto Spencer's cock, Tim did more for his self-confidence than a hundred heartfelt compliments. Lying with words was easy; it was a lot harder to lie with bodies.

"Fuck...Spenc—ah! This...God, you feel so good."

That's not to say the words were unappreciated.

Eventually, Spencer decided to be a bit daring. He let go of Tim's hips and began to explore the soft, sweat-slicked skin of his back. Tim's lean muscles clenched under his hands, and Spencer groaned out loud. He loved being in Tim's position; he knew what it was like, what he was feeling, what *Spencer* was making him feel. Lust took over, and any thoughts he might have had about keeping Tim hard enough to have a go at him later disappeared. Tim was *going* to come. He was going to *make* Tim come.

Spencer grabbed Tim's hard, leaking cock and started to stroke.

It took a bit to get the technique down, his rhythm stopping and starting as he got the hang of managing these new sensations and desires. Spencer was surprised at how good he was at this, at least if Tim's now-incoherent moan-groan-pleas were any indication. It was a sexual rush, one he'd never experienced, and when Tim's hole clenched hard around him as his cock spilled all over the bedspread, he knew this was something he'd want again and again.

Spencer started coming almost at the same time Tim did, and when they were done they both collapsed onto the bed in exhaustion, Spencer on top of Tim, his slowly softening cock still inside.

Insideinsideinside. I came inside. Holy shiiiiiit.

"That," Spencer said breathlessly into Tim's back, "was fun."

Tim hummed in contentment. "So, does that mean you want to do it again?"

"Hell yeah. Imma hit this—" He yawned, then gave the general area around Tim's ass a lazy slap. "*All* the time."

Tim let out a breathy laugh. "One time screwing me, and you turned into a top. I feel like I should be proud."

"What the hell are you going on about?" Spencer thought about sitting up and crossing his arms so Tim could get the full effect of all the 'bitch please' he was throwing at him right now, but he was way too comfortable to bother. "Spencer Kent is *no* top."

"Good to know."

"Actually, I'm such a bottom that you need to even out my bottom ratio by fucking me *twice* every time I fuck you."

"Do I?"

"Yep."

"What if I'm too tired?"

"Sorry, I don't make the rules. You've gotta—" *Oh shit, he moved, I'm falling.* He slid off Tim's sweat-slicked back, his half-soft cock pulling out with a soft *thwup*. "Urg. You've gotta—"

In a move smoother than anything Spencer would have been capable of minutes after getting the fucking of a lifetime, Tim quickly turned onto his side and pulled him into a cuddle. Their rapidly cooling, damp, cummy groins squished together. It was perfect.

"You're so adorable," Tim said, his face half buried in Spencer's hair. "I love you."

Spencer closed his eyes and went limp. *Yeah. That's what you gotta do.*

"I love you too."

Tim's arms tightened around him.

Spencer blissfully fell asleep in the wet spot.

Chapter Eighteen

The bell rang, loud and shrill as only school bells can be, signaling the end of Spencer's last class of the day.

"Okay everyone, before you leave, I'm gonna remind you again about how amazingly generous I've been by telling you what your Christmas break assignment is going to be a whole week early. If you procrastinate and don't touch it until break begins in just five short days, you'll only have yourselves to blame for ruining your time off with evil, evil schoolwork." He took a quick look at his students, making a note of which ones didn't seem to be listening. Those would be the ones who, despite being very clear all year about his rule of obviously rushed assignments not being accepted, would probably wait until the day before break ended to start their homework. He was torn between hoping they proved him wrong or hoping they didn't so he could keep his near-perfect Lazy Student Pick Rate intact.

"That's it," he said, waving his hand magnanimously. "You may leave."

It was the end of the day, so even the biggest lit nerds in his class wasted little time in getting out of the room. Which meant, in no time at all, every single distraction Spencer had been holding on to all day long was gone, and everything he'd been trying to avoid thinking about came roaring back. He sat down behind his desk, dropped his head on his day planner, and sighed.

The bullying hadn't stopped.

In fact, in a twist of dramatic irony Spencer might have appreciated if he'd been reading it in a book, it turned out Connor had been right all along; getting the Henderson kids in trouble only made them come after Connor ever harder. The one saving grace was they hadn't touched his son again. There had been no more blood to clean up and no more bruises that needed to heal, but a small part of Spencer almost would have preferred that to coming home to Connor sobbing in his room or on the couch almost every day since Dean and Julie got off suspension. At least if he had some blood on his face Corbin might have done something about it instead of shrugging his fat fucking shoulders and saying, "There's only so much I can do, Spencer. It's your son's word against theirs," like the fucking coward he was. But no, all they did was corner Connor in the bathroom or some other out-of-the-way place and tear into him with words instead of fists. Spencer knew what that felt like. He knew how much damage teenagers could do with words. He'd spent almost every day of his middle and high school years fighting back tears and desperately hoping he could get through the day without attracting anyone's attention, and his stomach roiled when he thought about his kid going through the same shit. The worst part was he couldn't do anything about it. He had no power to suspend students outside the grade he taught, and Corbin had already warned him about going after the little shits with the few punishments he was allowed to hand out. Which was all kinds of bullshit. People like Steph McConnell couldn't get fired, but he was getting warned not to drag a couple of teenage sociopaths in for lunch detention so his kid could have forty-five minutes of peace? How was that fair?

Spencer's forehead started to throb where it was pressed against the day planner, so he crossed his arms and rested his head on them instead. Hell, even if he did pull the Hendersons in for lunch, the problem wouldn't be solved; it would probably only make things worse. He felt like he was climbing a glacier, and every time he thought he might reach the top, his feet hit a slick spot and he went tumbling back down to the bottom. Nothing he tried helped.

Spencer groaned into his arms. The overly loud clock hanging above the door to his room was mocking him, *tick tick ticking* away the seconds until Christmas break. Spencer needed to have this shit solved by then. This was going to be their first Christmas together with Tim, something he and Connor both needed, in their own way. Spencer needed the sense of permanence and tradition Christmas always brought. No matter what had been going on in his life, he'd always spent Christmas with the people he loved the most, and he so desperately wanted Tim to be a part of that. Part of him still felt like he could lose Tim at any moment and spending the most important family holiday in Spencer's year with his son and his boyfriend would go a long way to soothing those fears. Connor needed Christmas for much the same reasons; the holiday had always been a peaceful time for the kid, and the week or so leading up to it had always been filled with excitement and anticipation. But not this year. This year Connor was too busy scurrying through the halls and flinching at everyone who approached him. Even the promise of a whole ten days away from school for Christmas break wasn't helping. Spencer had always been a natural pessimist, and Connor was too much his son not to obsess over what would happen when that break ended.

And, to be honest, Spencer worried about the same thing. That fear and helplessness would be a giant fucking pall cast over Christmas. It would be impossible for them to enjoy the holiday, and Tim was too observant not to notice. Dean and Julie Henderson were about to ruin Christmas.

If Spencer had been a girl, his life would be a Hallmark movie.

The sound of his door opening during what was still technically school hours had his head shooting up as he tried to twist his face into an expression that didn't radiate frustrated despair. When he saw Steph McConnell slip into his classroom, he scowled, annoyed that he'd put effort into making himself presentable for her.

"And here I thought my day couldn't possibly get worse."

"Well, that was rude," Steph said as she closed the door behind her.

"Oh. I'm sorry. I didn't mean to say that out loud," Spencer said, not even trying to sound sincere.

"Spencer—"

"Oh God, my name sounds so wrong coming out of your mouth. It's Mr. Kent to you. Wait, no, you probably make those poor kids call you 'Ms. McConnell' when you're scarring them for life; I don't want you calling me Mr. Kent either. Just don't address me at—"

"*Spencer*, I—"

"And it's just as gross as the first time. Seriously, please don't do that again. If you say my name three times you might actually steal my soul."

"Spencer!" She was glaring at him now.

"Oh, look at that," Spencer said, grinning. "My soul's still here. Crisis averted! Since we're done here, the door's that way. Don't let it touch your ass on the way out; I don't want to have to disinfect it."

"Jesus Christ," she said, staring at him in disbelief. "Why I thought I could talk to you like a normal human I have no idea."

"I don't know either. Have you been taking human lessons?" Spencer cocked his head. "Is that why you're here? To practice?"

"I'm—"

"Because you should probably start with 'not molesting kids' before moving onto 'conversing with words.'"

"You know not a single one of those accusations was ever proven."

"She says with all the conviction of a bad actor on *SVU*."

Hm. Apparently internal angst does wonders for my witty snark. Good to know.

Steph's face twisted into a sneer, any pretense of civility she might have come in with sloughing away like rain off a windshield. "I just want you to know," she said, enunciating every word, "that I absolutely loathe you."

"The feeling is completely mutual."

They both glared at each other in a frozen tableau of mutual disdain before Steph broke eye contact. Spencer's childish glee at winning their stare-off was short-lived though. Steph took a moment to visibly collect herself before taking a deep breath and making eye contact once again.

"I came in here for a reason," she said, her voice impressively even considering the two small spots of furious red still staining her cheeks. "Not to fight with you."

"I literally could not possibly care less about whatever—"

"I heard all about what's going on with your son."

Never had Spencer been more grateful to be sitting down. He wasn't exactly sure what would have happened if he'd been standing, but it was probably a toss-up between collapsing like some Victorian maiden with the vapors or leaping across the desk, fists flying. He'd mostly been trying to get a rise out of Steph before when he acted disgusted when she said his name, but hearing her talk about Connor actually made his stomach roil.

"What are you talking about?" he asked, gritting his teeth at the slight shakiness he could hear in his words

Steph put her hands on his desk, leaning over until Spencer had to tilt his head up to keep his eyes on her face. "The Henderson kids are giving him trouble, right?"

God, the way she said it, like it didn't matter, like it was just another schoolyard *thing* that happened every day, made his whole body clench.

"I don't know what you're talking about," he snapped. He'd lie down in traffic before he turned his son into gossip fodder for Steph McConnell. Part of him knew he wasn't hiding even a small portion of how much this conversation bothered him, knew that this was most likely the exact reaction she came here to provoke, but he couldn't play cool and unaffected. Not now. All he could do was endure until she got bored of needling him and left.

"Of course you do," she said patiently. "It's not that easy to keep a secret in this school, especially when Corbin's office might as well be made out of rice paper for all the sound it blocks."

"And why," he said, "are you talking about my son at all?"

She studied him for a long moment, then moved back, getting just far enough out of his personal space he could almost relax.

"Look," she said. "I know this might be hard for you to believe, but I actually came here today to help you."

Spencer didn't even try to hold back his scoff.

"I'm being serious," Steph said. She left an obvious opening for him to respond, but he wasn't going to play her game. If she had something to say, she could say it without getting whatever reaction she wanted from him.

"Bullshit," he said, then grimaced.

Goddammit.

"Not at all." She looked smug. She sounded smug. Spencer had never hated her more than he did right then.

"If you have a point, can you just get to it?"

To Spencer's surprise, she did.

"I don't know if you know this, but I coach the field hockey team along with being a full-time teacher," she said with the air of someone expecting to impress. Spencer managed to keep from rolling his eyes, barely. Steph pouted at his lack of reaction. "Look, I've known the Hendersons for years. Julie Henderson has played for me every year since she's been in this school. She's good too. Good enough to keep playing in college. And I happen to know that she's desperately hoping to get a scholarship."

"So, she's a talented jock bully," Spencer said flatly. "Wow. That's unique."

Steph crossed her arms and let out an annoyed huff. "Fine. Forget subtlety. I can get Julie to leave your son alone by threatening to kick her off the team if she doesn't. Her brother, while cute enough with those eyes and his little faux-gangsta getup, has always been a follower. If she stops, he'll stop, and your boy will have a nice, bully-free time at school. All I want in return is for you to tell Corbin you're no longer interested in room 210. Is that clear enough for you?"

Spencer could not believe what he was hearing. "Are you..." He glanced around and leaned toward her. "Are you on something right now?"

It was a serious question too. Not even Steph McConnell could seriously be thinking about threatening the entire future of a student she'd apparently mentored for *years* just because she wanted a better classroom. No one in their right mind would be that disgustingly unprofessional, or just plain *disgusting*, without some kind of substance fucking their head up.

Right?

Steph leaned in as well, her eyes hard as she stared directly at Spencer. "I want that room," she said. "And I want to take it from *you*. There is nothing I'm not willing to do to get it."

Spencer stared in complete disbelief. "What the hell is *wrong* with you?"

"You!"

"*Me*?"

"Yes, you. You're what's wrong with me. You've *always* been what's wrong with me."

What the hell does that even mean? What the hell have I ever done to her? Well, besides...

"Is..." Spencer cleared his throat. "Is this because I wouldn't fuck you?"

Those two splotches of color on her cheeks flared back to life. "It's because I *hate you!*" she said, her face twisting into something ugly and bitter. Spencer had no idea how to respond. Sure, he'd never liked Steph and, their first meeting notwithstanding, Steph had obviously felt the same way, but he had no idea of the sheer level of loathing she'd been hiding. It didn't matter how he felt about her, or that he'd never respected her opinion about anything; being on the receiving end of such intense, unshielded hatred made him feel small and lost.

"What did I ever do to you?" he asked, his voice weak.

"Everything!" The word exploded out of her, as if she'd been desperately waiting for just that question. "Ever since you started working here, you've treated me like I was something you stepped in. No civility. No professional courtesy. Not even the smallest attempt to hide your disgust. You walk around here as gay as you want, terrifying and threatening your students, and *I'm* the one everyone looks down on? And why? Because a few overprotective parents called the cops on me once or twice? I was never convicted of anything. I was never even formally arrested! And everyone just assumes I'm guilty? How is that fair?"

Spencer thought about bringing up OJ Simpson or Casey Anthony, but she barely left enough time between sentences to take a breath, let alone for him to go into how the justice system sometimes fails to lock up obviously guilty people.

"And then you aren't even here three years and suddenly you have higher test scores than me, and everyone won't shut up about how funny and nice you are and everyone just loves you even though you treat your students like crap."

Really? People actually said they liked me? Because they sure as hell never said that to me.

"But that's fine. Because even if everyone hates me and thinks the sun shines out your ass, you're never going to get the recognition you want. I'm going to take it—no.

Even better. You're going to *give it* to me. Hand it to me, even. Right now. And then you're going to have to spend the rest of your career knowing I have the best classroom in the school, and every single new teacher who comes here won't know anything about me other than that I have 210, and that makes me the *best*. So don't even pretend like you're not going to accept my offer. I've heard you and Cassandra talking about how much you love your little *raisin* enough times to know better."

Spencer flinched when he heard his cute nickname for Connor pass her lips. How long had she been eavesdropping on his conversations? Better question, how long had she been building up this fantasyland where Spencer was the super popular Teacher of the Year and she was the unfairly maligned outcast? Which was such bullshit Spencer didn't even know where to start. He wondered if this was how people felt when they found out they had a stalker. Because this kind of obsession with shit that *never happened* was scary.

Aside from Cass, he had exactly zero friends at this school. Every shred of professional recognition he'd ever gotten from *anybody* he'd had to scrape and claw for. He was always too young or too short to be taken seriously; too hard on his students or too casual with them; he gave too many writing assignments and not enough tests; he spent hours making up assignments that challenged kids to think for themselves and hours more of his life reading and grading and trying to give commentary that was actually useful, instead of xeroxing a bunch of multiple-choice tests that would take a fraction of the time to grade; he'd gotten into *shouting matches* with Corbin over their reliance on standardized testing. *Nothing* in his professional life had ever been handed to him, and no one in this school deserved 210 more than he did.

Which was why a large part of him absolutely hated that Steph was right.

"I can't give you the room," Spencer said. He took a second to memorize the way her face twisted into outraged disbelief. Maybe looking back on this moment would help later when he had to deal with her being a smug cunt for the rest of eternity. "All I can do is tell Corbin I don't want it. I can't promise he won't give it to someone else, and I'm not telling him anything until you talk to Julie and the bullying stops, but..." He cleared his throat. "But if it does stop, then I'll tell Corbin I'm not accepting the room."

Steph pursed her lips. "You're lying."

Spencer sighed. "No, I'm not." She started to argue, and he quickly cut her off. "Look, if I don't give up the room you can just tell Julie you're not gonna threaten to kick her off the team if she beats up my kid again. You actually have the upper hand here, so don't get your panties in a twist about what I'm gonna do. If anything, I should be the one worrying about *you* fucking me over."

Steph frowned like she hadn't considered any of what he'd said until right then. "How do you know I won't?"

If there had been even a shred of her earlier hate or spite in her voice, Spencer would have called the whole thing off. Instead, when all he heard was genuine curiosity tinged with the barest hint of confusion, he decided to answer honestly.

"Because I think you're a despicable waste of humanity who should be in jail. And you hate me right back. But you also know how much Connor means to me, and even though you know seeing him hurt is a thousand times worse to me than giving up a classroom, you still offered to help me protect him." He shrugged. "No matter how young I look, I'm not a teenager anymore. I'm aware there's no such thing as a person who's 100 percent irredeemably evil, just like there's no such thing as a person who's 100 percent good. There are probably much easier ways for you to get teenage boys into bed, so I believe there's a reason you spent all that time and money to become a teacher, beyond the obvious one. There has to be a reason you coach a girl's field-hockey team when you could just go home at the end of the day and relax like the rest of us. I have to trust there's at least enough humanity in you that you don't want to see these kids getting hurt."

Spencer felt ill even implying that what she did didn't hurt kids, but he was pretty sure that was exactly how she thought. She didn't seem like the kind of person to get off on actively hurting children. In her mind, she was probably doing them a favor. It didn't change the reality of the situation, and it didn't change how disgusting of a person she was, but it was something. An island of morality in a sea of filth.

She seemed surprised by his honest assessment, and maybe that worked in his favor too. The villain of her self-constructed fairy tale finally giving the heroine her due.

Whatever.

"Also." He pushed out of his chair and stood as tall as he could, staring into Steph's eyes with every ounce of stubborn determination he possessed. "If you don't keep your end of this agreement, I will spend the rest of my life making every second you spend in this city a living hell. If you think people hate you now, that's nothing compared to how they're going to feel about you when I'm through. I'll follow you everywhere. I'll mortgage my house and spend every cent of what I get on the best cameras and audio equipment I can find. I'll record you every time you come within ten feet of an underage boy. If you touch them, or flirt with them, or take them off for a private whatever the fuck you call it, I'll send those tapes to everyone I can think of. The cops and the FBI and the media will be *drowning* in the amount of footage I send them. I'll mail them to your house. I'll find out where every single member of your family lives and mail them there too. I'll mail them to your old college professors. I'll mail them off to the local papers of whatever town you came from so everyone you grew up with will know exactly what little Stephanie McConnell grew up to be. There won't be a single person in your life who won't know what you are. And I don't care how good the teacher's unions are, when I'm done with you there won't be a single school district in this country that will want to touch you with a ten-foot pole. And if you think I won't, if you think I'm just saying all this to scare you and there's no way I'll ever follow through, think back to all those conversations you spied on over the years. Think about everything you overheard that made you so sure I would do anything to protect my son, and then realize that no matter what I might have said, it's *nothing* compared to how I feel inside. I will destroy you with a smile, Steph McConnell, if you don't keep your word."

Spencer knew he was less than intimidating to most adults. That was fine. He didn't need Steph to be intimidated.

He just needed her to believe him.

"So," he said, extending his hand across the desk. "Do we have a deal?"

Steph said absolutely nothing.

But she shook his hand all the same.

*

The best thing about Tim's job was, even though he had to get up during the ungodly pre-dawn hours of the morning, once noon hit, the rest of the day belonged to him. And while that would change once the new semester started and he had to drive three hours each way to get to classes, right now it meant he could always be at Spencer's house when Connor got home, an arrangement that seemed to make everyone involved happy. Spencer liked knowing that his son wouldn't be going home to an empty house, Connor liked having someone to come home to, and Tim...

Tim absolutely loved how domestic it all was. He honestly didn't know how he was going to cope when classes started.

For now, though, he'd settled nicely into a routine he loved.

Then, one day, Spencer came home from school and everything changed.

It began subtly at first, a small fluttery pressure in Tim's stomach as Spencer walked over to Connor without a word and pulled him into a tight hug. The pressure built as Spencer pressed a dozen kisses into his son's hair, and it rose up into Tim's heart as Spencer began to speak. He told Connor he was safe. That he would never have to worry about Dean and Julie again. That he could go to school and learn and skip homework and barely pass tests and be stressed and miserable for all the right reasons, instead of being made that way by circumstances no one should have to endure. It was such a *Spencer* explanation that even Connor couldn't be upset by his lack of tact. He threw his arms around his dad and hugged him so tightly Spencer's face started to turn red. The pressure inside Tim began to blossom, slowly taking shape as Spencer reached over and dragged Tim into their hug. It expanded as Connor wrapped one of his arms around Tim's waist too without even thinking about it. As if it were something they did all the time. As if this was another in a long line of situations where Tim was a necessary part of Connor and Spencer's happiness.

As if they were a family.

The feeling simmered for a while, as they held their embrace for several long minutes; as Connor slowly pulled and wiped at his eyes with an embarrassed flush to his cheeks; as Spencer kissed Tim lightly on the corner of his mouth before letting him go; as they shared a quiet dinner in front of the TV, the first one in weeks that didn't carry an undercurrent of tension and worry and dread. It simmered until dinner ended and Connor disappeared into his bedroom while Spencer pulled Tim into what might as well have been theirs with as many nights a week as he stayed over. It simmered until Spencer locked them behind a closed door and told him everything he hadn't told Connor. About McConnell and her offer, about Spencer's answer and his threats. Tim listened in awe as Spencer outlined the exact circumstances that had led to him giving up the professional recognition he desperately craved so his son could walk through school without being afraid. And when he finished, the feeling finally bloomed—exploded really; that is if something so quiet could be classified as an explosion. In the end, it wasn't really a feeling at all. More a long overdue realization that Tim's life had been changed forever. A realization that came in the form of a single sentence running over and over again through Tim's head.

Someday I'm going to marry this man.

Perhaps that shouldn't have surprised him considering how committed he was to both Spencer and Connor, but it did. And with this realization came another: that the different compartments holding each part of his life could no longer be kept shut. Spencer and Connor weren't just part of his life anymore; they were the whole thing.

And it was long past time Tim shared his life with the people he loved.

After a long period of time where he and Spencer kissed and spoke quietly and kissed some more, he managed to make his excuses and slip away into the bathroom. Probably not the best setting for what he had in mind, but it was the closest bit of privacy he could get.

Surprisingly, his fingers didn't tremble in the slightest as he pulled out his phone and called home.

"Hello?" his mother answered on the second ring.

"Hey, Mom."

"Timothy! I wasn't expecting you to call today! This is such a nice surprise, hearing my baby's voice."

If she had said those words to him even a few hours ago, Tim would have read in them a subtle rebuke; a chastisement for ignoring his poor mother for so long that hearing his voice was something to be noted. Today he only smiled at the fondness he heard in her voice, and realized he missed her too.

"Yeah. It's nice to talk to you too, Mom."

"So, what did you call for?" she asked in the absent way she did when she was splitting her focus. Probably on dinner. His dad usually got home from work in the evening, so dinners at home tended to be late.

What a coincidence.

"I was just wondering," he said, "what time do you think Christmas dinner will be this year?"

Tim heard the tinny, metallic sound of a utensil being dropped. "What?" she squawked. "Timothy! Does this mean…"

"Yes, Mamma," he said. "I'll be home for Christmas."

"Oh, Timothy! I'm so happy!"

There wasn't a trace of smugness in her voice, only happiness and relief, and something in Tim's chest eased. His mom really did love him. Maybe he should have been giving her more credit all along.

"I am too, Mom. Actually, I—I have some people I want you to meet. Is it okay if I bring them?"

"People? What people? Did you make some new friends?"

"Something like that." Tim grinned as an idea popped into his head. It might not be the smoothest way to break the news, but he knew his mom. Once she calmed down, this would be a story she'd take special delight in telling for *years*.

"Tell me," he said. "How do you feel about grandchildren?"

As the expected screams and cries and demands to *"tell me what you mean by that right now, young man"* came through the phone, Tim smiled so wide his cheeks started aching as he wiped away a few tears of his own. He could see his future stretching in front of him as clearly as if it were right outside the bathroom window.

And for the first time in a long while, he couldn't wait to meet it.

Epilogue

Tim pulled his scarf tighter around his neck as a sudden gust of icy wind kicked up. Shivering, he picked up the pace, pushing through the throng of people still clogging the sidewalks even though it was 9:00 p.m. on Christmas Eve. Not that he could judge them, really, especially since, going by the grocery bags he could see weighed down by a familiar rectangular shape, he wasn't the only one out braving the New York City winter because someone hadn't bought enough eggnog.

Personally, he blamed Connor. That boy inhaled the stuff like it was air.

Although, Tim thought as the wind kicked up again, it would probably be better if it *were* air. Eggnog had to be warmer than the ice crystals currently passing for an atmosphere. Despite the cold Tim couldn't help smiling. *I've been with Spencer so long I'm starting to sound like him.* It was a surprisingly warm thought, and since Tim could use any warmth he could get, he let himself sink into happy memories as he trudged through the slush covered sidewalks.

It had been a year since the first Christmas they'd all spent with his parents, and Tim had surprisingly little to complain about when it came to his life these days. His commute might be awful, and sometimes there were nights where he crashed on the couch of one of his friends who lived by ISU instead of driving all the way home to the house he now shared with Connor and Spencer, but his doctorate was coming along well. Dr. Payton was patient and encouraging and nothing less than 100 percent supportive when some Connor-related emergency kept him at home, as long as it didn't happen too often. He made it clear he thought Tim would make a great child psychologist, something even Spencer couldn't find fault with.

(Spencer hated Dr. Payton. He thought he was a stuck-up prick who looked down on Spencer for being a lowly high school teacher. It was ridiculous, because Dr. Payton had never been anything but pleasant in either of their company, but on the rare occasions he stopped by their house for dinner Spencer was always especially aggressive in bed that night, so Tim had kind of been dragging his feet on figuring out what the issue was.)

Another thing Spencer couldn't find fault with was what happened with Edward Carmichael. Despite how invincible he'd always seemed to Tim, Professor Inappropriate had finally gotten fired a few months ago after multiple former students sued him, and the university, for sexual harassment and coercion. Tim was even able to get in on the lawsuit, which would hopefully help him pay off his student loans if they won, and he'd made a few new friends during their lawyer meetings and the biweekly meetups most of them had fallen into to bitch about Carmichael. Tim had never been more grateful he hadn't given in to his advances after hearing some of their stories. Carmichael apparently liked taking secretly recorded videos and pictures as blackmail material, sometimes keeping his students on the hook for years for "favors" even after they earned their doctorate. There was a legal case being developed against him too, and Tim had offered to give testimony if the prosecution wanted him. Even if none of them ended up with any money from the lawsuit, Tim still had high hopes that Carmichael would find himself in jail one day. Some of the things he'd heard Carmichael forced his students to do made Tim sick to think about.

Slightly less traumatizing was the fact that Connor's puberty was moving right along at a clip. He'd even had a huge sexuality crisis earlier in the year that had gone on for months and involved all three of them as Connor had desperately tried to figure out what he was. Tim had spent most of his nights trying to talk Connor down from his increasingly frequent panic attacks, as well as comforting a slightly traumatized Spencer, who wasn't taking this latest evidence of Connor's growing up well at all. Which was a shame, because he had a lot more experience struggling with his sexuality than Tim did, and he probably would have been able to help Connor more. They'd muddled through though. Spencer curling up in the corner and doing his best to come to terms with the fact that his little boy was very quickly rocketing into adulthood, and Tim doing his best to understand why figuring out who he was attracted to was so upsetting to Connor. He'd never really gotten a coherent answer, but a few months earlier Connor had calmed down significantly, and these days he spent most of his free time flirting with a trans girl he'd met online.

"Because that just clears his sexuality right up," Spencer had grumbled when he found out. Tim had rolled his eyes but otherwise ignored him. Spencer would never be the most tactful or politically correct person, but he never said anything disparaging to Connor about his first tentative steps toward teenage romance, so Tim wasn't going to make a big deal out of it.

As for Spencer himself? He was probably the part of Tim's life that had changed the least over the last year. He still wore his adorable cardigans. He still despaired over his hair, grimaced every time he looked in a mirror, and forgot to shower on his days off. He still had the same job. He still taught in the same classroom. (And so did Steph McConnell, something Spencer had laughed himself into a coughing fit over when he'd heard. In the end, after Spencer turned it down, 210 had gone to the next most senior ninth-grade teacher after Benjamin Rasputin, a woman who was two years away from getting her pension. Spencer didn't want to jinx things, but he'd quietly confessed to Tim he thought Corbin might offer him the room again after she retired. By then Connor would be in college, and there would be nothing McConnell or anyone else could do to make him give 210 up again.)

Spencer was Tim's rock. The one thing Tim could always depend on to be there no matter what else was going on. Which, considering how they met, was something Tim still occasionally had trouble wrapping his mind around. But that was okay. Things didn't need to make sense or be logical for them to be true.

Spencer was the truest thing in Tim's life. And he wouldn't have it any other way.

And speaking of Spencer...

Tim could hear his boyfriend's laugh echoing down the hall as he made his way to his parent's apartment. For a person as shy as Spencer could be at times, his voice easily carried through the heavy apartment door, over the obnoxiously loud Christmas music the neighbors would be complaining about in an hour or two, and even the chattering of Tim's own teeth. He picked up his pace and entered the apartment.

Even though he felt like something that had been half defrosted in the microwave, the scene he walked in on did more to warm him than even his parents' overworked space heater.

Everything was almost exactly the way Spencer had described on that long-ago night when they first confessed their love to each other. Tim's mom raced back and forth from the kitchen to the living room, somehow managing to refill drinks, hold up a conversation with Spencer's mom, and pluck the bag of eggnog out of Tim's hand without seeming to slow down at all. Both Tim and Spencer's dads sat talking in front of the TV, an old black-and-white movie no one was watching playing quietly in the background. Two families who didn't know of each other's existence before this time last year had come together as easily as raindrops joined with the water in a lake. Walls, whether of brick or cellophane, no longer had any place in their lives. Of course, not everything went the way Spencer thought it would—their dads actually had disturbingly similar opinions on politics, and everyone loved the casserole Spencer's mom brought. And while Tim's mom did nag them about moving to New York, Tim was pretty sure it was just to keep up appearances. His parents visited Chicago enough these days that moving wasn't necessary. Tim wasn't sure if he was insulted or charmed that they mainly came out to see Connor. Although, when he thought about it, he was mostly happy that Conner seemed to love them just as much as they loved him.

Even if his mom had taken to leaving brochures for NYU behind every time they left, despite Connor only being in tenth grade.

An insistent tugging at his jacket brought him back to the present.

"Jesus Christ," Spencer said as he yanked off Tim's winter coat and unwound his scarf. "You're soaked. Was the only grocery store open at the bottom of the harbor?"

"It started snowing on the way back."

"I can see that." Spencer ran his fingers through Tim's hair, then grimaced when they came back wet. "Get those shoes off so we can sit you in front of the space heater before you get hypothermia." He paused. "Oh my God, I think I'm actually turning into your mom. What the fuck?"

Tim grinned, and suddenly it struck him that this was a perfect moment. His family was together, bigger than he'd ever thought it could be and all the happier and closer for it. The holiday he used to dread every year had become the one he anticipated the most. His parents were in their element, talking and cooking and spreading the feeling of family, one sheet of gingerbread cookies and impassioned rant about Congress at a time. Connor, his son in every way that mattered, was curled up next to the space heater, a contented smile on his face and a slight flush to his cheeks suggesting the nonalcoholic eggnog wasn't the only kind he'd gotten into. Tim's heart swelled as he thought about the stocking hanging not even six feet from Connor's head, and the piece of paper inside, carefully folded in an innocuously festive box, that allowed Tim to claim his son in the legal way as well.

And then there was Spencer, the man he loved more than anything in the world, standing in front of him in an aggressively purple Christmas sweater covered in reindeer skeletons and skulls with Santa hats, staring up at him with dawning suspicion in his eyes.

"Oh no," Spencer said. "Don't you dare give me that look. If you put your cold hands anywhere on my body, I swear to God I'll smother you in your sleep tonight."

Yeah. Tim's heart began to pound in his chest. *This is the perfect moment I've been waiting for.*

Spencer started to back away, but Tim grabbed his wrist.

"No! Don't—"

Tim dropped to one knee.

Spencer's eyes went saucer-wide, his words bit off by a wet, coughing wheeze.

On the edge of his awareness, Tim realized he was now the center of attention. His mom and Spencer's were clutching each other in the kitchen doorway, tears already streaming down their cheeks. Their dads were watching over the backs of their armchairs with quiet approval on their faces and a telling, watery shine to their eyes. Connor was mostly in the same position, warm and slightly drunk and the only person who wasn't really surprised, since Tim had asked for his permission weeks ago. As if in echo of his previous approval, he grinned at Tim and shot him a big double thumbs-up.

But most of Tim's attention was on Spencer, his boyfriend, his motivation, his role model in fatherhood, and absolute love of his life, whose face was so red Tim was sure he'd forgotten how to breathe.

Absolutely perfect.

Tim took the small box he'd been carrying around for days out of his pocket and flicked it open.

Inside was a slender silver ring.

"Spencer—"

"Yes!"

Spencer blushed as everyone laughed.

Tim smiled so wide it hurt. "Not even gonna let me ask?"

"No. Yes. Yes!" Spencer broke off, shaking his head as everyone laughed again. When he looked back at Tim, his smile was wild and his eyes were glistening. He pulled his arm back just enough to be able to grab the hand that had been holding his wrist.

"Go ahead," Spencer said, squeezing tightly as happy tears began to slide down his cheeks. "Ask."

"Spencer Kent," Tim said. The entire room held its breath, waiting for the first words of what they no doubt expected to be a flowery, romantic proposal. Much later, when his mother smacked him on the shoulder and complained about what he said, he'd make sure to tell her how much Spencer hated overwrought romanticism. "Wanna get married?"

Spencer grinned. "*Fuck* yes."

About the Author

Dan lives in Ohio (as people do) with his husband and the most adorable little rescue dog ever. His three favorite things are *The Empire Strikes Back*, winter, and RPGs. His least favorite thing is pizza. Since the age of twelve, it's been his dream to write something good enough to get published and, after over a decade of unforgivable procrastination, he actually managed to get it done. Thankfully, what he finally ended up writing turned out much better than the Spider-Man and Eminem fan fiction he wrote in sixth grade. His new dream, which will hopefully take less time to achieve, is to own two Netherland Dwarf bunnies named Bunnedict Thumperbatch and Attila the Bun.

Email: danwritesthings@gmail.com

Twitter: @DanWingreen

Also Available from NineStar Press

Connect with NineStar Press

www.ninestarpress.com

www.facebook.com/ninestarpress

www.facebook.com/groups/NineStarNiche

www.twitter.com/ninestarpress

www.tumblr.com/blog/ninestarpress